Crown of Flames and Ash
COURTS OF AETHERIA
BOOK TWO

G.K. DEROSA

Copyright © 2024 Mystic Rose Press

All Rights Reserved. This book may not be reproduced, in whole or in part, in any form or by any means, including photocopying, recording, or by any information storage and retrieval system known or hereafter invented, without written permission from the publisher, Mystic Rose Press.

Print ISBN: 9798345101537

Cover Designer: Seventhstar Art
Interior Art: Samaiya Art

Published in 2024 by Mystic Rose Press
Palm Beach, Florida
www.gkderosa.com

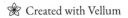 Created with Vellum

To the incredible Samaiya for creating all the beautiful art in this book and so many others. Thank you for bringing my characters and worlds to life!
~ GK

CROWN OF FLAMES AND ASH

Contents

Chapter 1	1
Chapter 2	7
Chapter 3	13
Chapter 4	20
Chapter 5	26
Chapter 6	33
Chapter 7	39
Chapter 8	46
Chapter 9	52
Chapter 10	59
Chapter 11	66
Chapter 12	73
Chapter 13	79
Chapter 14	85
Chapter 15	93
Chapter 16	99
Chapter 17	105
Chapter 18	111
Chapter 19	117
Chapter 20	124
Chapter 21	131
Chapter 22	140
Chapter 23	146
Chapter 24	154
Chapter 25	162
Chapter 26	168
Chapter 27	176
Chapter 28	184
Chapter 29	190
Chapter 30	198
Chapter 31	205
Chapter 32	211

Chapter 33	218
Chapter 34	225
Chapter 35	231
Chapter 36	237
Chapter 37	243
Chapter 38	249
Chapter 39	257
Chapter 40	263
Chapter 41	271
Chapter 42	278
Chapter 43	284
Chapter 44	291
Chapter 45	298
Chapter 46	304
Chapter 47	311
Chapter 48	318
Chapter 49	324
Chapter 50	331
Chapter 51	339
Chapter 52	344
Chapter 53	350
Chapter 54	360
Chapter 55	366
Chapter 56	373
Chapter 57	380
Chapter 58	387
Chapter 59	395
Chapter 60	403
Chapter 61	410
Chapter 62	418
Chapter 63	426
Chapter 64	432
Guide to the Courts of Aetheria	441
Also by G.K. DeRosa	445
Acknowledgments	449
About the Author	451

Kingdom of Aetheria

- Darkmania Falls
- Court of Ethereal Light
- Luminoc River
- Arcanum Citadel
- Conservatory of Luce
- Court of Umbral Shadows
- The Shadowmere Sea
- Alucians Mountains
- Feywood Forests
- Feywood
- The Wilds

Chapter One

R*eign*

Noxus, what had I done?

Pure hatred emanated from Aelia's gaze, those twin pools of silvery-blue glaring up at me. The wind lashed strands of platinum hair across her face as she balanced upon Solanthus's jagged spine. Her skyrider hovered only a few yards away from the slate dragon and my gods' damned brother. Pain like I'd never experienced scorched through my chest, slicing into my heart at that look. She would never forgive me for this betrayal. I could feel it with every shred of my being. Her fury pulsed around her form like a sentient creature, white-hot and frantic. Why the realms hadn't I admitted the truth when I'd had the chance?

I never meant for her to find out like this. I had hoped to protect her from all of it. Hoped to sort things out with my father before she would ever need to hear about any of it—and then *I* could have told her everything.

The battle raged around us, a steady drumbeat of flapping wings, along with the clash of *nox* and *rais* filling the air with heady power. Screams, cries, weapons clashing, all of it blurred in the distance over the manic timbre of my pulse.

"Aelia, please..." I reached for her, but she recoiled, the reaction another stab to the heart. She staggered farther back along the sharp ridges of Solanthus's backbone and fear wrenched my gut in a vice. "Be careful—"

"You lied to me for *months*," she hissed.

"I lied to everyone."

"I don't care about everyone, Reign. You lied to *me*!" She clenched her teeth, swallowing down a sob, and my gut clenched in return, her pain creating a visceral reaction in my body. "I trusted you, I fell—"

"Please, let me explain." I crept closer, but her hand flew up, fingertips glistening in golden light.

"Stay. Away. From me."

A dark chuckle resonated over my shoulder, and the all-consuming desperation, the pain, the fear, the regret, all of it morphed into fury. Fucking, Ruhl. This was all his fault. I spun around, rage blossoming in my chest. I felt it as the silver cuffs reacted, searing my skin as my *nox* rose, fueling the burgeoning wrath.

He sat astride his dragon, a smug grin across his face. "Did you really think you could keep the truth from her, brother?" Ruhl's smirk only further fired up my temper.

"Shut your mouth," I snarled. "You know nothing about her, and worse, nothing about me."

"I'm truly hurt, Reign." He lifted his hand to his heart. "Despite our differences, all my life I've looked up to you. Dom, too. This forced time apart has been awful for all of us." His dark gaze lifted over my shoulder to Aelia, and I widened my stance, my shadow wings unfurling, hoping to shield her from his hostile scrutiny. "So, is she the one Father has been searching for? We've all heard about the powerless Kin who destroyed the

Luminous Maze. Arcanum has been abuzz with rumors. Of course, they don't know—"

"No!" I snapped. "She is *not* the one."

"But she clearly means something to you." His dark brow arched.

I lifted my arms and pushed back my sleeves. "She's my freedom from these damned manacles."

"Oh, is that it?"

"Yes," I hissed, even as I prayed Aelia would understand it to be a ruse.

"So I shouldn't tell Father the good news—"

"No! She is not the child spoken of in the prophecy, Ruhl."

I could feel Aelia inching closer, her soft footfalls gliding across Sol's back. I released a shadow and guided it toward her ear. "I know I don't deserve it, but please, just trust me one last time, princess. Once this is over, I will tell you everything and you can despise me as I deserve, but I will *not* let you die today. And if my brother learns the truth, he will kill you."

A faint grunt reached my sensitive ears before her quiet steps fell away. I heaved out a breath, focusing my attention on my ruthless sibling. "If I wasn't bound by these damned manacles, I would have full access to my powers. You have no idea the torture I've endured with my *nox* bottled up. I would do anything to get these off."

"It certainly seems that way. A second ago, I was certain you'd attack your own flesh and blood."

"It's the buildup of *nox*, Ruhl. It's driving me mad."

"Hmm." He rubbed his chin, a mischievous gaze lighting up his pitch orbs. He clearly was not buying my bullshit. Ruhl may have been many things, but stupid wasn't one of them.

"Now, let's finish this battle so we can all go home." I motioned to the ensuing chaos still unfolding around us. My brother wasn't wrong before. Arcanum had clearly won the battle today. The Light forces were petering out and barely any Conservatory skyriders remained midair.

Draven would have to retreat with his tail between his legs or suffer the loss of the majority of the first-year class.

"Go claim your victory, brother," I shouted. *And leave Aelia the fuck alone.*

His eyes darted over my shoulder once again before his gaze settled on me. "Are you at least bedding the girl? You must be getting something out of this..."

I could feel Aelia bristle behind me. "For the love of Noxus, now is not the time, Ruhl," I snapped.

"You know, bringing the mysterious Kin back to Arcanum would score me maximum points with Malakar."

"You know very well kidnapping Conservatory students is not permitted in the first-term battle." As the years continued, anything became fair game, as I recalled.

"And I'm sure you remember, I'm not much of a rule-follower. And besides, Malakar is just unhinged enough to allow it. I'd say he might even reward me for it."

He likely wasn't wrong there. "Maybe... But, if you choose to try and take her, just know you'll have to go through me first." My shadows whirled into a frenzy, *nox* brimming to the surface. Darkness slithered over my skin, the respite from the gods' forsaken sun only strengthening my reserves. I'd always been stronger than my brother, and he knew it just as well as I.

"All that simply to get those pretty little bangles off?" He cocked his head as he regarded me.

"Yes," I snarled. "The Kin's life means my freedom." In more ways than even I could comprehend.

Ruhl loosed a breath and shook his head. "Fine, fine. I'll simply have to find some other first-year to drag back to the Citadel."

"No!" Aelia barreled by me, and I barely got a shadow around her waist before she launched herself at my brother, her hands splayed and flames flickering from her palms.

"Behave," I hissed as my shadows spun tighter around her.

She still clasped the dagger in her fist, the crystal gleaming beneath the faint light. Hopefully, Ruhl didn't catch the delicate glint. Aelia struggled and groaned as my shadows twisted around her body. She could easily slice at the dark tendrils to free herself, but I prayed to all the gods she wouldn't.

A sharp horn blared across the smoky mid-air battlefield, and the vicious snarls and pitiful moans and cries fell away. The darkness pervading the campus began to lift as the Shadow skyriders turned toward the Luminoc River. Streaks of brilliant light crisscrossed the Conservatory as light once again attempted to reign supreme.

"I suppose you lucked out this time, Kin." Ruhl's narrowed glare lanced over Aelia, and every muscle in my body coiled in response, ready to strike.

A disturbing certainty flickered through my mind: I would kill my own brother for her.

And he would deserve it. Phantom's voice invaded my consciousness, her familiar timbre a soothing balm to the turmoil.

Don't you think that's a bit harsh, old girl? I scanned the horizon for her sleek, obsidian form. She hovered just above the Alucian Mountains, slowly circling. Bringing her here today was a huge risk, but losing Aelia was a greater one, still.

Phantom huffed. *Not at all. It is natural for Fae males to go to any lengths to protect their—*

Don't say it.

Just because you forbid me to say it doesn't make it untrue. You will have to accept it eventually.

Perhaps you missed the last few minutes of the exchange with Ruhl? Aelia will never accept the call now.

Maybe, or maybe not.

The connection between us cut off, and I focused my attention to my brother. He still stared at the furious female glaring up at him. Her aura was a fiery mix of ochre, magenta and crimson, like the radiant dawn itself.

"I look forward to meeting you again, Aelia Ravenwood."

Ruhl dipped his head, a snide smirk tugging at his lips. "My brother is right, though, for, now, I must claim my victory." He paused and dark shadows coiled around his dragon. "Strength from Darkness, Power through Pain, Arcanum Citadel has won the day."

The slate dragon's wings beat the air, propelling them into the smoky blue. The moment he ascended, the tightness in my chest began to dissipate. I heaved in a breath and recalled the shadows keeping Aelia prisoner.

The instant she was freed, she whirled on me. "I hate you."

"As well you should, princess."

"Stop calling me that," she hissed. "We are not friends, you are not my mentor, you are not my *anything*."

"I wish that were true," I murmured under my breath. My life was a thousand times less complicated before this female fell into my orbit. I wished I could simply forget her, but I knew in my soul I never could. She'd already ingrained herself deep into my marrow, and I couldn't carve her out if I tried. As if I wanted to...

Aelia slipped by me and dropped to sit between her dragon's wing bones. "Take us down, Sol," she commanded. "I cannot suffer another moment in *his* presence."

Her skyrider angled his wings toward the ground, and his bumpy spine fell away from beneath my boots. My own wings of shadow began to flap, saving me from a painful freefall. I floated in the air for a long minute, watching as Sol's glittering scales zipped toward the ground.

Aelia never looked back. Not once.

Chapter Two

A *elia*

I would not spend another day drowning in misery in bed. Rolling over, I reached for a tissue and blew my nose, then wiped the remaining tears from my cheeks. I also refused to cry for another sun-blessed minute. Reign Darkthorn was not worthy of my tears. No male was, as far as I was concerned.

The draping vines curled overhead, dancing on a non-existent breeze. The myriads of colorful flora surrounding my bed had been my constant companion during these dark days. Hazarding a peek at the scroll on my nightstand, I watched as a glimmer of light danced across the parchment. *I should read it...* Instead, I closed my eyes and lay back against the plush pillow.

I could have easily slept for a week if given the opportunity. Not only was I physically drained after the endless weeks of the Ethereal Trials and the grand epic failure that was the end of the term battle with Arcanum, but I was emotionally exhausted as well. But I refused to give into the all-consuming sensations for a moment longer. Instead of facing Reign's betrayal and the suffocating emotions that came with them, I'd bury it all in the darkest recesses of my fragile heart and hide my head beneath the pillow.

Yes, that sounded perfectly rational. No, I would no longer be that fragile, powerless Kin ruled by her emotions. I would become stone, hard and unyielding—anything to survive what came next.

I yanked the coverlet over my head as images of the battle from three nights ago zipped across my subconscious. Every night the confrontation with Reign's brother, Ruhl, plagued my dreams. No matter how hard I attempted to free myself of the heart-wrenching memory, it haunted me all the same.

I would never forgive Reign's betrayal.

And still, a part of me, a part I absolutely despised, longed for him. I told myself it was closure I needed. He'd promised answers, but I'd refused him at every chance, in turn, denying myself that closure. For now, my heart was leading the way and I'd have to wait a bit longer for that resolution, it seemed. Poor Rue had become my temporary guard, shooing away my professor—well, former professor, as I'm determined him to be—every time he darkened our doorway.

Thank the goddess the term had finally come to an end, and we would be granted a moment of respite.

The only thing that kept my broken heart pumping was the knowledge that I'd finally get to see Aidan after four long months. I slid my hand beneath my nightgown and felt for the gold medallion my adoptive father had gifted me what felt like a lifetime ago now.

Would this visit back to Feywood finally give me the answers I've been seeking?

I thumbed the warm medal, the delicate etching beneath my finger kindling a memory from the day I was taken from my home.

"*What does it say?*"

Aidan cleared his throat, his eyes dipping to his folded hands. "I'm afraid I'm not sure. I believe it is in the old tongue of Faerish. I wish I could say I had it made for you, Aelia, but I stumbled across it in the village a few months ago. Raysa must have guided me to your gift for this special day."

There was one male on this campus who I knew was very familiar with Faerish. Too bad I wasn't speaking to him. After all these months here, I wasn't sure why I'd never shown Reign my necklace. Perhaps some dark part of me knew he wasn't to be trusted. Squeezing my eyes closed, I banished all thoughts of my traitorous prof—ex-professor.

I only hoped Aidan would be more forthcoming upon my return.

The creak of the dormitory door opening sent my head spinning toward the sound. I stared, my heart in my throat, as it slowly inched open. Reign hadn't dared to use his mystical access to enter, but what if...?

"Finally, you're awake!" Rue bounded into the chamber, that irrepressible grin firmly in place. Even the loss against Arcanum hadn't dulled her cheery disposition.

I mumbled a hello before burying my head into the pillow once again.

"Aelia! Enough of this." The pitter-patter of her tiny feet echoed an instant before the coverlet was ripped off my head. "So, we lost against Arcanum. It's no reason to behave like this."

And still another reason I refused to emerge from my bed. I hated lying to my friend more than anything. As angry as I was at Reign, I couldn't divulge his secret. Which likely made me a complete imbecile. If a prince of the Shadow Court had infiltrated this academy, it could only be for nefarious reasons.

And yet, I kept my mouth shut, possibly putting everyone I cared about in danger. Okay, it was only Rue, Symon, and Heaton that I cared anything about at this horrid place, but still.

"Aelia! You cannot continue like this." She ran her hand

over my hair, the unexpected display of affection only increasing the guilt. In my short time dwelling within the courts of the Fae, I'd come to see how rare genuine caring was—and showing fondness, rarer still.

Drawing in a breath, I rolled over and faced my friend. "It's not only the loss against Arcanum…"

"I gathered as much since you've refused your favorite professor admittance into our chamber for days, and yet he still sulks at our door."

"He does?" Gods, I hated how hopeful I sounded.

"Reign was out there when I came in just a moment ago."

I forced myself to sit up and squash the flutter of hope that had my heart in a tizzy. Let him wait out there forever.

She squeezed my hand, and a prickle of heat blossomed behind my lids. "Maybe if you just told me what happened between you two, it would help."

I slowly shook my head, clenching my teeth. *Do not cry.* I promised myself I would not shed another tear for that lying bastard.

"Well, I'm here when you're ready to talk."

Nodding slowly, I murmured, "Thank you, Rue."

"Cheers, my dear." She stood and trotted over to her closet. I watched as she pulled out a large carpet bag, humming a happy tune. "I suppose we should start packing. I don't know about you, but I cannot wait for this break."

Oh, gods, yes. For a moment, I'd completely forgotten. An entire week at home in Feywood was exactly what I needed to remove all traces of Reign from my mind. *And heart.*

"You're right, it's time." Running a hand through my disheveled locks, I forced myself to the edge of the bed. Rue was right. I needed to pack. I couldn't wait to see the look on Aidan's face when I arrived atop Sol. All of Feywood would be in an uproar.

You know I won't be able to remain in Feywood. Sol's voice skittered through my thoughts. *There won't be enough food to survive for a whole week without ravaging their meager supplies.*

I know. But you'll be nearby, right?

You know I'm never far, Aelia.

Sol's deep voice was like a balm to my aching heart. He'd been surprisingly quiet as of late. He claimed it was because he'd been forced to fly farther from Fae lands to hunt, but I had a feeling there was more to it. Perhaps, he'd open up along our journey home.

Just call for me when you're ready to depart. I'll be hunting along the border to prepare for the flight back.

Have you ever been to Feywood, Sol?

Of course, I have. There aren't many places along the immense continent of Crescentia that I haven't explored in my many lifetimes.

Right. Sometimes I forgot that though Sol's body was new, his soul had been reincarnated dozens of times. *What about the Wilds? Are the beasts as horrifying as they say?*

Nothing is frightening to a dragon, little Kin.

That wasn't quite the answer I was searching for so I tried again. *Are the Wilds as dangerous as the Fae claim?*

Why do I have a feeling if I answer that it will only lead to more questions?

Because you know me well and are fully aware how inquisitive I am.

Almost fatally so.

A rueful chuckle slid out. *I'm not going to run into the Wilds to confirm your answer if that's what you're afraid of.*

I just told you dragons aren't afraid of anything.

There must be something...

Sol snorted, the sound vibrating through my skull. I could practically see the plumes of smoke rising from his enormous nostrils. *Perhaps, one day I'll tell you.*

His reply stunned me to silence. I truly believed there was nothing the great Solanthus, the Sun Chaser feared. I remained quiet, reveling in the faint pulsing of the bond that stretched between us. I was just beginning to feel hints of my skyrider's emotions, whereas he could sense everything from me, which most of the time simply proved embarrassing. Maybe that was why he'd been distant lately. He was likely fed up with my aggressive pining for a certain Shadow Fae professor.

Now, get packing, Aelia. I hope to arrive in Feywood before nightfall.

Yes, sir!

I could practically hear his smile across our mental link. Nightfall... Goodness, it would be odd to see the sunset and sunrise once more. Reign wasn't the only one who missed the moon and the stars. There was nothing more beautiful than the twinkling orbs nestled across the midnight sky. It reminded me of Reign's eyes—

No. No. No. I banished the thought from my mind and stomped toward my closet. It was time to go home.

Chapter Three

Aelia

The lush greenery of Feywood Forest stretched out below us, and for the first time in months, the dragon-sized weight on my shoulders lifted. I was almost home. Safe and sound with Aidan, where I could spend the next week without the constant threat of jealous Fae students, without having to constantly look over my shoulder.

Goddess, it would be glorious.

I patted the dagger strapped to my hip and for a few precious moments, all was right in the world. Even memories of Reign would not spoil my homecoming.

With some death-defying maneuvering, I'd managed to escape my dormitory without running into my now-ex-professor. According to Rue, he'd been rooted outside the door all day. My getaway had involved sneaking out through the window and leaping onto Sol's awaiting back.

As we soared above campus, I could have sworn I felt his

furious shadows on our tail, but once I steered Sol into the Court of Umbral Shadows to test my theory, the sensations sputtered away. Though, I could have imagined the whole thing.

Once I was certain I'd lost my shadow tail, I guided Sol back toward the light of Ethereal lands which rimmed the Feywood Forest.

Where to, Aelia?

I narrowed my eyes to make out the land miles below before I remembered there was an easier way. Calling on my *rais*, the tip of my finger began to glow, and I traced a symbol in the air. The celestial glyph burned to life, amplifying my mortal vision. The ground below was suddenly clear, each detail perfectly magnified. *Just past those trees to the right. Do you see the small cottage ahead?*

The one with the white smoke coming from the chimney?

Yes. Our home stood at the foot of Feywood Forest, just south of the border between the two courts. Excitement brewed in my belly, a flutter of nerves suddenly battling my insides. I hadn't seen Aidan in months. How would he look? How had he fared all this time without me?

Sol angled his wings toward the ground, the flap of his mighty appendages slowing. *I'll land in the field to the right. We don't want to startle your adoptive father.*

Oh yes, good thinking. I was so excited I was not thinking clearly. A dragon landing beside our cottage would likely send poor Aidan to an early grave. It was a pity I hadn't been permitted to send word of my arrival.

As Sol slowly descended, circling the wide swath of land beside our home, I took it all in. The last rays of sunlight sinking into the horizon, bathing Feywood in a riot of warm ochre and deep magenta. Goddess, after months of endless light, I'd forgotten how beautiful a true sunset was.

A blast of brilliant light streaked across my peripheral

vision, and Sol banked to the left, the scorching flare just missing his right wing.

A warning would have been nice, Aelia! Sol growled through our bond.

What in all the realms?

Another wave of searing light surged in our direction. I gripped onto Sol's wing bones as he veered yet again, barely escaping the assault.

My head swiveled over my shoulder in the direction of the flash of *rais*. The front door of our cottage was swung open, and Aidan stood in the doorway, long silver hair blowing on the breeze and both hands splayed out toward the sky. Blazing ethereal light emanated from his palms.

No... it couldn't be. A tangle of disbelief and amazement lit up my insides as I attempted to process what I was seeing. Aidan with *rais*? How could it be? All this time, he'd lied. An invisible hand fisted around my battered heart.

"For Fae's sake... *Aidan!*" I finally shouted when the initial shock waned. "It's me, Aelia."

My adoptive father's pale gray eyes widened, mirroring the curve of his lips. "By the goddess, Aelia..." He dropped his hands, gaze intent on me.

Sol swooped down, landing a few yards away from the chicken coop. The poor little things trembled with fear as my dragon's talons hit the ground, vibrating the earth.

I leapt off his back and raced toward Aidan, who still stood frozen in the doorway. I wasn't certain who was more surprised at the moment, him or me. A flicker of light still shimmered along his fingertips, his arms at his sides.

"You're Light Fae." I whispered the confession as if it were my own. How could he have kept this secret from me my entire life? Another devastating tangle of shock and betrayal surged through my system. Of course I'd assumed he'd been keeping things from me all along, but this?

"And you have a dragon." His bulging eyes razed over Sol's

immense form. "I thought for sure he belonged to one of the royals..."

"He's my bonded skyrider." I pointed toward the gigantic golden beast. "Aidan, meet Solanthus, the Sun Chaser."

Aidan's complexion grew paler, still, until finally his head dipped. Sol mirrored the faint movement, and I watched the pair as if I were some intrusive bystander.

Do you two know each other? I shot the question through our mental link, hoping Sol would be more candid than the man who raised me, who'd apparently lied to me for two decades.

No, I do not. Sol's answer was clipped and far from satisfying.

"Well, *estellira*, after all this time, are you going to offer me a hug at least?" Aidan held out his arms, and despite the flare of irritation at him having kept this enormous secret from me, hearing him call me "little star" knocked away some of the anger, and I fell into his embrace. I would be angry later. "Welcome home, Aelia." He held me tight against his warm chest, his familiar scent filling my nostrils and immediately setting my heart at ease.

"I missed you so much, Aidan." Hot tears burned the corners of my eyes, and for once, I let them fall unhindered. Because today, I didn't have to be strong. I didn't have to be Aelia, carved of stone. I was home.

I sat across the rickety table from Aidan inside our quaint cottage with my fingers laced around the warm mug of tea. Everything was exactly as it had been when I left four months ago—and yet, it couldn't have been more different. Aidan was Light Fae, and I was... who knows what. I couldn't keep my gaze from darting to the tips of my adoptive father's rounded ears. Round not pointed. How was it possible?

After the initial pleasantries, we'd found ourselves sitting here in silence.

"You cannot keep the truth from me any longer, Aidan." I'd already attempted to extract an explanation more than once, but had been rebuffed each time.

"I simply cannot say more, Aelia," he muttered, light eyes fixed to the cup in front of him.

"*More*? You haven't said anything!" I shouted. "If I hadn't caught you using *rais*, would you have even admitted you were Light Fae?"

His lips pressed together.

"You wouldn't have, would you?" I slammed my palm against the worn table and the legs shuddered. "Goddess, this is so unfair. I deserve the truth, damn it."

"To what end, *estellira*? Do you not understand that there is a reason for all of this? That the lengths we went through to protect you—"

"We?" My voice hitched at the word.

Aidan huffed out a breath and dragged his hand through his long, silvering-white hair. It was now neatly tied back as he always wore it. Somehow seeing him like this made the surreal moment seem less so.

"Who is *we*?" I repeated when he remained silent.

"The people who loved you most in this world."

My breath hitched, all the air siphoning from my lungs in one swoop. "You knew my parents?" I rasped.

His head slowly dipped.

"How could you keep this from me? How could you lie to me all this time?" I shot up, anger rushing my veins. Good gods, first Reign, now Aidan? Was anything in my life real?

"It was only to protect you, Aelia!" Aidan rose, mirroring my pose. "I'd lie to you a hundred times over if it meant keeping you safe. That is what I was charged to do. It's been my greatest honor."

"What? Lying to me?"

"You know that is not at all what I meant." Exasperation laced his tone.

"And by whom? Who are my parents? Why did they send me away? Who did I need to be kept safe from?"

"It is not my place to share."

I threw my hands in the air, frustration filling my being. "Aidan, you cannot be serious. You are the only link to my past, and you're telling me that it's not your place to share? Then whose place is it?" I stomped around the small kitchen area, my strides growing angrier with each step. "Are my parents truly dead? Or was that a lie as well?"

"I cannot say..." he growled in irritation, whether it be at me and my questions or the situation in its entirety, I couldn't be sure.

"Gods, I cannot believe this, Aidan!" I dragged my hands through my hair, tugging at the long, blonde streak. "First, I discover I'm Light Fae, but once I arrive at the Conservatory, my powers are mysteriously lacking. And yet somehow, in the presence of my Shadow Fae professor, my finicky *rais* blooms. He has all these theories about me, but I'll never know if any are true because he's been lying to me all along as well—" I snap my mouth shut as my spiraling musings bubble out without my control.

"The Fae male who came to collect you?" His light brows arched.

"Yes."

"Why is a Shadow Fae teaching at the Conservatory?"

"Honestly, I have no idea, Aidan, because every word that comes out of his mouth is a lie, much like yours." I clenched my jaw to keep the slew of curses at bay. A part of me understood his misguided attempts in protecting me, but the other part was too furious about all the lies to even attempt to see reason. I sprinted toward the door, anxious to take in a breath of fresh air. "I need to go before I say something I'll regret." I paused with my hand on the handle and spun back, a last bit of hope unfurling inside me. "Unless there's something you'd like to tell me?"

A sigh parted his lips as his head slowly shook from side to side. "I'm sorry, *estellira*. It is safer for you to despise me than for the truth to see the light of day."

A tornado of fury and pain whirled through my chest. I pressed my hand to the spot in an attempt to alleviate the ache before I turned to the door and stormed out. How could the two men I cared most about in this world have been lying to me all along?

Chapter Four

Aelia

This was not at all how I'd imagined my one-week respite to start. Aidan refused to disclose any detail of my past, and in turn, I refused to speak to him. It had been three torturous days of silence and meaningful glares. Crouching in front of the chicken coop, I half-heartedly tossed a handful of feed and sighed. "At least you little ones are happy to see me." I clucked at the fluffy yellow chicks as they stuffed their tiny beaks with kernels, chirping happily.

Of course Aidan's happy to see you, little Kin. Sol's grumpy voice sailed through my mind.

Then why won't he tell me the truth? I fully realized I was whining; even in my head I could hear the irritating twinge.

I believe he's given you the answer to that question, regardless of whether or not you like the answer. It is for your safety.

"It's not fair!" I blurted, startling the chickens. They

squawked their displeasure before continuing with their feasting.

It may not seem fair, Aelia, but often, difficult decisions must be made for the greater good.

So you agree with him? Indignation fired up my mental tone.

There is one thing that I understand clearly. That man cares deeply for you, and if he's willing to suffer your wrath, the secret he has kept from you all these years must truly be worth his continued silence.

Now you're going to tell me Reign lied for my own good too.

I never mentioned the Shadow Fae. His tone turned surlier still. In fact, he hadn't mentioned Reign at all since the battle. I apparently was the only fool who couldn't get him out of my damned head.

Whatever... Where are you, anyway? I hated to admit it, but after the constant hustle and bustle at the Conservatory, this sudden quiet had me uneasy. And lonely.

Soaring over the Court of Ethereal Light, on my way back toward Feywood.

Good. I could use a flight to take my mind off things.

You may want to warn your fellow Kin in the village. I've already received more than my fair share of fearful gazes.

Not fun being stared at, is it? I hadn't hazarded a walk through the village since my return, but I couldn't imagine the relief of once again being able to amble freely without the constant stares at my rounded ears and odd hair.

I am a dragon, Aelia. I live under perpetual scrutiny by all—Fae, Kin and wild beasts alike.

A twinge of regret stabbed at my heart. Gods, I was being selfish. I'd been so wrapped up in my own misery I hadn't once considered my skyrider. As one of the few remaining dragons, he lived under perpetual attention. *I'm sorry, Sol. And not just for being so insensitive, but for my overall behavior in the last few days. I'm just so—*

Hurt. He spoke the word softly, stilling my thoughts.

Heartbroken, devastated, furious... The list went on and on.

If it's any consolation, the Shadow Fae is in no better condition.

My heart kicked at my ribs, and I sucked in a breath. *How do you know?* Raysa, I hated how eager I sounded.

I told you I was flying over Light Fae territory. I may have seen the good professor wreaking havoc across the Conservatory lands.

Doing what, exactly?

Let's simply say he wasn't in control of his nox, *and half of the academy had been plunged in darkness.*

The corners of my lips lifted into a begrudging smile. Draven would certainly not be pleased, especially since those silver cuffs were supposed to keep Reign's *nox* in check.

Do you feel better now, little Kin?

Maybe. Yes. A tiny bit.

It was easier to pretend everything with Reign was a lie—that the moments we shared weren't real. Those lingering glances, the whispered confessions, the feel of his body protecting mine—all just illusions. But a deep, dark part of me knew the truth. Despite my lack of experience with males, this connection between us was more real than anything I had ever felt before. And, unless I was completely clueless, the same could be said for him.

But none of that mattered because he'd betrayed me, lied to me again and again.

Not to mention the fact that he was a prince of the Court of Umbral Shadows, our greatest enemy.

Despite the feelings we may have had, we could *never* be together.

I'll be back in Feywood in a quarter of an hour. Sol's reply interrupted my dismal musings. I huffed out a breath, forcing my thoughts back to the happy chicks.

See you soon. My life was so much simpler a few months ago.

All that mattered in my little world was right here. Patting each of the chicks a quick goodbye, I closed the coop and stood, brushing the excess feed from my breeches.

The reassuring sound of flapping wings tilted my gaze to the sky. Well, that was quick. I searched the pale blue for Sol's gilded form, but instead of my dragon, two other familiar creatures emerged from between the clouds.

"Greetings from the Court of Ethereal Light!" Rue waved wildly atop Windy, with Sy aboard Griff right behind her.

"We've come to spend a few days with our favorite round-eared friend!" Symon threw me a wink as his gryphon's wings slowed their frantic beating.

"Oh, my goddess!" I squealed as I ran toward my friends. "What are you two doing here?" A beaming smile stretched across my face as the pair landed only a few yards from the cottage.

Rue leapt off her mount and raced toward me, long, curly hair billowing out behind her and arms spread wide. She pulled me into a hug, and for the first time in days, my heart felt full once again. Symon embraced me from behind, his nose blatantly nuzzling my ear. "Kin sandwich, my favorite!"

I couldn't help but laugh at my ludicrous friend.

"I hope you don't mind we came without a proper invitation." Rue held me out to arm's length, and Sy finally released me.

"Not at all. This is the best surprise ever."

Sy clapped his hands, bouncing on his toes and causing a wisp of blonde hair to come loose from its neat tie at his nape. "I was hoping you'd say that. You did promise me a proper tour of Kin lands and all the round-eared females I could get my hands on."

I smacked my friend on the back of the head, smiling. "You are absolutely incorrigible."

"Incorrigible? Let's hope the Kin females find me absolutely adorable."

"Oh, I'm sure they will." I wrapped one arm around Sy's back and weaved the other through the crook in Rue's arm, then I tugged them both toward the cottage. "Come on, I want you two to meet Aidan."

※

An hour later and my adoptive father was spinning jokes alongside my two Fae friends around the kitchen table. I supposed I shouldn't have been so surprised since he was, in fact, one of them. How long had he been posing as a mere Kin to protect me? And why were his ears round like mine? What sort of magic could be powerful enough to conceal those pointy tips?

A sobering thought crossed my mind as I watched the three of them and their lighthearted banter: Aidan had given up a life of luxury at court to live at the foot of the perilous Wilds and toil in the fields for the past twenty years. For me.

A wave of guilt crashed over me as I regarded the man who had raised me in a whole new light. Stars, I was beyond self-absorbed. Aidan had given up everything for me for some ungodly reason, and here I was, furious at him for it.

Reaching across the battered old tabletop, I squeezed Aidan's hand. "I'm sorry," I mouthed over my teacup as Sy regaled us with a tale of his failed attempts at wooing a Kin female on his last visit to Feywood.

My adoptive father offered me an indulgent smile. "No, I am sincerely sorry, *estellira*," he whispered. "And I pray that one day, I will be able to tell you everything. But for now, I hope it is enough to know that you were, and are, truly loved."

I nodded, blinking quickly to keep the tears at bay. My fingers drifted up to the medallion on my chest. As I traced the engraving, I couldn't help but consider its true origin. Was it simply another one of the lies Aidan had concocted to keep me safe? Forcing the slew of questions to the back of my mind, I drew in a breath. I simply had to trust Aidan as I always had. Once my friends had left, I'd properly apologize for my terrible behavior and thank the man who'd so selflessly raised me all these years. Perhaps, Sol was right, and some secrets were worth keeping.

Sy's big hand smacked my back, jerking me from my thoughts. "So, where will you take me tonight? I want to sample the local Feywood female delicacies with a native."

I nearly choked on my tea.

"Oh, yes, me too!" Rue blurted. "I've never been with a Kin either!"

"What about Devin?" I speared my roommate with a look.

She waved a dismissive hand, a smirk playing on her pouty lips. "Oh, Aelia, Devin and I are free to do as we please. We have an entire week apart, after all."

An entire week? I feared it would take me lifetimes to move past what Reign and I almost had, much less if we'd made it to the level of intimacy Rue and Devin had.

"You should take them to Faerie's Flagon," Aidan interjected.

Rue clapped her hands, bouncing in the chair. "Oh, Raysa, that sounds perfect!"

Chapter Five

R *eign*

"*Noxus*, will nothing remove these blasted bangles?" I roared as I levered the blade of Aelia's dagger—the one she still didn't know I had, or that was even missing—beneath the silver cuff encircling my wrist. Fury rushed my veins, that invisible force a constant in the days since the battle with Arcanum. I couldn't eat, couldn't sleep. An itch had buried deep within my skin, and there was nothing I could do to scratch it.

And now with Aelia gone to Feywood, I had nothing to focus my attention on besides these damned things. Anything to keep my mind occupied, to force my thoughts away from *her*. After days of waiting at her door, and nights spent in the shadows of her chamber, I was going absolutely mad. I had to speak to her; I had to explain...

Explain what? That my entire life had been dedicated to seeking out and destroying her?

So romantic, Reign.

Shaking my head free of the ludicrous thoughts, I concentrated once again on the task at hand. The mysterious crystal encrusted in the hilt of the dagger glimmered in the faint light of my chamber, heating against my skin, but the mystical metal held strong. Or rather, the spell that kept the full breadth of my powers bound did.

If Gideon was right about the origin of Aelia's daggers, they should have been able to break past a *rais*-imbued spell crafted by the semi-competent headmaster. Draven's power was far from impressive. It didn't make any gods' damned sense.

I forced the tip of the blade farther beneath the cuff and the sharp edge sliced across my skin. I bit out a curse as blood dribbled down my forearm. But it did nothing to halt my determination. I would get these sun-cursed manacles off or slit my wrists trying.

Clenching my teeth, I gritted out obscenities as I continued my attempts and still failed to pry off the cuffs. "Fuck!" I hissed and hurled the dagger across the chamber. It sailed through the sliver of space between the dark curtains and smashed against the stained-glass window. Shards of deep crimson and ochre scattered across the floor, landing alongside the dagger.

I strode toward the broken window, the familiar thrumming of air squeezing through the crack raising the hair at my nape. Shoving aside the heavy curtain, my eyes narrowed on the mass of darkness looming closer.

What in all the courts?

With the rare hour of twilight overhead, casting shadows across the light-filled lands, the slate dragon hovered closer, just beyond the wards surrounding the Conservatory. My *nox* lurched to the surface, tendrils of night buzzing around my form.

Standing beneath the ornate arch, I wrenched the windows open and loosed one of my shadows to deliver a message to the intruder.

"What are you doing here, Ruhl?"

Even from this distance, I could just make out the twitch in my sibling's mouth. "Is that any way to greet your dear brother?"

"Dear? It's been four years and you never dared cross the Luminoc to visit before. And now, twice in a week? Did Father send you?" A whisper of fear lanced through my chest. Had Ruhl told the king about Aelia? Thank the gods, she was far away from here.

"I have my own mind, Reign. I'm not simply Father's heir."

I snorted on a laugh. Our entire lives Ruhl had been groomed to take the place of mighty King Tenebris of Umber, while I was trained for one thing only: to seek out and kill the child of twilight.

A child of twilight, born from the dance of light and dark, shall emerge with the power to reshape destinies. From the celestial embrace and the shadow's whisper, a harbinger of cosmic balance shall be brought forth.

A fateful choice awaits her - to heal or to harm, to nurture or annihilate. Her every step shall resonate through realms, influencing the very fabric of existence.

When the child of twilight shall come of age, her choices, guided by the celestial and obscured by shadows, shall determine the fate of worlds. Whether she becomes a beacon of hope or a harbinger of oblivion, the child of twilight shall be the catalyst of an epochal choice - to bring forth a new dawn or plunge all into eternal dusk.

The words of the prophecy rang out in my mind, each syllable permanently entrenched in my skull. Father had forced me to recite it over and over again as he pummeled me with waves of *nox*.

It was because of it that I grew strong, more powerful than the great Shadow heir.

"Then why did you come?" I growled.

"Simply to check on you." Ruhl's dragon hovered closer, a

hairsbreadth from the shimmering wards. "Come, let's go for a ride. Surely, Phantom isn't far. I'd like her to formally meet Mordrin, Eternal Nightbringer."

I barely restrained an eyeroll. That was why he'd come. Since I'd been chosen by my skyrider all those years ago, every dragon male had sought to claim her. Dragons were rare in Aetheria, and females, even more so. My brother should've known by now that Phantom was not interested in finding a mate.

I'd rather bite Mordrin's cocky head off than fly by his side. Phantom's words brushed through my consciousness right on cue.

Don't you have better things to do than listen in on my thoughts, old girl?

Unfortunately, not. Trust me, there are many things I'd prefer to do than listen to you wallowing in self-pity. Aelia this and Aelia that...

Enough.

Her chuckle rumbled deep in my chest, filling the vacant cavity. Nothing but a gaping hole remained since Aelia's hasty departure.

Will you come or not? I cannot suffer Ruhl's company without you.

So you would force me to suffer it too?

Yes, that's your duty as my bonded skyrider.

It seems Noxus did not choose well for me.

Now it was my turn to laugh, a deep belly one I hadn't experienced since the dreaded battle. *Come on now, you know you miss me.*

Sadly, I do, but it is only out of sheer boredom and desperation.

"Phantom will be here shortly," I whispered through my shadows. "But she has already warned me that she has zero interest in your new skyrider."

"What makes you think Mordrin would be interested anyway?" my arrogant brother shot back.

"Because he's a dragon and *male*."

Thank Noxus, Phantom appeared across the horizon, putting an end to our conversation. Summoning my shadows, they curled into wings around my back. I leapt out the window and caught the faint breeze, my wings propelling me toward the two awaiting dragons along the border.

Once I was seated across Phantom's back, my shadows receded and I released a shuddering breath. Now, beyond the Conservatory's wards, using my powers was taxing, despite the glorious feel of the cool night.

"How do you do it, brother?" Ruhl's dark gaze twisted in my direction. "To live among the enemy for so many years? To have your *nox* bound? To suffer the humiliation…"

I raised my hand, cutting off his ramblings before I loosed a shadow to silence him more permanently. Given our ten-year age difference, my younger brother and I were never close, but he seemed to grow more irritating by the day. "It's my duty, Ruhl. Just as you have yours. And mine is to avert the utter ruin of our courts."

"By finding the child of twilight."

"Yes."

"And you're certain the Kin, Aelia Ravenwood, is not the one?"

My *nox* surged to the surface, the fury his words sparked eclipsing the power of the manacles. "I already told you…"

He lifted a hand, donning a placating smile. "Yes, you have. I'm simply not certain I understand what it is between you then." He motioned at the swirl of darkness I hadn't realized surrounded me. "Only mere mention of the girl has you in a tizzy."

"It's lust you're seeing, little brother," I gritted out. "You would recognize it if you'd ever experienced a proper bedding."

Ruhl threw back his head and laughed.

My brother was predictable, at least. There was nothing like talk of females to get his mind off important issues. He, much like I had been at his age, was quite adept at capturing female attention. Whether it was his title or something more, no one could be certain.

"Trust me, I have never had any complaints in that department."

I shrugged nonchalantly. "But have the females?"

Ruhl clucked his tongue. "I know what you're doing, big brother, and it's not going to work. I *will* find out the truth about you and that little Kin sooner or later. Besides, the new term is soon to begin, and you know what that means."

Curses, I did. Which explained part of my foul temper. Of all the ill-timed moments for Aelia to refuse to speak to me. She would need my help this term more than ever.

A tornado of shadows whipped around my form, stretching across Phantom's wide expanse. "If you set your sights on her, Ruhl—"

"Relax, brother, I won't kill your precious Kin. Besides, if she *is* the child of the prophecy, Father will make you do it yourself." He tossed me a sneer. "Now, tell me, is it true what they say about Kin? That the pleasure is magnified?"

My thoughts flittered back in time unwittingly. To the feel of Aelia's soft form beneath me, the touch of every curve, the sound of her faint moans as I tasted her, but mostly to the wild drumbeats of my heart and the strengthening tethers lacing around my staggering, battered organ. I hadn't even claimed her yet, and already I was certain she was mine.

But fate had other plans for us.

"No," I finally grumbled with my brother's expectant gaze boring into the side of my face. "It was much like being with any other female."

I'd never told such a blatant lie in my life, which spoke volumes, since nearly every word I'd spewed in the past four years held some sort of untruth. With the depressing reality boring down on me, I lapsed into silence.

When Aelia returned, I would have to find a way to earn her forgiveness. The prospect of life without her was unbearable; the darkness was suffocating, and even the brightest light had lost its luster.

Chapter Six

Aelia

"I love you guys," I slurred, holding up my flagon of berl, a sorry rendition of the lager Heaton had brought from the outskirts of the Court of Ethereal Light. The Kin version was distilled from the remnants of the wheat we harvested for the Fae. It was much less potent, but tonight, I'd consumed more than my body weight in the stuff.

"We love you too!" Rue and Sy smothered me in a tangle of arms. They'd also enjoyed copious quantities of the Kin specialty.

A happy jig hummed along in the background, two of Feywood's famous fiddlers striking up a tune that had the entire pub on their feet. Holding up my skirts with my free hand, I attempted the intricate steps. Step, step, turn and kick. In my mind, I was the star of the dancefloor, but judging by the squeals coming from Sy as I stomped on his toes, perhaps I wasn't quite as coordinated as I imagined.

But none of that mattered right now, because for the first time in a week, I could breathe. My heart skipped along happily, and all thoughts of Reign were pushed to the corners of my hazy mind.

"By the gods, Aelia, is that you?" A familiar voice spun my head to the outer rim of the circle that had formed around us.

A head of fiery crimson emerged from the crowd, a smile forming across freckled cheeks. "Edgert?"

Dropping the tankard on the bar top, I launched myself at my old friend. His arms laced around my waist as he spun me in a circle. "I cannot believe it's really you, Aelia. We all heard you were sent to that gods' forsaken Conservatory, and I'd feared the worst." Gently lowering me to the dusty ground, he held me out to arm's length. "I'm so relieved to see you alive and well."

"I'm relieved to be alive." I snorted on a laugh. "I can quite honestly say I'm as surprised as you are to find myself still breathing."

Rue cut in between us, a beaming smile on her face. "Oh, Mother Raysa, is this *the* Edgert?"

I nodded quickly, snagging my bottom lip between my teeth. I still couldn't believe I'd told Rue the sad story of my first kiss with none other than the redhead standing in front of me.

"Edgert, this is my roommate at Luce, Rue Liteschild—"

"Roommate and best friend." She held out her hand as Edgert stared at her pointy ears.

"And I'm Symon Light—" Sy's jaw snapped shut. He was likely remembering the trouble he had last time he'd visited, simply because of his last name. The Lightspires owned much of the farmland in Feywood, which meant most of the Kin here spent their lives working his family's fields. "Just call me Sy."

"Pleased to meet you both." Edgert eyed my new friends warily, and I couldn't really blame him. All our lives we'd been raised with this idealistic notion of the Fae; that they were greater than us and we were barely worthy to stand in their radiant presence.

A few other males I'd grown up with approached, emboldened by Edgert's advance. They each offered me their greetings before circling Rue, watching my Light Fae friend in utter fascination.

As we all chatted, catching up with my old acquaintances, Rue curled her hand around Edgert's friend Myron's bicep and tugged him to the center of the dancefloor. "Come on, Ron, show me how it's done."

His head twisted toward me, hazel eyes alight in fear as my friend dragged him away.

"Don't worry, Myron, she'll take it easy on you."

Sy chuckled, weaving his arm through mine. "A hundred gildings says she'll have that Kin in her bed before the night is out."

"I may be slightly intoxicated, but I'm no fool, Symon," I slurred. "And only a complete idiot would take that bet."

Sy's finger traced the rounded tip of my ear, and a faint sigh pursed his lips. "Touché, my friend. Since you *are* slightly intoxicated, should we make this the night we take our relationship to the next level?"

"I'd have to be much more inebriated for that to *ever* happen."

"You are an evil, little thing, dashing my hopes like that!" He pouted, pushing out his bottom lip, and I couldn't deny how utterly adorable he appeared.

"Oh, Sy, you know I love you." I curled my arms around his neck and backed him to the dancefloor. "Fear not, I'll find the round-eared Kin for you." Scanning the gathered crowd, my gaze landed on a chestnut-haired female. Gertrude Hollowood. Perfect.

Shimmying my way toward the girl, I pulled Symon along with me. Her eyes widened at our approach, a sharp breath hissing past her fuchsia-tinted lips. "Hi Gertie, nice to see you again."

"Oh, Aelia, I'm so glad you're all right." Her curious gaze flickered between Sy and me.

"I'm alive, at least." I gave her my best smile. "I'd like to introduce you to my friend Symon. He's an excellent dancer, and I was hoping you could teach him the steps? I seem to have two left feet tonight."

"Of course, I'd be honored."

Sy's brow arched, a mischievous gleam in his lilac irises as he extended a hand. "A pleasure, darling." Gertie's hand closed around it, her cheeks burning a bright crimson as she led him to the center of the bustling dancefloor.

With both my friends happily occupied, I turned toward the bar to reclaim my flagon. I was suddenly parched. As I squeezed through the twirling bodies, the boisterous atmosphere perked up my dwindling mirth. I reached for the tankard and a hand closed around my own.

"I believe you owe me a dance, Miss Aelia." Edgert grinned at me, a drink in his free hand.

"Miss?"

"Well, I'm not certain how to address you, now that you've become one of them."

My head whipped back and forth. "I am not one of *them*."

His gaze raced across my chest to where a sliver of my Light Fae mark was exposed. It glimmered beneath the flickering candlelight overhead. "That gods-blessed symbol would say otherwise."

How could I tell him I had no idea who I truly was? I no longer felt like a mere Kin, but I was not Light Fae either. Would I ever fit in anywhere?

"Does it matter what I am?" I brought the mug to my lips and gulped down the remainder.

A grin lit up his amber eyes as he watched. "Of course not. You'll always be Aelia Ravenwood to me."

In that moment, that was all I wanted to hear. A smile melted across my lips as I glanced up at good old Edgert. "Let's dance." I wrapped my hand around his and tugged him onto the dusty, wood-planked floor. After only a few steps, the lively tune slowed, and his arms circled my waist, pulling me into his chest. He felt safe and familiar. Perhaps, I'd been foolish before in not giving my faithful friend a chance. He'd always made his feelings for me obvious, unlike a certain lying, bastard Shadow Fae professor.

We danced for a while, our bodies moving to the sharp twang of the fiddle. I kept one eye on my friends, each one completely enthralled by their partners. At least Rue and Sy would make unforgettable memories on this trip to Feywood. I could only imagine what they would say about finally bedding a Kin, because the way things were going, neither was far from their goal.

"It's so good to see you again, Aelia." Edgert's words drew my attention back to my partner. His palm cupped my cheek, his light touch, sweet and gentle. "I must admit, I feared I'd never see you again. It was quite a sobering thought."

"I had moments at the academy I believed I'd never see anyone ever again," I admitted. The berl had certainly loosened my tongue.

His gaze dipped to the Light Fae mark once again, and a rueful smile flitted across his face. "It appears Raysa truly has blessed you."

If he only knew what I'd endured, I'm not certain he'd feel the same way. I shrugged, not wishing to delve into the tumultuous past few months. The only thing that interested me in the moment was the bottom of my flagon.

Maybe if I drank enough, Rue and Sy wouldn't be the only ones with a memorable stay in Feywood. Perhaps it was time to rid myself of this cursed virginity, once and for all. If Reign wouldn't take it, I'd offer it to a more worthy male.

Tipping my chin up to meet Edgert's warm gaze, I

convinced myself this was what I wanted. He'd always been kind and respectful, and he certainly was pleasing to look at. Why shouldn't I?

"Aelia, all this time apart and the terrifying thought of losing you, it made me think—" Edgert's words fell away as his lips brushed mine.

The touch was so light I barely felt it. Not only had my lips felt little, my heart felt less still. It was nothing like the fiery surge I'd experienced simply standing within Reign's proximity. Goddess, how could I be so stupid? As if one drunken night with Edgert could possibly erase my feelings for Reign?

I could never be so lucky. Nor could I be so unfair to Edgert.

I pressed my palms to my friend's chest, slowly shaking my head. "I'm sorry, I can't."

He froze beneath my touch, cheeks burning a rosy hue, eclipsing the familiar freckles. "No, no, it's my fault. I never should have been so bold."

Staggering back a step, I pointed over my shoulder to the door. "I need a bit of fresh air. I may have overdone it with the berl." Signaling toward my friends, I murmured, "Would you let them know I'll be outside if they look for me?"

Edgert nodded, his mouth a grim line. "Of course."

Spinning around, I sprinted for the door, bumping into warm bodies, my steps more unsure than the ragged beats of my heart.

Chapter Seven

A*elia*

Hidden beneath the thick canopy of leaves from the encroaching forest, I drew in a much-needed breath. I leaned against the massive trunk of an old willow and cocked my head to the dark sky. Through the tangle of twisted branches, a bright full moon appeared, and beside it, a myriad of twinkling stars. Each one reminded me of Reign and that unfathomable midnight gaze. What a fool I'd been to have not seen the truth all along. Curses, I'd even called him the prince of shadows once.

Prince Reign of Umber, heir to the great King Tenebris of the Court of Umbral Shadows.

As I savored the bitter taste of his royal title on my tongue, a sobering thought streaked across my mind. In that mid-air chaotic exchange with Prince Ruhl, he'd called himself the heir.

I am Prince Ruhl of Umbra, heir to King Tenebris of the

Court of Umbral Shadows. And the male standing so protectively in front of you is my eldest brother, Prince Reign.

If Reign was the eldest, why wouldn't he be the heir to the king?

So many unanswered questions. My lips twisted as I regarded the night sky, the endless obsidian stretching toward the Fae Courts to the north, to where that former professor of mine was apparently raining shadows. Had Reign returned to his home for the break? Was he too staring up at the same sky? Or was he trapped on Light Fae soil, playing the role of eager professor?

Shaking my head, I attempted to dislodge all thoughts of the duplicitous Fae. *It does not matter what he is doing, Aelia, because he is no longer any concern of yours.* No matter how many times I repeated the phrase to myself, my foolish heart could not seem to process the change of course.

The door to the pub squealed open, calling my attention to the familiar forms stumbling out.

"There you are, Aelia!" Rue sprang forward but her steps faltered thanks to the copious amounts of berl. Somehow, Sy weaved an arm around her before she fell, but he was in no better state.

The two toppled to the ground in a heap of legs and laughter. Mud coated the earth, immediately blanketing the pair in a layer of dark sludge. The absurdly comical sight brought a smile to my face as I marched toward my drunken friends. After the mini-kiss with Edgert and the ensuing sobering thoughts of Reign, my pleasant buzz had all but fizzled away. Standing over them, I waggled my brows. "It seems as if the two of you had fun tonight."

"So much fun," Rue purred.

"And the night is still young!" Sy grabbed my arm and pulled me on top of them. His sly fingers found my most ticklish spot, just under my ribs, and before long, I was squirming and cackling right along with them.

"Who knew rolling around in the dirt could be so fun?" Rue laughed.

"Oh, I knew." Sy flashed my roommate a smirk, lilac eyes glittering with mirth.

Symon finally released me, and I sat up, lifting my skirts so they would not become even more caked in mud. "What happened to Myron and Gertie?" I glanced from one to the other.

Rue raised a dismissive hand. "We didn't come all this way to Feywood simply to take advantage of unsuspecting Kin. We came to be with our friend."

"Speak for yourself," Sy grumbled.

I dug my elbow into his side, and he doubled over, laughing. "I jest, my little round-eared friend. You know no other Kin could compare to you, as no other ear is so perfectly round and tempting..." He stroked the tip of my ear affectionately.

"Oh, stop!" I wriggled free of his touch and forced myself up. "Well, if you're certain you won't be taking any company home, we should probably start back." The threat of the Wilds had been drilled into me since birth, and lingering outside at the height of a full moon was never wise.

It was a pity we had sent my friends' skyriders off to hunt with Sol. A quick flight home would have been preferable to the hike we were about to endure back to the cottage.

"Lead the way, oh knowledgeable one." Sy dipped into an elaborate bow, pale blue moonbeams highlighting his flaxen hair.

The walk home passed quickly enough, filled with Sy and Rue's easy banter. Symon was convinced he'd broken his curse with Kin and would surely succeed in claiming one upon his next visit. Surprisingly, Rue admitted she missed Devin. I half-listened to their stories, a part of my mind wandering. In only two days, we'd return to the academy. I hated to acknowledge that a tiny part of me was eager. The other, more sensible part was terrified, and rightly so.

Heaton had warned us that each term would be more difficult than the last.

The rustle of branches jerked my attention to the tree line to our right. Despite the berl, both Symon and Rue reacted as quickly as I did. All three of us spun in the direction of the sound, my dagger already unsheathed, *rais* blooming along my friends' fingertips. Though my *rais* had certainly come a long way, I still preferred the use of my favorite weapon.

"War is nearly upon us. The courts will not be able to hide the truth for much longer." The words were so faint, I wasn't certain I'd heard them correctly. My head whirled between my two friends, but neither seemed to have heard the ominous whispers. Was I simply hearing things again, like in the final trial?

"Who's there?" I hissed.

"I told you we never should have come this close to the village," a male voice grumbled.

"I had to piss," replied another.

"Come out from there and show yourselves," I shouted, clenching the dagger in my fist.

Two forms emerged from the bowels of the forest, pushing aside gnarled branches until the males were revealed. I immediately recognized the distinctive alabaster uniforms of the Royal Guardians from the Court of Ethereal Light.

"Lawson?" Rue yelped, lively blue eyes wide.

It only took me an instant to recognize the name.

"Rue, what are you doing here?" The tall male with pale silver hair gaped.

Without responding, my friend launched herself at her eldest brother, her squeals of happiness echoing through the quiet woods.

"Oh, Lawson Liteschild!" Sy's eyes widened in understanding. "I thought her brother was stationed in the eastern parts of the Court of Umbral Shadows, near the Shadowmere Sea," he whispered.

"As did Rue."

As the siblings spoke in hushed whispers, Sy approached the other Light Fae male in uniform. "Hello, sir. I'm Symon Lightspire, initiate at the Conservatory of Luce, and who might you be?"

The Fae dipped his head. "Gareth Glower, graduated from the Conservatory with Lawson here just last year." His eyes darted to mine, first to my dark hair and then rounded ears, before settling on the glimmer of the mark along my chest. "And you are?"

"Aelia Ravenwood, also an initiate."

"And Light Fae," Sy added proudly.

The Royal Guardian's brows knitted as he regarded me. Anything he may have wanted to say died on his tongue when Rue bounded into the center of the conversation, hauling her brother along with her. She held onto his arm tightly, as if he might disappear if she released him.

"This is my brother, Lawson. Law, my roommate, Aelia, and our friend, Symon."

I offered a tight smile. There was something about his wary gaze that had unease churning in my gut.

"They're patrolling the border along the Wilds," Rue explained.

"Why, has something happened?" I blurted.

Lawson shook his head, but again, there was something about his expression that didn't evoke much confidence.

"Law, if you know something, you must tell us." Rue tugged at her brother's arm. "Aelia's adoptive father lives near the border. She's worried for his safety, that's all."

The tight set of his jaw softened a touch. The elder Liteschild's gaze held nothing of the warmth of his younger siblings'. Had he always been like that, or was it the result of his training at the Conservatory?

"There's nothing solid I can share, but there are rumors—"

"Watch your tongue," Gareth snapped, cutting him off. "You know the information is confidential."

Lawson turned to his companion. "She's my sister, Gareth, and she'll be one of us before long. They all will." He paused, blowing out a breath. "Raysa, willing," he murmured softly.

"There's nothing to tell," Gareth muttered. "All we've heard are unsubstantiated reports."

"About what, exactly?" I stepped closer to the Royal Guardians, that hint of unease only growing more potent with this strained exchange.

"Movement across the border."

A carousel of images raced across my mind of terrifying creatures making their way toward the edges of Feywood. "Then you must stop the beasts," I cried. Memories of the blood-thirsty gloomwhisper came next, flitting to the surface, and fear for Aidan constricted my lungs. "The Kin here are powerless. They'll be slaughtered."

The Royal Guardians exchanged a hesitant gaze.

"Please, Law," said Rue, "if you know something, you must tell us."

"I don't know anything." He turned his pale blue eyes on me. "Just tell this Aidan fellow to be prepared for anything. There are much worse things beyond the borders than the frightening beasties they told us about as children."

I swallowed hard, forcing down the lump in my throat.

"We have to go, Lawson." Gareth signaled toward the forest. "The commander will have wondered what's happened to us."

Rue's brother nodded. "He's right. We'll have to say our goodbyes now." He curled his arm around his sister's shoulders and drew her into a hasty embrace.

"But we barely had a chance to catch up." Rue stared up at her brother, eyes glossy.

"I hope to be home upon the Spring Solstice."

"That's six months from now, Law."

He bent down and cupped Rue's cheek, harsh lines cutting

into his jaw. "I know, and if the gods are good, we'll both survive that long." With a quick wave over his shoulder to the rest of us, he spun around and marched toward the edge of the forest.

We watched the Royal Guardians for a long moment, with their broad shoulders and gleaming white uniforms, until the darkness swallowed them whole.

Chapter Eight

Aelia

The remainder of the week flew by much faster than it had started. As I stood in the washroom, drawing a brush through my hair and staring at my reflection, I couldn't believe my time home had already come to an end.

More than that, it was nearly impossible to comprehend that only a few months ago, I'd stood at this very mirror when I discovered the Light Fae mark—or what I later discovered was a Light Fae mark, but which had started out as odd, angry slashes. Pulling the collar of my tunic down, I found the mysterious medallion Aidan had gifted me. If only I could find the answers I sought... Then my fingers moved farther, tracing the pattern of glittering swirls beneath my collarbone.

Why did you choose me Raysa? Who am I?

You do understand that the goddess in her infinite abilities cannot answer you, correct? Sol's gruff voice interrupted my musings.

Yes, you impertinent dragon, of course I understand. And stop listening in to my personal ponderings!

I'm trying, Aelia, but at times, you make it quite difficult.

The familiar pounding of air just beyond the flimsy cottage walls had my head instinctively tilting skyward. Except, in the small washroom I found only a dark, thatched ceiling, instead of the immense skylight I was accustomed to at the Conservatory. A tremor shook the earth beneath my feet a moment later, and Sol's presence bloated my chest.

I've arrived.

I guessed as much. We don't often have earthquakes in Feywood, thank the gods.

Very funny, little Kin. I will wait for you beneath the cover of the trees. No need to terrify more villagers.

I think most have grown accustomed to you by now.

I'm not so sure about that. Your neighbor with the sprawling farmlands gave me the evil eye when I glanced at his goats.

That's completely understandable.

I suppose. In any case, call for me once you've said your goodbyes.

A knot of emotion tightened my throat at the prospect of leaving Aidan once again. *Will do. Thanks, Sol.*

At least Aidan and I had been on good terms for the last few days. Once Rue and Symon left, I spent every waking moment with him. The only thing we had left to do together was my favorite pastime. Pulling my wild hair into a tie at the top of my head, I hurried out of the washroom.

My dagger was already strapped to my hip, and a buzz of excitement pulsed through my hands. In the past few days, I'd used little *rais*, the occasional hum of power equal to the sensations I experienced while on Light Fae land. There was clearly something to Reign's theories about my powers as nothing spurred my reluctant *rais* to life like standing upon Shadow Fae soil. Dismissing the pointless thoughts for now, I hurried outside to find Aidan awaiting patiently as always at the field adjacent to our cottage. The straw-filled targets stood ten yards away, and already my fingers itched for my blade.

"Are you ready, Aelia?" Aidan's long hair was swept into a neat tie, as he typically wore it.

"Always." I moved beside him and drew in a breath before unsheathing my dagger. I thumbed the hilt, the warmth of the crystal beneath sending pops of energy across my skin. I barely held my tongue, wishing I could ask Aidan more questions about its origin.

"Where's your other dagger?"

Aidan's question froze the blood in my veins. I spun at him, jaw nearly unhinged. "*Other* dagger?"

His light brows furrowed as he regarded me. "I gifted you two blades on your sixteenth birthday, *estellira*. You left for the Conservatory with both, do you not recall?"

By the goddess, I did not. My thoughts swirled back in time, to every moment I used my dagger while at the academy. Each and every memory only held one.

Memory... Reign!

"That no good, lying, cheating Shadow Fae," I snarled. "I'm going to murder him!"

"Your professor?"

My head bounced up and down. "Reign's shadows can infiltrate a Fae's mind. They can twist and alter memories..." Oh gods, what other thoughts had he stolen from me?

"It takes an extremely powerful Shadow Fae to manipulate memories. Who is this male?"

For some insane reason, I hadn't even told Aidan the truth about Reign's royal blood. Perhaps, I did it as punishment for his refusal to tell me about my own mysterious beginnings. And even now, I simply couldn't force the words from my mouth.

Had Reign manipulated me somehow? Had he forced me into a binding agreement without my knowledge?

"Aelia?"

"I don't know," I finally muttered.

Aidan's hands curled around my shoulders, squeezing. "It is imperative you locate the second dagger."

"Because of the infernium vein?" I blurted. Blasted loose tongue. I supposed I couldn't blame it on the alcohol this time.

Aidan blanched, his weary eyes bulging. "How did you know?"

"Since you refuse to tell me anything, I've been forced to undertake my own research." Again, I was not certain why I kept Reign's name out of it. Embarrassment? Guilt? Now that I knew Aidan was Light Fae, I was certain he'd disapprove of the entirely inappropriate relationship with my ex-professor. And he wouldn't be wrong. Clearly, he was not to be trusted.

"*Estellira*, I am begging you to stop." Those light gray eyes seared into mine. "Delving into your past will only shatter the future you deserve. You must trust me." His hands slid down my shoulders and curled around my palms. "Please, promise me you will look no further."

I willed my mouth to form the words, but I simply couldn't. It was one thing to accept that Aidan would not tell me the truth, but to agree not to seek it out myself? It was too much.

"I can't..." I murmured. "Aidan, do you realize what you're asking of me? To turn my back on my past, to forsake the person I was destined to become?"

"If you do not stop, *estellira*, you will not survive long enough to see that day."

The breath caught in my throat and icy frost coated my veins at his words, rushing through every inch of me. A blade in the gut would have pierced me less deeply.

"I suppose I'll have to risk it then."

Aidan blew out a breath, his shoulders sagging, but a rueful smile curled the corner of his lip. "I wouldn't expect anything less from you. You are as stubborn as the day is long and fearless to a fault. You are so much like them..."

Emotion quickened my breaths, hot tears suddenly stinging my eyes. "...I am?" I choked out.

Aidan nodded slowly. "And they would be ever so proud of the woman you've become."

I threw my arms around his neck and pulled him into an embrace. "Thank you," I whispered.

"No, thank you, *estellira*. Raising you has been my greatest honor." He slowly released me, holding me out to arm's length. "Now, let's get some practice in before that dragon whisks you back to the Conservatory."

I nodded and curled my fingers around the hilt of my dagger once more. "I promise I'll find the other blade, Aidan. And no one will discover their secrets."

"I know you will." He signaled toward the target across the field. "Now, throw."

The soaring alabaster turrets of the Conservatory of Luce loomed closer with each flap of Sol's mighty wings. My heart kicked at my ribs, my pulse matching the thundering tempo.

Reign was a dead Fae.

Despite wishing nothing more than to keep my distance from the duplicitous male, I'd have to deal with his newest treachery immediately. How could he steal one of my daggers and erase it from my memory?

A flicker of fear kindled deep in my core. What if he'd given my dagger to his father, the king? That infernium blade had the power to destroy Light Fae...

Oh, please, Raysa, no. I would never forgive myself.

Fate weaves her own plans for us, little Kin. You must not be so hard on yourself. Much is beyond your control.

Are you saying I'm powerless to fix this, Sol?

I suppose only time will tell.

Sol's wings angled toward the lush campus below, and we

began our descent. With the whipping winds tossing hair across my face, I hazarded a glance over my shoulder at the dark citadel across the river. It loomed dangerously along the border, its obsidian walls gleaming beneath the moonlight.

I should have known never to trust anyone bred in that darkness.

Chapter Nine

A*elia*

The campus was quiet, an eerie stillness descending upon the sun-soaked land. It was early still and most of the students had yet to return from the term break. Once I'd landed upon Light Fae soil, it took me only moments to track down my former Shadow Fae professor. His distinctive aura called to me, that whirling darkness like a magnet yanking me into his all-consuming orbit.

Standing across the training field, I halted my rushed footsteps as I took him in at a safe distance for the first time in over a week. The withering sun kissed his bare shoulders, illuminating the beads of sweat across his torso as he arced his sword high above his head. Every dip and valley of his perfectly carved form glinted in the sunlight. Wild tumbles of dark hair fell across his brow, each strand exactly as I remembered it. I could practically feel it's silky touch between my fingers. His full lips were pursed, scruffy jaw clenched into a hard line as he battled his own shadows, swinging the broadsword in mighty arcs.

Each nerve in my body lit up at the sight of him, happily humming at his mere presence. I gritted my teeth, forcing down the unwanted sensations. *I am Aelia, carved of stone.* I had hoped the time apart would dampen this strange connection between us, but it seemed to have the opposite effect.

Raysa, it was unfair how much I missed him.

As I stood there on the edge of the field, every muscle urged me forward. I could barely keep my feet from launching myself at him. Curling my twitchy fingers into fists, I reminded myself that not only had Reign lied to me about who he was, he'd also stolen one of my beloved daggers and altered my memories. Who knew what else he'd done?

A swirl of anger blossomed in my chest, and I clutched on to it for dear life as I marched toward him. He must have heard me as I stomped along the crisp grass, but he never spared me a glance. Instead, his shadows grew more furious, churning around his body like a tornado of pure night.

"Reign," I growled as I stood just beyond the whipping strands of darkness.

He spun around, sword held high over his head. His mouth curved ever so slightly, and he drew in a breath, as if he were drinking me in. That dark gaze raked over me, those eyes more lethal than the wild shadows encircling his form.

Reign swallowed hard, his Adam's apple jogging along the column of his throat. His eyes found mine and held me there, captive. "Aelia..."

It was unfair how a single word uttered from those lips could pierce my very soul; his voice wrapping around my name with the power to shatter me in one breath. It took everything I had not to falter, to suppress the overwhelming urge to spring into his arms. I knew it was what he wanted, I could feel it in his burning gaze.

At some point, I'd learned to read this enigmatic male. He

may have lied to me for months, but *this* was real. Just as real as the fact that he was a prince, son of the King of the Umbral Court, and a masterful liar.

My hand skimmed the dagger at my thigh, and I clenched my fingers around the hilt. "Where is my other dagger?" I hissed.

The storm of shadows subsided, and the intensity of Reign's gaze faltered. His lips parted, but not a sound came out.

I held onto the anger, the betrayal, focusing on it with all my might. "Where is it, Reign?"

His shoulders sagged, and a rush of air surged past his lips. "It's safe," he murmured.

"How *could* you?" I snarled. "You had no right to take it from me, to squirm your way into my thoughts and steal my memories!"

"I know…" His eyes dropped to the verdant grass between us. He paused as if counting every single blade. "Do you remember when it happened?" Those blazing pitch orbs lifted tentatively.

"No," I snapped. "Aidan reminded me I was missing one when we went to practice this morning. If I hadn't returned home, I never would have known. You had no intention of returning it to me, did you?"

Reign crept closer, and I took a step back. "I only did it to protect you—"

"Stop!" I threw my hand up, and *rais* zipped through my veins, illuminating my fingertips. "I'm tired of the lies, Reign. I *can't*."

"They weren't all lies, princess," he whispered, the haunted look in his eyes tearing at my insides.

"It doesn't matter. One enormous lie is enough to obliterate all the tiny truths."

He held out his hand, and a shadow slithered from his fingertips and raced across my shoulders. The icy touch sent goosebumps cascading down my arms. "Then, please, allow me to tell you the truth."

I shook my head and attempted to wriggle free of the dark tendril. "It's too late."

"It's never too late." He closed the distance between us in one long stride, and his familiar heady scent infiltrated my nostrils, blanketing my body. His hand caressed my cheek before I had the sense to stop him. "Please, princess, do you want me to beg?"

The possibility was thrilling. To have the great Shadow Fae prince on his knees for me?

"All I ask is that you allow me the opportunity to explain. Once I have told you everything, I will accept whatever choice you make."

"Why should I gift you the choice you never gave me?" My voice trembled, revealing the depth of the impact he had on me.

"Because you are an infinitely better person than I." A lopsided smile tipped up one side of his mouth.

His shadows danced around us, cocooning us in a web of darkness. I barely felt my chin dip, so little was my control around this intoxicating male. Those wicked minions curled around my head, whispering as they weaved around me.

A faint pressure penetrated my skull, and my thoughts became hazy. The sprawling sunlit field vanished for an instant before another familiar scene coalesced around us. We were still on the training field, but in a new location, dead center instead of on the outskirts. Reign stood in front of me, but he was no longer shirtless and soaked in sweat.

I glanced down at the *two* daggers strapped to my waist, then to my tunic and fighting leathers. Reign also wore his typical training uniform, in all black from head to toe. He paced in front of me, shouting about something.

Wait... I recognized this scene, this very discussion.

Reign stalked closer, pinning me against a wall of shadows. "I don't give a sun's ray about Draven. But you—"

I stood staring at him as the familiar scene from months ago unfolded again before me.

"*Me, what?*" I repeated the words I'd said to him all those weeks ago, moments after he'd erased Rue's memories of my daggers.

"*Fuck it.*" *Reign's hand snaked around my neck and yanked my lips to his. A gasp escaped as he claimed my mouth, swallowed up in the tangle of rage and desire.*

By the gods... I watched the scene, jaw gaping. Present Aelia knew I should pull away, but past Aelia was too consumed in the moment. I should let this play out... I needed to find out the truth.

Reign's mouth moved over mine as his fingers delved into the hair at my nape. Gods, he tasted just as I'd remembered, like the most glorious starlit night. He laced his free hand around my waist and brought me flush against the hard planes of his body. His arousal pressed into my belly, inciting a wave of heat in my lower half.

Goddess, how had he managed to erase this from my memory?

"*Reign...*" *I whispered against his mouth.*

"*Mmm, princess. You have no idea what you do to me.*"

He tilted my head to deepen the kiss, and all restraint was lost as I gave into his heated touch. The kiss stretched on, the fiery sensations lighting up every corner of my being. It simply wasn't fair that one person could yield that much power over my body. Much too soon, Reign sucked in a desperate breath and ripped his mouth free of mine.

I stared up at him, confusion clouding the lusty haze, my chest heaving. "*Reign?*"

"*I—I'm sorry.*" *He pressed a gentle kiss to my forehead, and his shadows slithered across my form, twisting and churning.* "*I never should have—*"

"What are you doing?" My eyes widened in panic.

"It won't hurt, I promise."

His shadows slithered through my mind, and I could feel them weaving the new memories, the ones that annihilated the heated kiss and erased my memories of the second dagger. He planted a new scene, a terribly embarrassing one in which I blurted my feelings for him, and he brutally rebuffed me.

None of it had been real.

I'd never admitted the truth of my feelings, and Reign had never denied me.

He'd kissed me months before I thought he had. All that time believing my feelings were unrequited...

But why take away my dagger? I reminded myself to focus on the purpose of this entire exercise, the missing dagger, not that fiery kiss or our twisted relationship.

Blinking quickly, the scene from the past dissipated and the training field of the present appeared once again. Reign still stood in front of me, an expectant look on his unfairly handsome face.

"You kissed me," I blurted.

The dagger. The dagger. Focus, damn it.

"And you stole my dagger from my memories!"

"Only to ensure that if anything happened to yours, I could keep the other safe. I'd hoped if Gideon had more time with it, he could discover something more useful." He clenched his jaw, a tendon flaring across his dark stubbled cheek. "And I kissed you because you were all I could think about. Every waking moment, every breath, you consumed my thoughts. And yes, I'm a selfish bastard who takes what he wants, consequences be damned. I couldn't fight the pull any longer, and in that moment, nothing else mattered but having you."

My resolve crumbled at the declaration, at the fire in his eyes as he admitted the truth. And it was the truth, I could feel it in the marrow of my bones.

"You've done something to me, Aelia... anything that mattered before means nothing now. All I want is to keep you safe, and for me to do that, I need you to trust me again."

Tears burned my eyes, threatening to spill over. Gods, I wanted to trust him. There was nothing I wanted more than to fall into his embrace, to sink into his familiar feel and forget everything.

But even if I could forgive him for the lies, we could still never be together. He was a prince of the Shadow Fae, and I was no one. Kin? Light Fae? The child of twilight? I had yet to discover the truth about anything. What future could we possibly have?

"Aelia, please." He reached for me, but I staggered back, my knees already wobbling.

"I can't." I spun around, forcing my feet into motion. Tears streamed down my cheeks as I raced across the field, running from the male who meant everything to me, and the only person who had the power to utterly ruin me.

Chapter Ten

"Rise and shine, sleepy Fae."

The sweet tune pulled me from the haze of Noxus's cold embrace. My lids fluttered and slowly opened, taking in the gold ringlets cascading around Rue's familiar face.

"Is it morning already?" I grumbled.

She bounced up from the corner of my bed and fluttered around happily. Sometimes I could have sworn my lively roommate was already sun-blessed with ethereal wings. "Not only is it morning, but it's also the first day of the new term."

Internally, I winced.

I'd barely survived the first term, and that was with considerable help from my former professor. The same professor who I now had to keep my distance from at all costs. I simply couldn't trust myself around him. It was as if all logic vanished in his presence, only my naïve, foolish heart controlling my actions.

On a positive note, after I'd fled the field yesterday, sobbing like a fool, once I'd returned to my dormitory, I had found my missing dagger back in its hiding spot in the nightstand. Reign must have sent one of his shadow minions to return it. Seeing it again had nearly brought me to tears once more.

"Did you see our new classes?" Rue bounded closer with my scroll tucked beneath her arm, diverting my attention. She unrolled it across the bed as I forced myself to sit up. A glittering penmanship flickered across the parchment.

Aelia Ravenwood
Designation: First-year, Second Term
Squad: Flare
Squad Leader: Heaton Liteschild
Classes:
Luminous Enchantments
Aurora Weaving
Lightweaver's Craft
Offensive Flight
Combat
Shadow Arts

Daily Instructions:
Report to the Hall of Luminescence for the first day gathering at nine hundred hours.

My stomach pitched at the sight of the final two classes. Combat and Shadow Arts. There was only one professor on campus who taught those courses. It appeared that the male I was determined to erase from my life was to once again become a daily fixture. Sometimes the goddess seemed so unfair. "Why must we take Combat and Shadow Arts again this term?"

"I hate to break it to you, A, but we take those classes every term, every year."

A dramatic groan dribbled out and I dropped back onto the mattress, burying my face in the pillow.

"Oh, no, you don't. You're not doing this again." Rue dragged the blanket down, then pulled the fluffy cushion out from under me.

"Hey!" I squealed and curled into a ball on the bare mattress.

"I will not allow you to spend another minute pining over that good-for-nothing Shadow Fae professor."

Speaking of that liar, Reign had forced me to become one, too. In an effort to keep his secret—which I still couldn't comprehend why I continued to do so—I'd spun a white lie while in Feywood explaining the strained relationship between the good professor and me.

I had told my friends I'd admitted the truth of my feelings, and Reign had rebuffed me. I was embarrassed and hurt, and now had no desire to be in the presence of the insufferable male. The lie had been inspired by the truth, only now I knew none of it had ever happened. *Would that make me a double-liar?* Rue drew me from my thoughts as she continued her pep talk.

"Come on, Aelia. Nothing has changed, really." She waved a nonchalant hand. "Do you have any idea how many males I've been forced to see after having my heart broken?"

I raised a skeptical brow. If anyone was breaking hearts around here, it was my naughty vixen of a roommate.

"What?" She shrugged as she plopped down beside me. "I too have been scorned by an unwilling Fae or two."

"I find that impossible to believe."

She curled her arm around my shoulder and squeezed. "I swear it upon the goddess herself, and anyway, the point is, the best way to move past the hurt is to forget it existed in the first place. And the best way to do *that* is by finding someone else."

My roommate's cavalier attitude toward Fae of the opposite sex suddenly rang with more meaning. Had Rue been so hurt at some time that she chose to mask her feelings by filling her bed with males she didn't care about?

"I don't know if I can do that..."

Her light eyes twinkled with mischief. "And I know just the Fae. Someone who is already crazy about you."

I shook my head, whipping it from side to side. "Oh no, I couldn't, Rue. I would never use Heaton like that." Just the fact that she was offering him as a consolation prize had my gut churning.

Her brows knitted as she regarded me. "I didn't say anything about *using* my brother, Aelia. He genuinely cares for you, and I thought maybe you could learn to feel the same for him." Her arm fell loose from my shoulders.

"Oh, goddess, I'm sorry, Rue, that came out wrong. Any female would be beyond lucky to have Heaton."

"Then why aren't you interested?"

Because Reign has my heart in a vice, his strangling hold the most wicked of tortures. Every breath, every heartbeat belonged to him and him alone. The confession, even within the dark recesses of my mind, was disquieting.

"It's too soon," I finally murmured, my voice barely a whisper. "No matter how much I want to forget Reign, how much I want to move on and give someone else a chance, he's always there, haunting my thoughts, pulling me back."

Rue sighed, placing a comforting hand on my shoulder. "Love can be complicated and painful, but you deserve someone who treats you right, who makes you happy. I know Heaton could be that man for you."

I nodded, feeling the weight of her words. "I just need time to sort through everything. My feelings for Reign... they're not something I can easily ignore." They seemed impossible, if I was being honest with myself.

"I understand," Rue said softly. "Just promise me you'll take care of yourself and keep an open mind. Maybe one day, you'll find someone who can love you the way you deserve."

I smiled faintly. "Thank you, Rue. I promise."

"Now, get up out of that bed and let's get ready. It's nearly time for the gathering."

One thing I had not missed in the slightest during my time away was the curious stares and hateful glares from my classmates. As I settled into the seat in the second row of the grand hall, I wished I could disappear into it. The loss against Arcanum Citadel had been a brutal blow, and though I had little to do with it, I again found myself the object of everyone's hatred.

A few had witnessed the mid-air spectacle of our Shadow Fae professor and his dragon. Though his shadows had concealed most of the exchange, they could not have missed his enormous skyrider coming to what appeared to be my rescue. Unless Reign had somehow managed to erase all their memories?

The whole disastrous event had only kindled more rumors of the lowly Kin who not only seemed to have Professor Darkthorn's favor but who had also consorted with the enemy. After the battle, everyone on campus had recognized Ruhl, the heir to the Court of Umbral Shadows when his mighty dragon descended and he claimed the win for Arcanum. I could practically hear their thoughts as inquisitive, distrustful gazes lanced over me.

Why did the prince of shadows let her live?
Why does the professor dote on her so?
Why was she chosen by a dragon?

They were questions that often plagued my thoughts as well.

"Welcome back, Aelia." Heaton offered a kind smile as he scooted into the seat beside me. His presence was oddly comforting, the broad expanse of his shoulders shielding me from some of the worst glares.

"Cheers, Heaton." I countered with a smile of my own.

"I hope you enjoyed the break and had some time to rest up."

"I did."

Rue leaned across my lap and waggled her brows at her brother. "She sure did. After our big night out in Feywood and the tankards of berl she consumed, she slept nearly the entire following day away." Her head fell back as she released a cackle.

Heat blanketed my cheeks at the hazy memories of that night. "I wasn't the only one."

Sy poked his head between us, leaning forward from the row behind. "Aelia certainly was not. We were all two sheets to the moon from that oddly potent Kin draught."

"Well, I'm sorry to have missed it." A rueful smile peeled back the corners of Heaton's lips. "If someone had invited me," he said, looking pointedly at his sister, "I would have gladly jumped aboard Nigel to join you in the south."

I regarded him for a long moment, picturing him mounted upon his ligel flying beside the rest of us, as Sy recounted the stories of our drunken escapades in Feywood. Heaton was remarkably handsome with high cheekbones, full lips, and that silky, flaxen hair that fell to his shoulders. As I took in the familiar features, my thoughts turned to our encounter with Lawson and the other Royal Guardian. Had Rue shared their cryptic responses with her brother? When I'd mentioned it to Aidan, he'd taken it lightly, dismissing my worry. What truly lay beyond the border in the Wilds?

Dismissing the dark thoughts, I focused my attention to Heaton once again. He watched Symon, amusement in the tilt of his lips. Rue's brother was kind, honorable and—*not Reign*. That was the male's only discernable flaw.

As if my thoughts had summoned the dark Fae, a familiar prickle danced its way up my spine. Despite my most valiant attempts to keep my gaze focused on Symon's lively tale, my traitorous eyes twisted over my shoulder.

A cloud of umbral shadows pierced the blanket of luminescent light that flooded the hall. My breath hitched at the sight of him. The prince of shadows, as he would now forever be referred to—serving as a constant reminder of his true origins—

stalked through the grand chamber. The twinkling flames of the chandelier shriveled and then all but extinguished at his menacing sight.

My pulse escalated with each step closer, my heartbeat pounding in time with each footfall. Reign appeared as the epitome of the dark royal today in a double-breasted midnight coat that trailed the length of his long legs. His shadow minions twisted around his form, coating him in a layer of impenetrable darkness.

As if he'd sensed my stare, those starlit eyes chased to mine. They blazed with the intensity of Raysa's blessed sun, radiant and infinite as they settled over me. Then traveled to the male at my side. A flurry of *nox* pummeled into me, Reign's overwhelming power pushing against me, as if it were attempting to physically create space between Heaton and me. Those eyes seared to mine, but before I was helplessly trapped in that hypnotic gaze, I forced my head to pivot, to once again focus on my friends. As I tuned into the conversation, Symon was recounting his epic success wooing my friend, Gertrude. Zephyr and Silvan, two of the males from Flare Squad, listened intently. Apparently, a round-eared conquest, even of only the kissing variety, was of the utmost importance in this circle.

A throat cleared, the harsh, gravelly sound turning my attention, along with the rest of my groups', to the dais, only a few rows in front of us. Draven stood at the pulpit, the shards of radiant beams streaming in from the skylight bathing the headmaster in a heavenly glow. "Initiates, silence, please. It is time to face the punishment for your disastrous failure."

Chapter Eleven

Bile crawled its way up my throat as the headmaster's words echoed across the now silent hall. My gaze unwittingly darted to meet Reign's. He sat at the edge of his high-backed chair, a tendon feathering across his scruffy cheek. *Look at me.* I willed the bastard to meet my questioning glare, but he didn't move a muscle. I was not even certain he was breathing.

It was as if the entire chamber held its breath.

"Due to your resounding failure in the end of term battle with Arcanum Citadel, I have conjured a most fitting punishment." His menacing ivy gaze lanced across the quiet room, ensuring he had the full attention of every Fae in attendance before continuing. "Clearly, the majority of you are weak. At this Conservatory, we do not allow the feeble to survive. So starting tomorrow, for the next five days, I am abolishing the code of conduct."

A wave of gasps rippled across the hall.

"I don't care if you kill each other until only one stands. You first-years are an embarrassment to this sacred institution," he growled.

"He cannot be serious," Rue whispered.

Fear's claws dug into my heart, piercing my already faltering organ. I would be the number one target. Everyone here assumed I was weak.

"Oh, but he is," Heaton gritted out. "It's not the first time he's doled out such punishments for the students' failures." Our team leader's eyes dimmed, his expression haunted.

What had Draven put Heaton through when he was an initiate?

"Perhaps after the fragile have been weeded out, you will have a chance to win this term's Umbral Trials."

Umbral Trials? I thought the trials were over...

A sneer curled the headmaster's lips, his willowy mustache twisting with his mouth. "For those of you unfamiliar with the next set of trials, these will be conducted in a slightly different manner. This term, you won't simply be competing against your fellow classmates, but also with your adversaries across the river."

All the remaining air squeezed from my lungs as I processed his words. We'd be fighting against Arcanum, and more specifically, Ruhl, the heir to the Shadow throne. And after our encounter last time, I had a feeling this upcoming battle would be a personal one.

Curses...

How would I ever survive this?

A hand shot up a few seats away, drawing my attention to the long, golden-haired male. Belmore's expression morphed into something truly wicked as his eyes flitted to mine before swiveling to face the headmaster.

"Yes, Mr. Dawnbrook?" Draven drawled.

"Just so that we're clear, with no code of conduct in place, we are free to strengthen our teams in any manner possible?"

"Yes, that is exactly what I said, Belmore. Separate the wheat from the chaff and each squad will become the stronger for it."

Having grown up tending the fields of the powerful Fae, I was quite familiar with the old agrarian saying. And judging by Belmore's eager grin, I was the first he'd set his eyes on for elimination. Little did he know, I was no frail shaft of wheat, and I had no intention of returning to Feywood in an urn.

So flashing Belmore a feral grin, I mouthed, "May the strongest survive."

As we marched across campus, my faithful friends flanked my sides. A part of me was embarrassed that my friends had such little trust in my survival, but the other part, the logical one, was thankful for their dedication.

"You two realize the forfeiture of the code of conduct does not begin until tomorrow, right?"

Rue only inched closer, weaving her arm through mine as she often did in a show of support. "Of course we do, A, but there's still Lucian and Kian to take into consideration. Wherever Belmore is, those two cannot be far."

I grimaced at mention of the two males from Scorch Squad who enjoyed torturing me as a pastime. And with the forced distance I'd instituted with Reign, I was fairly certain they would no longer keep their distance.

"Aelia..." That deep voice sent my entire body into upheaval.

"Keep walking," I muttered to my friends.

"But Reign—"

I whipped my head at Symon throwing him a scathing glare.

"Oh, right, sorry. I forgot we weren't speaking *The Dark One's* name." He flung his arm around my shoulder and picked up the pace toward the banquet hall.

"Aelia Ravenwood," he barked, harsher this time. Goosebumps cascaded down my spine at the ferocious edge to his tone.

A coil of darkness inched across the back of my neck before wrapping around my throat, briefly halting my forward motion. "I am still your professor, princess, and you will obey me." His whispered snarl froze the blood in my veins.

The momentary pause was enough for Reign to gain on us. He coalesced from the shadows, wings of night towering over his head. "Both of you, leave." He eyed Rue then Sy and lifted his chin.

"You can't speak to them like that," I hissed.

"I can, and I just did." Those bottomless spheres of pure, icy onyx fixed on my friends. "Miss Liteschild and Mr. Lightspire, unless you'd like to spend the evening with me as life-sized targets for my umbral blades, I suggest you leave us, now."

Sy's panicked gaze lifted to mine, but to her credit, the mask of calm on Rue's face never faltered. Perhaps it was because she'd seen the softer side of our professor when he insisted on sleeping in our dorm to keep me "safe", or maybe she was simply that much of a badass.

Exhaling a sharp breath, I wriggled free of my friends' hold. "Go ahead, I'll be fine."

"Are you sure?" Rue gripped my hand, her hold surprisingly strong given its petite size.

"Yes." I hoped it sounded more convincing to her than it had across my own ears.

"We'll wait for you in the banquet hall." After squeezing my hand, Rue's reassuring smile flipped into a frown as she turned to face our professor. "I'll be watching you."

Reign's lips twitched, and the hard set of his jaw faltered for an instant before that icy mask slid back into place. "I'll see you on the training field, Miss Liteschild."

With a grunt, my best friend spun on her heel and tugged Symon along with her. Just when I didn't think I could possibly appreciate my best friend any more, she did something like that. I'd truly been Raysa-blessed to have found her.

The moment Rue and Sy disappeared within the crowd of students headed for the banquet hall, a wall of shadows rose up, enclosing Reign and me in a murky haze. Those familiar wisps slid over my skin, inciting a prickle of goosebumps. Steeling my spine, I searched for a strength I did not seem to possess around this male. Still, I slapped my hands on my hips and glared up at the looming Shadow Fae with false bravado. "What was so urgent you had to interrupt my supper?"

His eyes narrowed as they regarded me. "As I recall, you never ate much at dinnertime."

"Because of you." I rose to my tiptoes and speared my finger into his unyielding chest. "Because *you* forced me to train every night, and if I'd eaten like I wanted, I would have ended up spewing the contents of my stomach all over your shiny boots."

"It wouldn't have been the first time." A crooked grin tipped up the corner of one side of the perfect bow. My heart skipped and stuttered at the twinkle it brought to his fathomless irises.

"No." I shook my head and dropped back down to my heels as memories of the time he carried me to my chamber after I'd been poisoned ransacked my mind. We had been so close to giving into temptation that night... "You are not allowed to do this. You cannot simply shoot me a flirty grin and assume I'll forget everything that's happened."

The smile was instantly smothered beneath a positively tortured scowl, and I couldn't help the satisfaction that crept in. I wanted him to be miserable, just as distraught as I was because of his damned betrayal.

"That's not what I'm trying to do." He paced a quick circle within the orb of increasingly frenzied shadows and dragged his hand through his unruly head of hair. "Noxus, I cannot seem to do anything right when it comes to you."

"Then just leave me alone, Reign."

He shook his head, a torrent of emotions flashing across the endless night of his eyes. "I cannot." He gritted his teeth and muttered a curse. "Trust me, princess, if I possessed the willpower, I would have stayed away from you long ago."

Despite the soft, tortured tone, the words stung.

"Because you believe I'm this child of twilight," I spat.

His eyes widened and a sliver of night burst from his palm, wrapping around my mouth. "You cannot speak those words aloud," he growled. "You have no idea how dangerous they are."

"No, I suppose I don't," I mumbled around the mystical gag.

"I told you I would explain everything, and I still wish to, but I cannot here. There is still so much you don't understand, so much I can't figure out. There's the matter of your daggers, and your elusive *rais*—"

I raised my hand cutting him off. It took every ounce of willpower I had to force the next words from my mouth, because really, there was nothing I wished for more than to understand all of it. But I knew spending more time alone with Reign would only lead to my doom. As it was, my fragile heart could barely stand to be near him. "I don't want to know anymore."

His shadow slid from my lips and returned to its master, burrowing in his dark cloak. "But Aelia—"

"No," I hissed. "This is what I want. Can you at least respect my wishes?"

"No!" The response erupted through his clenched teeth, as if he hadn't expected the outburst. He obliterated the little distance remaining between us, his hands closing over my shoulders, fingers digging into my skin. "Because respecting your wishes means risking your safety, and I'm sorry Aelia, but to me, there is nothing more important than your life."

Overwhelming emotion tightened my throat, and hot tears threatened to spill over. Instead of giving in to the ache, I latched on to the pain until it blossomed and twisted into something darker. I attempted to wriggle free of his hold, but his fingers only tightened the more I squirmed.

"Please, Aelia, the next five days will be brutal. It's imperative you understand what is at stake."

"Let *go* of me." The anger grew more powerful, bloating my chest. A flicker of *rais* flared in my gut, and energy rushed my veins, exploding through my fingertips. The brilliant light cut through Reign's shadows and pummeled into the infuriating male, sending him flying beyond the circle of darkness.

By the time I blinked, the shadows had fallen away and Reign was splayed out across the field beside the Hall of Luminescence. He lifted his head, confusion curving his mouth into a capital O. Shaking it off, he slowly pushed himself up, and a slow smile crept across his face. "Nicely done, princess."

Knotting my arms across my chest, I spun toward the banquet hall, eager to leave him far behind. But one of those damned shadows flitted beside me, whispering its master's words.

"You may not be ready to hear the truth yet, and I will respect that. But I refuse to let you suffer for my failings. Whether you like it or not, I will stand by your side and protect you for as long as I draw breath. I have made countless mistakes in my life, Aelia, but none weigh heavier on my soul than hiding the truth from you."

Reign's shadow messenger slithered away, but his words echoed in my mind long after.

Chapter Twelve

Reign

R I stood in the middle of the field, the sun's relentless rays boring down on me, and watched Aelia march toward the Hall of Elysia. I had pretended to give her some space, as she wished, but I'd follow her into the banquet hall cloaked in shadows all the same.

That little Kin was the most stubborn, willful, frustrating, incredible... The litany of adjectives took a turn for the positive, and I halted my mind's useless wanderings. An entire week apart, and whatever this was blossoming between us had only grown stronger.

Since her return, it felt as if I had to physically restrain myself to keep my legs from instinctively moving toward her. And if I caught her—

Shaking my head, I loosened the completely inappropriate thoughts that had become a constant companion. Ever since that night in my chambers, before everything went to hell. Every second replayed in my mind—every guarded look, each heated touch, all the sweet sounds I coaxed from those pillowy lips. My heart stomped out a manic beat, battering my ribcage at the fiery memories.

Realms, what if Elisa was correct?

My thoughts flitted to my conversation with the healer all those weeks ago when Aelia had nearly died in the Skyrider Flight.

"Are you familiar with the cuorem?"

"Excuse me?"

She leaned closer and whispered, *"The cuorem bond? Have you ever heard of it?"*

My brows slammed together, her words like a vice grip around my lungs. The cuorem...twin flames. I searched my memories for what little was known about the Fae mate bond. A profound and mystical connection believed to exist between two souls, making them perfect counterparts of one another.

A true cuorem bond had not been seen in decades between Fae, and between Fae of opposing courts? It was simply unheard of. It couldn't be.

Unless...

Unless, Aelia truly *was* the child of twilight, a blend of Light and Shadow. Our bond could be from the Shadow side. But then why hadn't her *nox* emerged?

Maybe... No, it couldn't be. I would not *allow* it to be. Because if it were true, all my training, all the years of torture at my father's hands, it had all been for this moment. To find *her*. To kill *her*.

I would take my own life before fulfilling my duty.

"Professor Darkthorn." A deep, gruff voice set my shadows into a tailspin. Oh, Noxus, save me from this insufferable male.

Glancing up, the headmaster's beady eyes latched on to mine. He marched down the steps of the Hall of Luminescence, his billowing robes trailing across the marble stairs.

"Yes, Draven?"

The corners of his eyes narrowed, deep crevices wrinkling his pale skin at my informal tone. "I wish to speak to you."

"Well, here I am." I stretched out my arms, *nox* curling

around my form, twisting and weaving. After the failed battle with Arcanum, I did not find myself in the headmaster's good graces. As such, I cared not if he observed my blossoming *nox*.

I'd been forced to skulk into his mind, along with that of nearly the entire first-year class and a few other professors, to erase all traces of Phantom. Or at least, I hoped I found everyone... I'd been so depleted of my powers after, I could barely stand. Still, I found my way to Aelia's dormitory in a vain attempt to explain my inexplicable past. That obstinate little thing had managed to evade me at every turn until she and Sol departed for Feywood, her having taken avoidance to a whole new level by leaping out of her window. It had been an excruciating week apart. Thank the gods for Phantom and her never-ending patience as I dove headfirst into a desperate spiral.

If Draven knew the skyrider bond was still intact, he would have forced me to procure her. And knowing the twisted male, he would have fashioned a matching pair of cuffs for my dragon. Phantom would never have stood for that.

Besides the stunt I pulled with Aelia, the old bastard blamed me for the first-years' loss. He insisted I hadn't trained them well enough, hadn't been as brutal as needed. As such, he had warned me that if I did not step it up this term, I would find myself without a position at the academy come the next.

Little did he know, I had no reason to stay any longer.

Except for *her*.

Draven snapped his fingers inches from my nose, and it occurred to me I'd been silent for too long.

"Hmm?"

"I said, has the second term curriculum for the first-years been prepared?"

I pointed at my temple and grinned. "It's all right here, headmaster."

"That is not good enough, Darkthorn. I need these initiates challenged. I must have a guaranteed win against Malakar this term. He's been a thorn in my side for far too long. I want Arcanum taken down."

"And they will be," I huffed out. The only positive to all of this was that with Draven's focus across the river, he'd mentioned little about Aelia. Perhaps Ruhl's appearance had been fortuitous, after all. If my secret hadn't emerged, if her focus hadn't been taken away from the battle, who knew what sort of attention Aelia would have mustered atop Sol in the final trial.

If I had it my way, I would scoop Aelia into my arms and fly her far away from here. My chest tightened at the thought, invisible bands encircling my dark, hollow heart. It seemed to beat quicker now, to rejoice in a life that was nothing but darkness before. To hell with the Conservatory, with the prophecy, with the blasted kings... None of it mattered anymore, nothing but her.

Fuck. It had to be the budding cuorem bond. There was no other logical explanation.

Another close call... if I had bedded Aelia that night, the way things had been headed, the bond would have formed, or at least, that was how I remembered it solidifying based on the ancient tomes I'd read at the Arcanum library. That overwhelming sensation I felt the first time we kissed, one I'd never felt before with any other female—and gods knew I'd had plenty of opportunity—must have been when it was first triggered. We would have been tethered together for life, and that was a fate I was certain Aelia did not deserve.

But did I want it all the same?

"Reign, are you even listening to a word I've said?"

My brows furrowed as I regarded the silver-haired Fae. Had he been speaking? "Yes, of course I am."

"Good, because King Elian will be here next week."

"Excuse me?" I blurted. It took all the years of discipline I'd been forced to master to maintain the mask of calm.

"He wishes to personally address the entire Conservatory as to the situation along the border with the Wilds. It appears the fourth-years may be called into service sooner than expected."

Before graduation? "Has the situation truly grown that treacherous?" And to think Aelia was alone near the volatile boundary only a few days ago. My heart pitched up my throat at the thought.

"I suppose we'll all find out soon enough."

"And you believe it wise for the king to come while the first-years are at each other's throats with the temporary lifting of the code of conduct?"

A devious grin curled up his trailing mustache. "It's the perfect opportunity for His Ethereal Highness to see exactly what sort of ruthless talent we house here at the Conservatory."

I grunted, shaking my head. If the code truly was lifted, that meant that Aelia and I could—

Gnawing on my bottom lip so hard I drew blood, I tossed aside the ludicrous thought. *She won't even speak to you, imbecile.* The dark voice sounded suspiciously like that of my father. What did it matter that for a few short days the rules forbidding student and teacher relations would be no more? Clearly, that was not the headmaster's intent. He wished only to allow the first-years to tear each other apart.

"Do you have a problem with my methods, Darkthorn?"

I momentarily lost control of my tongue as I loomed over the simpering idiot. "It only seems to me that if the situation along the border is so dire, it would behoove us to conserve as many bodies as possible. Should a war erupt, we will be found greatly lacking."

"Not if you do your job right," he snapped.

For a Fae who lived through the Two Hundred Years War, the male seemed to lack even the most basic understanding of battle. But I would not win this argument today, and I had more pressing matters to attend to, anyway. I vowed to remain at Aelia's side until this newest threat had passed, and I would keep my word. "As you say, headmaster," I gritted out. "Now, if you'll excuse me, my supper is waiting."

Without waiting for a dismissal, I trekked across the field toward the Hall of Elysia, quickening my strides with every step that got me closer to Aelia.

Chapter Thirteen

A*elia*

"Oh, for Fae's sake!" My hands shot out, clenching the doorframe before I toppled over the hulking form splayed out across the threshold of my dormitory. "Reign!" I growled. Had he not listened to a word I said yesterday?

Standing on her tiptoes, Rue poked her head over my shoulder. "Did you sleep out there all night, professor?"

Grumbling a curse, Reign rolled over, dark eyes peering up at me. "If I did, it is of no one's concern but my own."

I pointed at the dozens of first-years emerging from their dormitories and beginning to litter the halls. "I'm fairly certain it will be everyone's concern before long."

He shrugged, sitting up against the wall. "The code of conduct has officially been lifted. For all the other students know, we could have met for a midnight tryst." Those infernally irritating spheres of pure night glistened with mischief.

I blew out a sigh of frustration. I would never be rid of my dark shadow, which meant I would never be freed of these crushing feelings.

"I think I will leave you two to discuss this alone." Rue stepped over Reign, hugging her satchel to her chest. Before my roommate was swallowed up by the wave of students, she whirled at our professor. "Can I count on you to ensure Aelia reaches her first class safely?"

The bastard prince rose to his feet, displaying his impressively towering form. As if to prove his worth, a storm of shadows darkened his ominous aura as his lips curved into a grin. "Always," he replied.

"Will you be all right, A?" Her lively eyes darted between the two of us. "Or do I need to accompany the two of you?"

"Of course, I'll be fine. I'm not a child. I am perfectly capable of fending for myself against any foe." I threw a meaningful glare at my stalker as I revealed both blades now sheathed at my sides.

Rue waggled her slim fingers at me as she closed the door behind her. "Wonderful, see you in class!"

I hovered in the doorway for an endless moment, strangling the strap of my satchel. Reign leaned casually against the wall a few feet away from me, and still, that overpowering presence pressed into me. I refused to meet his gaze, despite the burning sensation seeping across my cheek. Only one male's look was capable of that.

"You cannot keep doing this, Reign," I finally hissed out. A few students threw curious gazes in our direction, but after last term, they'd become accustomed to seeing the Shadow Fae professor glued to my side. I could only imagine the rumors.

"It's a free campus. I can sleep wherever I wish."

"No, you can't. Not if it's in front of *my* door. And after I told you that I didn't want to be anywhere near you."

"You are my acquisition, and I will do whatever it takes—"

"Oh, goddess, so we're back to that?"

He spun around, pinning me against the door, a cloak of shadows chasing his form. "If that's all you will allow, then yes!"

"Allow? You make it seem as if I have any say in this, at all."

Reign loomed closer, his body suddenly flush against my own, making me regret my decision to remain in the doorway. My breath hitched at his proximity, at his musky scent flooding my nostrils. Heat raced across my body at the familiar feel of him. The chatter and frenzied footfalls of the busy hallway all fell away as his shadows whipped around us, shrouding us in a bubble all our own.

"Logic tells me to stay far away from you," I gritted out once we were encompassed in his cool shadows. "But I, too, find myself in a hopeless battle to keep my distance. You speak of restraint and control, and I cannot seem to grasp the meaning of either of those words when you're near." My treacherous body melted into his as if confirming my confession, leaning into his solid form. Stars, I hated how little composure I could summon around him.

"Then don't, princess," he whispered, lips inches from the shell of my rounded ear.

"I have to, Reign. I can feel it in my soul, you will be my ultimate undoing."

"But our downfall would be ever so sweet." His nose brushed my ear, his warm breath spilling down my neck. "Come away with me."

My head snapped back, shock compelling my hands to push him out to arm's length so that I could truly look at him. "What?"

"Let me take you far away from here. You threatened that once, do you remember? Jumping aboard Sol and flying to a distant land. Now, I am asking you to do just that, but with me. To pretend that I am only Reign Darkthorn, your dedicated professor and caring mentor, and whatever else you'll allow me to be."

I would have laughed if it weren't for the tempest of emotion surging in his unwavering gaze.

"And you are only Aelia Ravenwood, a powerless—no, a power*ful* Kin from Feywood. Please, princess, let's pretend and be the happier for it."

"And deny who we are for the rest of our lives?"

"I can do that. I've been doing it for the past four years, and for a reason not of my own making. And now for a purely selfish one? To live the remainder of my days with you? A hundred times yes."

My heart kicked at my ribs, each word carving into my soul, to be emblazoned there for all eternity. But I couldn't allow my feeble heart to guide all my choices. I'd already given into it before and paid the price. "And what of your father, the king? Of your duty? And what of Aidan? I cannot simply abandon him. If I escape from Luce, he will bear the burden of my betrayal."

"We will figure it out, somehow, Aelia. I will ensure Aidan is safe, I promise you."

"How can you promise that when you yourself have been banished from your own court? How does the heir to the Court of Umbral Shadows even manage that?"

His dark brows furrowed, lips twisting.

And a splash of understanding crashed over me. "Wait... you weren't banished at all, were you? It was all part of this elaborate ruse. But why?" My head spun, lungs constricting at the realization. I raised my hand, and it required all my strength to press it against Reign's chest and push him away. "No, never mind. I don't actually wish to know. I'm sorry, Reign, but I simply cannot be with someone I cannot trust." Anger blossomed, but I forced a breath through my tightening lungs, even as a scream built in my throat. "My entire life up until this point has been a lie, and until I can begin to decipher between what is real and what is not, you and I can never be."

Reign's broad shoulders rounded, the heartbreaking hope

on his face slipping away. My heart shattered bit-by-devastating-bit as his expression shuttered, the starlight in his eyes dimming before nothing but pure midnight remained.

I was certain he would disappear in that cloak of shadows as he frequently did when we fought. Only this time, he simply remained frozen in place. An endless moment of silence passed between us, and with each lingering second, the knot in my throat grew more overwhelming. I needed to be away from his all-consuming presence so that I could shout and sob in peace.

But I had no such luxury today, because in a moment, I would officially be late for my first class of the new term.

I forced my feet, which seemed to have grown roots into the wooden floorboards, to move forward, but Reign remained steadfast. "Excuse me," I murmured.

"No." His shadows darkened, their icy *nox* skimming over my skin.

"Reign, I will be late for Professor Lumen's class, and as it is, I don't know the difference between *Aurora Weaving* and *Luminous Enchantments*. Who knows what my punishment will be?"

"I would never let anyone lay a hand on you, princess."

I squeezed my eyes closed in a feeble attempt to escape that scrutinizing gaze. Just as I could read him, I was certain he had learned my tells as well. And despite the convincing words I spewed, I hovered on a knife's edge, an inch from falling into his arms.

"I can accept that you do not trust me yet, but you need to understand that I will do everything in my power to earn that trust back. You will likely hate me for it, but I will not leave your side until I succeed." My eyes snapped open at his words. A rueful grin now slanted Reign's lips softening his hardened expression. A tendril of *nox* snaked around my throat, gently caressing my sensitive skin and raising a swell of goosebumps. Reign drew closer, his lips a hairsbreadth from my own. "Because from the moment I dragged you from that hovel in

Feywood, you became mine, Aelia Ravenwood. I may not have wanted to admit it then, for numerous reasons, but the gods have chosen you for me, and I will be damned if I throw away their generous gift."

An icy chill raced up my spine, my entire body shuddering at the intensity of his declaration. Good gods, the power this male held with that tongue. Heaving in a breath, I allowed myself to fully meet his burning gaze. I could see the truth of his sentiments in his eyes, in that pulsing aura. And a part of me reveled in it. Because Raysa, I *needed* to trust him again. I wanted it more than anything in this sun-cursed court.

"Fine," I murmured.

"Good." Reign's warm breath skated over my lips. He slowly backed away, and the encroaching darkness moved with him. Once he was at a safe distance, a smile crawled across that bewitching mouth. "Now, let's get you to class, princess."

Chapter Fourteen

A*elia*

Professor Lumen regarded me in horror over the rim of his circular spectacles as I fought my uncontrollable *rais*. In the past hour, I'd learned that *Luminous Enchantments* required a level of control I had yet to master. Imbuing objects with light magic for enhanced abilities and protections sounded simple enough in theory, but when only a tiny trickle of *rais* was needed and mine came out in floods of wild power, it resulted in the creation of an enormous man-eating plant, intent on the destruction of its maker, instead of the innocuous daisy meant to provide its owner with enhanced speed.

"That's enough, Miss Ravenwood," the professor barked from across the great hall. "We cannot risk yet another disaster today."

With a huff of resignation I returned to my seat before glancing up at the enormous skylight I'd recently added to the chamber. Streams of vibrant light streaked into the hole I'd blown through the roof of the Hall of Luce, echoing its namesake. Who knew after a week of bottling up my *rais*, the results would be so catastrophic?

"Professor Darkthorn, if you would be so kind?" Lumen ticked his head at my dark shadow. He emerged from the corner of the hall, his shadows streaking from his fingertips like bloodthirsty wraiths. They twisted and coiled around the monstrous daisy, siphoning out the overabundance of *rais* I'd imbued it with.

"So creepy," Sy whispered as we watched the plant shrink back to its original size and the influx of *nox* return to its owner.

"Agreed." Rue's head bounced up and down.

Once Reign had slunk back to his hiding spot again and Lumen's attention was on the next student, I hissed out a curse and spun on my roommate. "And you said things would be easier this term."

"She lied. Clearly." Sy threw me a smirk. "I'm afraid every term, every year, will only get harder for us all, unfortunately." He reached for my ear, but with my foul temper flaring, I swatted him away.

"I'm never going to master my goddess damned powers."

"Don't say that," Rue hissed. "You don't want to anger Raysa."

"I'm fairly certain it's too late for that." I leaned my chin on the desk and rolled my eyes.

"Are you kidding me, A?" Rue reached for the collar of my tunic, tugging it down. The glittering Light Fae mark twinkled along my pale skin. "The goddess *chose* you among all the other Kin of Feywood. That does not happen by accident."

"Light Fae," Symon interjected.

"What?" Rue pivoted to face him.

"You said Raysa chose Aelia among all the other Kin of Feywood, but clearly, she's Light Fae. I mean, just because Aidan won't admit the truth—"

Throwing my hand up, I called upon my *rais* and drew a

familiar shape in the air. The celestial glyph sparked to life, immediately silencing my big-mouthed friend. Despite Reign's apparent disappearance, I knew very well he was still lurking in the shadows, and I had yet to tell him the truth about Aidan.

If I was being perfectly honest, I was afraid to. A part of me was certain that if he knew Aidan held the key to my mysterious origins, he'd stop at nothing to force it out of him. And given my professor's ruthless tendencies, I resolved keeping it a secret was the best course of action, despite my own eagerness to learn the truth.

I threw Symon a glare, pressing my finger to my lips, and his jaw clamped shut. Waving my finger in the air once more, I removed the silencing glyph, praying to all the gods Reign hadn't heard my friend's slip of tongue.

"Well, you've certainly gotten a hang of celestial glyphs," Sy muttered.

"Why, thank you, my friend." I dipped my head into an elaborate bow. "And that was mostly thanks to your tireless tutelage."

"And now the round-eared student surpasses the teacher." He clucked his teeth, grinning sheepishly.

"Very well, initiates," Professor Lumen's voice boomed across the chamber, amplified by the ordinary pen he held in his hand which Ariadne had imbued with *rais*. "That's enough for today, you are all dismissed."

She stood beside him, an obnoxious smile spreading her pink lips, Belmore hovering protectively behind her. They truly believed themselves to be the power couple of the Conservatory —or of the initiates, at any rate.

Belmore's frosty gaze swiveled in my direction, and my hand instinctively reached for my dagger. Dagg*ers*, plural. Now that I had both back in my possession, I felt whole once more. Or at least as whole as I'd ever been.

"You know," Rue whispered, eyeing my blades, "I was

thinking about it, and perhaps, hiding from Belmore, Kian, Lucian and those other Fae imbeciles is the wrong approach."

"What are you saying?"

"Maybe we should take the offensive and rid the Conservatory of them."

Excitement flared, waking my wounded heart, and I leveled my gaze on the cocky Fae male. "It's not a bad suggestion." Then, that weak Kin sensibility kicked in, reminding me it was wrong to instigate a fight. And judging by the wicked gleam in my roommate's eyes, it wasn't just a fight she was looking for, but the end of a war.

"What do you say, little Kin?" Symon draped an arm around my shoulders, his nose nuzzling my ear.

Could I, in good conscience, take the life of one of my classmates, unprovoked?

Likely not. Even if it was well-deserved.

"Oh, I can't," I grumbled.

"Told you." Sy threw Rue a mischievous grin and held out his other hand, palm up. "That'll be five gildings, please."

I reached up and smacked my friend in the shoulder. Hard. "You took bets on this?"

"Oh, Aelia..." Rue weaved her arm through mine and tugged me toward the exit of the hall. "You're too good to be at this Conservatory. You're much more kind-hearted than even the best of us."

"And that would be you two? I truly am in trouble now."

My friends laughed, and I joined in for a moment of lightheartedness. It felt good after the stress of the first day. Only four months to go, and I would have survived my first academic year at the Conservatory. Raysa, help me!

><

After my epic defeat in the classroom, I decided it was time to spend some one-on-one time with my *rais*. I'd simply start with the basics, practicing like I used to do with Reign. As I walked past the gymnasium, I cast a quick glance over my shoulder. To his credit, my professor was keeping to his word by maintaining his distance. I could always sense his aura nearby, but he kept to the shadows and limited engagement.

I hated how much comfort his quiet presence brought. Gripping my dagger in my fist, I reminded myself for the umpteenth occasion how many times he'd lied to me. I had to stay strong, regardless of all the things he'd said to me just that morning. Compelling my feet forward, I continued on to the outskirts of the campus, behind the gymnasium. If I would be taming my volatile *rais*, I needed to be as far away from everyone as possible.

I'd never wandered this far from campus before by myself, always preferring to remain within the busier sections, but today, I craved the solitude. Here, I could pretend I was back in Feywood, in the field behind our old cottage, training with Aidan.

As I turned the corner around the grand hall that held the gymnasium, the encircling grove stretched out before me radiating an otherworldly beauty. The air was infused with the soft, sweet fragrance of blooming flowers, mingling with the fresh scent of dew-kissed grass. Towering trees with silver-barked trunks and leaves that shimmered like emeralds formed a protective canopy, allowing only the gentlest rays of sunlight to filter through and dapple the ground in a mesmerizing dance of light and shadow.

Rais hummed beneath my skin, the serene haven of nature drawing it to the surface. Closing my eyes, I focused on the kiss of sunlight across my bare shoulders and the embers of energy in my core. As the power grew steadily, my lids fluttered open and I focused on the constant buzz. Holding my hands out, palms up, a flicker of light danced across my fingertips. A smile stretched across my face as I watched the shimmering spectacle.

"Okay, you can do this, Aelia." My thoughts flew back in

time, not to Aidan, but to Reign, all those months ago. *Imagine a balloon in the farthest depths of your core. You can blow harder to inflate it, or you can release some of that air so that it becomes more manageable.*

I imagined the balloon growing bigger, but only slightly so, and power thrummed through my veins. The flicker along my palms blossomed into a fiercely burning orb between them. The heat skimmed my flesh, warming my skin all the way up to my elbows. Before the energy grew out of control, I pictured that balloon and released a bit of air. The glowing sphere tapered, and I shifted it around my palms before tossing it from one hand to the other.

I could do this. I was in control.

A slow clap echoed from behind me, shattering my concentration. The gilded bubble burst, and my *rais* receded to the depths of my core once more. Spinning around, I scanned the grove for the source of the interruption.

Two familiar heads of blonde hair bobbed between the trees, and my heart sank. Belmore's gaze caught mine first, a snide grin twisting his lips. Kian snarled as he emerged from behind his friend, only accentuating the gruesome scar that ran from his forehead down across his upper lip. Courtesy of my Shadow Fae protector.

As if my thoughts had summoned him, a whisper of darkness curled around my neck, raising the hairs on my nape. I could feel his unspoken question in the frantic state of his shadow minion.

"I've got this," I whisper-hissed and unsheathed one of my daggers. The dark wraith settled across my shoulders, but still, I could feel its master's overwhelming unease.

"What a fortuitous meeting," Belmore crooned as he crept closer.

"Fortuitous? I thought you would have been planning this encounter from the moment Draven nullified the code of conduct." I paused, a smirk slanting my lips. "Let's be honest, we both know you've wished for this moment ever since initiation day." I ran my finger over my rounded ear then pivoted my gaze to his pointy one. A faint scar still remained along the tip, only widening my smile.

"How very conceited of you. As if you are that important to me. That little incident was forgotten moments after it occurred."

"Oh, really?" I grunted. "Is that why you sent Lucian and Kian after me?"

Belmore's gaze swiveled to his friend. "I cannot be held responsible for their actions."

Kian's smile turned angelic, the picture of innocence. But now that scar Reign had gifted him marked the monster that lay beneath the beautiful surface.

"I was there, you imbecile," I hissed. "You told them to welcome me to the academy."

Belmore shrugged. "I only meant for them to show you a good time. I figured you'd be pleased. It isn't often a Kin like you would get the chance to associate with Light Fae males."

Kian chuckled, his thin lips twisting. "And it would have been a great time had you only given us the chance."

"In fact, I haven't seen you with any males since your arrival. Are you not attracted to males? Do you prefer the fairer sex?"

"Oh, shut up, Belmore. Enough of the idle chit-chat, let's get this over with." Clenching my dagger in one fist, I flashed him the blade.

"Be very careful, Aelia." Reign's warning hissed through his shadow, reminding me of his ever-watchful presence. I had been pleasantly surprised he hadn't interrupted sooner. *"If either of those males discover what your daggers can do, I will be forced to end them. And I will enjoy every moment of it."*

I wouldn't say I was exactly sorry to hear that.

As if he had read my mind, he added, *"On second thought,*

show them what your daggers can do so we can be done with them once and for all."

"Reign..."

"You think that measly dagger can defeat our *rais*?" Belmore's words drew me from our whispered conversation. He chuckled as his entire body lit up, energy pulsing around his form.

"No, but this can." I splayed my free hand, calling on the power lingering just below the surface and *rais* burst from my palm. The wave of pure light crashed over the males, sending both sprawling across the lawn.

Shaking his head to drive off the daze, Belmore muttered a curse. He pushed off the grass, leaping to his feet despite the shock embedded in his fine features. "You are going to regret that, Kin."

"I've found there's little I feel remorse for in life, Belmore. In fact, it's only when I failed to act that I've regretted it. And I'm tired of fighting you." I nodded to his friend. "And you, Kian. There are much worse things out there beyond this university. So if you choose to act upon this silly revenge plot, let's finish it today." I seared them with my steeliest glare, hoping they'd fall for the icy edge to my tone. I had no desire to kill either of them, but I also couldn't spend the rest of my days at the Conservatory looking over my shoulder.

"Well said, princess." Reign's silky voice caressed the shell of my ear. "But know, if they lay a hand on you, I will gut them from spine to sternum."

Belmore's shoulders rounded, the dark glint in his ivy-green eyes receding. I lowered my dagger at his faltering resolve. He was my teammate, after all, and if we wanted to survive this year, our best chance lay in working together.

As I basked in the momentary respite, Kian lunged.

Chapter Fifteen

A*elia*

"Shield, princess!" Reign's cry hissed across my eardrum a second before Kian's luminous blade would have sunk into my chest. And an instant before my *rais* burst to life, enclosing me in an impenetrable radiant orb.

Kian's ethereal weapon bounced off the protective sphere, propelling both him and the blade across the grass.

Belmore watched, stunned, indecision warring across his furrowed brow.

"Don't do this, Belmore," I growled. "We are a team, despite the rules of conduct. We must work together this term to battle our foes across the river. I've proven myself over and over again. I am not weak, and I will fight."

Kian pushed himself off the ground, breathing heavily. A wicked gleam flashed across his light azure eyes as he stalked toward me. "Don't listen to her, Belmore. She's not like us. The Kin doesn't deserve to be here, to fight for a place as a Royal

Guardian. We are the best of the Court of Ethereal Light, and she is *nothing*."

"Shut that male up before I do something you'll regret." Reign's whisper only magnified the anger flaring in my chest.

I dropped the shield, daring Kian to make a move. The blasted male leapt at me once more, releasing a barrage of luminous arrows. I ducked and weaved through the onslaught. But one arrowhead struck true, piercing my bare upper arm.

A growl vibrated the shadow already encircling me, and a frenzy of dark tendrils joined it and coiled around me.

"No," I whisper-hissed. "Kian is mine."

Wincing, I plucked out the arrowhead crafted of pure light and blood trickled down my arm. It stung like a mother Fae. While I was momentarily distracted by the injury, Kian sensed his opportunity and leapt at the chance. A radiant spear hissed from his fingertips, seemingly guided by Raysa herself. I barely managed to summon my shield up in time.

This time the clash of power sent a tremor straight through to my bone marrow. The protective bubble burst and I staggered back as Kian continued his onslaught, now with his fists.

"Aelia, I cannot simply sit here and watch this—"

"Quiet!" I hissed, cutting off Reign's menacing growl.

Kian's fist slammed into my cheek and twinkling stars consumed my vision. I bit out a curse, staggering back another step.

"Give up, Kin. You don't belong here," Kian snarled.

"Princess, finish that insufferable male, or I swear to all the gods, I will do it for you."

"I am Light Fae, just like you," I growled, and sparks of energy lit up my flesh. The medallion hanging below my collarbone warmed, heating my skin, and that well of power broke loose. Like a dam, raw energy bled through my bones, the intensity so overwhelming a shriek burst from my lips. Sheathing my dagger, my hands shot out, unbidden, and fiery tendrils of light uncoiled from my fingertips. Like Reign's wraithlike shadows, they curled around Kian and hoisted him off the ground.

A familiar deep growl echoed in the distance, but Reign's snarl was drowned out by the roar of my thundering heartbeat. My minions of pure light spun around Kian, a long coil curling around his throat. Brilliant light blanketed my vision, coating everything in an unearthly glow. My thoughts grew fuzzy, the influx of *rais* all-consuming. That deep voice edged the corners of my subconscious, the familiar timbre tethering me to the present. My gaze flicked up to the flailing Kian. He kicked and screamed, fingers clawing at the glittering, ghostly binds.

I could feel the smile melt across my lips. He deserved this, had earned a dance with death after what he put me through. Uncontrollable power filled my chest, then every corner of my being. My entire body pulsed with energy, an inconceivable force fueled by anger and months of fear at the hands of these ruthless Fae.

I was Aelia, carved of stone, and I would never be weak again.

"Aelia, no!" A hand wrapped around my arm, jerking me around to face a pair of blue eyes. Belmore? Genuine fear flashed across that typically icy gaze. "Please, don't."

"*Please?*" I nearly choked on the word, remembering how little effect my pleas had on him or his friends when I had uttered it. The great Belmore begging me not to kill his friend?

"Release him, and I swear I'll make sure he never comes after you again."

The heady onslaught of power began to subside, and I blinked quickly, clearing my hazy mind. "And what about you or Lucian?" I stammered.

Kian continued to flail mid-air, his face a deep crimson shade as he clawed at the tethers of light holding him captive.

"None of us. I'll even swear an oath if that's what you require." He held out his hand and I stared at it, warily. How could I trust him after everything?

I felt it an instant before it happened, the shift in the air, the prickle of the tiny hairs at my nape. I spun around as a cord of light slithered toward me, wrapping around my neck. Kian had managed to wriggle a finger free of my restraints, and he now held onto the magical construct by the tips of his fingers.

The rope tightened, and I choked on a gasp.

From the corner of my eye, I felt *him* emerge from the shadows. Reign erupted from the very ether, a feral snarl on his lips and pure darkness whirling around his massive form. *No.* Before one of his wicked minions slithered off his arms, I reached for my dagger and hurled it at the glowing tether keeping me captive.

The moment the blade touched the beam of light, the mystical rope shriveled. The suffocating clamp around my neck fell away, and Kian's *rais* disintegrated into a pile of ash. I drew in a breath of sun-blessed air, slowing the frantic thundering of my heart, as Reign appeared at my side.

"You truly wish to test my restraint, don't you, princess?" he snapped.

"I told you I could handle him."

The hint of a smile ghosted across his lips, and my heart flipflopped at the gorgeous sight.

Shaking my head, I scanned the grove for Belmore, and it was only then that I noticed the oppressive silence. Where was Kian? Spinning toward the spot in which the Fae had hung moments ago, I found Belmore on his knees beside his friend's crumpled form.

I took a step, but Reign leapt in front of me, blocking my forward movement. "Get out of my way."

He slowly shook his head.

Rising to my tiptoes to see over his broad shoulders, I could just make out Belmore now standing over a rapidly expanding pool of crimson.

"No..." I rasped. "Wha—what did I do?" I attempted to push past Reign again, but he widened his stance, an immoveable object between my mounting fear and the truth of what I'd done. "Let me by!" I shouted.

"No. You do not need to see that."

"See what?" I ducked under his arm and wriggled free.

"You killed him," Belmore called out before I took my next step. "I don't even understand how..." He circled the body, running a hand through his pale blonde strands that had come loose from the neat tie.

Reign's arm curled across my chest, preventing my escape. "Your dagger," he whispered. "When you threw it, it cut through his *rais* and kept going..."

"*I* really killed him?" My voice trembled, a mixture of anguish and rage.

"And now," Reign whispered, "I'll have to deal with Belmore."

"No!" I shouted, my hands curling around the collar of Reign's tunic as I frantically spun to face him. "You cannot."

"He saw what your blasted dagger did to Kian's *rais*."

With Reign's arm wrapped tightly across my back, holding me to him, I peered around his hulking form. He had maneuvered to use himself as a physical barrier, turning us so that our positions were now reversed. Belmore still stared at the ground as my eyes found his, expression pinched and light brows furrowed. "He has no idea what he saw."

"Are you willing to risk it?" he growled.

Blowing out a frustrated breath, I gritted out, "Wipe his memory clean, then."

His eyes narrowed, a sneer crossing the perfect bow of his lips. "So now it's okay to tamper with someone's memories?"

"Yes, Reign. It's only not okay for you to wipe *my* memories!"

He shook his head, a rueful smile tugging at the corners of his mouth.

"I would much rather you delve into his twisted mind than kill him outright." I inched closer, an unnamable force compelling my boots toward Kian's still form, regardless of Reign's hulking body still wedged between us.

"Even after all he put you through?"

My head slowly dipped. Technically, it was Lucian and Kian, but the point was moot either way. I simply couldn't sentence someone to death, guilty or not. My gaze latched onto Kian's unmoving form, then to the hilt protruding from his heart. I squeezed my eyes closed as the wave of remorse threatened to pull me under. I hadn't meant to plunge that dagger into Kian's chest. Not really...

Right? Gods, that power was all-consuming. I'd never experienced anything like it. What was happening to me?

Chapter Sixteen

A*elia*

My heart was so heavy with guilt I'd been unable to drag myself out of bed this morning. Sunlight streamed through the skylight overhead, dappled rays forcing my eyes closed. Burying my head under the covers, I wished for the blasted sun to sink across the river and never return. I'd lied to Rue at Reign's insistence, telling her I was ill because, according to the masterful liar, *the fewer souls that knew what happened to Kian the better.* Lies came as easily to him as breathing. I must never forget that.

Missing Aurora Weaving with Professor Gleamer would surely come back to haunt me, but I simply couldn't summon the courage to face Belmore. Or worse, Lucian. Did they know their friend was dead?

After Reign's shadows obliterated Belmore's memories of the entire incident, he hauled Kian's body over his shoulder and shot across the river, those dark wings forming a shroud around the fallen Light Fae.

Oh, gods, the whole thing was simply awful.

Of all my regrets from that fateful morning, the one that hurt the most was Reign forcing Belmore to forget that instant of indecision before the chaos ensued. For a moment, I was certain I'd won him over, and now, all would be forgotten.

A prickle of awareness lifted the hair on the back of my neck. I shoved the covers back as that all-consuming presence filled my room. In the form of shadows.

"Get out, Reign," I snarled. "Neither you nor your murky minions are welcome in my chamber."

The cluster of shadows—Reign, but not Reign in physical form—twisted and hissed, as if truly insulted by my words. "Good morning to you, too, princess." His words echoed across the dark whorl.

"I have no desire to see you."

"Precisely why I'm not actually here."

"Or speak to you," I spat, sliding beneath the coverlet. "Just go away."

"Alas, I cannot. As if your sparkling personality wasn't enough of a draw, I've been tasked by the headmaster to continue in my efforts—"

"Of stalking?"

"I prefer the term personal bodyguard, but whatever you wish."

I re-emerged from beneath the covers, irritation puckering my brow. "And what if I refuse your constant presence?" My gaze flitted across the room in search of those damnable speaking shadows. Now I just felt silly shouting at the indistinct haze. "Just come out already, Reign. This is ridiculous."

My professor materialized from the whirling darkness, shadowtraveling from gods knew where, all sharp angles and lethal stares. "You cannot refuse, Aelia, just as I cannot. We do not have the luxury of denying the headmaster."

"Well, I certainly *cannot*, but you? A prince?"

Those midnight irises narrowed as he stalked closer, a finger pressed to his lips. Within the space of a heartbeat, his shadows blossomed, cloaking us in their icy touch. "Careful, princess." He eyed the hanging vines curling around my bed, forming the canopy of colorful flora. "You never know who might be listening."

His words sent a chill up my spine, and I stood, my gaze darting to the nightstand where my daggers were not so well-hidden.

Reign's dark gaze raked over my flimsy nightgown, as if he hadn't seen me in it many times before when he kept watch overnight on my settee. That piercing stare warmed my cheeks and forced my arms up, knotting across my chest. He cleared his throat, his shifting boots causing the floorboards to let out an ominous creak. "About your daggers," he muttered, "we need to find a more secure location to house them."

"*We?*"

"It is our secret, is it not?" He inched closer, those shadows spinning tighter between us. "As you love to remind me, I would be in as much trouble as you for not disclosing their existence."

"Why do you do it?" My eyes drifted to the spot beneath his tunic, to where the mark of the banished marred his flesh. "Why remain here and pretend to cower beneath Draven's boot? Hostage to those cuffs?"

"I will always be where you are."

It was as if the male had a direct link to my soul, every word piercing straight to my marrow. Raysa, I despised it. Hated how weak I felt around him, how out of control. And mostly, I hated myself for wanting what I should despise.

"So that you may betray me when the time is right?" I spat.

"Aelia, you know I would never—"

I staggered back a step as he moved to reach for me and hit the foot of my bed. My body could not stand to be in this close a proximity to this Fae and still succeed in forming coherent thoughts. "And how would I know—" I stopped myself, taking a deep breath to gather myself. "You know what? Never mind. Why did you come in the first place?" I finally managed.

The corner of his lip curled. "Are you finally ready to hear the truth?"

No, of course not. But instead of speaking the truth, I replied, "I suppose ignorance isn't always bliss. And since I plan on remaining in my chambers until this cursed code of conduct ban has come to an end, I suppose I have the time to listen."

"Thank the gods." He erased the space between us, his hand settling on the small of my back, the chill from his palm penetrating the thin fabric of my sleeping gown. The faint touch sent a jolt of awareness straight through me. I wriggled free of his hold, the deliberate move requiring everything I had to escape that intoxicating sensation. He held his offending hand up and motioned toward the sitting area by the hearth. "I only want you to be comfortable."

"Before you deliver the death blow?"

The corner of his lip twitched as we traversed the chamber. "So dramatic, princess."

"I wouldn't expect anything less from the prince of shadows." As I spoke the words, realization crashed into me like a tidal wave, overwhelming and inescapable, leaving no part of me untouched. "Wait, is that why you've always called me princess? It was some sort of ironic twist?"

His expression shuttered as he folded onto the settee across from the crackling hearth.

"Tell me," I snapped as I plopped down beside him, unaware my traitorous body had inched so close to his. I scooted over, attempting to create some much-needed space.

"It was not spoken in irony." Those impenetrable orbs of night focused on the fire, avoiding my gaze entirely. "I had mistakenly assumed that the day I was sent to acquire you would be like any other mission. I had been sent on countless tasks to seek out worthy Light Fae for the Crown, but I had never encountered anyone quite like you. Your radiance was undeniable, but it was the brilliance within that truly captivated me. I had never beheld a fiercer soul. While most royals are entitled and lazy, bred in a world of indulgence, you were different. A true princess must be as lethal as she is well-mannered, and I could see that in you, from the fire blazing within those mesmerizing pools of iridescent silver-blue." He paused, his eyes finally chasing to mine. "You may have been raised a simple Kin, Aelia, but you possess the soul of a princess."

I swallowed hard, my throat suddenly much too dry. Why did he have to spout out those beautiful, terrible words that streaked straight to my heart and forced me to question everything?

"So, it wasn't ironic?" I blurted, if only to dispel the building tension coating the air.

A rueful chuckle pursed his lips. "No, princess, it most certainly was not."

I sat back in the settee, relaxing the tense set of my shoulders and allowing them to gingerly rest against the cushion.

"Are you ready now?"

I nodded quickly before I could think better of it. I could only escape the truth for so long before it came for me, a thief in the night to steal the false sense of security I'd built around myself.

Reign released a slow breath before pivoting to angle his body toward mine. His knee brushed my thigh, and sparks ignited across my bare skin. I jerked from the contact, crossing my legs to avoid further accidental touching. As it was, I could barely focus with him so close. His wild, musky scent assaulted my senses and interrupted the steady thrumming of my heart.

Apparently, the effect was mutual, because despite the slight part of his lips, Reign had yet to mutter a word.

"Well?" I finally forced out.

A wry smile appeared, lighting up the gloom in those fathomless irises. "I've spent countless nights practicing this very speech, and now that the moment has come, I find myself at a complete loss for words."

"Just tell me, Reign. You were right, I must know the truth. Hiding from it isn't going to serve me well in the end."

His shoulders rounded, a sharp exhale puckering his lips. "My entire life has been focused on duty, on a single essential mission forced upon me by my father. That task has guided my steps for as long as I can remember, practically since I was old enough to wield a sword."

He lapsed into silence once more, the hard set of his jaw like stone.

"And that is?" I finally blurted, the quiet having grown unbearable.

"To find and destroy the child of twilight."

Chapter Seventeen

R *eign*

The moment I spoke the dreaded words, the crushing weight I'd been forced to carry for all these months began to dissipate. I'd wanted to admit the truth to Aelia since the moment I suspected she could be the one. The desire to protect her, to prove she wasn't the child of the prophecy had become all-consuming. But the more I observed, the more time I spent with her, I only seemed to achieve the opposite.

"...Destroy?" Aelia's whispered question drew me from my musings. She had stiffened beside me, her brilliant aura dimming. Her breaths quickened, as if sitting beside me were suddenly painful.

I reached for her hand, tentatively, my fingers barely brushing her palm. While she did not return the gesture, I was comforted by the fact that she didn't bolt for the door either. "You've heard the prophecy yourself," I whispered. "The destruction it speaks of must be avoided at all costs. Or, at least, that was how my father understood it."

"So he tasked you to come to the Court of Ethereal Light to find this child?"

I nodded slowly, impressed by her calm. "My father has been searching for this pivotal Fae since the seers pronounced the prophecy looming ever closer over two decades ago." Coincidentally, just before Aelia's birth. "He has long curated his web of spies within the Court of Umbral Shadows, but he had yet to establish a solid foothold across the river."

"So he sent you…"

"A seer foresaw the epochal moment approaching, which hastened the king's resolve."

"And then he pretended to banish you and forged that false brand to fool the Light Fae?"

I winced as memories of the mystical branding carving into my chest surged to the surface. Screams ricocheted through my skull, and the noxious odor of burnt flesh infiltrated my nostrils. The toxic smell had lingered for hours… A bitter laugh tumbled out. "There was nothing false about the banishment or the branding, princess. King Tenebris had to ensure his plan was infallible. The entirety of the Shadow Court believes I was exiled, a traitor to the realm."

Stunned horror curved those perfect lips, the ones I could barely restrain myself from capturing. Even while reliving my painful past, it was difficult to focus on anything but her. "But why?" she rasped. "What was your alleged sin?"

"It was no sin of my own, princess, but rather that of my father and some 'whore', as the queen calls her."

Understanding widened her eyes, and she expelled a sharp breath.

"That's right. There is a reason Prince Ruhl is the heir to the throne, despite the fact that I was the firstborn. I am King Tenebris's bastard child."

Aelia regarded me for a long moment, as if she couldn't

quite believe my words. She was not the only one. In all the times I'd practiced this speech in the darkness of my room, I had never intended on divulging quite so much. But this female held an inexplicable power over me, one I was helpless to resist. I yearned to lay bare my broken soul before her, hoping to all the gods she would mend the shattered pieces, that she would accept me, brokenness and all.

"Reign…" Unshed tears glistened in her eyes, and my chest ached at the pain in that gaze. For me. Even after all the lies, she still felt something for me; even if it was only pity, I would take it for now. Pity was better than hate—or worst of all, apathy.

"You must know that despite keeping the truth from you, I've also kept all my theories from my father. From the moment I met you, I suspected, but I would never betray you to him."

"Why not? Isn't that what you were bred for? To find this child and put an end to the threat to our realm?"

"Because, Aelia, you are everything. You are the light that banishes the darkness within me, the hope I never thought I could find. You are my reason, my anchor, and I will protect you with every fiber of my being, until I no longer draw breath."

Her cheeks burned an enticing crimson, stilling my tongue to admire her fierce beauty for a moment longer.

Then, unable to stop myself, I continued.

"And I refuse to believe that you would be that 'harbinger of oblivion' or the Fae to 'plunge all into eternal dusk.'" I shook my head, my resolve, my certainty growing with every word that tumbled free. "On the contrary, I believe you will determine the fate of our worlds as a beacon of hope."

A tear finally lost the fight and spilled over, tracing the soft curve of her cheek. Tentatively, I reached for her and swept it away. Then I pressed my thumb, now coated with her tear, to my lips. For now, it was the closest I could get to tasting her, but I vowed in that moment that one day, she would be mine. Completely.

Her chest heaved, whether from the touch or the subsequent action, I wasn't certain, but the anger in her gaze fell away, her expression softening. "How can you say those things when you barely know me?"

"That's not true, Aelia. In the past few months we've spent together, not only have I come to understand your true nature, but I've also memorized every facet of your soul. If you truly are this child of twilight, you will bring forth nothing but good to this realm. And I will remain by your side, steadfast against any who stand against you."

Aelia regarded me with that unguarded expression I hadn't witnessed since that dreaded battle, and it did nothing but embolden my tongue.

"Whether you'll have me or not," I added. A wicked grin parted my lips, the one that always made her breaths come more quickly. I stole a glance at her chest, at the wild thrumming beneath the thin linen, confirming my musings, and my grin transformed into a smile of satisfaction.

Because I felt the certainty deep within my bones; the gods had gifted me this extraordinary female, and though fate denied us the chance to be together right now, our paths were destined to intertwine for all eternity. I would wait for that moment, no matter how long it took, for she was worth every second of longing and every sacrifice.

"You are rather difficult to evade." A bittersweet smile splashed across her face. "As I imagine your father must be."

"Mmm." She wasn't wrong, but my foremost concern at the moment was my brother. As soon as he was pitted against Aelia in the Umbral Trials, he would discover her secret. It was inevitable. "Let me worry about him, along with my brother."

"What if Ruhl discovers the truth?"

"We must do everything in our power to ensure that *does not* happen. My brother and I do not exactly have the best relationship."

"I gathered as much."

"You cannot use your daggers in the trials against Arcanum, Aelia. Draven has informed me King Elian will be arriving any day now; hiding your blossoming powers from the royal is critical. If anyone catches whiff of your daggers' origins, I'll be forced to annihilate the entire class of initiates—realms, the bloody king, included."

"Reign..." she growled.

"Or wipe their memories, which would be extremely taxing."

Her expression grew somber as she crossed her arms over her chest, then asked a question I wasn't expecting at that moment, but knew was inevitable. "Where did you hide Kian's body?"

"Somewhere no one will ever find him."

A haunted look darkened the spark in her silver-blue eyes.

"Do not spend a minute grieving his loss, Aelia. He is not worth it."

Her head fell back against the settee, and after what felt like an age, she loosed a slow breath, turning her head to face me. "Is that it, Reign? You swear there are no more secrets now?"

I'd confessed it all, with the exception of Elisa's conjectures about the cuorem. But before I even considered revealing the possibility of a practically extinct fated mate bond, I needed to win her trust back. It was the key to claiming her heart.

"Yes," I replied resolutely. "No more secrets."

"Good." That hint of a smile was enough to set my cold, dark heart aflutter. "But that doesn't mean I forgive you, Reign Darkthorn."

"Understood, princess." I pinched a lock of ebony hair entwined with a strand of platinum, and twirled it around my finger. "It seems as if I'll have quite a bit of groveling to do before I earn that mercy."

"*Quite* a lot."

"Since you've already missed your classes for the day, how

about I start by escorting you and Solanthus to Phantom's most favorite hunting ground?"

Her eyes lit up to shimmering orbs of cobalt as she leapt to her feet. "Phantom would do that for Sol?"

"Why wouldn't she?"

Her slim shoulders lifted slowly. "It didn't seem as if they were very fond of each other."

"That's only because Solanthus and Phantom were mates in another life, and it didn't end well."

Aelia's brows jumped to her hairline as she regarded me unbelievingly. "Reign! How could you keep that piece of vital information from me? You just said no more secrets!"

"I forgot." I shrugged nonchalantly as I ushered her toward the door.

"Tell me everything."

Chapter Eighteen

A*elia*

You're certain Phantom knows I'll be here? The twinge of apprehension in my skyrider's tone speared straight through my heart. It was so unlike him. He shifted beneath me, his talons digging into the earth below. His eyes were pinned to the line of darkness separating Light Fae lands from the endless night beyond. We awaited along the western border of Aetheria nestled within the Alucian Mountains where the realm joined the rest of the continent of Crescentia, the kingdom of Mysthallia resting ahead of us to the west. Here, dusk was nearly upon us, as only the Raysa-kissed lands were blessed with eternal light.

"Yes, she knows." I spoke the words aloud, but in a hushed tone to express the reverence they deserved.

Reign had refused to share the details of our dragons' disastrous pairing, but this time I couldn't blame his reticence. It wasn't his secret to share. I only hoped Sol would feel comfortable enough to entrust me with the truth.

"Are you nervous about seeing her?" I hedged.

His long reptilian neck swung around so those luminous golden irises met mine. *That traitorous Shadow Fae told you, didn't he?*

"He didn't tell me much of anything. Only that the two of you had a past."

I cannot believe she would tell him...

"She's his bonded skyrider, Sol. They share important things like that." I hoped he could hear the flare of annoyance in my tone, because it wasn't the first time I felt as if he were keeping secrets from me.

Aelia, I have never lied to you.

"Maybe not, but I know for a fact you've omitted important details. Like when you teamed up with Reign to keep me from the battle with Arcanum."

That was different, it was for your safety.

"For someone who doesn't approve of Reign, you certainly sound a lot like him." I paused, nibbling on my bottom lip. "Wait, did you know who he was?"

He snorted and plumes of silver smoke floated into the air. *If I had, I never would have allowed him near you.*

"But you and Phantom can speak telepathically, couldn't you sense him since they're bonded?"

Phantom is rather adept at blocking me. Even through the mental link, the bitter edge laced his tone.

"Can you please tell me what happened between you?" The question was easier than the one I really wanted answered. What did he know about the twilight prophecy? Despite Sol being only a few months old in this lifetime, he'd lived countless lives before. Did the memories bleed over from one life to the next?

I would really prefer not to.

"Fine, since you refuse to tell me about that, then what do you know about the twilight prophecy?"

He shifted beneath me, his enormous ribs expanding as he huffed out a breath. *Cursed, Shadow Fae bastard. He told you that too, didn't he?*

"He did. Along with the fact that his father assigned him the task of searching out the child and destroying her—or him. Why didn't you tell me?"

Oh, Aelia, do you have any idea how many prophecies have existed in the centuries I've lived? Seers are capricious, and their divinations, even more so. No one knows for certain if this child exists or ever will.

"So you don't believe I am that child?"

His shoulders lifted, and I squeezed my thighs to keep from losing my seat. *I honestly do not know, Aelia. But if Reign believes you are, that is all that matters. You must keep your distance at all costs.*

"He swears he hasn't told his father anything about me."

Then you're a fool to believe him.

"Sol!" I cried out, shocked.

I apologize for my bluntness, Aelia, but he is the son of King Tenebris, one of the most notorious tyrants in Aetheria's history. Only King Helroth of the Court of Infernal Night was more ruthless. Even if Reign does not wish you harm, he will have no choice but to succumb to his sire's wishes.

A dagger to the heart would not have cut as deeply as those words. I loved Sol, valued his opinion and trusted him with my life, such was the magic of the skyrider bond. So it seemed prudent that I take his words into account. I'd been fighting my impulses to give in to Reign, to forgive him, from the moment he professed the truth. Perhaps, he truly was unworthy of my trust.

"Sol, I don't know what to do. When I find myself in Reign's proximity, I lose all common sense. I forget everything he's done, everything he is. It's as if the Spellbinders of

Mysthallia have cast an incantation over me whenever he is near."

He released a long, suffering breath and shook his head. *Sometimes we are simply powerless to fight what the gods have preordained.*

"Like with you and Phantom?" I flashed a quick smile.

Aelia...

"Just tell me, Sol."

He snorted and golden flames lit up the darkening sky of Mysthallia. *Only if you promise to remain ever vigilant around that Shadow Fae.*

"Always."

There honestly isn't much to tell. We discovered we were mates in a previous reincarnation during the time of the Two Hundred Years' War. It was a terrible time to be alive, and even more so as a dragon. The Fae sought to use us for our power, and we became nothing more than vehicles of destruction. They pitted us against us each other, forcing us to fight.

In that reincarnation, I was not born into the life of a bonded skyrider. I was a wild dragon, as most were hundreds of years ago. It's only been in the past few decades that the academies were established, and the gods deigned to bless their most formidable students with skyriders.

On the eve of the war, I was claimed by a formidable Light Fae, while Phantom already belonged to a Shadow Fae female across the river. Once the fighting broke out, we were torn apart.

Forcing mates to live without each other is the cruelest of all tortures. It can drive one mad...

He paused for a long moment, the silence echoing the solemnity of his mood. I waited with bated breath as an onslaught of emotions surged through our mystical bond. Typically, I felt little from his side. He'd learned to block the influx of sentiments from leaking through long ago, whereas I had no such control.

One evening, in the heat of battle, she attacked me. We were both out of our minds with bloodlust, and the forced time apart had meddled with our sanity. In retrospect, I doubt she even knew what she was doing, but that momentary distraction allowed another foe to swoop in, which led to my ultimate demise, along with that of my rider.

I gasped, the inappropriate sound unstoppable. "I thought you said you'd never lost a rider."

We were speaking of the battles with Arcanum, and this was long before that, little one. And technically, my rider perished a bit after that particular clash, but I often blame my death on his eventual demise. Had I been there to protect him...

"And as a result, you blame Phantom."

I did. For a very long time, after each reincarnation since then. But when Arcanum attacked the academy and I was too far to reach you, I had no other choice but ask for her assistance. She enlisted Reign's aid in keeping you safe. I suppose it was her way of atoning for past wrongs.

He fell silent once again, and I took it as the end of our conversation. I searched for words, something to comfort the tremendous beast whose heart, it appeared, was just as fragile as my own, despite the fearsome outer shell. Nothing could encompass the turmoil of emotions battering my chest.

So instead, I leaned across the enormous dragon's neck and patted his sleek scales. A deep chuffing sound vibrated his barrel chest, and we awaited in silence until Phantom's onyx wings darkened the skyline.

"There they are," I whispered.

Guard your heart, little Kin, as I will guard mine.

As if it were that easy. It had been a futile attempt from the moment I set foot upon this sun-cursed soil. While Sol's gaze remained fixed upon the soaring obsidian beast hurtling ever closer, I wondered if he, too, waged a constant battle with his own heart when his former mate was near.

And was a dragon mate bond severed upon death, or did it truly link their souls for all eternity?

As Phantom's wings slowed and angled toward the peak where Sol was perched, Reign's dark gaze locked onto mine. My breaths quickened, my pulse racing as I took him in, even from this distance. My heart staggered, then somersaulted, crashing against my ribcage with that one heated look. In that moment, I knew my answer.

For the first time in as long as I could remember, I wished I were simply a powerless, mortal Kin, because I wasn't certain I could survive an eternity battling my feelings for Reign. The intensity of his gaze, the undeniable pull between us—it was a war I was afraid I might lose, and yet, I couldn't bring myself to retreat.

Chapter Nineteen

elia

"I have sort of mixed emotions." Rue slammed her Luminous Enchantments book closed when Professor Lumen stepped off the stage.

"How could they be mixed? I'm thrilled it's the final day before the code of conduct goes back into effect." I glanced over my shoulder at Belmore and Ariadne as I stood and swung my satchel over my shoulder. Neither had made an overt move in the past few days, but that was likely due to my ever-present Shadow Fae protector. Even now, I could feel him looming in the dark corners of the chamber. "It's exhausting having to look over one's shoulder all the time."

"I hate to state the obvious, my round-eared friend," Symon interjected, curling his arm around my shoulders and steering me toward the door of the grand hall, "but you'll still have to be wary of the initiates from the other teams starting tomorrow."

"And, let's not forget that before long, our training will

begin across the river." Rue ticked her head through the doorway. From beneath the arch, the towering fortress of obsidian cast ominous shadows along the Luminoc.

"Well, now you've just gone and squashed my appetite completely."

"I'm still starved," said Sy with a cheeky grin. "What about you, Rue?" He waggled his light brows at my roommate. "Aelia mentioned you never returned to your chambers last night. Were you making up for lost time with Devin?"

Rue shot me an unexpected scowl before turning her attention to our grinning friend. "Where I spend my evenings is none of your business. And jealousy does not suit you, Master Lightspire." She knotted her arms over her chest, unamused, as he folded over laughing. "Besides, Aelia is the one who disappeared with our Shadow Fae professor for hours just the other night."

Symon released me and pressed his palm to his chest dramatically. "*What*? Have you two lovebirds made up?"

"Of course not," I hissed. "We would've had to have been together in the first place to make up." Thoughts of our flight on dragonback across Aetheria scurried to the forefront of my mind. It had been perfect. Dangerously so. Despite Reign's admissions, beautiful words and heartfelt promises, the fact remained that his purpose in life was to kill me. Possibly. If I was this supposed child of twilight. And I planned to heed Sol's warnings. "Besides, he's still my professor and any sort of relationship is strictly forbidden." Not to mention the fact that he was the bastard Shadow Fae prince, but I couldn't exactly explain that to my friends.

"Not for the next twelve hours." Rue's lips curled into a devious grin. "Since the code of conduct is currently not in effect, you could technically *be* with your professor..."

Heat swam across my cheeks as Rue's meaning became resoundingly clear.

"No, I couldn't..."

"But Aelia, don't you think it's time? Despite Reign's behavior, I've seen the way he looks at you. It is as if it's truly painful to breathe in your presence. And he would be the perfect one to—"

"Rue..." I hissed, throwing my hand up. As much as I wanted to be upset at my friend for her insistence, she truly had no idea about anything that had transpired between us. And that was my fault for keeping it all a secret.

"I feel terribly lost in this conversation," Sy quipped.

"It's nothing," I blurted, my attention focused on Rue. "And there is nothing between Reign and me, except for a completely professional professor/student relationship."

Rue rolled her eyes, a sigh parting her lips. "You can deny it all you want, but it doesn't make it any less true. Whatever this spat is between you, I'm certain you'll both move past it." She lifted her chin, signaling behind me, and I cocked my head over my shoulder to find a tendril of darkness hovering only a few feet away. "You see? That is not typical professor behavior."

"He's simply overly controlling and slightly paranoid about his prized acquisition."

Symon snorted. "Professor Gleamer has never offered me a hint of the attention Reign showers you with."

"He's just competitive and refuses to lose against the other professors."

"I suppose we'll find out soon enough," said Rue.

"What do you mean?"

"It's the start of a new term. Surely, Reign will have a new acquisition before long. Then we'll see just how much attention his new initiate gets."

My stomach twisted at the mere thought of having to share Reign's attentions with another student. Especially a female. *Stop it, Aelia. Don't be ridiculous.* "I'm sure he will treat this new first-year with equal enthusiasm," I claimed, lifting my chin.

"Gods, you are so *blind*, A!" Rue released an exasperated laugh.

"So what did you do with the good professor the other night?" Symon asked, thankfully somewhat changing the subject. "Are you back to private training?"

"In a manner, yes. We took Sol and Pyra out for a flight around the realm. Offensive flight lessons start next week, after all." Raysa, I hated lying to them yet again. But I couldn't very well tell them of Reign's dragon after he'd confessed to wiping the entire campus's memory of it or about the history she and Sol shared.

Just thinking about it had my gut churning. To think Sol spent countless lifetimes believing Phantom had betrayed him. The flight across Mysthallia had gone smoothly, but I hadn't noticed any interactions between the two. Then again, if they had been engaging in internal conversations, I wouldn't have been the wiser. I made a mental note to ask Reign more about it the next time we were alone.

"Speaking of the dark Fae..." A smirk spread across Symon's face, and I didn't need to turn around to know who had appeared from the ether.

"Good evening, initiates."

"Professor." Rue flashed him her teeth, and it only made me love her more.

Drawing in a steadying breath, I spun around to face the shadow prince. What a pair we made, the shadow prince and the Kin princess. I nearly laughed at my own joke.

"With training for the Umbral Trials set to begin next week, and King Elian's visit nearly upon us, it is time to resume our evening sessions, Aelia. It will be imperative if you have any hopes of defeating your Shadow Fae rivals."

"We appreciate the vote of confidence, professor." Rue's light eyes twinkled with a devious smile.

"Unlike the two of you, Aelia has had little time to learn control of her *rais*."

"And it's so selfless of you to take time out of your busy schedule to help her."

Oh, gods, I was going to kill my best friend. Heat flushed my cheeks, reaching all the way to the rounded tips of my ears.

"Watch yourself, Miss Liteschild," Reign growled. "Alluding to any sort of impropriety could lead to Aelia's expulsion or worse."

"It's not my friend I believe to be acting improperly." She flashed him a sneer, and Reign's shadows spun into a turmoil. Before either did something they would surely regret, I moved to my professor's side, weaving an arm through his, and instantly the wild buzzing of darkness subsided.

"Let's get this training over with." Offering my friends a quick wave, I hauled him toward the training field before he could bite out another word.

We marched around the gymnasium, to a quiet spot between the great hall and the encroaching woods. As soon as we were beyond earshot, Reign's dark gaze whirled upon me. "Does she know?"

"Know what, professor? You'll have to be a little more specific. There's an entire treasure trove of secrets I'm currently keeping from my friends."

"About any of it, the prophecy, your daggers, my bloodline... *us*?" He paused before the last word, slowly drawing it out.

"There is no *us*, remember? Impropriety and all?" I knotted my arms across my chest, the insignificant barrier between us helping to slow my escalating pulse.

"Technically, not true until daybreak when the code of conduct goes back into effect."

And there it went. My heartbeats skyrocketed once more at his insinuation. "Good gods, are you and Rue tuned into the same mental channel today?"

"So, she does know..."

"She suspects there may be something between us. The

constant shadows pervading our room may have something to do with it."

"I must do better then, especially with King Elian's imminent arrival." A silly part of me hated to hear him say it. I was a complete fool. Of course, we must keep whatever this thing was between us a secret. *Nothing. There is nothing between you and there never could be.* That cursed voice reminded me.

"Yes, you must."

He crept closer and power swept over me, pushing at my dwindling restraints.

I staggered back a step, my shoulders hitting the alabaster outer wall of the gymnasium. "Shouldn't we go inside to begin training?"

His mouth twitched into a smile at my apparent discomfort. "On second thought, perhaps today we could train in a different venue."

My eyes flickered over his shoulder to the threatening onyx turrets of the citadel across the river. It seemed like a lifetime had passed since I'd felt the cool rush of night over my skin. "Yes," I whispered.

His dark brows knitted. "How do you know what I have in mind?"

"Because every time you speak of the Umbral Court, the trace of a smile slashes across your face and lights up the darkness in your eyes."

"I hadn't realized I'd become so easy to read." The smirk only grew more brazen. "I'll have to work on that as well." He paused, lifting his hand and brushing my cheek with his knuckles. The contact was ever so brief, but still, the slight touch had awareness prickling across every inch of my skin. "But I'm glad to hear you are paying such close attention to my lips."

Rolling my eyes, I slid out from my precarious position. Being trapped between a wall and Reign's unyielding form never led to anything good. "Will you be shadowtraveling us there, professor?"

"No, not today, Aelia. Your official training has begun." Dark shadows slid off his arms, coiling around his form and only accentuating his ominous smile. "Race you there."

"You cannot be serious?"

"No time to waste, initiate. I'll even give you a head start."

Son of a Fae. Gritting my teeth to keep the curse from bubbling out, I darted around the grinning bastard and sprinted across the lawn.

Chapter Twenty

elia

Sweat poured from my brow, every muscle screaming for me to stop the torture as Reign pummeled me with wave after wave of *nox*. But alongside the pain there was something else. Something new and incredible, blossoming deep in my core.

We stood a stone's throw from the shore of the Shadowmere Sea. It was the first time I'd beheld the dark, murky waters, lit by starlight. But there had been little time to take in its beauty.

"Just a little longer, princess, and you'll get your reward."

Reign had been taunting me with this reward for the past few hours. "It better be damned good, professor."

"Oh, trust me, Aelia, it will be." A glint of amusement set his pitch irises ablaze as he released another surge of impenetrable darkness.

For the hundredth time today, my fingers twitched for the familiar feel of my blades. As Reign was adamant I did not use them for the upcoming trials, he forbade me to use them while training. But once every ounce of *rais* was drained, there was nothing I wished for more than the fury of my daggers to combat his incessant *nox*.

Not for the first time, I marveled at Reign's ability to wield so much power with those cuffs dampening his abilities. The Light Fae had no idea how lucky they were that Reign's birthright had been stolen due to his impure blood. He would have been an unstoppable force as King of the Umbral Court.

"What's Ruhl like?" I blurted as I summoned another luminous shield.

Reign's shadows poked and prodded at the protective bubble, unable to pierce my *rais*. "You need to focus, princess."

"I am focusing. I am quite adept at multi-tasking."

Heaving out a frustrated breath, he recalled his shadows, the murky minions sinking back into his flesh. "He's a lot like you, actually. Impulsive, stubborn, powerful..."

"He sounds lovely."

Reign rolled his eyes, then swept the dark tangle of hair that had fallen forward during our strenuous training from his brow. After another twenty minutes of torture, he heaved out a breath and crept closer. "I suppose you have finally earned your reward."

I bounced on my tiptoes before reminding myself to temper my expectations. At this point, I had no idea what to expect. Besides, the streak of pain that lanced up my spine at the sudden movement had me gritting my teeth. "So what is it?"

He stalked closer, erasing the space between us. Before I could utter a word, he swept me into his arms. The sharp tang of sweat and musk clung to the minute space between us, and still I found myself breathing him in, drawing in the familiar musky smell of him.

"What are you doing?" I managed on an exhale.

"Taking you to your reward."

Reign's shadows slid across my skin, the icy tendrils raising the hair on the back of my neck. They whirled around us both, the darkness expanding until we were blanketed in a cocoon of pure night. Then the dark field fell away, blurring in the background as we shot through the ether.

My stomach catapulted against my spine as we hurtled through the void, only Reign's firm grip keeping the anxiety at bay. It had been a while since I'd shadowtraveled, and I'd nearly forgotten the thrill it brought.

Nearly as quickly as it had started, the darkness began to fall away, revealing a completely new scene. "We're here." Reign slowly released me, and my boots hit the soft ground beneath.

Under the shroud of night, a small island coalesced before us, cloaked in an eerie, haunting beauty. The inky black waters of the Shadowmere Sea lapped gently at the rocky shoreline ahead, similar to where we had just come from, yet altogether different. Its surface was barely disturbed, reflecting the faintest glimmers of starlight like scattered shards of obsidian. Shadows danced and flickered along the edges of the island, the interplay of light and dark creating an ever-shifting mosaic of deep grays and silvers.

"Where are we?" I whispered, as if my voice could shatter the unearthly beauty if I spoke too loudly.

"A small isle off the coast of the realm. It's uninhabited."

"Let me guess, another one of your haunts from your days at Arcanum?"

He nodded. "The need to find a place of solace during those dark years was essential to my survival."

My bleeding heart pinched at his words, and more, at the darkness etched into his features. He never spoke much about his years at the citadel unless I prodded, and judging by his haunted gaze, tonight was not the time to delve into those memories.

Instead, I focused on the beauty stretching before me. Twisted, ancient trees with gnarled branches reached skyward, their silhouettes stark against the backdrop of the night sky.

Their leaves, dark and glossy, whispered on the wind as it rustled through the dense foliage. I dropped down to the carpet of soft, dark moss and jerked off my boots, eager to feel the white sand along the shoreline between my toes.

"I wish you would have told me to bring a bathing suit."

A devious smile parted his lips, setting his teeth aglow beneath the moonlight as he folded his immense form beside me. "Perhaps I'd hoped for a repeat of our night in the mystical pond all those months ago."

A shiver rippled up my spine at the heated memories. Instead of indulging in the warmth it kindled, I sharpened my glare. "So you wish me to be poisoned?"

"Aelia..." he growled. "I had hoped to spend some time with you. For us to enjoy a few hours of rare peace in the tranquil waters before the chaos of the Umbral Trials begin."

"Where I'll surely be poisoned." A bitter laugh slipped out.

"I wish I could say it could never happen, but I promised to no longer lie to you."

"Something to look forward to, then." With a sigh of resignation, I stuffed my socks into my boots and rose. My breeches would certainly not make for the most comfortable swimming attire, but if I peeled them off, it would leave me in only my tunic, which barely covered my behind.

"You're going to swim like that?" Reign arched a dark brow as he pulled his tunic over his head.

Every ounce of moisture in my mouth disappeared as I took in the sight of his perfect form glistening beneath the moonlight. Waves of dark hair fell across his broad shoulders, calling my attention to the runes along his arms, which I then followed back up and over to the dark slashes on his chest. The mark of the banished, which had not been magically placed, as I'd assumed, but painfully inflicted by his tyrant of a father.

My fingers twitched to reach out and touch him, to run my fingertips over the fine dips and valleys of his torso, to explore the canvas of tanned skin and mystical markings. Instead, I curled my fingers into a tight fist and forced my gaze to the ground. "Yes," I finally murmured.

"Suit yourself, but our return trip will not be very pleasant in those wet breeches."

I lifted my gaze once more to tell him to mind his own business when he began to unlace his own leathers. *Oh, no, no.* Squeezing my eyes closed, I waited until I heard the unmistakable sound of his trousers hitting the soft earth.

"You can open your eyes, princess. I'm still wearing my underclothes. I haven't forgotten about your delicate sensibilities, despite your clearly Fae blood."

I snuck a peek through slitted lids, and once I confirmed he was telling the truth, I opened my eyes all the way. Still, those undershorts left little to the imagination, so I kept my gaze pinned to his, determined to not let my eyes drift—no matter how much they seemed to want to. Mirth flashed across those dark spheres as he clearly noticed my flustered state.

"If you'd like, I can close my eyes so that you may at least remove your breeches. Once you are fully immersed beneath the dark waters, I assure you I will be unable to make out any details."

"No, it's fine."

"Why must you be so stubborn?" he growled. "When will you embrace your Fae heritage?"

"Oh, I'm not Fae enough because I refuse to bare myself to you?"

"No, Aelia, that is not what I meant. Sometimes I just wonder if you're the one blocking your powers."

I slapped my hands on my hips and glared up at the insufferable male. "So if I strip down, it will magically unbind whatever is blocking my *rais*?"

Reign stalked toward me, a tendon feathering his jaw. "I don't know. Maybe! Would you try it if I believed it were?"

"No!" I squealed. "Because I cannot trust that it's not merely a ploy to see me naked."

Reign barked out a laugh, the rumble of his bare chest causing the runes across his torso to vibrate. "Trust me, princess, if I was that desperate to see you naked, I'd find another way." The jagged edge to his tone sent fire licking down my belly.

I knew we were treading dangerous waters, and still I continued, helpless to still my traitorous tongue. "You believe yourself to be that irresistible?"

He inched closer, and my feet propelled me forward, guided by that unnamable force between us. "Mmm, I do." His tongue jutted out, gliding across his bottom lip, and gods, I wanted it to be my tongue across his lip. "Because you can deny it all you want, but I see the desire in the widening of your pupils, the ever-quickening rise and fall of your chest." He paused and his nostrils flared. "I can even scent it in the air."

I squeezed my thighs together to quell the burgeoning heat. "My physical reactions have no bearing here. I'm not an animal driven only by lust, and that is all there is between us. Because without trust, there could never be anything more."

The amusement in his eyes vanished, the twinkle of light evaporating in a slow blink. His entire posture stiffened as he regarded me, the weight of his gaze so powerful it fixed me to the spot, thick roots wrapping around my legs and digging deep into the earth.

"Do you really feel that way?" he whispered a long minute later.

"I must protect my heart at all costs, Reign." I laced my arms around my torso in an effort to keep myself from falling apart.

"And that is what I want to do."

"But you haven't earned the right."

His chin dropped, and he drew in a lengthy breath. "Then I will continue to try."

I waited for more, but he turned on his heel and marched toward the lapping waves, leaving me exhausted and alone.

Why did all of our encounters end like this? Why couldn't I simply give in to the overwhelming need to be with him?

The answer was simple: I was terrified.

A dark shadow blotted out the moonlight, and I lifted my gaze skyward just in time to see a wave of dragonfire setting the night ablaze.

"Aelia, watch out!"

Chapter Twenty-One

A*elia*

Reign's shout awakened that energy trapped deep in the dark recesses of my soul. A radiant shield bloomed around me, the ethereal light so brilliant I was forced to close my eyes from the sheer intensity of it. The silver flames licked across the protective sphere and fiery heat filled the bubble.

The molten surge rushed my veins, lighting up my insides in pure agony. Intense pressure squeezed my skull, vibrating my temples. Oh, gods, I couldn't hold the shield for a second longer. The torrent of flames continued, the steady onslaught cracking through my faltering *rais*.

This wasn't working. I had to try something else or I would die. Searching my core, I summoned my dwindling *rais* and followed the faint glimmering filaments that connected me to my skyrider. I'd never attempted to channel Sol's power, not even in the trials. I'd been too frightened by its sheer volume, but perhaps today was the day.

Aelia, are you all right? Sol's voice trickled through my subconscious the moment I gave those ethereal strings a pull.

Just fine, but I could use a little power boost.

Do you need me?

No, I believe I can handle him.

Him, who?

Sol, please, I'm a little busy here.

Cutting off our mental connection, I tapped into the well of power that was Solanthus, the Sun Chaser, calling all that energy into one hand. A heady surge zipped down my arm and rushed through my fingertips. Splaying my hand, I pointed to the sky, in the general direction of the gray dragon wielding those blistering flames. Gritting my teeth, I focused the energy, and a solar flare burst to life in my palm.

I launched the sphere of pure *rais* into the deluge of silver flames, and a spine-tingling roar ricocheted across the night sky. The sweltering blaze fell away instantly. I gulped in a breath, and the moment the flames vanished, my shield popped, my power having reached its apparent limit. I dropped to the ground, my knees hitting the earth with a thud, and the air remaining in my lungs fled.

Another roar echoed overhead, calling my attention to the smaller dark-winged form soaring toward the gray dragon and the rider I now saw on its back. *Ruhl.* It had to be.

Reign's shadow wings propelled him into the sky, and his dark minions surged over the slate beast, inundating him in hissing, writhing tendrils. A moment later, the creature's wings angled toward the earth, and the rider and his mount began their descent.

A prickle of unease descended along with them, and I thanked Raysa I never shed my breeches. Meeting the Shadow heir in nothing but my underthings would have been far from ideal.

A moment later, Reign coalesced beside me, my focus so fixed on the dragon coming from above, I barely noticed his shadows before they were upon me. At least he was back in his breeches once more, although his shirt hadn't made a reappearance. "Are you all right?" The panic in his eyes was palpable. Forcing down the emotion threatening to clog my airway, I nodded quickly.

"What is Ruhl doing here?" I rasped out.

"I have no idea, but we are about to find out. I forced him to ground Mordrin."

"The dragon?"

"Yes. Now please, princess, for the love of Noxus, play along with whatever I say, despite how unpleasant it may sound. Do you understand?"

"Fine," I gritted out. "But don't get used to it."

Everything all right now? Sol's anxious voice invaded my thoughts. *Or must I resort to contacting Phantom once more?*

No, I'm fine. Thanks for the power boost.

Keeping one eye on the descending dragon, I took a moment to assess the glut of power I'd siphoned from my skyrider. It felt different somehow. *That wasn't* rais *that I drew from you, was it?*

It was not. As I told you before, dragons are neither light nor dark. We possess a balance of all the gods' powers.

So you wield rais *and* nox?

Yes, as well as the lesser known zar. *You are familiar with the banished god, Zaroth?*

I'd heard the name at some point in my studies, but I'd barely learned anything about Raysa or Noxus, let alone Zaroth, throughout the subpar education I'd received as a Kin. *Not really,* I finally admitted.

As it seems as though you're still otherwise engaged, I'll have to postpone the history lesson for another day. Suffice it to say, our power is the perfect amalgamation of those of all the gods. Which is why dragons reign supreme.

I snorted on a laugh. *Of course, Sol. It makes absolute sense.*

Be safe, little Kin, and do not hesitate to call on me should the need arise. I'm nearby now.

Thanks, Sol. As our connection grew dim, I mulled over his cryptic words. From what little I recalled, Zaroth was the son of Noxus, and he was revered by the now-extinct third Fae realm, the Court of Infernal Night.

The mighty whoosh of dragon wings tore me free of my musings and turned my attention toward the enormous beast alighting only a few yards away. As his talons hit the ground, my knees shook from the tremor that ran beneath the soft earth. Reign reached for me, but I batted his hand away. The last thing I needed was for his brother to think me weak.

As the younger Shadow prince leapt off his mount, my fingers twitched for the daggers Reign refused to allow me to wield.

"Well, isn't this a fortuitous coincidence?" Ruhl flashed a cocky smile as he strode toward us, the grin reminding me so much of Reign's it was unnerving. "I apologize for that unfortunate mishap with the fire. Mordrin thought he'd found himself a Light Fae snack. I never would have allowed it if I'd known it was you, Miss Ravenwood."

At the sound of my surname on his lips, an errant thought zipped through my subconscious. What was my true last name? If I was born Light Fae, I was certainly not a -wood like all the other Kin.

"Now that you know it is Aelia, you can be on your merry way then, brother." Reign's deep growl forced my thoughts back to our present predicament. A tendon beneath his scruffy cheek feathered, the tension rolling off his stiff form in waves.

Ruhl waved a dismissive hand. "And miss the opportunity to spend a little quality time with my favorite brother and his new girl?"

The elder prince narrowed his eyes. "If it wasn't apparent, that was exactly what Aelia and I were attempting to do. Spend some time *alone* together." His arm roped around my waist as he tucked me into his side.

Oh, gods, no. This was what he wanted me to agree to?

"Ah, a lovers' escape?"

"Yes," he gritted out.

"Difficult to bed your student on campus, then, brother?" Ruhl's dark eyes glittered with mischief beneath the moonlight.

A snarl worked its way up my throat, but Reign's arm tightened around my middle, an unspoken reminder of my promise to go along with this farce.

"Don't be an ass," Reign barked.

"Apologies, my lady." The Shadow heir dipped into an exaggerated bow. "You know, Reign, if I didn't know any better, I would think the lovely Aelia barely tolerates your presence." He inched closer, dark shadows buzzing around his form. "As it is, her aura is an inky black. Hardly what I'd expect from a pair of lovers out on a moonlit stroll."

"In case you forgot, your dragon attacked me only moments ago," I bit out. "An incident like that does nothing for my mood."

Ruhl chuckled, the sound sharper than the warmth carried in Reign's laughter. "Fair enough, Miss Ravenwood." He waved a hand in our direction. "But I would still feel more convinced of this pairing if I could witness a demonstration."

"Enough," Reign growled, his body surging forward. If it wasn't for the hold around my waist, I was certain he would have launched himself at his brother. "You will not speak to her like that."

"So protective over your paramour, brother."

I could feel every muscle in Reign's body coiled to strike, and I knew a battle between the two Shadow princes could be deadly for us all, especially with Mordrin looming nearby. Steeling my resolve, I gritted out, "I suppose it's true what they say about us Kin." Batting my lashes, I attempted my most seductive pose as I leaned into Reign more fully. "Once you bed a Kin, none other will do." I ran my fingers up his still bare chest, and his shadows swirled in delight. They weaved between my fingers, sending icy chills across my skin.

Ruhl barked out a laugh as he watched us. "I suppose I'll have to experience it for myself one day, then." He stepped closer still and offered a hand. "Perhaps, you'd be willing to share, brother?"

Reign was nothing more than a blur as he launched himself at his brother, his shadows morphing into those enormous wings, and his hand curled around his throat. "I. Do. Not. Share." He punctuated each word with the tightening of his fist. Ruhl choked out a breath, his cheeks darkening beneath the brilliant moon. "You would do well to remember that, little brother, if you value your life. Aelia is *mine*, and if you believe that I would ever let you touch her, you're more deluded than I thought."

"And if you," his brother rasped out, "are deluded enough to believe I don't know that there is something more going on here between the two of you, you are the fool." Reign's fingers tightened, his white knuckles gleaming as he lifted Ruhl off the ground. "Now, release the future heir or suffer Mordrin's wrath." The dragon perked up, its smoldering silver eyes intent on Reign. A low growl permeated the thick air, and I prayed Phantom was close by. "And don't think for a moment I won't share this new development with Father."

"Oh, I don't doubt that, Ruhl. That's what you always do, isn't it? Run to Father when you cannot win your own fight." He slowly released his hold, dropping his brother back to the ground. "Tell Father what you will about the female I'm bedding. I'm sure he'll find it incredibly interesting that you risked my position at the Conservatory by spilling our secrets."

The young prince paled and staggered back a step.

So he hadn't told the king any of it. Interesting... At least my secret would be safe for now. If I truly was this child of twilight, which I still refused to believe.

Ruhl cleared his throat, straightening the collar of his rumpled tunic. He wagged a finger at his brother. "You know what? You're right. Father does not need to know *everything*... Surely, he would care little about the female you've invited into your bed. Just be careful she doesn't bear you little bastards." A wicked grin curled the corners of his lips. Then he pivoted that dark gaze to me. "When he bores of you, as he inevitably will, Miss Ravenwood, I would be more than happy to introduce you to the true pleasures of life. I assure you I am a far more skilled lover than my brother. He's much too tense, too restrained."

A chill skirted up my spine at the sinful sparkle in those bottomless orbs. But even still, I couldn't let him have the last word.

"Funny, I wouldn't say he's too anything in that regard."

His brows rose in surprise for a moment before he dipped into another bow, those eyes pinned to mine. "I look forward to our next encounter, in the Umbral Trials."

An unexpected flare of heat settled low in my belly. Raysa, what was it with these Shadow males, and why was my body such a traitorous little thing?

Ruhl spun on his heel, then darted up Mordrin's leg, and the two were airborne seconds later. I blew out a breath of relief the moment the dragon's wingbeats pounded the night sky.

Reign pivoted toward me, those ominous shadows stretched out around his imposing form. "I swear to the gods I'm going to murder him."

"You can't," I hissed.

"It's only a matter of time until he learns the truth, Aelia. And when he does—"

"What truth? We don't even know if I am this child of twilight!" Frustration puckered my brow. "It's been months, and we are no closer to discovering the truth."

"I know that!" he roared, the tendrils of darkness whipping into a fury around him. "You don't think I suffer with that failure every day?" The shadows grew thicker, more dense, swallowing me up in their icy embrace. "If only there was a way to determine, undeniably, if the prophecy referred to you, I wouldn't live in this constant state of agony, with the fear that you could be taken from me. That I could be forced by my father—"

A prickle of awareness drew my gaze overhead, and my feet moved of their own accord, my arms curling around Reign's neck as the darkness enveloped us. My mouth captured his, lips crashing with such force, our teeth clashed. Fiery heat surged through my blood, the onslaught more powerful than Mordrin's dragonfire. He snagged my bottom lip between his teeth, nibbling on the pillowy flesh until I was certain he'd draw blood. And still, I couldn't force myself away. His hands slid down my back, cradling my behind and pressing me flush against the hard planes of his body. Good gods, this was not supposed to happen. He staggered forward, a male drunk on lust, walking me back and pinning me against a rough bark, devouring every inch of me.

Beneath the thick canopy of leaves and the whirling tornado of Reign's shadows, I was certain we were now concealed from watchful eyes, and yet, I continued to give into the moment, unable to tear my body away from his. As his kisses grew more desperate, and my own body ached for release, my traitorous hips arched toward his growing arousal.

"Mmm, princess," he whispered against my lips. "You have no idea what you do to me..." He paused to lean back just enough to trap me in that hypnotic gaze. "What I wouldn't give to claim every inch of you beneath the starlit sky."

My breath hitched, a gasp escaping my swollen lips. We weren't supposed to be doing any of this. It was only meant to be a distraction. "Mordrin was flying overhead," I managed to get out.

His dark brows furrowed, those piercing irises finally releasing me to scan the sky above. A long minute later, his eyes met mine once more. "That was why you kissed me? It was all part of the ruse?"

"You told me to follow your lead..."

He staggered back, his shadows disappearing back into his skin. He huffed out a rueful chuckle, shaking his head. "I should have known."

"I'm sorry if you thought—"

"No, don't apologize. What did I tell you about apologizing the first day we met?"

"It makes one look weak."

He nodded. "And you, Aelia Ravenwood, are anything but weak. But you are damned obstinate." He dragged a hand through his disheveled midnight locks, the ones my fingers longed to run through again. "You will never forgive me, will you?"

I swallowed hard, my mouth, still burning from his heated kisses, puckering. Before, I believed perhaps I could, but he was right, I wasn't weak anymore. I was Aelia, carved of stone, and our fate was a cursed one. "I don't know that I can," I finally murmured, my heart shattering as I forced out each word.

Chapter Twenty-Two

Thank the gods the code of conduct was back in place, because my protective shadow had gone into hiding since our return from the deserted isle days ago. A swirling void had blossomed in my chest in Reign's absence. I reminded myself it was what I wanted, but still, the ache grew worse. We could never be together, so keeping our distance was the best strategy. As I kept reminding myself. Being in close proximity proved much too difficult, and now that I was once again relatively safe, there was no need for my overprotective professor to spend every moment guarding me.

"Any questions about the mentorship program?" Heaton's voice tore me from my internal musings. Mottled shadows darkened the soft skin around his eyes, and there was something about the rounding of his shoulders that betrayed his exhaustion. Heaton had been oddly absent this term, along with most of the fourth years. I'd seen them flying off in the odd hour of twilight more than once this past week. I'd asked Rue if she knew where they were going, but apparently her brother had been sworn to secrecy.

And now, our team leader had summoned Flare Squad to the small auditorium in the Hall of Glory for a pre-class meeting.

"I wonder who I'll get as a mentor." Rue jabbed her elbow into my side. "I hope it's not Gleamer, he's dreadfully boring."

"Ten gildings says Aelia ends up with Darkthorn." Sy poked his head between us from the row behind.

"I wouldn't be so sure about that," I muttered.

"Are you two fighting again?"

I shot my round-eared-obsessed friend a scowl. "We've simply decided it's best if we kept our distance going forward."

"Right..." Rue whispered. "Anyway, Draven will be assigning the pairings, so ultimately it's up to him."

My stomach bottomed out at her words. Maybe I should have been listening to Heaton's speech more closely. If the headmaster was still set on Reign spying on me, he could very well appoint him as my mentor.

Ariadne's hand shot up a few seats over. "Can we make a specific request for a professor?"

"I'm afraid not," Heaton replied.

Wonderful. I suppose that meant we wouldn't be able to switch if we didn't approve of Draven's choice either.

"Trust that our headmaster will be guided by Raysa when making this important choice. Your mentor will lead you through your remaining years at the academy. It is not a position taken lightly."

As Heaton's words echoed in the background, it occurred to me I'd never heard Reign mention any of his other mentees, or acquisitions, for that matter. A pit of dread formed in my gut at the insinuation. Were they all dead?

"One more thing before you are dismissed for morning classes. King Elian will arrive on campus tomorrow. He will be here to observe as you train for the Umbral Trials, which will begin in one week's time."

"Great," I murmured.

"Don't worry, A, you've got this." Rue squeezed my shoulder and offered her typical bright smile.

It wasn't so much the trials I was dreading, but rather facing a certain student across the river. There was something about Ruhl that had warning bells ringing, and yet, I couldn't help the curiosity that came along with it. I needed to know more about the heir to the Shadow throne.

"Not to be the bearer of bad news," said Sy, appearing between us once again, "but I've heard the trials will be even more difficult this term due to this year's special attendee."

"The prince of the Court of Umbral Shadows," Rue grumbled.

"What do you know about him?" I attempted nonchalance, but even I could hear that the pitch in my voice had risen a few notches.

Rue shrugged. "The royals tend to keep their offspring out of the public eye as much as possible. No one even knew he'd been enlisted in Arcanum until the final battle last term."

Glad to hear I wasn't the only one.

"He was ruthless mid-air," Sy interjected. "And that dragon, even more so."

"I cannot wait for Sol to take him on in the Skyrider Battle." Rue clapped her hands as I groaned internally. Heaton shot his sister a narrowed glare, and she tucked her hands beneath her thighs.

"If there are no more questions," said Heaton, pausing for a long minute, "you'll find the name of your mentor in your scroll tomorrow morning." He scanned the remaining members of Flare Squad. "Then you are all dismissed."

Belmore straddled me on the mat, his knees boring into my ribs and his hand wrapped around my throat. My arms were pinned to my sides, and only my fingers were free enough to give an occasional wiggle. I heaved out a breath, my lungs tight from the strain. And to think, if Reign hadn't erased his memories of the other day, would my teammate and I be on better terms? Or would this stalemate have continued?

My *rais* flickered to the surface, desperate to let loose on this bastard Fae squeezing the remaining air from my lungs, but our Combat professor had been adamant. No *rais* today. A part of me was certain Reign had concocted this rule just for me. To force me to bolster my other skills so I wouldn't be so reliant on my powers when they failed me, or worse, when they grew uncontrollable.

"Come on, A!" Rue's shout of reassurance drew me from my wandering thoughts.

I bucked my hips, but Belmore remained rooted atop me like an ancient willow, roots dug deep beneath the earth.

"Come on, little Kin," the Light Fae rasped, dipping low so his spittle sprayed across my face. "Show us the mettle borne in the wilds of Feywood."

"If you insist." I smiled sweetly as my fingers crept down my side in search of the dagger hidden beneath my waistband.

Reign had said no *rais*, but he'd never said anything about weapons.

My fingertips found the familiar cold metal and wrapped around the hilt. Before I could release the blade from the sheath, an icy shadow crawled across the shell of my ear.

"No daggers, either, princess," Reign hissed, his voice so clear it felt as if he stood right beside me instead of across the gymnasium.

Son of a Fae. Releasing the hilt, I glared up at Belmore, his brawny form pinning me to the mat.

"Still waiting..." A cocky grin slashed across his perfectly carved features.

"Punch him in the balls!" Sy cried out. "He deserves it!"

I barely restrained a wild chuckle from spilling free.

"Shut your mouth, Lightspire," Belmore gritted out. "You're nothing but a rounded-ear, Kin-loving traitor."

"Enough, gentleFae!" our Combat professor roared across the chamber. "Too much chatter and not enough fighting." He stalked closer, eyes intent on the enormous male holding me down. "Aelia, finish him or tap out."

Belmore snorted on a laugh, his big form vibrating with mirth. "She's not even close, professor."

Reign's dark glare followed the movement of Belmore's body until it landed on his thighs, or more specifically, his crotch, where it draped across my lower half. His nostrils flared, and a wave of shadows surged from his skin, circling his form in a mad tempest.

Belmore dropped down again so his body was flush against mine, completely oblivious to the chaos unfolding behind him. "I've got her flat on her back, like a good Kin whore," he whispered against the shell of my ear.

Oh, Raysa, he did not just say that.

A dark tendril zipped by, hissing, and Reign's little messenger minion whispered, "Get that Fae off you or I will be forced to remove him myself. Trust me, princess, you will not be happy with the results." The feral edge to his tone had every single hair on my body standing at attention.

Focusing my scrambled thoughts, I glared up at Belmore. With his weight shifted, now sprawled on top of me, his enormous Light Fae head weighing him down, I was able to get the leverage I needed. If I only had a little help. Searching my core for the *rais* brimming over, I channeled the energy to my lower half. Please, let this work. Technically, I wasn't using my *rais* to subdue him with a solar flare or to protect from his assault with a shield—instead, I only needed a hint of that power to strengthen me physically. Much like when we used celestial glyphs to enhance our abilities.

Rais flowed through my veins, the power a heady tangle of energy with no point of release. Heat surged through every inch of my being, and I channeled all that fire into my pelvis. With an explosion of energy, I vaulted my hips. Belmore's eyes widened, jaw nearly unhinging as I launched him, arms flailing, across the entire gymnasium.

"Woohoo!" Sy and Rue shouted, their applause echoing across the now silent auditorium.

All of Flare team stared with matching expressions of shock as Belmore pushed himself off the floor and staggered toward the exit.

Reign appeared beside me as I smoothed out my crumpled tunic and rose. I fully expected a reprimand, as he must have surely noticed I'd gone against his instructions. Instead, a wry grin melted across his face. "It was about time," he ground out.

Rue and Symon surrounded us a second later, each spouting out congratulations. "That'll teach him to mess with you, A." Rue gave me a squeeze.

"I say we finish him off in the next trial." Symon's eyes flashed, a bloodthirsty expression carving into his jaw. "It will be such chaos in the first trial against Arcanum, I doubt anyone will notice."

It still struck me in times like these how different I was from these Fae. Despite the Light Fae blood clearly running through my veins, I would never be like them. I simply couldn't take pleasure in the kill. I doubted I ever would.

"Let's focus on the Arcanum students," I muttered. "We don't need to battle each other as well." Shaking my head, I turned toward the door.

Perhaps I'd only been deceiving myself into believing I could ever truly be Aelia, carved of stone.

Chapter Twenty-Three

Professor Reign Darkthorn.

I stared at the glittering letters penned across the parchment and released a groan.

"What's wrong?" Rue darted over, peering over my shoulder as I continued to gape at the mystical scroll stretched out across my nightstand. A faint chuckle escaped her lips before she clapped her hand over her mouth. "I'm sorry, A, but it was inevitable that Reign would be chosen as your mentor, don't you think?" She folded down beside me on the soft mattress.

"No," I gritted out. "I did not think." Or, at least, I'd prayed to the goddess it wouldn't be. Every time I attempted to draw space between us, fate bounded in and erased every damned line. It truly seemed as if destiny was drawing us together.

Then why in all the realms did I continue to fight it?

"Well, better Reign than Professor Litehaus," Rue huffed.

"He's so ancient it takes him a half hour simply to get out one sentence."

Squeezing my roommate's shoulder, I offered a smile. "Just think of all the wisdom you'll glean from the centuries of knowledge he holds."

Rue snorted on a laugh. "Right. Or he'll simply bore me to death, severely cutting short my time at the Conservatory."

"It's certainly not the worst way to go." I tossed her a smirk. There were countless more gruesome ways to meet your demise at the academy, and I feared I'd only witnessed a select few.

"Enough of this dismal chatter." Rue bounded to her feet and hauled me up along with her. "It's time to see the king!"

This time, I managed to suppress the groan of dread. In my time at Luce, I'd learned the Ethereal royal was well-loved by the people. It seemed I was the only one skeptical of the bright and shiny male. Or perhaps, it was only that I'd been spending too much time with his Shadow Fae enemy.

How could I have not seen the truth about Reign's royal blood earlier? All the insider knowledge he held of the courts should have been a clear give away. Noxus, I'd been so blind.

Forcing my feet toward the armoire, I selected a light tunic and a pair of comfortable leggings before peeling off my nightgown. "Why do you suppose he's returned?" I mumbled over my shoulder. "I thought Heaton said King Elian didn't often bless us with his divine presence."

Rue sauntered from her closet in a sumptuous gown crafted from the finest gossamer silk. The fabric was so delicate and translucent that it caught and reflected the light with every movement, creating a soft, glowing aura. I stared at my friend for a long moment before I realized she'd been talking, and I'd missed it entirely.

"Are you okay, A?" She waved her petite hand an inch from my nose.

"You look beautiful!"

"Oh, this old thing?" Rue twirled around in a circle and the mesmerizing color of her trailing skirts shifted subtly between hues of pale gold, ivory, and a shimmering silver, reminiscent of the first light of dawn breaking over the tranquil horizon of Feywood.

My tattered tunic and worn leggings suddenly seemed terribly inadequate. "I thought we were training after the audience with the king?"

She shrugged. "Maybe, but I can always change if that is the case."

I eyed my friend as she smoothed down her voluminous skirts. "Is there something else going on that you haven't told me about, Rue?"

Fingering the intricately adorned iridescent crystals across the bodice, her smile slowly crumbled. "It's Devin," she breathed out. "He's been seeing Mariana from Burn Squad."

My brows furrowed as I attempted to conjure an image of the girl. Not that it mattered what she looked like, all the Fae were beautiful. "But I thought things weren't serious between the two of you." I bit my tongue instead of pointing out that she'd spent the evening with a Kin only a few weeks ago.

"They aren't *supposed* to be serious." She flopped down onto my bed with a sigh. "And then I saw them together yesterday after dinner and I was... jealous. It's not a feeling I am at all familiar with, and now I simply don't know what to do."

"Oh, Rue, I'm sorry." I drew her hand in my lap as I sat down beside her. "Maybe you should tell him how you feel. Perhaps, he too, would like an exclusive relationship and is afraid you'd deny him."

"Maybe..."

"Regardless, once Devin has a look at you in *that* gown, he'll surely dismiss any thoughts of plain old Mariana."

A half smile flashed across Rue's sullen face before she leaned her head on my shoulder. "I hope you're right. I don't enjoy this feeling at all."

"Love is certainly not for the faint of heart."

Rue glanced up at me, glittering eyes meeting mine. "Oh, goodness, I cannot love Devin, it's simply impossible."

"Why?"

"I don't believe I've ever loved a male, nor had I planned on it happening any time soon. In the life we've chosen, forming meaningful relationships is nothing more than an inconvenience."

I nodded slowly, feeling the truth of her words but hating them all the same. "Come on, we must get going, or we'll be late."

Light cascaded from the high, vaulted ceilings of the Hall of Luce, refracting through prisms of crystal that hung like chandeliers, casting a thousand rainbows that danced across the marble floors. As we filed into the glistening chamber, a familiar head of blonde hair popped up among the masses. Heaton's gentle smile lit up the deep azure of his eyes. I'd barely seen our team leader since my return to the academy, and as he strode toward us, I was surprised to realize how much I'd missed him.

"Hello, ladies." Heaton dipped into a dramatic bow. "You look beautiful today, Aelia," he said before pivoting to his sister, "And you certainly dressed up for the audience with the king today, Rue. Did you believe there to be a ball?"

"Where have you been, Heat?" Rue's lips puckered as she stared up at her brother, completely ignoring his comment. "We've barely seen you all term."

The warm smile fell away, replaced by a cold mask I'd often seen on many a Light Fae, but never our team leader. "Some of the fourth-years have been tasked with extra duties as of late."

"What sort of extra duties?" I blurted.

The icy mask hardened. "I'm afraid I'm not at liberty to say."

"Not you too, Heaton? First, Lawson acts all secretive, refusing to divulge anything of importance, and now you?"

"I apologize. Truly, I wish I could."

An apology? Raysa, this must be serious. Even the affable Heaton rarely offered those words.

"Come, I've saved Flare team a row in the front." He motioned toward the dozens of impeccably lined rows of gilded chairs.

Curses, of course he had.

Reluctantly, I followed our team leader to the second row where the rest of Flare Squad already sat waiting. I squeezed by Belmore and Ariadne, half expecting a dagger in the back as I passed, but when none came, I found an empty seat beside Symon while Rue was sandwiched between Zephyr and Silvan, her billowing, iridescent gown cascading over the edges of the seat. She immediately picked up a conversation with Silvan, grinning wickedly as she ran her fingers across his arm.

I hazarded a peek over my shoulder and, sure enough, found Devin only a few rows behind us seated with the traitorous Mariana. In truth, I had nothing against the girl up until this very moment. Unlike some of the other Fae females, she'd never been overtly unkind. But if she was Rue's enemy, she would automatically become mine.

Casting one last disapproving glance in Devin's direction, I swiveled around to face the front.

Sy leaned over and whispered, "Is there a formal ball you and I were not invited to?" His mischievous gaze lanced in Rue's direction.

Shaking my head, I bit down on my tongue to keep from giggling. "She's only trying to look her best to outshine a certain member of Burn Squad."

"Ah, more trouble in paradise for you females, then?" He cast a quick glance back at Devin and Mariana. "Why you girls insist on these silly dalliances is beyond me. We males like to keep it simple."

"Is that why you prefer the company of males?"

"In some respects, yes. But as you know, I do not discriminate. At times, a purely sexual encounter is much simpler with another male. There isn't all that pesky emotion involved." He shrugged and sat back in the chair.

"Perhaps I should attempt a meaningless sexual encounter."

Symon's head fell back, a sharp cackle piercing the hushed murmurs of the hall. Dozens of curious glances whipped in our direction, sending a wave of heat across my cheeks. Sy lifted an apologetic hand before returning to our conversation. "You could never pull it off, my little Kin."

"How do you know?" I huffed indignantly.

"Because I know you." His fingers lifted to my ear, trailing the rounded curve. "But if by some miracle, you decided to give it a try, I am more than happy to oblige."

Now I was the one suppressing the wild cackle. "I could never risk what we have for one meaningless night."

He breathed out a dramatic sigh. "I cannot say I'm surprised, but still, thoroughly disappointed." Bumping his shoulder against mine, he offered a reassuring smile. "Still, the offer stands."

If he only knew I'd yet to lie with a male, I was sure he'd be less willing. Everyone knew a female's first time was important, a moment not easily forgotten.

Dark tendrils of power permeated the air an instant before heavy footfalls resounded across the marble floor. My new mentor strode down the aisle, his overwhelming *nox* filling the immense hall. I could feel his burning gaze lancing across my cheek as he stalked by, but I refused to meet it. I would be forced to submit to it soon enough since Reign was to be my mentor. According to the headmaster, we would spend countless hours with our special counselor leading up to the Umbral Trials and beyond. Not that I was unfamiliar with one-on-one training with Reign, but I'd foolishly hoped to keep it at a minimum this term.

A shiver of awareness suddenly darted up my spine, and I canted my neck toward the back of the hall. The grand double doors, carved from luminous whitewood and inlaid with gold, swung open of their own accord as King Elian crossed the entryway. His presence was like the dawn breaking over the horizon, an aura of pure, radiant light surrounding him. A troop of Royal Guardians moved into step behind the royal as he strode forward. His tall, regal figure was clad in a robe of the finest silk, woven with threads of sunlight, shimmering in hues of gold and silver.

As he walked by, the very air seemed to hum with energy; a soft, melodic resonance that matched the quiet power that radiated from him. When the king reached the dais, he paused, his gaze sweeping across those assembled, his presence commanding. Those piercing turquoise eyes pivoted, finding my gaze and holding for an endless moment. A crackle of energy pulsed in the air. Or had I imagined it? The light around him intensified, casting the entire hall into a brilliant glow, as if the very walls reflected his inner radiance, as if the hall itself bowed to his presence. And most of the Fae already had. I was the only one still standing.

"Aelia," Heaton hissed from a few chairs down. "Bow."

Forcing my chin to dip, I drew free of his gaze long enough to attempt a curtsy. Once I straightened, the king had moved up the steps of the dais. Reign's dark eyes met mine, and a wicked smirk touched his lips. Had he bowed to the king? What an insult to the enemy royal, and all this time, Reign was compelled to play the game.

"Welcome your Ethereal Highness, King Elian." The headmaster's voice boomed across the silent chamber. "We are once again honored to behold your presence."

King Elian offered a half smile before taking Draven's place at the pulpit. "Students of the Conservatory of Luce, my brothers and sisters in light, today I stand before you not as your king, but as a guardian of all that we hold dear. The air grows heavy with the whispers of conflict; the shadows lengthen at our borders, and the Wilds—once a distant menace—now stir with dark intent. The time has come for us to face the truth that we have all felt looming on the horizon: war is upon us."

A wave of gasps rolled across the assembly.

"The Court of Umbral Shadows, our ancient adversary, have gathered their strength, honed their dark arts, and now they seek to plunge our world into darkness. They believe that by extinguishing our light, they will secure their dominion over all the realms. But they are mistaken. For every shadow they cast and every blow they strike, we shall meet with unwavering strength."

Reign's dark gaze chased to mine, his head slowly turning from side to side. The move would have been imperceptible had I not been so attuned to the male. Why would the king lie about an upcoming war?

"But it is not only the Court of Umbral Shadows that we must contend with. The creatures of the Wilds, long a threat kept at bay by our vigilance, have grown bolder. They sense the discord between our courts, and like predators smelling blood, they seek to exploit it." He paused, reveling in the awe inspired by his words. "It is time to stand together. We must harness the power of our blessed light, not just to defend, but to drive back the darkness. So let the Court of Umbral Shadows come. Let the creatures of the Wilds rise. We will meet them with the fury of a thousand suns, and we will show them that Raysa's light cannot be extinguished. Not while we stand together."

Wild applause rang out, echoing across the cavernous space.

Chapter Twenty-Four

A^{elia}

King Elian's rousing speech echoed through my mind long after the royal had left the dais. He made it seem as if we were truly on the brink of war—and yet, nothing confirmed his foreboding words.

I remained in my seat long after we'd been dismissed, the weight of the king's monologue, along with the impending meeting with my mentor keeping my behind firmly in place.

"Aelia? Everyone has long gone." Heaton stood at the end of the row, light eyes intent on mine.

"Is it true what he said about the war?" I had been in the Umbral Court only a week ago and nothing had seemed out of the ordinary. And wouldn't Reign have mentioned if his father was plotting to 'plunge our world into darkness,' as King Elian had put it?

Our team leader slumped into the chair closest to him and dragged his hand through the errant blonde strands which had come loose from the neat tie at his nape. "I suppose it must be if it came from the royal's lips." He shrugged, a look of defeat boring into his handsome face. "There must always be an enemy, Aelia. If not, what would be the purpose of these academies? Perhaps the idea of war is more important for stability between the courts than the enemy itself."

I took a long minute to process his words before I voiced the question lingering in the back of my mind. "Did Rue tell you that we saw Lawson along the border of the Wilds?"

He nodded slowly, as if the faint movement were painful.

"He, too, insinuated that something was brewing across the boundary, but in all my years in Feywood, I have yet to spy a single terrifying beast."

"I wish I could tell you more, Aelia. All I know is that the fourth-years are being called to graduate early to patrol the borders. I, myself, have been chosen for early graduation."

"What? No..." I slid across the seats separating us and peered up at him. "How soon?"

"I'm not certain. It could be as soon as next week." He blew out a slow breath.

A sliver of my heart crumbled, not only for him but for Rue as well. How would she take the news? "But the Umbral Trails... you're our team leader."

"I will be sure you all have the training necessary to succeed in my absence."

"I don't want another team leader, I want you." I inched closer, my emotions suddenly overwhelming.

"Oh, Aelia," he whispered, head tilting to mine. "You've never wanted me. Despite my best efforts." A rueful smile crawled across his lips.

"Maybe not in that way," I mumbled. "But you are the best Fae male I know, and we need you here."

"I wish I had a say in the matter." His hand lifted to my cheek, thumb gently brushing my skin.

"You must promise to stay safe out there, and to return to

us..." Heat lashed behind my eyes, emotion tightening my throat. He'd been the first Fae to be kind to me.

"I still have some time, Aelia, there's no need to say our goodbyes just yet."

Blinking quickly to keep the tears at bay, I leaned forward and pressed a kiss to Heaton's forehead.

The sharp sound of a throat clearing at the back of the hall ripped my lips from his warm skin. *Oh, gods, no, not him.* "It is not wise to keep your mentor waiting on the first day, Miss Ravenwood."

Heaton's hand curled around mine as I stood. "Good luck," he whispered.

"I'll certainly need it." Especially now that Reign had seen that kiss and surely misinterpreted it for something more. Releasing my team leader's hand, I slipped through the row and marched up the aisle.

Reign's shadows loomed aggressively, a torrent of night whipping around his ominous form. An inky coil surged forward as I approached, its icy touch skimming up my arm before settling across my shoulders. Every single hair on my body stood at attention.

"You better be careful, princess." Reign's menacing voice hissed through his dark messenger. "I have little control over my shadows when it comes to other males touching what is mine."

Lifting my gaze to meet his lethal one, I lengthened my stride, anxious to have this confrontation over with. "I am not *yours*," I snarled, lifting to my tiptoes to jab a finger into his chest.

I barely registered Heaton's quiet footsteps in the far corner of the chamber as he crept out of the hall.

"Smart man." Reign's murderous glare chased after Heaton's retreating form.

"You cannot act like this." I gripped the collar of his tunic, pulling him closer until his eyes locked with mine. "We will never be together, Reign. Not because I don't wish for a different fate, but because the reality we face won't change. No matter how desperately we might want to, we cannot undo the hand we have been dealt."

"So you wish to be with *him*?"

"No..." *Gods, I wish to be with* you, *because I'm clearly a masochist.* Somehow, I managed to keep the confession from sliding past my gritted teeth. "Heaton is my friend. A friend who may be forced to graduate early because of some war with the Umbral Court I'm not certain even exists."

"It does not exist," he huffed out. "And I do not understand why King Elian continues to torment his people with the idea of it."

"And the Wilds?"

Reign shrugged. "I am not certain. It's been years since I set foot in the deserted lands of the south." Crossing his thick arms over his chest, his eyes dropped to his boots.

We stood there for a long moment, neither speaking, neither moving. Except for those shadows. They still circled me like wild, ravenous dogs.

I finally forced the dreaded words out, only because I needed an answer before I even considered the possibility. "Would you be able to handle it if I *were* interested in another male?"

His eyes jerked to mine, and a flash of fury streaked across those fathomless spheres of starlight. "No. Unless if by handling it, you meant squeezing the life out of the poor bastard with my *nox*." A savage grin twitched his lips.

"Then I suppose it's a good thing there is no one I have set my sights on." I paused and sucked in my bottom lip. "Yet."

"For the love of Noxus, princess, I beg of you to keep it that way. For both our sakes."

My silly heart fluttered at the intensity in his gaze, at the wild frenzy of his twisting shadows. How could I ever consider another when it was only Reign who made my soul tremble with desire?

My mentor offered his arm, cocking a dark brow. "Come, we have training to do, mentee. In a short week, you'll be facing Ruhl across the river, and it is my duty to ensure you survive."

※

"Remember, keep that unpredictable *rais* of yours contained, princess." Reign's shadow slid across the shell of my ear, delivering his message before returning to its home in the dark folds of his cloak a yard away. He ticked his head toward the steps of the Hall of Luce where the king and his entourage watched the initiates train.

"I'm trying," I called back as I unleashed a dozen luminous blades at that smug smile. "Innocent enough?" I mumbled under my breath. His shadows sliced through the air, curling around my projectiles, but a few met their mark all the same.

Thanks to that sensitive Fae hearing, he must have heard my reply, either that or he read my lips. It would explain that unyielding gaze now focused solely on my mouth. I refused to consider any other reason for that hunger in his eyes because as Sol suggested I was guarding my heart above all else.

Returning my focus to training, I glanced around the field at the dozens of first-years taking turns sparring with their mentors. It suddenly occurred to me that I was the only initiate who wasn't forced to share a mentor with at least two other students.

Calling back the burgeoning *rais* strumming through my veins, I dropped my defensive stance and marched toward my professor. "Why do you only have one mentee?"

"Because I do not wish to waste my valuable time on sub-par students."

I wasn't sure if I should be proud of the compliment or insulted on behalf of the rest of the Light Fae student body. "Surely, there was some other first-year worthy of your time."

"Not in the four years since my arrival."

"What? You've never mentored another student?"

He shook his head. "Need I repeat my explanation once again?"

"So you only did this for me?"

His lips twisted before settling into a hard line. "I would have volunteered anyway, but as Draven forcibly suggested it, it wasn't necessary for me to do so."

"He still suspects me?"

"Of what, I cannot be sure yet, but the prophecy is still the most likely option."

"Of course it is." That goddess-cursed prophecy seemed to be the main cause for many of the issues I faced these days. I released a dramatic sigh and flopped down onto the soft grass.

"What are you doing, princess? *He* is watching."

I cast a casual glance over my shoulder to find the king's penetrating gaze fixed in our direction. "Am I not allowed a water break?" I pointed at the waterskin across the lawn.

With a dramatic eyeroll, Reign released one of his shadows, which darted across the field, returning with my water seconds later. "Do you wish for King Elian to believe I'm *your* lap dog too?" A glint of amusement sparked in those midnight orbs.

"It would certainly do nothing to raise his opinion of me." I smirked.

"You're right on that count. I am certainly not one of his most favored professors."

I lowered my voice to a mere whisper. "How does he not know who you really are?"

He dropped down beside me. "The children of the royals are typically kept hidden from prying eyes of the enemy court. And even more so when they are of questionable parentage. When I attended Arcanum, I did not receive quite the same fuss my brother has. No one knew who I was. If I hadn't bonded Phantom, no one would have thought twice about me."

I prickled at the insult as if it had been levied upon me. Despite the hard mask Reign wore, I could tell his impure bloodline weighed heavily on the proud Fae. "I suppose it's a good thing you weren't recognized, then."

"Always so optimistic, my little Kin." A wry smile spread his lips for an instant before it faded once more.

I took a long sip from the waterskin and glanced up at the enigmatic male. There had been something else I'd been curious about. "What of your other acquisitions? I know you've had others over the years. So what's happened to them?"

"They're all dead."

The breath caught in my throat as I pictured dozens of dead Light Fae sent to their homes in gilded urns.

"And I vowed that would never happen with you."

"Before or after you knew—or rather suspected—who I was?"

"From the moment you passed through the Veil of Judgement, and I saw something in you that was glaringly missing in all the others."

"And what would that be?"

"There was a fire in you," he said, his voice low and steady. "A defiance that refused to be snuffed out, even when faced with the impossible. The others... they were strong, yes, but they lacked that spark, that will to survive no matter the cost. But you, Aelia, you have the spirit of a warrior, the heart of a queen. From that moment, I knew you were different. I knew you were the one worth saving."

His words sent a shiver down my spine, the weight of his admission settling over me. This wasn't just about survival anymore—this was about something far greater, something that connected us in ways I still couldn't understand.

A long moment of silence passed between us as I slowly sipped the cool water, mulling over his words. No one had ever thought so highly of me; maybe Aidan, but he'd never spoken the sentiment aloud, much less so candidly.

"I have another one coming soon," Reign finally whispered.

"Another acquisition?"

He nodded. "The beginning of the term is my least favorite time of the year."

"Do you know anything about the new student?"

"Only that they are female, and I am to retrieve her from the northern part of the court, near the border along the Darkmania Falls, actually."

My thoughts whirled back in time to our visit to the mystical cascades and our night spent in the caves. Squeezing my eyes closed, I buried the fond memories and focused on his quiet words. "A female?" An unexpected twinge of jealousy speared me between the ribs.

"Will you be able to *handle* that, princess?" He threw my earlier question back at me with an amused glint in his eyes.

"Of course, I will. I'm very capable of sharing your attention." Even as I spoke the words, I could feel the lie through my teeth.

"Good. Now get up, you've had more than enough rest."

Chapter Twenty-Five

A*elia*

The whipping winds lashed dark hair across my face as Sol drew lazy circles just above the Conservatory. Both Symon and Rue flew a few yards below us aboard their mounts, Griff and Windy. Neither the hippogriff nor the Pegasus were able to fly quite as high as my dragon, but we still attempted an occasional joy ride together.

It was only in quiet moments like these that I felt truly free.

The week of training flew by in a flurry of clashing *rais* and *nox*, with a dash of broadswords and a sprinkle of mid-air combat. My body was battered and my ego bruised, but I felt more confident in my abilities than ever before. With nightly clandestine visits to the Shadow Court with my mentor, my *rais* was blooming.

Reign was more convinced than ever that *nox* was the key to unblocking my hidden potential. If only we could escape Draven's watchful eye long enough to visit a Spellbinder in

Mysthallia, he was certain we could discover the truth of my origins. I had yet to confess what I'd learned from Aidan upon my visit home, and I had no intention of ever doing so.

Sol angled his wings and slowed their gentle flaps to glide alongside the others, drawing me from my internal musings. Griff and Windy finally seemed at ease beside my giant golden beast. It had taken months, but their fears of ending up between Sol's razor-sharp teeth were finally assuaged.

"I'm so nervous about tomorrow," Rue squealed over the winds.

Tomorrow was the official start to the Umbral Trials, though our first competition would not take place until the following day. According to Reign, tomorrow was more about the pomp and circumstance. There was even a grand banquet and ball scheduled for the evening. We would finally meet the headmaster of Arcanum, along with all the Shadow Fae first-years. Though we'd already encountered them in battle at the end of last term, we had never been formally introduced.

With the exception of Ruhl, of course. But no one knew of our encounter upon dragonback at the end of term battle, and especially not of the one on the deserted isle. A whisper of fear crawled up my spine as those cold, dark eyes flitted to the forefront of my mind. For half-brothers, the heirs of the Umbral Court shared a striking resemblance. And something else too... That unnamable quality that had immediately drawn me to Reign, somehow tethered me to Ruhl.

"You have nothing to worry about," Symon replied, returning my thoughts to the present. "We will slaughter those Shadow Fae."

"Like at the final term battle?" I blurted.

"That was different." Sy's light brows furrowed. "Those cheating bastards had an unfair advantage because they attacked days early. This time, we will be prepared."

"I hope you're right."

Rue pointed across the endless blue toward the mountains in the north. "Is that Reign?"

I pivoted to follow her line of sight, and sure enough, my mentor appeared atop Pyra with a blonde female pressed to his back. That surge of jealousy I'd experienced before filled my chest, like a tidal wave breaking across the shore.

"And who is that with him?" Sy squinted, holding his hand above his brow to shield his eyes from the sun's brilliant rays.

"It must be his new acquisition." I prayed my voice came out steadier than it felt.

Rue's eyes widened as her head swiveled back and forth between me and the approaching phoenix.

"Finally, a new female." Symon's smile stretched from pointy-ear to pointy-ear.

"You've already tired of the entire student body?" I bit out, harsher than intended, but the tangle of emotions twisting my gut had put me in a foul mood.

"There can never be too many bodies, my little round-eared friend."

"You're absolutely hopeless."

He shrugged, that mischievous grin only growing wider.

I watched, held utterly captive, as Reign neared, his head cocked back to deliver an occasional word to his new acquisition. What was he telling her? Would he wish the gods be with her as he'd said to me upon my arrival at the Veil of Judgement? Would the female survive?

A multitude of questions peppered my thoughts as Reign soared by without so much as a passing glance in my direction.

"Oh yes, she's gorgeous," Symon purred as they zipped past us.

"Symon!" Rue reprimanded.

"What?" His oblivious gaze bounced between us before understanding finally dawned on the unaware male. "Oh, but she's nothing compared to you, Aelia. Clearly, not competition.

And I'm not simply saying that because of your ears." He shot me a wink, but I could barely manage a smile in return.

Good gods, what had gotten into me?

Only the gods know, Aelia. Sol's voice interrupted my mental musings. He'd been remarkably quiet today. In fact, not only today, but ever since that flight with Phantom a couple weeks ago.

I am not jealous.

I never said you were.

How's Phantom? It was an underhanded attack, and I knew it well. Still, the thought escaped.

Plumes of silver smoke drifted from his nostrils as he snorted beneath me. *I wouldn't know. I have not spoken to her.*

I'm sorry, I shouldn't have asked.

It's fine, Aelia. I have had many decades to sort through her betrayal. I only hope it does not take quite so long for you to do the same with Reign.

Ouch. I deserved that.

"Come on, let's go meet the professor's new acquisition." Symon pointed toward the Hall of Glory. "She made it through the Veil!"

I should have been happy for the female, but instead, I found myself wishing the opposite were true. Raysa, what was happening to me? How could I wish death upon this stranger?

Shall we? Sol's question lingered in my mind for a long minute before I finally answered.

Yes, I suppose we should get it over with.

Sol angled us toward the lush earth below, and with each measured flap of his wings, my anxiety grew. As if my bonded dragon could feel my apprehension, which he likely could, he moved so slowly we were the last to arrive. By the time Sol's talons hit the ground, Rue and Symon were already chatting with the new initiate.

I begrudgingly slid down Sol's extended leg, moving toward

the foursome where they hovered around the sparkling fountain at a sluggish pace.

Be nice. Sol's chuckle vibrated across my skull.

Just wait until the next time we see Phantom.

Slamming down the link on our mental connection before he had a chance to reply, I donned my sweetest smile as I approached.

"Oh, here's Aelia!" Rue reached for me, pulling me into the semi-circle inspecting our new colleague. "This is Liora Brighton, Reign's newest acquisition."

The tall blonde with a cute bob cocked a light brow when her scrutinizing gaze caught on my rounded ear.

"I am his acquisition *and* mentee," I added, my tone laced with a sliver of spite. I didn't miss the twitch in Reign's mouth at my outburst.

"Oh, I didn't know they allowed Kin to attend the Conservatory."

I drew back the corner of my tunic, displaying the Light symbol upon my chest. "I bear the mark of Raysa, hand drawn by the goddess herself upon my twentieth birthday. Can you say the same?"

The female's cheeks rosied, matching the soft pink of her lips, and I despised the fact that it only made the stunning Fae more attractive. "No, I'm afraid not. I was born with my mark, along with my pointed ears." She ran her finger across the silver and gold circlets running up to the sharp tip.

Reign cleared his throat. "Now that you've all met, I must escort Miss Brighton to her dormitory."

"Must you, right now?" I blurted. "I was hoping to go over some defensive flight exercises prior to tomorrow." I motioned over my shoulder at Sol who still stood on the flight field.

"Perhaps later, Miss Ravenwood." *Miss Ravenwood*? He dipped his head and led Liora up the steps of the hall as a flush of fury pummeled my insides at the abrupt dismissal.

Was I being childish? Perhaps. Did I care in that moment?

Not one bit. "Very well, I'll wait for you in my chambers, then," I called out.

Reign spun at me, his eyes wide and a hint of crimson kissing his cheeks. Liora mirrored his movements, watching the exchange eagerly. Even Rue and Sy had gone silent. Again, my mentor cleared his throat, a hitch in the awkward sound. "I will meet you at the flight field after supper. I will need a few hours to get Liora settled, much as I did with you on your first day." With that, he scurried up the steps, his shadows snaking across his form, like a big coward, before I could counter.

"Whoa, Aelia, down girl." Symon nudged me with his shoulder. "Will you be pissing on your mentor next?"

The heat of embarrassment crawled across my face until I was certain I was as red as the stain on Rue's lips.

"Oh, leave her alone, Sy." My roommate curled an arm around my shoulders and steered me toward the stone pathway to the Hall of Elysia. I was in no mood to eat, but anything was better than standing here in shame.

Chapter Twenty-Six

A*elia*

"We mustn't really attend the ball afterward, must we?" I glanced across the room at Rue as she slipped into yet another gorgeous gown. The idea of spending the evening consorting with the students of Arcanum as if they hadn't slaughtered half of our own last term was utterly repulsive.

"We do, and you know it. Headmaster Draven made it perfectly clear."

"But why? What is the point of it all? Why pretend we are at peace with our neighbors across the river when the king says we are on the brink of war?"

Rue slowly shook her head, releasing a long breath. "Because that is simply how it's always been done." She sauntered closer on her heels and spun around. "Now lace me up, please."

I hadn't dared to inquire if Devin had asked her to attend the ball together. I wasn't even certain if that was how it was done. If it was a mandatory event, did one even need an escort?

I certainly did not.

Not that my usual escort could be bothered to do so if I had wanted him to.

Once Rue was perfectly fitted in her corset, I turned to my own armoire. Now I understood why the academy had filled our closets with luxurious ballgowns. I'd learned that not only would there be a grand celebration this evening, but also one to commemorate the end of the trials and crown the winners.

"Definitely the gold one." Rue stood behind me on tiptoes peering over my shoulder.

I fingered the opulent fabric, the silk like rose petals between my fingertips. As I pulled the gown from the dim closet, it shimmered with an ethereal radiance, crafted from the finest gossamer silk that seemed to be spun from pure sunlight.

"Oh, yes, put it on!"

I slipped into the gown and held up the corset top as Rue got to work on the elaborate laces. The bodice was intricately adorned with tiny, iridescent crystals that sparkled like dew on morning flowers. The skirt flowed like liquid light, cascading in soft, sweeping waves to the ground. It was the most glorious gown I'd ever seen.

Rue squealed when the final lace was tied, but she wasn't quite finished with me yet. After taking a brush to my unruly hair and thoroughly powdering and primping me, she took a step back. A beaming smile spread across her dainty features. "Go take a look in the mirror. You look absolutely ravishing."

Rushing across the room, anticipation quickened my heartbeat. With every step, the gown seemed to float around me, as though it had a life of its own, trailing a faint, shimmering mist in its wake.

When I reached the mirror, I could barely recognize the female in front of me—no, the Light Fae. I felt like a living embodiment of the beauty and power of light, a radiant being descended from the heavens. The necklace Aidan had gifted me on my twentieth birthday glinted beneath the steady stream of light from above. I fingered the worn medallion, and it warmed beneath my touch.

Rue appeared beside me and gently tapped beneath my chin. "No gawking, A. You have always been beautiful inside and out, and you must own it."

A bittersweet chuckle escaped as I continued to stare at my reflection. As difficult as the last term had been, I couldn't deny all I'd gained by coming here. I was no longer the powerless Kin from Feywood. I was Aelia Ravenwood, Light Fae. I still may have had much to learn, but I would never go back.

Rue offered her arm, that big grin still firmly in place. "Shall we?"

"Yes, we shall. Let's show those Shadow Fae who rules this side of the Luminoc."

※

I stared in absolute awe as we crossed the threshold into the Hall of Luminescence. The entire first floor had been converted into a sprawling chamber of beauty, light and magic. Towering crystal columns stretched endlessly toward the skylight, each one catching and refracting light in a dazzling display of rainbows. The floor, made of polished opalescent marble, gleamed underfoot, creating the illusion that one was gliding across the surface of a calm, celestial sea.

"Realms, how did they do this?" I breathed.

"An overabundance of *rais*." A shadow curled across the shell of my ear, delivering his master's message an instant before the prince of shadows appeared. He moved beside Rue and me, all sharp edges and dark formal wear. I refused to ogle the perfect cut of his jacket across those broad shoulders, the way the material clung to his powerful form like liquid midnight.

My mentor had been too busy with his new acquisition to

show up for our defensive flight training yesterday. Instead, he'd sent Professor Lumen in his place. To say that I'd been a little peeved was putting it mildly.

Reign, on the other hand, looked perfectly giddy as his heated gaze raked over me. His jaw ticked, lips parting as if to speak, but a familiar voice cut him off.

"Please be seated." Headmaster Draven's deep tenor boomed across the chamber as students, Light and Shadow Fae alike, filled the hall. A clear divide of light and dark stood in sharp contrast, diverting my attention from the resplendent scenery. I scanned the room in search of another shadow prince, but to my relief, the only one I could spy stood inches away from me. Much too close for my comfort. His buzzing shadows whirled between us, thickening the air with *nox*.

"As soon as everyone is seated," Draven announced as he stood upon a raised platform that stretched the length of the far wall, "Headmaster Malakar and I will say a few words, then our sun-blessed king himself shall honor us with his wisdom to commemorate this grand occasion." A dark-haired male with a thick mustache stood beside the headmaster, a tornado of shadows coiling around his form. A sinister scar bisected his cheek, the jagged edges seemingly created by a serrated blade. A prickle of unease zipped up my spine at the sight of Arcanum's headmaster. From everything I'd heard from Reign, he was far worse than Draven.

Turning my attention back to the room, I perused the dozens of tables that had been set up across the space, encircling what I assumed was the dance floor. A soft melody filled the air, confirming my unspoken thoughts. Did the administration honestly believe we would dance with the enemy?

Rue pointed across the hall at a long banquet table filled with blonde heads. "Look, there's Heat. Let's go sit with our squad."

I followed behind my roommate, weaving between tables of familiar faces along the right side of the hall. All eight squads were assembled, the first-years adorned in gowns and suits that rivaled the beauty of the chamber. My dark shadow loomed behind me, inching closer with every step. Before we reached Heaton, I whirled on Reign, and he nearly barreled right into me. Instead, his hands came around my waist to steady himself.

A hiss escaped through my clenched teeth at the accidental touch. It took me a moment to focus my thoughts as he slowly released me and took a step back. "Where is your new acquisition?" I rasped out. "Shouldn't you be accompanying *her* this evening?"

"Perhaps, but instead I'm here with you."

"Why? You didn't seem concerned about me last night when you missed our training session to, I assume, remain with your acquisition."

"I *was* concerned, which was why I sent Lumen."

I knotted my arms across my chest, as if they could somehow protect me from the raging indignation.

"I suggest you quickly move past whatever has your emotions twisted and focus on the fact that the prince will be here tonight."

I barely resisted the urge to punch him in that royal nose. *Whatever has my emotions twisted*? He could not be serious.

"Aelia, sit down, the king is arriving." Heaton's sharp whisper turned my attention to my team leader and the rest of the squad where they were already seated.

As I glanced around the room, I noticed Reign and I were among the few still standing. Wonderful. Nothing like calling more attention to myself. As it was, with my dark, unbound hair, I seemed to be seated on the wrong side of the divide. I dropped down into the closest empty seat and found myself beside Belmore. Raysa, help me.

At least Reign finally skulked away, disappearing among the ranks of the Conservatory's faculty. As we awaited the arrival of King Elian, I glanced at the empty table to our left. It was the only one in the entire hall devoid of students. I was seconds away from asking Belmore if he knew who the table had been reserved for when a familiar ethereal presence filled the hall.

The right half of the chamber stood and bowed as his Ethereal Highness strode in, while the other portion of the room diverted their gazes as if standing too close to the sun may permanently blind them.

I'd been so enrapt by the beauty of the hall and my own issues with Reign, I'd been completely oblivious to the thick tension in the air. A heady tangle of *nox* and *rais* skimmed over my skin, drawing my own powers to the surface. Here we all were, in the same room, together, Light and Shadow, enemies.

King Elian's heavy footfalls jerked my attention to the dais as he joined the headmaster. As always, the Light royal beamed with radiant energy as if Raysa herself had bathed him in her heavenly luminescence.

The two headmasters moved to the pulpit and Draven stepped up, clearing his throat. "Here we are, once again, on the eve of the Umbral Trials. I will keep this speech short as tonight is for celebration, not reliving our dark history." He cast a glance in Malakar's direction. "As you know, the training you all receive at both academies is essential to the ongoing peace between our courts. If it were not for this perfect balance, war would ensue. And we certainly would not want that, now, would we?"

A rush of murmurs crawled through the hall.

Malakar moved in front of Draven and the left half of the chamber seemed to tense. "Of course we would not," he replied, a wicked gleam in his eye. "My old friend Draven is correct. What we accomplish at the universities is of the utmost importance. And I expect Arcanum to show our neighbors on this side of the river just how seriously we take that duty."

A roar of applause exploded across the Shadow Fae section of the chamber.

A sharp keening sound turned everyone's attention to the back of the hall. The grand doors whipped open and a cloud of pure, inky night seeped in. The very air seemed to shift, the brilliance of the room dimming as if the light itself recoiled from an ominous presence. A figure of imposing darkness, tall and regal, with an aura that exuded power and an unsettling stillness emerged from the shadows. The male's midnight-black robes, woven from the shadows of the deepest night, clung to his form like a living entity, rippling with an almost imperceptible movement, as if they were a part of the darkness itself.

"Noxus's nuts," Belmore gritted out. "What is *he* doing here?"

My gaze chased to Reign's, whose face had become a hard, impenetrable mask. His eyes refused to meet mine, instead locked on to the intimidating male stalking down the aisle. He could only be one person: King Tenebris of Umbra.

The king's face, pale and chiseled like cold marble, bore a look of serene confidence, the sharp angles of his cheekbones and jawline casting shadows that seemed deeper than they should be. His eyes were his most striking feature—deep, fathomless pools of pitch-black, absorbing all light and reflecting nothing. They were voids, betraying no emotion, unlike those of his eldest son. When those eyes swept over the hall, they left a trail of unease in their wake, as though they could see into the very souls of those who dared meet his gaze.

I finally forced my attention to the front of the room, to our own king whose expression seemed cut from glass. "Tenebris," he growled. "What brings you to my side of the Luminoc?" A warm golden glow vibrated around the royal as if his *rais* was mere moments from detonating.

"I thought it only fair since my heir was to attend the ceremony. In fact, I invite you to join us in Arcanum at the end of the term. I assure you the celebration will be just as grand, if not more so." He raised his hands as he slowly circled, a stream of shadows trailing in his wake. When he stepped to the side, Ruhl appeared from the void. His gaze flickered in my direction, but to his credit, never once did it twitch toward his half-brother on the dais. Reign, too, remained an unreadable mask of calm. I supposed after so many years, his duplicitousness had become second nature.

"Mmm," King Elian muttered. "You are of course welcome in my court for the remainder of the day."

"And no more, I'm sure." Tenebris smirked, the curve of his lips reminding me so much of Reign, I was certain surely someone else would notice the uncanny resemblance. He moved toward the dais, and a wave of shadows pursued, both his own and those of his Umbral Guards, the Shadow version of Royal Guardians.

While King Tenebris strode right past me and stalked up the steps to stand beside Elian on the dais, Ruhl settled at the empty table beside ours. I waited for more Arcanum students to fill the remaining spots, but not a soul moved in his direction.

Interesting...

Draven stood frozen in front of the pulpit, a hard line replacing his typical sneer. A long minute later, King Elian cleared his throat and approached the headmaster. "Shall we continue?"

His head dipped, his long beard trailing the folds of his robes. "Yes, of course, Your Ethereal Highness, the hall is yours."

Chapter Twenty-Seven

R*eign*

What in all the realms was King Tenebris doing here?

My pulse hammered in my ears like a relentless drum as my eyes razed over my father in slow motion.

I do not wish to see your face until your mission is complete, do you understand me, Reign?

Yes, my king.

Four long years. And, still, that voice plagued my dreams, as if it were yesterday. Squeezing my eyes closed, I banished the dark thoughts. I was not the same male that left the Fortress of Umbral Shadows all those years ago. My gaze flickered unwillingly to Aelia, to where she sat only inches away from Ruhl. She looked completely ravishing, more radiant than the blessed dawn breaking across the Umbral Court. *She* had changed me, perhaps even more so than my four lengthy years at the Conservatory.

Tenebris shifted beside King Elian, his familiar shadows

twitching with impatience. Being forced to stand by quietly and listen to his enemy drone on must be the wickedest of tortures for Father. I nearly laughed out loud. But no, this was not the time for mirth.

This was the first time the Shadow King had crossed the divide in ages. This was no coincidence. As King Elian concluded his speech, I cast a covert glance across the dais in my brother's direction. Had he told Father about Aelia? That sniveling, ingratiating bastard would pay if that were the case.

"And now, without further ado," the king's voice trounced over my murderous thoughts, "let the celebrations begin!"

The moment the king of Ethereal Light stepped off the platform with his retinue of guards, Father followed. He hadn't hazarded a single glance in my direction, thank the gods. Now I simply had to ensure Aelia did not catch his eye either.

Before I even had the chance to leave the dais and reach the table Flare Squad occupied, Ruhl crossed the divide between the Shadow and Light students, marching a path straight for Aelia.

Curses. What was he doing?

A smooth smile slipped into place as he extended a hand, and Aelia... *accepted* it.

Noxus, what has come over *her*?

I picked up my pace, but before I made it off the platform, Draven intercepted my escape, planting himself between Aelia and me. "May I have a word with you, Darkthorn?" he hissed in my ear.

"Right now?" I barked right back.

"Yes." His long, wrinkly fingers curled around my forearm, and he ticked his head to the chairs lining the left side of the dais.

For the love of Noxus...

I followed him toward the seating area with one eye remaining on Aelia and Ruhl. "What is it?" I snarled as I flopped down on the chair.

"Did you know anything about this?" His beady eyes seared into mine as he waggled a long finger at me.

"Of course not," I growled. "You know very well, per the banishment, I have no information as to the comings and goings of the Shadow royals."

"Why do you suppose he's here then?"

"I don't know!"

Draven's eyes narrowed to incensed slits. "Watch yourself, Darkthorn. Remember you remain here only while you prove yourself useful."

Amending my tone, I whispered, "How could I forget, headmaster?" I rose, straightening to my full height so I towered over the ancient Light Fae. "Now, are we quite finished?"

"Yes," he hissed. "But I urge you to keep an eye on the king and his heir while they are on Light Fae land."

"Of course." I spun toward the steps, but his hand caught my arm once more before I could escape.

"And one more thing, Darkthorn, if he appears to hold particular interest in any of our students, take note."

"Why would he do that?"

"I do not know yet."

"Anyone in particular?" I held my breath as I waited for his reply.

"The Kin."

Those two words lanced through my insides like twin daggers to the gut. Draven knew. He must. And there was only one reason that could be: King Elian had charged him with finding the child of twilight. I'd suspected all along, but this essentially served as confirmation. Why else would Draven believe my father to be interested in a lowly Kin?

The answer was simple, only the royals were privy to the secrets of the sacred seers.

"There's a reason I appointed you as her mentor." Draven's hushed words carried me back to the present.

"Then let me go so I may find her."

He must have read the desperation in my expression because his own soured. "I warn you again, Darkthorn, if I catch a whiff of the slightest bit of impropriety between you and the girl..."

"Yes, yes, I am perfectly aware, Draven." I shook free of his hold and marched across the dais and down the steps with Aelia in my sights all the while. She still stood beside Ruhl, the pair whispering like old friends.

It took every ounce of restraint I possessed to keep my shadows from lunging at my brother and forcibly peeling his body from hers. But anything I did would only call attention to her, and knowing my father, he had his shadow spies crawling across the chamber.

"Miss Ravenwood," I called out, at least a yard before reaching her. Her head pivoted in my direction and Ruhl's eagerly followed. "There is an important matter I must discuss with you."

"Can't this wait, professor?" Ruhl's dark gaze glinted with mischief. "This is supposed to be a celebration after all, is it not? I was only just beginning to enjoy your prized pupil's company."

"Feel free to celebrate without her, young prince." I couldn't conceal the biting edge to my tone. As it was, I could barely contain my *nox* from ripping free. Seeing him with Aelia, and with my father here, it was tearing at every scrap of restraint I possessed. My hand curled around her arm, reveling in her familiar feel.

For once, she did not fight me. Instead, she followed obediently as I toted her toward a shadowed corner of the grand ballroom, only after confirming my father's attention was elsewhere.

The moment we were alone, I called upon my *nox*, drowning us in a sea of darkness. Her shoulders trembled as the onyx tendrils danced across her skin, and goosebumps rippled down her bare arms. I couldn't help but stare now that we were alone, away from inquisitive gazes. "You look like a goddess draped in starlight, Aelia," I breathed. "Every movement you make sends ripples of light through the room, as if you were made of the essence of the stars themselves."

Her wide eyes lifted to mine, mouth curving in surprise. "Th—thank you," she finally whispered. "Is that the urgent matter you had to discuss with me?" Her lip twitched, setting off a sparkle in those silver-blue eyes.

"I wish it were as simple as that."

"Then what is it?"

"First of all, I couldn't stand the sight of you in my brother's presence," I growled. "What were you speaking of?"

"Ruhl was apologizing, actually."

I barked out a laugh, unable to control my tongue. "The heir to the great Shadow King? Apologize?"

"Yes, about the mishap with Mordrin that night on the island. He honestly seemed genuine, sincere even." Her slim shoulders lifted.

"Don't tell me you were naive enough to believe it?"

"I don't know," she murmured. A beat of silence passed before her jaw worked once more. "What else was so urgent? Was it about your father?"

I nodded slowly. "I believe he's here for the same reason King Elian has been snooping around the academy."

"So... not because of your brother?"

I shook my head. "Father would never be so paternal, not even for his grand heir."

"I hate this, Reign. I feel as if I'm walking on eggshells, constantly waiting for the sky to fall. So what if I am this child? Perhaps, I should just throw myself at King Elian's mercy."

"*No*," I snarled. "Never." My hands moved of their own accord, gripping her arms more fully.

"What could he possibly do to me?"

"It's not Elian I'm worried about, it's Tenebris." Because, gods, if he knew the truth...

"There's something else, something you're still not telling me, isn't there?"

"No," I gritted out, forcing a tempered mask. "I simply cannot fathom what either ruler would do if they discovered the truth, and I cannot risk it." My hands moved lower of their own accord, drawing her closer. "I will not lose you."

She heaved out a breath as her body grew closer to mine, and stunningly, she melted into my hold. "I'm so tired of fighting this, Reign."

"Then just give in."

The hard line of her lips softened, a faint smile appearing. Perhaps, it was that bout of unexpected jealousy at seeing me with Liora that had caused this change. Had I known envy was the way to get her to come around, I would have started flirting with other females long ago.

Her head tipped up, eyes meeting mine. "What are we doing, Reign?"

"Dancing?" I took her hand in mine, holding it close between us, then laced my other arm around her waist, drawing her even closer. The melodic hum of the mystical orchestra permeated my shadows, and I began to sway to the tune.

A rueful chuckle parted her lips as she reluctantly moved with me. "My life is in peril, once again, and you want to dance?"

"Aelia, in the short time I've known you, it seems as if your life is always, and will constantly be, in a state of peril." I dipped my forehead to hers, so our breaths mingled. "If you do not allow me moments like these, how will I ever prove myself to you?"

"It isn't your prowess on the dancefloor that needs to be proven."

"I know," I gritted out. "And I believe there is a way I can demonstrate my trustworthiness."

"Oh really?"

"Yes, actually, it was Liora's idea."

"Excuse me?" she squealed. "You've spoken to your new acquisition about *us*?"

She tried to pull back, but I simply tightened my arm around her, continuing our dance.

"No, of course not. But you have no idea how happy it makes me that you still believe there is an *us*."

She shook her head, rolling her eyes with a wry smile, but she stopped her attempts to flee, so I called it a victory. "So what is this grand idea from your illustrious new acquisition?"

"The female knows a surprising amount about spellcraft. She hails from the northwestern part of the court, near the border with Mysthallia. I'd considered taking you to see a Spellbinder once but feared it to be too risky—but now, it might be our only option."

"You still believe my powers are bound somehow?"

"I do. And I think that whatever is holding them back is the key to discovering more about your origins, and in turn, the prophecy."

"So what do you suggest?"

"In between the Umbral Trials, I will request for Draven to allow us an expedition off campus. As your mentor, the person responsible for your ultimate development, he will surely comply."

"You certainly have it all figured out, don't you?"

"Mmm, princess, I do." I pulled her closer still so our bodies were flush, and a faint gasp erupted from her perfect lips. Nuzzling the rounded curve of her ear, I breathed in her heady scent. "Now, upon the eve of yet another battle, for just a few moments, can we pretend to only be Reign and Aelia, like we did for that fateful night before we were interrupted?"

"I don't know..."

I pressed my finger to her lips, drowning her objections. "Try."

Her shoulders fell, body rounding against mine. I could feel the strain in her posture finally relax as she fully sank into me. It was oddly satisfying to feel how much she too had to fight this growing beast between us. It had been a while since I'd considered the effects of the cuorem, choosing rather to ignore the signs, but it was nearly impossible when I held her so close.

Everything else faded away as we clung to each other, swaying slowly to the soft, haunting melody that, along with my shadows, wrapped around us like a protective cocoon. Tomorrow, the trials would begin, and once more Aelia would be thrust into the heart of danger. I would be forced to mask my fear and watch her face every peril alone. But tonight, with her in my arms, I could hold on to the illusion that time had stopped, that dawn would never break, and that we could stay like this, safe and entwined, for eternity.

Chapter Twenty-Eight

Aelia

The murky waves of the Luminoc River lapped across the shore, a blustering wind splashing water across my boots. I stood beside Rue, Symon and the rest of Flare team, awaiting instructions, along with the other seven squads of initiates. Unlike the Ethereal Trials, we had not been given the list of events beforehand, so we were headed into the Court of Umbral Shadows blind.

Had I not become so habituated with overwhelming darkness on the other side of the river, I would have been twice as nervous. At least there had been one positive side to all my late-night excursions with Reign last term.

I bit back a smile as heated memories of the night before threatened to surge to the surface. I'd promised myself that the dance was the one single moment of weakness I would allow. Today, I was once again Aelia, carved of stone. If only I had my daggers, I would feel more the part.

Reign had again taken possession of them, and I wasn't sure what that said about my sanity that I let him. It was his attempt at forging trust between us, but I only felt bare and powerless without them.

No physical weapons were allowed in this trial, but he had assured me that my *rais* would be more than enough to see me through the day. Still, the familiar feel of a hilt in my palm would have done wonders for the onslaught of nerves.

"What do you suppose they'll have us do today?" Rue whispered.

"Didn't Heaton give you any idea?" Sy interjected before I could respond.

"No, he's not allowed. And besides, the trials vary from year to year."

Heaton's hard gaze flickered in our direction, and I offered a tight smile. The days with our team leader seemed measured. He'd been concerned that he would be shipped off to fight this imaginary war before the first trial, and so had I. At least he was here with us today. Right now, the little victories seemed to count as much as the big ones.

"Any news on Heaton's graduation?" I whispered to Rue.

"Not yet." She gritted her teeth and kept her eyes trained upon the encroaching darkness over the luminous bridge Professor Gleamer had conjured for today's event.

"I'm sorry," I murmured.

"Don't be sorry yet, A. At least he's still here."

Nodding slowly, her words echoing my thoughts, I pivoted my gaze to Heaton once again. He stood in the center of our team, an unfamiliar darkness carved into his jaw. He may not have been called to fight along the border of the Wilds just yet, but he frequently disappeared in the evenings aboard his ligel, returning in the morning visibly exhausted.

What was happening out there?

A cloud of inky darkness emerged along the opposite riverbank, and one-by-one they appeared. Our enemies, our competitors. Over a hundred of them, at least, came grouped in eight squads, much like we were, only our measly count was less than eighty.

"It truly isn't fair that we cannot travel through light as they do through shadow," Sy complained.

"And realms, they do seem advanced for first-years," Rue whispered. "I thought shadowtraveling was a senior level ability?"

"It is." My thoughts flew back to all the times I'd been transported through the murky ether with Reign. It had required a tremendous amount of *nox*, so how were first-years able to wield it already?

Headmaster Malakar coalesced from the cluster of students as I scanned the line for a certain prince. Despite squinting to make out their shadowy forms, I couldn't find Tenebris's heir. Which prince would I get today, the one whose dragon tried to scorch me on that desolate isle or the smooth, charming one I encountered last night at the banquet?

"Welcome to the first day of the Umbral Trials, initiates," Malakar shouted from across the river. A cruel smile flashed across the headmaster's face, curling the corners of his thick mustache. "I will not bore you with speeches as my colleague across the river did last night." The grin grew wider, more unhinged. "Instead, let us get right to it."

He took a step to the side, and an enormous metal sphere materialized from the shadow of the Citadel. "I present the Luminescent Gauntlet. Students, you must navigate this labyrinth that alternates between complete darkness and blinding light. The goal is to reach the heart of the labyrinth, where a sacred relic awaits—the key to passing the trial and advancing to the next round of the competition."

"How many rounds will there be in the trials?" I whispered to Rue.

"Typically, three or four."

"What if we don't advance?"

"We'll be disqualified."

"That sounds like the least of all evils," Symon interjected.

"Not exactly." She tipped her head to whisper between both our ears. "Those disqualified are forced to spend the remainder of the trial period at the opposing campus."

"You're shitting me..." Sy hissed, and a long moment of silence stretched between us.

"Are there any sort of rules that apply while we're there?" I blurted.

"In theory, we are meant to survive the stay, but who knows with those Shadow Fae..."

A heavy silence descended over us. A long minute later, Sy's lips quirked. "Something to stew over another day. Then again, perhaps I'll have better luck with the Shadow Fae females. Have you seen some of them? That dark hair, those mesmerizing onyx eyes..."

"Okay, we get it, they're gorgeous and exotic." I huffed out an irritated breath until my friend's fingers wrapped around a lock of my own raven hair.

"Just like you, my little Kin."

Heat burned my cheeks as I fought a smile. "You're impossible."

"Can you three be quiet?" Ariadne hissed, pressing a finger to her lips. "I'm trying to listen."

Belmore stood beside her, ever the doting boyfriend. At least he'd been so wrapped up in his little fling, he'd left me alone since the code of conduct slid back into place. A sneer twisted his lips, and as I forced my gaze away, I caught the glimpse of a pale blonde, shorn head of hair standing a row behind him. Wonderful, Lucian. Oddly, and luckily enough, I had yet to have an encounter with him this term. Besides passing sightings, the Light Fae had remained predominantly in the shadows.

Was it because of Kian? Did he have any idea what we'd done to his friend? No one had mentioned a word about his disappearance. Then again, students occasionally vanished around here, whether it was desertion or something else, no one ever talked about it. Lucian's mossy green eyes caught mine, and he lifted his index finger to his neck, slowly dragging it across his throat. His mouth twisted into a sinister smile. Well, it seemed as if my short-lived reprieve was about to come to an end.

"And now, if all the Light Fae initiates would kindly join us on this side of the river?" Malakar's voice put an end to all my dark contemplations about Lucian to focus on the new, more essential threat, the fierce Shadow Fae we were about to compete against.

The leader of Scorch Squad set foot atop the luminous bridge, the shifting substance made only of light and *rais* shimmering beneath his boots. Then his team followed, and I couldn't help but keep one eye on Lucian as he crossed over. Would he use this opportunity to finally stab me in the back while I was distracted by our real enemies?

"Flare Squad, let's move," Heaton announced, and we all stepped into line behind him.

For the first time since we'd congregated along the river, my head twisted over my shoulder in search of the one who shall not be named. For some reason, as we left the relative safety of the western bank, I needed the reassurance of his presence. Would Reign be permitted to join us on Shadow soil, or would he be forced to remain here, the banished traitor?

A flash of darkness snaked through the outskirts of the gathered squads, and as always, I could feel his aura without having to see his face. Those shadows were a constant—watching, waiting, protecting.

The moment my boot landed on Umbral soil, the invisible binds that often constricted my *rais* began to unravel. I could breathe more freely, and a rush of power surged to the surface. The medallion tucked beneath my tunic began to warm, quickening my pulse.

This wasn't the first time I'd felt my necklace react to my

burgeoning *rais*, but I'd never experienced it on this side of the river. Maybe it was time to share this development with my professor. If we truly were to go to Mysthallia to find a Spellbinder to break whatever this hold was over my powers, he needed to be privy to all the details.

As hesitant as I was to impart them...

"Welcome to the Court of Umbral Shadows, young Light Fae." Malakar stood in front of the enormous metallic globe with arms outstretched. "This will be the first trial of four you must master in the next four weeks. Should you fail, and not die, you will spend the remaining time as our guest at the Citadel." He waved his hand at the jagged, obsidian turrets that stretched to the midnight sky.

Then he turned to the troop of gathered Shadow Fae students. "The same is true for the lot of you. And may Noxus bless you if that is your fate." Muttered groans escaped from the Shadow side. "The rules are simple: there are none. Your only goal is to retrieve the artifacts as a team. There are fourteen sacred relics, and as you can see, there are sixteen teams. Therefore, two squads will come out of this empty-handed. You do not want to be one of them." A sharp keening sound sent my heart leaping up my throat, and a hidden door in the sphere glided open. "May the gods be with you."

Chapter Twenty-Nine

The chaotic shuffle of bodies drowned out the mad thumping of my heart against my ribs. "Come on, Aelia!" Rue's hand closed around mine and she dragged me toward the open door, where it was jammed with figures, both light and dark. I could feel the tension in the air as we stood at the threshold, the weight of what lay ahead pressing down on us.

"Flare Squad, follow me!" Heaton led the charge, pushing his way through the mass of bodies attempting to squeeze through the opening of the giant metal globe. "*Rais* at the ready," Heat called over his shoulder, his voice calm and authoritative, cutting through the tension like a blade. "We stick together, and no one goes off alone. This labyrinth will try to divide us, but we're stronger as a unit. Trust in your abilities and in each other."

Inky darkness poured forth and tendrils of night stretched beyond Heaton's large frame. A heady surge of *rais* flowed through our squad and a dozen ethereal blades blinked into existence, illuminating the black. My own luminous dagger materialized in my palm without much effort. It wasn't as comforting as my typical blades, but it would have to do for now.

"Which way do we go?" Ariadne pushed her way to the front to stand by Heaton, a glowing sphere in one hand and a light spear in the other.

A series of ramps and walkways stretched high into the cupola, shifting and twisting as blasts of light and streams of darkness wound around the metal globe.

"These artifacts could be anywhere," Belmore huffed.

"Well, there's nowhere to go but up." I tipped my head back and scanned the tangle of passageways. A scream ricocheted overhead, and my stomach lurched as a body plummeted from a level above. The female Light Fae hit the floor with a sickening smack, landing only a few yards from where I stood, her neck contorted at a gruesome angle.

"Oh, Raysa, bless her," Rue muttered.

I hazarded a quick peek at the girl. She looked familiar, though I didn't know her well, possibly from Burn Squad. We had spent more time with that team ever since Rue and Devin began seeing each other. Now with their relationship a bit unresolved, we'd stopped frequenting the Burn floor of the dormitories.

"Aelia's right," Heaton called out, returning our attention from the fallen Fae to the trial. "We must continue upwards." If we didn't want to join her in eternal rest in the arms of Noxus, we had to win. The idea of spending a week or more at Arcanum was motivation enough to speed up my sluggish movement. "This way." Heaton sprinted up a ramp to our right, in the opposite direction of the body splattered on the floor.

Ariadne and Belmore fell back, whispering amongst themselves so I took the opportunity to drag Rue and Symon past them, Sylvan and Zephyr. I would much rather Heaton's company anyway.

"How is it that you're allowed to lead us on this trial?" I asked as I moved into step beside him as my friends followed just behind.

"To ensure our Shadow Fae counterparts behave." A somber expression cut into his jaw. "They are given the same allowance when they attend events on our shores, but they do not always take advantage of them."

"I see." A moment of silence passed between us as he scanned the passage ahead. "Well, I'm glad you're here with us, Heaton."

"As am I, Aelia. I only hope I will be able to lead the team through all four trials."

"Still no word on when you might be called to the front lines?"

He gritted his teeth. "Not yet."

A cloud of sheer black swallowed up the mystical light from our weapons, and we were plunged into complete darkness. "Flare team, get ready for anything!" Heaton shouted.

A figure emerged from the shadows, a dark Fae female with a luminous blade protruding just beneath her collar bone. Dark blood trickled from her mouth as she staggered toward us.

"Oh, gods..."

"Help me," she rasped out, her hand reaching for my own.

She inched closer, and Symon's ethereal sword illuminated his palm.

"Take her out!" Belmore yelled.

"No. She's injured, can't you see that?"

"She wouldn't think twice about ending your life, you stupid Kin," he barked.

"Hey!" Rue cried and stepped between us. "Don't talk to her like that."

"Help me," the dark-haired female whispered, her voice faint.

My head pivoted to Heaton, eyes searching his weary ones. I couldn't leave her like this, and I certainly wouldn't allow one of these bloodthirsty fools to take her life. Our team leader's head slowly dipped, and I closed the distance between the female Fae and me. Blood dribbled down her chin as she watched me warily.

"I'm going to help you." Or at least I'd try. I'd seen Elisa perform the feat countless times, searing a wound with powerful light. "What's your name?"

"Clarys."

"Okay, Clarys, you're going to be just fine."

"We're wasting precious time," Belmore barked, and a few other members of the team echoed his sentiments. Zephyr and Silvan both nodded, attempting to move farther up the ramp.

"Go on without me, then, I'll meet up with you."

"No, we stay together," Heaton interjected. "Just do it, Aelia."

Gingerly, I reached for the blade of light and pulled it free. The female hunched over, hissing curses as dark, nearly black, blood spilled from her wound. Before she bled out, I lifted my palm and power flickered to the surface. Summoning my *rais,* that inexorable energy pulsed through my veins. I pressed my palm to the wound and the sizzle of charred flesh pierced the dense silence. The unmistakable odor reached my nostrils next, and my stomach churned. Holding my breath, I seared off the wound as the female clenched her teeth, but not a single cry erupted from her pinched lips.

Good gods, that had to have been horribly painful. How could she withstand it?

As the fiery heat in my hand died away, dark eyes lifted to mine. "Cheers," she gritted out. Before I could reply, she spun around and disappeared into the encroaching shadows.

Well, you're welcome.

"Now, if you're quite done saving our enemy," Belmore hissed as he stalked past me, "we have an artifact to find. I personally would rather die than spend a week in the hands of Arcanum students."

At least now if we did, perhaps someone would show us mercy as we'd shown them. Too much to wish for, surely.

"Let's move," Heaton commanded.

The darkness was so thick it felt like it was pressing in on us, suffocating in its intensity. We walked on in the interminable void for what felt like hours. I had to reignite my light, but I needed a moment to replenish the well of power in my core. That and the thought of what else might be waiting in the shadows, drawn to the illumination like moths to a flame, stilled my hand.

"Now, Aelia," Heaton urged quietly. "We need light to find the markers."

Taking a deep breath, I summoned a small orb of light in my palm, just enough to cast a soft glow around us. The darkness recoiled, revealing a narrow pathway lined with ancient stone walls that seemed to pulse with a faint, eerie glow. On the walls, faint glyphs flickered in and out of existence.

"Celestial glyphs!" I whisper-shouted.

"There!" Symon pointed to a glyph that flashed brighter than the others, a faint outline of an arrow etched into the stone. "That's our direction."

We moved cautiously, the light barely strong enough to cut through the thick darkness. The path twisted and turned, and every step felt like it could lead us farther into a trap. The silence was unnerving, broken only by our soft footsteps and the occasional drip of water echoing somewhere in the distance.

The darkness around us began to shift, pulling back as a blinding light burst forth from the walls, flooding the corridor in an overwhelming radiance. I winced, shielding my eyes as the light burned through my vision, turning everything into a blinding white void.

"Not too pleasant is it, my Light Fae friends." A familiar voice echoed just behind me. I twisted around and came nose to chest with Ruhl. His cool shadows coiled over his skin, dampening the overpowering light. "Hello, little Kin, so lovely to see you again," he whispered.

Even with the intense flare nearly blinding me, I caught Rue's eyes widening from my periphery as she watched our exchange. Heaton moved beside her, and a sword of pure *rais* appeared in his palm.

"Care for some assistance?" A mischievous grin split the Shadow prince's lips.

"Why would you help us?" I squealed.

"Because my team, Midnight Squad, has already found our relic, and I'm bored." He lifted a nonchalant shoulder. "Besides, if you get eliminated so soon, what fun would that be?"

I slapped my hands on my hips and glared at the cocky male. "What are you playing at, princey?"

"Nothing. I swear." He lifted his hands, palms up, the picture of innocence. "If you do not care for my assistance, I'll be happy to be on my merry way."

My eyes darted to Heaton's who slowly shook his head. Of course he wouldn't trust him. And why should I truly? But there it was again, that unnerving sensation that always accompanied Ruhl's presence.

"Have I ever lied to you, Aelia?"

Curses, it was as if he'd plucked the thoughts right out of my head.

"In fact, as I recall, I was the only one who told you the truth." Those shadows tightened around his form, like an armor of liquid night.

"Fine," I gritted out.

Ruhl sketched an elaborate bow. "At your service." He acted instantly, casting shadows that danced and twisted, creating a makeshift shield against the intense light. The contrast was disorienting, the blinding light against the pitch-black shadows making it hard to focus, hard to think.

"This way!" Heaton commanded, pointing toward a faintly

visible marker that flickered between the two extremes of light and dark.

Before following behind our team leader, I met Ruhl's glinting eyes. "Cheers," I murmured.

"Cheers, little Kin. Until we meet again." With that, the royal heir vanished into the ether. I half believed he'd never been there at all. Why would he help us?

"Aelia, come on!" Rue shouted.

I darted behind them, ducking beneath the shadowy veil and pressing forward. The heat from the incessant light was unbearable, despite the swirling shadows Ruhl had lent us. I could feel my energy draining as I struggled to keep my own light steady, guiding us through the chaos.

Just as I thought we'd cleared the blasted light, the ground beneath us began to tremble. A low rumble echoed behind us, and I glanced back just in time to see the walls closing in, the corridor narrowing dangerously.

"Run!" Heaton shouted.

We bolted up the ramp, the light and shadows shifting around us with every step. My heart pounded as we raced through the maze, every twist and turn a potential dead end. The walls seemed to have a mind of their own, moving to block our path, forcing us to change direction, again and again. It was as if the labyrinth was trying to separate us, the very air between us thickening, pushing us apart.

"We're close!" Symon yelled over his shoulder as he pointed at another luminescent marker up ahead. "Just a little farther!"

As we neared the glowing rune, the floor beneath us suddenly gave way. A scream ripped through my lips as we plunged into a freefall, the light and darkness spiraling around us in a chaotic blur.

"Rue! Symon!"

I screamed again, reaching out desperately for something, anything to hold on to, but there was nothing but the disorienting whirl of light and shadow.

Then, just as suddenly as we fell, we landed with a jarring thud, the ground solid beneath us once more. I groaned, pain flaring through my side when I hit the ground. Rolling over, I forced myself to stand, scanning the area for my friends.

"Heaton? Rue? Symon?" I called out, panic rising in my throat.

"We're here," Rue's voice came from my left, shaky but alive. A few other familiar voices muttered in the background. Ariadne and Belmore had survived the fall too. Lucky me.

Symon was already on his feet, helping Heaton up from where he'd fallen. We were bruised, battered, and exhausted, but we were still together.

"The heart of the labyrinth must be close," Heaton said, his voice rough. "We can't let it break us now."

I nodded, feeling a new resolve harden within me. The end was in sight—we just had to keep pushing forward, together. Drawing in one last, determined breath, I ignited my light again, stronger this time, banishing the darkness as Flare Squad moved as one toward the top of the Luminescent Gauntlet.

Chapter Thirty

A*elia*

The final level loomed just over our heads, and excitement quickened my footsteps as I followed behind Heaton. A steady pulse of energy ignited in the air, a mix of *rais* and *nox*; something with tremendous power. It had to be the sacred artifact.

"Psst," Rue whispered, moving up beside me. "Are you really not going to tell me what happened with you and the prince back there? Or explain why those shadows are following us?"

I hazarded a peek over my shoulder at the coiling darkness hovering in the air only a few yards behind our squad. At first, I'd thought they were part of the labyrinth, but as they traced our every move, the answer became evident.

I knew without a doubt they did not belong to Reign. I would recognize his dark minions anywhere. Which meant, there was only one other Shadow Fae they could belong to. Ruhl.

"I have no idea," I murmured lamely.

"A! You've got to be kidding me. They showed up shortly after the Shadow Fae prince miraculously assisted us. Why would he have done that, anyway?"

"Maybe because I helped one of his own?"

Her light eyes narrowed. "The prince does not seem like the type to be overly concerned about his teammates."

"Maybe none of us know him as well as we think. Perhaps we know nothing about the Shadow Fae at all!"

Rue's eyes widened, mouth curving and it occurred to me that perhaps I'd been a little overzealous on behalf of Shadow Fae—or of one, in particular.

"There!" Heaton's cry of excitement sent my head spinning away from my best friend and toward our team leader. He pointed up the next incline to a shimmering pedestal. Something glittered atop the marble slab, but it was too difficult to discern what from this angle.

"Oh, Raysa, we made it!" Rue squealed, thankfully forgetting all about our current topic of conversation.

"And not a moment too soon." Sy rubbed at his shoulder. "Everything hurts and my *rais* is nearly depleted from this infernal darkness."

Belmore raced up the ramp, hands outstretched.

"No, wait!" Heaton shouted as Belmore lunged for the artifact.

As his hands closed around the shimmering object, a blood-curdling scream tore from his mouth. The pungent odor of burnt flesh permeated the passageway, and the glowing stone toppled from his hands as he shrieked. The luminescent relic began to roll down the ramp as we all watched, frozen in place.

"Someone get it!" Ariadne cried.

No one moved. And it was no wonder. Belmore sat hunched on the floor nursing his scalded, blistering black flesh.

Before I could think better of it, I summoned my *rais* as my thoughts flickered back to one of last term's trials. Ethereal

Light Sculpting. It was one of my favorites. I balanced the sphere of luminous energy in my palm, then slowly stretched it using the other, thinning it out until I'd fashioned a lasso of sorts. Wrapping my hand around one end, I tossed the loop toward the fleeing artifact.

The circle of light landed just shy of the rolling relic.

Curses!

"Try again, Aelia," Heaton shouted.

Reeling in the rope of pure light, I drew in a steadying breath before drawing it over my head and releasing it once more. It sailed through the air, as if in slow motion, before it tangled with a tendril of darkness.

The wisps of light and dark dropped right on top of the radiant stone. I tugged on the rope and the lasso tightened, cinching around the iridescent prize.

"Aelia, you did it!" Symon squealed an inch from my ear.

I carefully pulled on the shimmering rope until the artifact sat at the tip of my boot.

"What is it?" Rue peered over my shoulder on tiptoes.

"It looks like some sort of glowing rock," said Sy.

Heaton appeared beside us, along with Belmore, still nursing his blackened hands, Ariadne, and the rest of the team. "Not just any rock, squad. It's the Valorite stone, a mystical artifact that measures one's courage and bravery. It is said that only those with impeccable strength of character may touch it."

"Why didn't you tell us that before?" Belmore grumbled.

"I'm afraid I'm only supposed to be here as your guide, team. There are certain things that I cannot disclose as your leader."

"Well, that's bullshit," Belmore hissed, blowing on his hands.

"It's the nature of the trials, unfortunately." Heaton curled an arm around my shoulders and rewarded me with a soft smile. "Well done, Aelia. I have no doubt you could have touched the artifact yourself, but it was smart thinking being cautious. That mindset will serve you well throughout the remainder of the trials."

"Ugh, of course, the little Kin is always *so* perfect." Ariadne rolled her eyes.

"It will do you well to remember that this is a team effort, Miss Bamberlight. You'll need each other in the weeks to come, and unfortunately, I may not always be here to guide you."

That pit of dread blossomed low in my belly once more.

"Come, now, we have the artifact, and that means Flare Squad has passed the first Umbral Trial. It is time to celebrate." Heaton squeezed me into his side as we began the slow descent to the entrance. I should have been happy, I deserved to celebrate, but I couldn't keep the unease at bay. Not only was the possibility that Heaton would not be with us in the second trial a great one, but also, there was that little shadow who'd directed my lasso and saved us in the last second.

Why would Ruhl help me? And worse, what would he require in return?

※

The evening's celebrations in Heaton's room were cut short by a sharp knock on the door. Dropping my goblet filled to the brim with lager, I spun toward the entryway. The hair on the back of my neck had already begun to bristle, signifying the approach of my new mentor.

Before Heaton made it to the entrance, the door swung open and none other than Reign darkened the threshold. What I had not been prepared for was the female at his side.

"What the realms is *she* doing here?" Rue spat as her gaze followed mine.

Symon unraveled his arms from around our shoulders. "Oh, come on, girls, the more the merrier."

Rue shoved our friend off the divan, and he slid to the floor in a tangle of long legs.

"Hey!" he grumbled.

"What is the matter with you?" Rue smacked the back of his head. "You know we are team Aelia and Reign."

"And don't you see that's exactly what I'm trying to do? If I manage to steal her attentions with my ruggedly handsome good looks then she'll leave the shady professor alone." He threw me a wink, the smirk setting off a twinkle in his light eyes.

"Oh, stop, both of you." I knotted my arms across my chest and sank into the soft settee. "What Reign does with his new acquisition is up to him."

"Well, he's coming this way," Sy whispered. "Don't worry, my little round-eared friend, I'll have the new female in my clutches in no time."

A cackle erupted through my pursed lips despite my best efforts. Gods, I loved Symon, despite his ridiculousness. In fact, it only made me love him more.

Reign's overpowering presence washed over me an instant before his looming shadow appeared over my shoulder. "May I have a word with you?" His deep voice traveled through his dark minion as he circled the shell of my ear.

"In private or along with your newest acquisition?" I whisper-hissed. "How many gildings do you have riding on *her* success?"

Both of my friends kept their gazes pinned straight ahead, but with their sensitive Fae hearing, I was certain they'd heard every bitter word. What did it matter, anyway?

Firm hands clamped down on my shoulders from behind, then icy shadows crawled beneath my underarms, and for an instant, I was completely weightless. Darkness consumed my vision for a long moment, until I was unceremoniously dropped onto the floor just outside Heaton's dormitory door.

A pair of blazing midnight irises found mine, and a haggard breath flitted across my lips. "What the stars happened in the gauntlet today?" he growled.

"What do you mean?"

"One of Ruhl's shadows sent me a message shortly after you finished."

"What did he say?"

"He said I owed him for saving my girlfriend."

A stupid grin crept across my face, and I clapped my hand over my mouth.

"Oh, you think this is funny, princess?" He pinned me to the wall, those shadows surging over me like a tidal wave. "You thought owing me a favor was bad, you would never survive Ruhl."

"I didn't ask him for help."

"It doesn't matter. He easily could have turned his favor against you."

"But he didn't..."

"This time." He pressed closer, those shadows like frenzied beasts as they swirled between us. "You cannot trust him."

"I don't," I spat. "But what I suppose you'll say next is that I can trust *you*?"

"Always." His jaw slammed shut, his mouth slanting into a hard line. He took a step back, and my lungs began to function once more, now that I could breathe air untainted with his musky scent.

I leaned against the wall, my entire body deflating. "Why did you bring *her*?" I muttered.

"I didn't *bring* Liora, Aelia. I ran into her along the way. She followed me, and I could hardly say no."

I stepped closer and gripped his jaw, fingers digging into his cheeks. "It's very simple. You merely move your mouth like this and say *no*..."

He swatted my hand away, the hint of a smile ghosting across the hard set of his jaw. "I suppose I have a weakness for my acquisitions."

"Bastard," I gritted out before spinning to the door.

"You're going back in?"

"I am."

"Since you have the day off tomorrow, I thought perhaps it would be the perfect time to go on a little trip across the border."

My pulse quickened as I whirled back around. "To Mysthallia?"

He nodded. "I've already gotten Draven's permission to give you a day of leave on top of tomorrow's respite. That leaves us two days to find the answers we need."

That familiar tangle of nerves surged in my belly. If we could find a way to break the spell, we would be one step closer to uncovering the truth of my past. But would it also confirm the dire truth of the prophecy?

"So, what do you say, princess?" He offered his hand, an unreadable expression on that brutally handsome face. "Are you ready to learn the truth?"

I drew in a deep breath and steadied my racing heart before I placed my palm in his. "I will be by tomorrow."

Chapter Thirty-One

I still don't understand why she had to come. Over the rush of wind, Sol's gravelly voice reverberated across my mind.

She is Reign's bonded skyrider, who he doesn't frequently get to see.

Because of the life of lies he's chosen to live.

It's not of his own choosing.

Oh, so you're defending him now? His tremendous wing flaps grew more agitated with each beat.

Yes. No! I don't know, Sol. It's complicated.

Ribbons of smoke erupted from his immense nostrils as he huffed out a frustrated breath. *Things are always complicated in matters of the heart, Aelia. You must be strong enough to discern the truth without relying on feeble emotion.*

Feeble? My emotions made me strong, they fueled the fire in my core, compelled me to act. Perhaps, not always wisely... but still. My fingers moved unbidden over the hilt of the dagger sheathed at my right hip. Reign had allowed me to bring one of my mysterious blades on the trip, while the other remained in his possession for safe keeping. I glanced over my shoulder at the shadow prince aboard Phantom only a few yards away. Our flight to Mysthallia had been surprisingly peaceful thus far.

Likely, because we'd remained silent throughout the voyage.

Instead, mostly Sol had occupied my thoughts mumbling about the hardships of enduring Phantom's presence. Why they couldn't simply kiss and make up was beyond me.

Things are never that simple and you know it, little Kin.

Stop listening to my private thoughts!

A tendril of darkness floated closer, drawing my attention away from our frustrating mental conversation to Reign's inky minion. It slid across the back of my neck, raising the tiny hairs across my arms.

"Once we reach the border, we'll have to ground our dragons." Reign's deep timbre reached my ears, as clear as if he stood right beside me. "The Spellbinders won't appreciate dragons coming into their lands."

It was embarrassing how little I knew of the neighboring territories that surrounded Aetheria. The continent of Crescentia was a large one, and my knowledge of the people beyond the border of the Alucian Mountains was scant. The three largest kingdoms beyond our courts were those of the Spellbinders, Wolvryn, and Immortalis, but besides their names, I had little idea of what went on in their respective realms of Mythallia, Lunaris, and Vesperis.

I supposed it was fortunate I was finally to visit one.

Phantom veered closer, her onyx wings nearly brushing Sol's with each flap. I could feel my dragon tense with each inch she drew closer. Did their new incarnations still feel the bond? Somehow, I hadn't managed the courage to ask, and I was certain he could feel my curiosity through our mental link, but he hadn't offered a response, which I took to mean he wouldn't appreciate my questioning.

"How will we travel to see this acquaintance of yours once we're across the border?" I called out across the blustering winds caused by the dragons' powerful wing beats.

"Mostly by foot I'm afraid. Unless we can commandeer one of the wild beasts that roams the valley at the foot of the Alucian range."

That didn't seem pleasant at all. "Why can't we shadowtravel?"

"Mysthallia has strong wards which make using large amounts of *nox* difficult. If it weren't for these blasted cuffs, I could likely manage it, but unfortunately…" He twisted the silver bangle around his wrist until angry red lines appeared beneath.

"Wonderful, so we'll be walking then."

"I'm so sorry to disappoint, *princess*."

A grin curved my lips at the familiar nickname and the disdain with which he'd growled it. It had been a long time since he'd used that inflection and, for some absurd reason, it brought a smile to my face. It revived memories of my arrival at the Conservatory and an easier time between us.

"And besides, it's not *my* acquaintance, it's a female friend of Gideon's."

"Your Shadow Fae friend from the Citadel?"

"That's right."

"Do Fae often associate with Spellbinders?" To my limited knowledge, not many of the kingdoms on the continent interacted.

His brow wrinkled, lips puckering in distaste. "Not at all."

"So how does Gideon know this female?"

"My, my, aren't we inquisitive today?"

"I'm always inquisitive."

"Fair enough, princess. But this isn't my story to tell. Suffice it to say, they had a chance encounter years ago and have kept in touch ever since."

"And you're certain she'll be able to help me?"

He gave a lazy shrug. "To be perfectly honest, I'm not certain about anything when it comes to you. You're quite perplexing."

"The same goes for you, prince of shadows." I offered a sweet smile, earning a scowl from my professor-turned-mentor.

The towering peaks of the Alucian Mountains stretched below us now, their snow-covered caps glistening beneath the mid-day sun. For a moment, I'd forgotten that once we crossed into Mysthallia the endless day would come to an end, and we would once again be slaves to the typical rise and fall of the celestial bodies. A part of me welcomed the kiss of cool night and the twinkle of a thousand stars that would come.

"Unfortunately, the time has come to ground our skyriders." Reign's voice drew me from my wandering thoughts. Night would come soon enough, but now, it was time to walk.

※

I kept my gaze pinned to the serene blue sky for a long minute after Sol's glittering form disappeared over the soaring peaks of the mountains. The two dragons split in opposite directions the moment they dropped us off in the shadow of the Mysthallian Valley. Despite the walls Sol erected across our bond, tiny hints of pain rolled through. How could Phantom's betrayal still run so deep after all this time? Shaking my head to dispel the pointless thoughts, I turned toward the stretch of verdant land before us.

From our perch atop a small hill, the sprawling landscape of Mythallia stretched out below us in its lush grandeur. Towering crystalline spires rose from the earth, their surfaces shimmering with an iridescent glow, forests of luminescent trees with leaves that sparkled like stars stretched across vast swathes of land and rivers of liquid light crisscrossed the realm, their waters gleaming with a soft, silvery radiance. It was breathtaking.

Now with my focus on the present, a thick hum of energy

pressed into my skin. I hazarded a glance at Reign from over my shoulder to where he stood, alert and tense, his shadows remarkably subdued.

Something alive with a vibrant and ever-changing pulse resonated through the air, as if woven into the very fabric of the land. "What is that?" I whispered.

"*Lys.*"

"Thank you, professor, for that very detailed explanation. Perhaps, you should reconsider your chosen profession."

A rueful grin parted his lips, and my duplicitous heart flip-flopped at the radiant sight.

"What is *lys*?"

"It is the power that Spellbinders wield, gifted to them by Elysira, the goddess of the occult." He nonchalantly hitched his pack with our supplies for the long trek higher up on his shoulder.

"Oh, so magic?"

Reign shook his head, grunting. "Yes, *princess*, magic." He brushed past me, his gaze intent on a shimmering orb at a great distance.

"What is that?"

"That is the Lysial Nexus that hovers above the capital city of Eldra. We want to stay well away from it if we have any hope of summoning our own muted powers. While it strengthens Spellbinders, it has the opposite effect for us Fae. Luckily, Melisara lives far from the sparkling center of the realm."

I certainly needed to brush up on my knowledge of our neighbors to the west. On the entire continent, honestly. I'd have to add it to my never-ending to-do list.

Reign offered a hand, and I begrudgingly accepted. The rough terrain of the mountainside might prove challenging. "Let's get moving, or we'll never reach Thalindra before nightfall."

His calloused hand closed around mine, and warm tingles alighted across my flesh. His eyes snapped to my own, searching for an answer I could not give. It must have been the *lys*. I buried the lie, tucking it away behind my teeth and followed Reign as we began the descent through the crumbling terrain.

At least the rest of the land appeared flat once we reached the valley except for those strange glassy spires. "What are those?" I pointed to the glittering, twisting rock formations below.

"Those are living conduits of mystical energy. Their shapes shift subtly in response to the ebb and flow of *lys* in the realm. Spellbinders draw power from the formations for their incantations."

"Wow..." I couldn't help the awe in my voice. The closer we moved, the more impressive they appeared. "There's something I don't understand," I huffed as Reign helped me maneuver across a particularly large boulder. "If you believe my *rais* is blocked by some incantation, and Spellbinders wield *lys*, how would they be able to help us?"

"Because some particularly powerful ones can siphon other forms of energy."

"So you believe this Spellbinder siphoned *rais* from a Fae to conjure the spell blocking my abilities?"

"It's a theory." He smirked.

"One of many, I'm sure."

His hold tightened around my hand as the descent grew steeper. "And it must have been siphoned from a very powerful Fae."

"Well, I hope this Melisara can finally give us the answers we seek."

"As do I, princess."

Chapter Thirty-Two

A*elia*

The ever-shifting landscape stretched on endlessly, and after hours of walking, it seemed as if we were no closer to Thalindra than when we started—despite Reign's assurances otherwise. The arid valley had long since given way to a lush forest teeming with luminous trees whose branches intertwined in intricate patterns that formed natural glowing runes. They appeared almost sentient, their roots deeply connected to the mystical forces of the land.

With darkness looming ever closer, the thick copse allowed little light to shine through. I never thought I'd miss the never-ending sunlight of the Ethereal Court, but as my footsteps grew wearier, I wished darkness would never come.

"Are we there yet?" I groused for the umpteenth time.

"Not yet, princess." Reign no longer held my hand, instead, I stumbled behind him, my muscles fatigued from exertion and my tummy grumbling for food.

With each step deeper into this forbidden realm, Reign's ever-present shadows grew dimmer. I occasionally performed a quick scan to determine the viability of my own *rais*, which was also dwindling. "How much farther?"

"Just a little longer. If we hadn't been forced to stop every half hour for snack breaks, we would have been there by now." Reign hauled the pack on his broad back further up his shoulder.

"I can't help it. I'm starved. With all this activity, I've burned much more energy than normal, and I'm in desperate need of replenishing."

"There she is, there's the spoiled little princess I remember."

"Oh, Fae you," I growled. "What do you know of hardship —" I bit back the rest of the sentence as slivers of his dismal story rushed my thoughts. I supposed for a prince, he hadn't exactly had the most comfortable upbringing.

We lapsed into silence as I focused on my footing once again, careful to avoid the maze of thick roots underfoot. According to the good professor, Melisara lived within the deepest parts of this forest. Whereas most of the powerful Spellbinders resided in the capital, she chose to live solitarily in this enchanted wood. Besides that meager bit of information, Reign hadn't disclosed much else about this mysterious female.

The chorus of birds and rustling leaves that had accompanied us this far was abruptly replaced by an oppressive silence that prickled the back of my neck. "So how do you know Gideon, anyway?" I blurted.

"He was a classmate from Arcanum." He slowed, and I lengthened my stride to catch up with his long ones. His eyes swiveled across the darkening woods, and that prickle of unease intensified at his pinched expression.

"Then why is he still there?" I continued, all the same. "If you are of the same age, he should have graduated years ago."

"Instead of joining the Umbral Guard, he opted to stay on

as a professor." Reign moved closer, every inch of my flesh aware of his sudden proximity.

"Oh, what a happy coincidence, both of you instructors at such fine Fae establishments."

He threw me a good eyeroll before his brows furrowed. "Those students are lucky to have him. I was lucky—" The thunder of heavy footfalls ripped the final words from Reign's mouth. "Get down!" His massive form pummeled me to the ground, the familiar feel of his icy shadows blanketing my body relieving a bit of the panic.

The whoosh of arrows zipped overhead, metal piercing thick trunks echoing through the air. Shards of wood splintered, landing in a blur all around us.

"Vandals," Reign snarled, his voice a dangerous growl. "Melisara warned Gideon the miscreants in these parts often dipped their arrowheads in poison, so stay down."

As the volley of arrows hissed through the air, I snuck a peek from beneath his muscled arm. Sure enough, each arrowhead was tipped with a sickly green substance that glistened ominously in the dappled sunlight.

Muffled voices grew closer, barely distinguishable over the frantic pounding of my heart. "We must move. Quietly and quickly," he hissed in my ear.

Dark shadows curled around us, the thick impenetrable ones that he often used to conceal us. "Go, now," he rasped out, a jagged edge to his tone that wasn't there a moment ago. Perspiration slickened his brow, and a sickly pallor coated his cheeks.

"What's wrong?" I whispered as he hauled me into a crouch.

"Nothing, just move."

We crept through the forest, staying as close to the ground as possible as the arrows continued their dance overhead. The underbrush suddenly erupted with movement, and dark figures emerged from the shadows, their faces obscured by hoods.

"Freeze." Reign's shadow whispered across the shell of my ear. I did as instructed, stilling on all fours behind a thick trunk. He positioned himself beside me so that I was nestled between his rigid form and the enormous tree.

"Where did they go?" A male voice hissed.

"They were here a moment ago," another one replied.

I pressed my side against the tree, hoping to disappear between it and Reign's icy shadows.

A cloaked male stood inches away from us, signaling toward the others. "Keep looking, they can't have gotten far." He lifted his long nose in the air and breathed in deeply. "They're not Spellbinders, that's for sure."

"Mortals?"

"No, I don't believe so. Either way, if they're in our land they must pay the tithe." He ticked his head to the encroaching darkness. "Find them."

The dozen or so hooded figures strode right past us, and I drew in a quick breath. I hadn't realized I'd momentarily stopped breathing. As their hushed voices began to fall away, I stretched out my legs, muscles cramping from the crouched position. The shadows flitting around us began to dissipate, and Reign blew out a ragged breath.

Sweat covered his brow, and a fine tremor coursed down to his hands.

A whisper of fear streaked up my spine at the sight. "Reign? What's wrong, damn it?"

"It's nothing. I'll be fine in a moment. I told you, using *nox* here is extremely taxing."

Oh gods, and here we were covered in a cozy blanket of it for the last few minutes. "Why would you do something so stupid?"

"To protect you," he snarled.

"We could have found another way," I muttered, the fire lacing my tone already dimming from his sweet reply. "Come on, let me help you up." I offered my hand, and his unfocused gaze suddenly sharpened.

"Aelia! You're bleeding..."

"I am?"

His fingers closed around my wrist and twisted, revealing a tiny cut across the top of my hand.

"It's nothing, barely a scratch."

Raw fury pulsed through his pitch irises as his eyes fixed on the wound. "It doesn't matter the size if the poison reaches your bloodstream." His nonexistent shadows whirled to life, whipping into a wild uproar.

"How do you know it's from the arrows? I could have scratched it on a twig or the bark of a tree as we were crawling."

He brought my hand up to his nose and drew in a deep breath, his lips twisting. "Fuck!" he hissed.

Oh, for the love of Raysa. "Now what?"

"Now, I have to get you to Melisara before the hallucinations start."

"Are you kidding me?"

Getting hauled into Reign's chest was my only reply. He cradled me in his arms, those shadows slithering over my suddenly warming skin. I could feel the strain in his body as he forced his legs forward. I only hoped we were as close to Melisara's home as he claimed.

The luminescent trees blurred across my peripheral vision as Reign moved faster. I waited for the onslaught of pain I'd endured when I'd been poisoned by the gloomwhisper, but it never came. Instead, only an enjoyable numbness tingled through my veins, drifting higher up to fog my mind. It was a pleasant haze, much like the one I experienced when I indulged in too much lager or Fae wine.

"This isn't so bad," I murmured, a strange, ethereal quality to my tone. "Much better than last time."

"I'm glad someone is enjoying this." His jaw was clenched so tight, a tendon feathered across his dark scruff.

"I don't think we have to rush, Reign. I feel fine; fantastic, even."

"That means it's spreading fast, princess," he growled, only lengthening his strides. His dwindling shadows spread across his back, and those wings of pure night coalesced. Instead of rising off the ground, we only moved faster, darting through the trees at lightning speed.

Another tremor raced through Reign's body, vibrating my own. Perspiration slickened his tunic, bleeding into my own.

That fear blossomed once again as memories of the last time he'd depleted his *nox* and passed out at the Darkmania Falls flickered to the surface. "Reign, please, slow down. You're going to over-exert yourself."

"I'm fine," he snarled. "You are the one who is injured."

"Neither of us will survive this if you pass out from the strain."

"I won't pass out, princess. I've survived much worse than this, trust me. And you are not dying today."

"Well, I certainly hope not."

"No, I mean the poison shouldn't be lethal. It only has some undesirable side effects. Though with you, I'm never quite sure what will happen."

"Like what?"

"I told you, hallucinations." He ticked his head at an enormous tree with roots that extended high into the air. "We're almost there."

I blinked quickly, wondering if I'd already started hallucinating, because from here, it appeared as if the tree was walking toward us. "Reign…"

"Yes?"

"Is that tree walking on its roots?"

"It is."

"Oh, thank the gods, I thought I was hallucinating already." I squeezed my eyes closed, then blinked rapidly in an attempt to clear the haze. "Why is it walking toward us?"

"I sent one of my shadows to deliver a message to Melisara about the vandal attack. My best guess is that the tree is our transportation."

Chapter Thirty-Three

R*eign*

A giggle escaped through Aelia's pursed lips as she wriggled in my arms. Her hand caressed the back of my neck, sending a wave of goosebumps cascading down my spine. Oh, *Noxus*, this female would be the death of me.

I never expected to spend the last portion of our trek to Melisara's cottage riding a tree with Aelia cradled in my arms, but I supposed it was much better than the alternative. As it was, my *nox* had reached dangerous levels of depletion. If it wasn't for my sheer determination, we would have had to endure the length of Aelia's hallucinations in that forest surrounded by vandals.

From the looks of her starry-eyed gaze, they had already begun. Her fingers found their way beneath my tunic and danced across my shoulder. The light touch had nerve-endings I had no idea existed springing to life.

"Aelia…" I growled.

Another high-pitched giggle. "What?"

"Stop that."

"Stop what?" She withdrew her fingers from my back only to crawl them up my nape and tangle in my hair. "Did you know that your hair feels like silk?" Her warm breath blew across the pointy tip of my ear, and heat raced to my breeches.

I cleared my throat, adjusting my position on the thick branch before a certain part of my anatomy became blatantly thick.

"I just want to run my fingers through it all the time, Reign. Can I, please?" Before I could reply, her fingers delved deeper into my hair and a groan erupted from her lips. "Oh, yes, just like I imagined it, the softest locks I've ever touched."

"Aelia, please..." I rasped out. I could already feel myself hardening, and every wiggle was only further tearing at my restraint.

Her hypnotic silver-blue eyes lifted to mine, a pout curving her full lips. "What? Do you not like it when I touch you?"

"No, I like it too much, princess."

Her head fell back as a cackle pierced the thickening air between us.

The lumbering gait of the tree slowed, and I released a breath of relief as the small cottage nestled deep within the heart of the enchanted forest came into view. The small, ivy-covered structure seemed almost a part of the forest itself, with its stone walls covered in vibrant green moss and creeping vines that bloomed with vibrant flowers.

"Thank the gods, we made it."

As the tree slowed to a halt, it lowered the branch we sat upon and gently deposited us onto the moist earth.

"Thank you, Mister Tree." Another giggle dribbled from the silly smile plastered across her face.

Shaking my head, I cradled Aelia tightly against my chest and walked up to the door, carved from ancient oak and etched with intricate runes that pulsed with a soft, amber light. It stood slightly ajar, so I peered through the opening.

"Melisara?"

"Is that you, Reign?" A female voice whispered from the depths of the cottage. "That was quicker than expected."

"Yes, it's us."

"Please, come in, I will be right out."

I stepped through the threshold, pushed the door open with my shoulder and scanned the deceivingly large space. Shelves lined the walls, overflowing with ancient tomes, scrolls, and jars filled with mysterious ingredients—dried herbs, glittering crystals, and rare artifacts. A large, circular table dominated the center of the room, its surface covered with an array of mystical tools, runes, crystal balls, and alchemical vials, each item humming with *lys*.

In the far corner of the cottage, hidden behind a curtain of shimmery crystals, a female stood at a bubbling cauldron. The scent of burning incense and fresh herbs hung from the beams of the low ceiling as she hummed a tune. Melisara's long, silver hair cascaded down her back in soft waves, catching the light like moonbeams.

"Wow," Aelia murmured. "This looks exactly as I'd imagined it." She unlaced her arm from around my neck and wriggled free of my hold. Despite my body aching from the loss of hers, I was thankful for the space. If I hoped to survive these next few hours, keeping my distance would be safest for us both.

"It's almost ready," Melisara called out over her shoulder. "Make yourselves comfortable."

Thank the gods.

After a quick stroll around the living area, Aelia plopped down on an upholstered divan then patted the cushion beside her. "Come sit with me, Reign. I'm exhausted." She leaned back, exposing the delicate column of her neck.

My feet moved of their own accord, helpless to deny her,

despite my proclamation of keeping my distance from only seconds ago. This female truly had me in a chokehold. I folded down beside her, and her head immediately dropped to my shoulder. A faint sigh pursed her lips, and the enticing sound had another wave of heat blossoming below with another type of warmth expanding in my chest.

"Can I sleep, Reigny?"

I snorted on a laugh, the unexpected sound shocking both of us. "No, not yet, princess. Wait until Melisara gives you the antidote."

"But I'm so tired..." She batted her lashes, the long, dark strands fanning porcelain skin. A rosy hue had settled over her cheeks, whether from the exertion or the poison I wasn't certain. The askalia plant from which the toxin was derived worked as a sedative on Spellbinders but had a wildly different effect on Fae, causing hallucinations, loss of inhibitions, and a general feeling of ecstasy. I couldn't imagine what it would do to Aelia.

"Ah, yes, here we are." Melisara emerged from the shadows, a figure of ethereal grace and quiet power. "You must be Reign and Aelia." She offered a pleasant smile. Though I'd never met the female, I'd heard many tales of her prowess from Gideon. He was utterly taken by her, and though they rarely saw each other anymore, the impression she'd left on my friend had been bone deep. And now, I understood why.

Melisara glided closer, moving with a fluidity that made her seem almost like a shadow drifting through the forest. She glanced up at me through the curtain of silver hair, and I met a face that seemed ageless, with high cheekbones and skin that glowed with a faint, inner luminescence.

She folded down beside us, cradling a stone chalice in her hands, and offered it to Aelia. "Drink this, child. It will hasten the effects of the toxin through your system."

Aelia's lips screwed into a pout as she eyed the vile-smelling concoction. "Do I have to?"

"If you do not, I'm afraid the effects could last for as long as twenty-four hours."

"And with it?" I asked.

"She should be back to normal in an hour, at most, and hopefully she'll sleep through the worst of it."

Taking the goblet from the female, I eyed the murky gray substance, and a stab of unease filled my gut. I was being foolish, I knew it well, but the sense of protectiveness over Aelia had been growing by the day. But if Gideon trusted Melisara, then so would I.

"Come now, Aelia, you must drink it." I brought the cup to her lips, and wary eyes met mine over the rim.

"It smells awful."

"The sooner the toxin is expelled from your system the quicker we can focus on the real reason for our visit."

"Okay," she huffed out. Her hand closed around mine as I tipped the contents into her mouth. Her lips contorted into a dramatic grimace as she swallowed it all down. "Oh, Raysa, that was disgusting."

Another goblet appeared in Melisara's hand before Aelia finished the sentence. "Water will help."

"Thank you for this," I whispered. "If it hadn't been for your warning, I never would have expected to encounter vandals on our journey."

"Yes, unfortunately, my sanctuary has been overrun with them the past few months. The disquiet in the capital has sent the less powerful castes seeking solace away from Eldra."

"What is happening?" With all the turmoil in Aetheria, the political rumblings of Mysthallia were the least of my concerns.

"The covens are always arguing about something, Reign, and it is the weak who suffer. Surely, you are familiar with the struggles, having grown up at court."

I slowly dipped my head. Melisara had no idea who I really was; to her I was merely Gideon's former schoolmate, and that was how it would remain.

"Oh, goddess, why is my head spinning?" Aelia's voice drew me to the present predicament. She crawled into my lap and my arms instinctively encircled her trembling form.

"Is this supposed to happen?" I barked at the Spellbinder.

"I'm afraid the poison's effects are unpredictable when it comes to Fae. It isn't often your kind ventures into our woods." She motioned toward an arched doorway. "Come, bring her into the guest sleeping quarters. If her powers have truly been bound by a spell, I will be unable to perform any examinations until she's recovered."

Dipping my head, I cradled Aelia in my arms once more and followed Melisara down the dimly lit hallway. With her head on my shoulder and her palm resting on my chest, my heart slammed against my ribcage in a desperate attempt to reach her. Good god, how much longer could I deny the obvious truth?

Are you familiar with the cuorem? Elisa's question from last term echoed in my mind, repeating in time with the slap of my footfalls. *It is said that those bound by the cuorem are predestined by the gods themselves, their spirits eternally entwined.*

And if Aelia were my mate? It wouldn't change a gods' damned thing between us.

How could the gods in their infinite wisdom do this to us?

The sound of a door creaking open stilled my dismal thoughts. Melisara stood in the doorway, motioning to a quaint chamber. Candles floated in the air, casting a soft, flickering light that danced across the room, illuminating the intricate patterns woven into the rug on the floor. In one corner sat a small, wooden bed covered with a colorfully embroidered quilt. Like the rest of the cottage, the scent of pungent incense and herbs clung to the air.

"Aelia may rest here for the night. I have a few matters to attend to while we wait for the effects of the toxin to pass. Please make yourself at home."

I found myself wanting to thank the female again but held my tongue this time. Despite the connotation of gratitude being different among the Spellbinders than the Fae, it was a hard ingrained habit, difficult to break.

Aelia's head lifted off my shoulder, her eyes widening as they took in the floating candles. "Wow, magic." Another giggle erupted, sparking shards of silver to come alive in her bright eyes.

I gently deposited her onto the bed, but her hand remained fastened to my own. I attempted to wiggle it free as I hovered over her, but her fingers only tightened around mine. "Stay with me," she whispered before she scooted to the corner of the bed.

Chapter Thirty-Four

R*eign*

"Aelia, I..."

"Please." She tugged on my hand, heated gaze fixed to mine, and my knees hit the edge of the mattress.

That one word had all my resolve crumbling. It was clear she was experiencing the effects of the poison, the diminished inhibitions, the heightened emotions, and who knew what else. If I allowed myself to lie with her, would I be able to control my deepest desires?

She had an excuse to behave this way, but what was mine?

With one more gentle tug, my knees buckled, and my resolve disintegrated. A heart-stopping smile crawled across her face as I settled in beside her, careful to keep some distance between us. Dropping my head to the pillow, my entire body was as stiff as a plank. As if she could sense my unease, a wicked grin replaced the satisfied smile. "Why do you look so uncomfortable, professor?"

I squirmed, rolling onto my stomach to hide the proof of my desire for the female that had turned my life upside down. "The bed is a bit small, don't you think?"

"No, I think it's perfect." She obliterated the carefully crafted distance I'd created, curling into my side.

"That's likely the hallucinations," I mumbled.

"Well, then they're the best damned hallucinations I've ever had." Her fingers dove beneath my tunic and once again roamed the planes of my back.

Every touch sent a fiery torrent licking up my spine. "Aelia..." I grumbled.

"What?"

"You know what."

She lifted her head from the pillow, propping her chin in her palm as those teasing eyes scrutinized me. "I thought you wanted to be with me?"

Gods, I did, I do. "You are not yourself right now."

"On the contrary, dear professor, I've never felt so much like myself—so free, so weightless and giddy—in my life. The vandals should bottle this poison and sell it. They'd make a lot more money than trying to rob innocent travelers of their coin."

A wry chuckle tumbled out as I reveled in the mirth of her expression, the twinkle in those twin silver-blue orbs. It wasn't often we shared moments like these anymore. And maybe she deserved it... just this one time.

As if she'd read my quickly crumbling resolve, her fingers climbed up my spine and settled on my neck. With a gentle tug, she coaxed my body to turn so that we were now flush against each other.

A shaky breath parted her lips when our lower halves met. Her gaze dipped between us, latching onto my growing arousal pressed against her belly. A mischievous smirk splashed across her face, tingeing the apples of her cheeks an enticing crimson. She inched closer, her lips a heartbeat away from mine, the rapid rise and fall of her chest brushing mine with each ragged inhale.

"Please, Reign..."

Noxus, I wasn't built for restraint. Her voice was still laced with a fevered pitch, her eyes glossed over from the toxin. Aelia was not in her right mind. I should not do this, not take advantage of this moment of weakness she'd surely regret. Then again, I was not a good Fae; I was arguably one of the worst. I was selfish, stubborn, and ruthless, willing to crush anyone who stood in my way. And in this moment, what I wanted more than anything was Aelia.

"Let's simply pretend again," she whispered.

So when her lips pressed closer, a questioning, unguarded expression in her eyes, I hurled my restraint into the abyss and closed the distance between us, claiming her mouth with the intensity I could no longer contain. And for one blissful moment, I pretended she truly was mine, and we *were* destined to be. Fuck the prophecy, the gods, the kings. Aelia was mine, and I was hers, fate be damned.

Despite knowing how wrong this was, how much I'd regret my feeble character in the morning, I threaded my fingers into the back of her nape and devoured her. I captured and claimed, exploring every inch of her mouth as I'd dreamt of doing since the first time our lips touched.

Soft moans echoed over the pounding of my heart and the rapid, rough breaths sailing between us. She rocked her hips against mine, driving her center over my arousal. "Oh, stars, Reign..." she groaned against my lips. "You make me feel incredible."

"Mmm, I was going to say the same to you, *princess*."

Her hand glided between us, moving down my torso and pausing at the laces of my breeches.

"Aelia..." I growled, the low, guttural sound more beast than man. "This is not a good idea."

"But I want to touch you."

For the love of Noxus... I deserved to spend the rest of my days basking in Raysa's sun-blessed splendor for what I was about to say. "Not today," I forced out.

"But why?" She pushed out her bottom lip as her hand cupped my arousal over my trousers.

A groan slid past my clenched teeth as I forced the words from my mouth. "Because the toxin is affecting your judgment."

"No, it's not," she whined. "I know exactly what I'm doing. In fact, I've always wanted to—"

I pressed a finger to her lips before I lost all self-control. "Soon, Aelia, but not here, not like this. Let me take care of you tonight."

Without free rein over my shadows, I would have to coax her pleasure the more traditional way. And gods, I couldn't wait to lure those sounds from her lips with my fingers, my tongue.

I rolled her onto her back, pinning her to the bed as I drew her tunic up over her head. Her eyes twinkled up at me, like a thousand stars across a moonlit sky. My starlight. Her breasts spilled over the top of her brassiere, and I dropped chaste kisses along the fine curves. Her back arched off the bed with each gentle touch, each languid lick. My arousal was heavy, straining against my breeches, but I pushed all thoughts of my discomfort aside, and focused only on her pleasure.

Aelia writhed beneath me, the sweet scent of her excitement filling the air and only urging me on. I crawled down her perfect form, licking and nibbling, tasting her as I dropped lower, fitting my knees between her legs. Painfully slowly, I dragged down her training leathers, the soft suede clinging to her skin, before I relieved her of her silky panties. Revealing milky white flesh beneath, I paused for an endless minute to take her in, to commit this moment to memory. I was a bastard because I knew that in any other situation, she would never have bared herself to me like this, but with her inhibitions subdued, she preened like a peacock beneath my adoring gaze.

"Gods, you are perfect, Aelia. The most incredibly exquisite female I've ever set eyes upon." And *mine*...

Her twitchy fingers found the hem of my tunic, lifting it up over my head. Her gaze settled on the mark of the banished, and her lips twisted, a light sheen coating her brilliant irises. "I hate that your father did that to you," she whispered, her voice nearly returned to her natural timbre once more. A tear glistened down her cheek, and the endless void that once existed in my chest bloomed with warmth.

"Don't cry for me, princess." I swept the errant tear from her soft skin and brought it between my lips. "I would never have met you if my father hadn't set those events in motion. And I would gladly endure the torture of a thousand banished marks just to have this one moment with you."

"Reign, I—"

"You don't have to say anything, Aelia. The poison would only tarnish the truth of your words. I will gladly wait for the real thing, even if it takes a lifetime." With that, I dropped between her legs and inhaled a deep breath of her natural perfume.

"Reign!" An airy giggle flitted between us as her fingers tangled in my hair. "What are you doing?"

"I'm committing your scent to memory, Aelia. It's common among m—lovers."

"It tickles!" she squealed.

I dropped kisses along her inner thigh, and she stilled, a soft moan replacing the nervous laughter. As I neared the hollow between her thighs, her anxious gaze latched onto mine, and her words from the last time we'd been intimate sprang to mind. Aelia had never been with another male. The gods had saved her for me, *my* mate. The heady thought streaked straight to my lower half, sending an electrifying pulse through my already painful arousal. I vowed in that moment that one day I would have all of Aelia, but that day could not be today because if the cuorem were real, the physical act of coupling would seal the bond. And I couldn't, in good conscience, allow that until we were certain of the truth. And until she knew and understood what that truth was.

Anxious eyes peered down at me, her bottom lip caught between her teeth.

"Has a male ever worshiped at the altar of your thighs?"

Another wave of brilliant crimson rushed her cheeks as she slowly shook her head.

"Then I consider myself a fortunate one to be the first to claim that title." *The first and the only, if the gods were good.* My free hand drifted up her torso, pinning her to the mattress, while my other one locked around her thigh. Licking my lips, I dropped between her legs and dragged my tongue across her center. "Tonight, I feast."

"Oh, my stars!" Aelia attempted to sit up, but I gently held her down, running my hand up her torso to fondle her breast. "Reign..." she moaned as I licked and nibbled, teased and thrusted. "My gods, this is absolute heaven."

A deep chuckle escaped, vibrating against her most sensitive region, and her legs quivered. "I'm just getting started, princess."

Chapter Thirty-Five

A*elia*

Oh, Raysa, this must be what the glorious afterlife feels like. With my hands knotted in Reign's silky locks, his head bobbing between my thighs, I was certain I'd died and gone to rest in Noxus's sweet embrace. Why had I denied myself this pleasure for so long?

And was that thing he was doing with his tongue normal?

My head fell back as molten fire surged my core. No, this was certainly not normal. Was it some strange effect of the poison? Likely not. If I was being perfectly honest with myself, the dizzying, euphoric feelings from earlier had long since receded. The moment Reign's lips had found mine, my senses had sharpened and the overpowering haze melted away. Had I taken advantage of the freeing sensations to explore a longtime coming reunion with Reign? Possibly.

This wasn't real, right? It was simply pretend. We could pretend for one incredible night that what was happening between us was only a result of the poison instead of facing the truth.

The truth was far too frightening: that I'd fallen in love with a ruthless Shadow Fae sworn to kill me.

Reign's tongue circled the taut bundle of nerves at my center and all other thoughts vanished. All that mattered was this moment and the surge of sensations raging across my body. I could feel every point of contact between us so acutely, as if I'd suddenly developed a sixth sense. Reign.

With each wicked lash of his tongue, invisible strands of power laced around my heart, binding me to this male. I'd tried and failed to fight this unnamable thing between us, but try as I might, we seemed inescapable. Every touch, every heated glance only tightened the grip he had on me, pulling me deeper into a web of dangerous desire and unavoidable fate. No matter how fiercely I resisted, it was clear—this connection between us was unbreakable, as undeniable as the stars in the night sky.

A wave of pleasure crashed over me, building, intensifying until only it existed. There was no Aelia, no Reign, no two separate entities, but only the thrilling rush of sensations between us. As if he could sense the pinnacle approaching, his tongue quickened, circling in a maddening tempo.

My head fell back when sparks of pleasure ignited in my spine and spilled through my veins as the fiery heat reached a devastating crescendo. My toes curled and raw ecstasy consumed me as my release flowed with Reign's name on my lips. My body trembled with the force of it, and in that moment, everything else vanished—the world, the dangers lurking just beyond, the weight of all that had come before.

Once I managed to open my eyes—I had no recollection of them having closed—I met a pair of starlit ones hovering over me. A relaxed grin softened the hard line of Reign's jaw as he regarded me, thoughtfully, silently. We remained like that, neither speaking, locked in each other's gazes for an impossibly long moment. And it was everything.

An endless minute later—or it could have been an hour later, for all I knew—Reign licked his lips and dropped a chaste kiss to my forehead. "Rest, princess. We still have much more to discover on our visit."

A thousand unanswered questions loomed between us, but I tucked them behind my teeth, keeping them hostage for now. A discussion would only lead to an inevitable fight, and I preferred to bask in the afterglow.

Exhaustion rose to the surface once more, threatening to pull me under. Reign swept a dark tendril of hair behind my ear, gently running his finger over the rounded tip before his massive form curled around me. "Sleep well, starlight."

His words were so quiet I wasn't certain I'd heard them correctly, and with the secure warmth of his body and the overpowering haze of sleep dragging me under, I couldn't find the words to ask where my new nickname had come from. So I gave into the overwhelming exhaustion, and my heavy lids slid closed.

Muffled voices dragged me from a fitful sleep, forcing my heavy lids open. Rolling over, I struggled to process the familiar timbres. It took a moment, but then I recognized them as Reign and the Spellbinder, Melisara. I forced myself up and slid to the edge of the mattress. A faint soreness emanated from between my legs and all at once, fiery memories of the night before surged to the surface.

Oh, gods, the things I'd allowed Reign to do to me. I had never been that intimate with any other male in my twenty years on this earth. And it had been incredible... A spark of heat kindled below as echoes of pleasure raced through my veins. Now that the toxin had fully retreated from my system, warmth flushed my cheeks at the vivid images springing to mind.

Stars, I'd practically thrown myself at him. How embarrassing.

Pushing myself to stand, I staggered to the door, the voices becoming more discernible with each step.

"She has no blood relatives that we know of." *Reign.*

"Then I'm afraid this will be a very difficult task." My recollections of Melisara were minimal, but that melodic tone definitely belonged to her.

"Gideon claims you are the best."

"I will do what I can. I only wish to temper your expectations, Reign."

My hand hovered over the delicate knob for a long moment, indecision paralyzing my movements. I truly wished to discover more about my past, but the fear that came along with it was at times insurmountable. If Aidan sought so desperately to keep my past hidden, perhaps breaking this spell was unwise after all.

The door whipped open, nearly crashing into my face. Reign leapt back, jerking the thick timber with him an instant before it cracked against my nose. "You're awake."

"I am." That cursed heat flushed my cheeks as those penetrating onyx spheres latched onto mine. I blinked quickly, attempting to banish the vivid image of those eyes searing into me from between my legs.

"How do you feel?" He crept closer and pushed the door closed behind him.

"Fine."

"No lingering effects of the poison?" His mouth curved into a feral smile.

"Not a single one." I staggered back a step. "In fact, whatever Melisara gave me last night seems to have wiped out *all* memories of the evening."

"Oh, really?" Reign took a measured step closer, and I mirrored one back. "You don't remember anything?"

I slowly shook my head.

"That's a shame." One of his shadows, the dark coil more

faint than normal, peeled off his form and crawled across my shoulder. "Because you missed out on the best night of your life. Your words, not mine," his dark minion whispered.

"I never said that," I blurted.

A sinful grin stretched across those perfect lips as his dark gaze raked over me. "That's what I thought, princess."

"You're insufferable. I thought you were a gentleFae." I crept back one final step before hitting the wooden footboard of the bed.

"I never claimed such a thing." He loomed over me, the slight whir of his dwindling shadows whipping around us. "In fact, I believe I've always said the opposite was true. That said, I never should have taken advantage of you as I did. I would apologize, but you know my feelings on the matter." His lips twitched, setting his eyes aflame.

"I'd hardly say *you* took advantage." If anything, I was the one to reap the rewards of my altered state.

"That's all I wanted to hear." A smug grin melted across his face as he offered me his hand. "Come now, princess, we have a binding spell to break."

"About that…"

His hand hung in the minute space between us.

"What if breaking this spell only makes matters worse?"

"How could it?"

"What if there were a very good reason to keep my powers bound?"

"Such as?"

"I don't know, Reign. I'm simply worried. And stop answering each of my questions with another question." I drew my bottom lip between my teeth, nibbling on the soft pillow. Perhaps I should have told him about Aidan and what I'd learned upon my trip home.

"Is there something else I should know, Aelia?" My real name on his lips only magnified the seriousness of his tone.

I didn't speak for a long moment, weighing the consequences of telling him the truth about Aidan. "There is something I haven't told you," I finally forced out. "But before I do, you must make another vow."

"Oh, must I?" His dark brow lifted into an incredulous arc.

Knotting my arms across my chest, I glared up at the infuriating Fae. "Or don't, and you'll simply have to remain in the dark."

"I'm trying to help you, don't you see that?" He clutched my shoulders, pinning me in that lethal gaze.

"Yes, but if I tell you what I've learned, I fear you will take matters into your own hands and hurt someone I care for in a single-minded attempt to help me."

He heaved out a frustrated breath.

"It certainly wouldn't be the first time," I added.

"Fine, princess. I'll make the vow. Just tell me what you've been keeping from me."

Chapter Thirty-Six

A *elia*

"Aidan is Light Fae," Reign barked, throwing his hands in the air, "and you've waited this entire term to share that vital piece of information with me?"

"Yes, because I feared for his life."

"We could have avoided this entire gods' forsaken trek into Mysthallia had I known!"

"No, we could not have." I closed the space between us and jabbed my finger into his chest. "And if you say that again, it won't be my finger but my dagger at your heart."

He rolled his eyes, a sharp exhale pursing his lips.

"If I hadn't forced you into taking a vow promising not to hurt Aidan, you would've used your shadows to torture the truth out of him. Don't pretend you wouldn't have…"

"It would have saved us all heaps of time and aggravation."

My thoughts swirled to the night before, and a pang of hurt

lanced through my chest. Time and aggravation, that was what I was to him? He must have noticed the twist of my lips, the momentary faltering, because he reached for me.

"Aelia, I didn't mean—"

I spun away before his hand closed around my arm. "It doesn't matter. We're here now, aren't we? So let's get this damned incantation over with. I'm anxious to get back to the Conservatory." Something I never thought I'd say. I marched to the door, still wearing my tunic and leathers from the night before, and wrenched the thick timber open.

Reign appeared at my side before I made it through the threshold. "If you truly are having reservations about this, Aelia, we need to discuss it now. Whatever Melisara finds, there will be no going back."

I stiffened my jaw, that damned indecision warring in my gut. I needed to know the truth, as terrifying as it was. "We've already come all this way, as you mentioned in your complaint, so we may as well complete our task."

"...Fine."

"Fine." I whirled on my heel and stalked into the living room, the scent of incense and wild herbs filling my nostrils.

Melisara glided toward me with a gentle smile on her lips, her robe swishing across the wooden floor in a hypnotic rhythm. "I'm glad to see you awake, child."

"Me too. Thank you for the hospitality."

"Of course. You were quite entertaining." Her lively eyes flickered between Reign and me. Oh gods, strike me down now.

"Come, I have everything prepared." She held out her hand, long slender fingers coaxing me forward. An enormous cast-iron cauldron sat atop the stone table in the middle of the room, bubbling and fizzing in a frenzy. The strangest part was that there was no fire beneath it. It simply simmered and boiled of its own accord.

Melisara led me to a cozy settee across the table, then

assumed her position beside the cauldron. Flickering candles hung in the air, suspended by nothing more than magic, or rather, *lys*. Reign flopped down beside me, eyeing the pungent concoction that sizzled and spat, expelling its grievances.

"First, I will confirm that you are in fact spellbound. Once I've ascertained that, I can go about finding the best way to break the enchantment."

"And if I decide I don't want the spell removed?" The words spilled out before I could stop them.

"That will be your choice, child. And to be perfectly honest, as I told Reign, there is no guarantee that I would be able to sever the binds of the incantation. It would depend on the many intricate details of its formulation."

"Just do what you can," Reign interjected.

"Very well, let's begin." She revealed a small, sharp dirk from the folds of her translucent robe. "First, I need blood."

Wonderful. Offering my palm, she slid the blade across my skin, leaving a thin trail of deep crimson.

"Now, hold your hand over the cauldron and squeeze it into a fist."

I did as instructed, the angry hissing and spitting growing more rabid with the addition of my blood.

"Very good." Her eyes slid closed, palms coming together as she hovered over the cauldron. "Ah, one more thing, this could be slightly unpleasant."

The pungent scent of herbs and something metallic heightened as I sat back on the settee, cradling my wounded hand. The dim light from the candles flickered ominously, casting long shadows against the walls, but it was the cauldron in front of me that drew my gaze. It sat bubbling, a thick, dark liquid swirling within it, tendrils of vapor snaking their way into the air like creeping fingers.

Melisara stood over it, her silver hair catching the faint light, her green eyes glowing unnaturally in the gloom. She chanted softly under her breath, words in a language I didn't understand, but that made the hairs on the back of my neck stand on end. The cauldron's agitation seemed to grow, the hissing and spitting increasing as the liquid within it turned a deep shade of crimson, thick like blood. My blood.

"Are you ready?" Melisara's voice was low, almost hypnotic, but there was a sharpness to it that snapped me out of my daze.

I nodded, my heart a raging war drum. That dread bloomed, but I forced it down, reminding myself I needed answers. If I was spellbound, I had to know.

Melisara dipped her fingers into the cauldron without flinching, scooping a handful of the viscous liquid into her palm. She approached slowly, her eyes locked onto mine with an intensity that made me want to look away. But I held her gaze as she knelt before me and smeared the warm, sticky substance across my forehead, drawing intricate symbols that tingled where they touched my skin.

"This part will hurt," she murmured, her voice both a warning and a promise.

Reign scooted closer, his thigh brushing mine, and his steady presence alone helped calm the fear.

Before I could respond, she pressed her fingers to the center of my chest, right above my heart and inches from my beloved medallion. A searing pain exploded from the spot, ripping through me like wildfire. I gasped and tried to pull away, but Melisara's hand stayed firm, pinning me in place with unnatural strength.

The pain intensified, sharp and biting, invisible claws tearing at my insides. My necklace vibrated, the medallion burning and scorching my skin. What in all the realms? My vision blurred as I tried to breathe through the agony, but every inhale was met with resistance, an invisible force wrapping around my lungs and squeezing the life out of me.

A warm band curled around my waist, anchoring me through the pain. A familiar presence blanketed my form, icy shadows dulling the invading powers. "I've got you, Aelia. You can do this..."

"Hold still," Melisara commanded, her voice now distant, merely an echoing in my mind.

The air around me shimmered, growing thick with *lys* as Melisara muttered more incantations, her voice weaving into the rhythm of the room. The candles flickered and died, plunging the cottage into darkness. Only the cauldron glowed now, its eerie light casting a sickly glow across Melisara's face. She appeared otherworldly, almost inhuman.

Through the fog of pain, I could feel something shift, a tug deep inside me. It was faint at first, but then it grew stronger, like invisible threads pulling at the edges of my mind. The pain sharpened, piercing every nerve as the magic worked its way deeper, unearthing whatever was hiding beneath my skin.

"Please—" I gasped, tears pricking the corners of my eyes.

"Quiet," Melisara murmured. "We're almost there."

Suddenly, the pressure inside me surged, and I cried out as something snapped. It wasn't physical—it was deeper, buried within the very essence of who I was. And then, I saw it: A flash of shadow, dark and insidious, coiled like a serpent around my heart. It slithered through my veins, its presence unmistakable, its grip tightening with every beat of my thundering organ.

Melisara's eyes widened, her hand trembling slightly as she withdrew her fingers from my chest. The dark tendrils lingered in the air, visible only for a moment before fading back into the shadows.

"You are indeed spellbound," Melisara whispered, her voice low, laced with something that sounded almost like fear.

The cauldron's bubbling slowed, its glow dimming as the magic faded. I collapsed against Reign, gasping for breath and covered in sweat, my entire body trembling from the pain and the revelation.

"By whom?" I rasped, my throat raw.

Melisara's face hardened, her lips pressing into a thin line.

"That, Aelia, is what we need to discover. But whoever bound you... their magic is powerful and dark. Very dark."

I shuddered as the memory of those shadowy tendrils, so much like Reign's dark minions, tightened in my mind.

"It's bound by *nox*, then?" Reign asked.

Melisara slowly shook her head. "No, it's *zar*."

Chapter Thirty-Seven

R*eign*

"That's impossible." With Aelia curled against me, I was forced to remain seated, otherwise, I would have been on my feet by now, pacing in mad circles around this gods' damned cauldron. Injecting a calmness I did not feel into my tone, I attempted to tame the mad fluttering of my pulse. "The Two Hundred Years' War ended well before Aelia was born. King Helroth, along with all Demon Fae of the Court of Infernal Night, were long dead. No one alive could have woven *zar* into that spell."

"And yet…" Melisara slowly shook her head.

"You've made a mistake."

"The cauldron does not lie, Reign, nor does her blood. Has it ever occurred to you arrogant Fae that the destruction you wreaked was not as complete as you'd imagined?" The Spellbinder's unnaturally bright eyes latched onto Aelia's fragile form pressed against me. A whirlwind of questions zipped through my mind, one less plausible than the last. None of this made any sense.

I thought for certain Aelia could have been born of Shadow Fae blood, but extinct Night Fae? Or were they...? So little was known of *zar* and the banished god, Zaroth.

What I was certain of was that no one must ever know; her very existence was treasonous.

Gently lifting Aelia from my lap and resting her against the cushioned settee, I rose, towering over the enchantress. "You must never speak of what you've discovered here today."

"How can I, when you forced me into a blood vow last night?"

"Only the gods know what you Spellbinders are capable of. I swear to you, Melisara, if you ever breathe a word of this to anyone, I will personally return and drag you back to Shadow Fae soil, where I will allow my shadows to have their way with you. And trust me when I say they've become unnaturally protective over Aelia. Once they've reduced your mind to pulp, I'll allow my dragon to feast upon you, starting with your fingers and toes. Do you understand me?"

The female's nostrils flared, her powerful *lys* surging to the surface. "If you weren't Gideon's friend, I would eject you from my home for such empty threats."

"Trust me, Melisara, there is nothing *empty* about them. I mean every single word. And if *you* weren't Gideon's friend, you would no longer be drawing breath in this world."

Her eyes flickered once again between Aelia and me. "I mean no harm to your mate."

I nearly choked on her final word. "She's not—"

She lifted a hand, a serene smile stretching across her pale features. "It makes no difference to me. As I've stated, I will take her secret to the grave or suffer the consequences."

"I am pleased to have reached an understanding." I turned to Aelia, stretched across the small settee, her eyes closed. Asleep like that, she suddenly seemed so vulnerable, *too* vulnerable. I crept closer, careful to avoid the squeaky floorboards, and pulled her into my arms. "Come, princess, I'm taking you home."

※

Standing on the top step of the Hall of Luce, I shielded my eyes from the mid-day glare and traced Aelia's quick footsteps across the lawn as she dueled against her friend. The obstinate little female never listened to me, always preferring to train against her roommate instead of a more challenging opponent. Not that the young Light Fae female wasn't formidable, but neither would push each other as hard as necessary.

And now with a handful of Shadow Fae first-years who'd failed the first trial loitering around the campus, finding a suitable sparring partner would be simple. With the next upcoming trial only a week away, now was not the time for coddling. If Aelia were to lose, she'd be forced to spend the remainder of the trials at Arcanum. I could not allow that to happen under any circumstances.

Stop staring at her. Phantom's familiar, rough voice skirted through my thoughts.

I'm not staring. As her mentor, I'm watching and taking notes to further her development. Not ogling her elegant, nimble form with heated memories of my mouth devouring the hollow between her thighs surging to the surface.

Liar.

I banished the sinful thoughts to the dark recesses where they belonged. Despite that incredible moment of reprieve, Aelia made it clear she still hadn't forgiven me. *What's got you in such a foul mood today, old girl?*

Perhaps, it was being forced to shuttle you and your little Kin across the Mysthallian border yesterday.

Or maybe it was seeing Solanthus again.

She snorted, and I could practically see the trails of smoke drifting from her nostrils. *What we had was in the past. It's long dead and buried, why unearth it now?*

You could apologize, you know. As I'd done with Aelia time and again, and still, she couldn't seem to get past my grave errors, but we weren't discussing me.

It would only open wounds that have long since festered.

Then the dragon mate bond hasn't transferred to your new bodies?

Silence.

Phantom...

You're in no place to criticize, my prince. Have you discussed the cuorem bond with Aelia?

Now it was my turn to bite my tongue—or my thoughts, in this case.

I didn't think so. Her smug chuckle vibrated through my mind.

It appeared we were both stubborn fools when it came to matters of the heart.

"Oh, there you are, professor." A light, airy voice spun my head over my shoulder, pulling my attention away from the internal conversation. My newest acquisition sauntered through the doors of the hall, a rucksack hanging from her slim shoulder. "The headmaster sent me to find you. I have exciting news."

"What's that?"

"I've done so well since my arrival, he's decided to transfer me to Flare Squad. Instead of taking part in the Ethereal Trials with my classmates, I'm to join in for the remainder of the Umbral Trials."

My brows slammed together as I regarded the first-year. While it was extremely rare for students to advance beyond their term, it did occasionally happen. Had I been so preoccupied with Aelia, I'd completely ignored Liora's potential?

She cocked her head, short blonde wisps fluttering across bright lavender irises. "Aren't you pleased?"

"Of course, I am." I offered a tight smile.

"Will you introduce me to the team?" She motioned across the field to where Heaton had the squad in formation, delivering what I was certain was a rousing speech.

"Yes, and it seems as though now would be the appropriate time."

Liora laced her arm through mine, and an odd undercurrent of energy zipped across my skin. My eyes snapped to hers, but her gaze remained fixed straight ahead, on a head of dark hair. "Won't it just be perfect having both of your acquisitions on the same team?"

After witnessing Aelia's last outburst when she and Liora were within proximity of each other, I wasn't quite sure. Still, I nodded as I led her across the grassy field.

Aelia's gaze lifted over Heaton's shoulder as we approached, eyes meeting mine before narrowing when they landed on the female at my side.

Heaton followed her line of sight, spinning around. "Ah, Professor Reign..."

"I hope I haven't interrupted your moving preparatory speech."

"No, of course not, I was simply informing my team that next week's trials will take place on Light Fae territory, granting them a slight reprieve."

"I have more good news to add, then."

Aelia's dark brows knitted as she regarded me, her eyes tapered at the corners as they darted between me and my new acquisition. I pulled my arm free of Liora's hold and faced the rest of the team. On either side of Aelia stood Rue and the Lightspire male. His curious, hungry gaze danced across the newest member of the squad. "Liora is to join Flare team, effective immediately."

A chorus of questions rang out, shrouded by a wave of murmurs and an occasional gasp. Even Heaton seemed surprised.

"Per Headmaster Draven," I added to the Flare team leader.

"Very well." The Liteschild male dipped his head, then turned to Liora. "Welcome to the team. We are pleased to have you."

Belmore's hand shot up, his wide jaw set in a hard line. "How is it fair that she is allowed to bypass the Ethereal Trials and everything else we were forced to endure in the first term?"

Liora bristled beside me, and I couldn't help but be reminded of Aelia's first day at the academy, and of the dagger she sent sailing through the ridiculous hoop at the top of Belmore's ear. But my new acquisition made no such move. Instead, she simply stood beside me, simmering.

"You can take that query up with the headmaster, Dawnbrook. It is not your place to question his motives, but by all means, please try." Heaton signaled down the path toward the Hall of Luminescence. "I'm sure he'd love a visit from you."

The arrogant Light Fae muttered a curse before slapping his arms across his chest. "Welcome to the team, Liora," he gritted out. "Just what we need, another outcast."

"Belmore," Heaton shouted, "need I remind you of the code of conduct amongst teammates?"

"No."

"Good." The team leader signaled to the line of first-years. "Liora, please join your squad. On Monday, you'll face the second Umbral Trial, the Mirror of Illusions, and I am here to tell you exactly what you must do to survive."

Chapter Thirty-Eight

A_{elia}

The week came and went in a blur of strenuous training and sleepless nights. Unlike the other trials we'd encountered, the Mirror of Illusions would test our mental strength.

According to Heaton, we would have to face and defeat mirror images of ourselves that reflected our inner fears and weaknesses. My fingers instinctively drifted up to my rounded ear. If only I'd learned the truth of my origins on our journey to Mysthallia, maybe I wouldn't have so many damned fears. The visit with Melisara had only left me with more unanswered questions.

As if my own concerns weren't enough, I could practically feel Reign's bleeding out from the tense set of his body, the twitch of his jaw, the deep furrow of his brow. He had spent the last two nights skulking over the border to Arcanum to meet with Gideon in hopes of finding answers about the inexplicable *zar* binding my powers.

So far, their efforts had proved fruitless.

An unnatural shift in the air drew my attention from my spiraling thoughts. That now familiar cloud of darkness blossomed along the foot of the Luminoc an instant before the horde of Shadow Fae first-years appeared on the river bank.

Rue bristled beside me, and her typically congenial expression morphed into something harder, fiercer today. Maybe I wasn't the only one with secrets. Beside her stood Sy, and just beyond, Liora. She'd been training with Flare team all week, and as much as I wanted to hate her, she'd been cordial, nice even.

The flood of hostile *nox* from the approaching Shadow Fae writhed across my skin, compelling my *rais* to the surface. Throwing my shoulders back, I stiffened at the influx of power, steeling my resolve. *Never show fear*. It was one of the first lessons Reign had attempted to instill when I arrived at the Conservatory. My eyes darted to the left where our professors stood behind the headmaster beneath the shade of an enormous weeping willow. As Malakar and his students marched closer, my fingers twitched for the daggers I should have had at my hips.

There were no weapons allowed today, the battle would be won with mental resilience alone. I only hoped my radiant energy would be enough to dispel the tangle of fears that would be magnified in those mirrors.

As the Arcanum initiates filed into a line across from us, a dark gaze caught mine. Prince Ruhl stood in the middle of the pack, a devious grin hitching up the corners of his lips and setting his pitch eyes ablaze. "Good luck," he mouthed.

The words were so unexpected that inexplicable heat flushed my cheeks. Instead of responding, I pivoted to the Hall of Luce, focusing my attention to where the trial would be held. Though we hadn't been informed of the details, Heaton had said the interior hall would be transformed for the event, much like for the grand Opening Night Ball. Only this time, instead of chandeliers and fineries, we'd be stepping into a battleground to face our greatest fears and inadequacies.

"First-years," Draven bellowed, and all eyes turned to the headmaster, including Ruhl's, saving me from their intense scrutiny. "Today, you will be facing off with the Mirror of Illusions, possibly your greatest foe yet. You will enter the hall in pairs, one student from Luce and one from Arcanum at a time. Light Fae must use their radiant energy to dispel the shadows of their fears, while Shadow Fae must embrace and manipulate their fears to overpower the illusions. You will have thirty minutes to complete this trial. Those who do not pass will spend the remainder of the trials at the opposite academy."

A frosty chill skirted up my spine at the mere idea of it.

Malakar stalked forward, a whirl of shadows following in his wake, nearly blanketing Headmaster Draven in darkness. "The first competitors to enter the hall will be: Prince Ruhl of Umbra and Aelia Ravenwood."

All the air caught in my throat, an embarrassing choking sound erupting from my depths. Rue's panicked gaze zipped to mine, her hand clamping around my clammy palm and offering a quick squeeze before releasing me. "You've got this," she whispered.

"Both of you, step forward," Malakar drawled. No title for the prince, no royal monikers were used this time. It seemed as if the prince truly was treated like any other at the Citadel.

I attempted to obey, but the soles of my boots seemed to have suddenly grown roots and buried deep into the ground. Ruhl's dark eyes caught mine from across the line, a taunting twist to his lips. He stepped forward, and a surge of *nox* crashed over me, compelling my own movements. My feet rushed forward of their own accord, and I heaved in a breath of relief. We met in the center of the line, our respective classmates on either side of us. In oddly perfect unison, we pivoted toward the open doors of the hall.

"I certainly hope your fears won't get the best of you today, Kin," Ruhl whispered as we marched toward the entrance.

His weak attempt at an insult only stiffened my spine, strengthening my resolve. "What fears?" I countered.

A sharp laugh vibrated his chest, the sound lacking the warmth of Reign's hard-won genuine chuckles. As if my thoughts had summoned the other Shadow royal, his dark gaze chased to mine from within the semi-circle of professors. He dipped his head, the movement so faint, I doubted anyone else would've noticed, myself included, had I not been so damned attuned to the male.

We reached the doorway and an icy blast of air raised the tiny hairs along my bare arms. Despite today's trial being a non-combative one, I still chose to wear my sleeveless tunic and fighting leathers for optimal range of motion.

"The time starts, now." Draven's deep voice echoed behind us.

A flicker of amusement flashed across Ruhl's face before he crossed the threshold. "See you on the other side, little Kin."

With one last, steadying breath, I willed my legs forward. The vast, circular hall was lined with hundreds of polished mirrors, each one shimmering faintly. I took another step, and my breath caught as the door sealed shut behind me with a soft hiss. *Relax, Aelia.* As I approached the center, the mirrors rippled and morphed, revealing hundreds of twisted, distorted versions of myself.

From the corner of my eye, I could just make out Ruhl already halfway down the immense room. I forced myself to focus, calling on my *rais*, building a wall of it, higher than the great peaks of the Alucian Mountains.

The chamber was unnervingly quiet, the only sound the faint hum of energy that vibrated through the air, as if the walls themselves were alive. The circular hall stretched endlessly, lined with hundreds of mirrors, each one gleaming in the dim, ethereal light. Their surfaces rippled like water, reflecting not just my appearance, but something deeper. Something far more dangerous.

As I took another measured step toward the center, my reflection flickered, twisting unnaturally. My eyes narrowed, heart thundering louder with every step. The farther I walked, the more the reflections distorted. The mirrors weren't just showing my face, they were showing my fears—twisting my features, distorting my essence. One moment I was bathed in light, then the next, dark shadows warped my features, plunging me into darkness. I could feel the pressure building in the chamber, the weight of my own insecurities pressing down on me like a suffocating blanket.

The prophecy.
The child of twilight.
Shadow Fae.
Light Fae.
Who are you, Aelia?

The wicked whispers twirled in the air, and my reflection suddenly froze. It wasn't my image staring back anymore. A version of myself, cruel and mocking, took form in the glass. Her lips curled into a sinister smile as she stepped out of the mirror, a strikingly beautiful version of myself with sharp pointed ears and incisors, her eyes filled with all the doubts and failures I fought so hard to bury.

A child of twilight, born from the dance of light and dark, shall emerge with the power to reshape destinies. That sinister voice, my own, echoed across the chamber.

Will you bring forth a new dawn or plunge all into eternal dusk?

A dark shadow raced across my peripheral vision, stealing the remaining air from my lungs. I whipped around to find Ruhl racing past. His hands were clapped over his ears, face twisted in fear.

"You don't belong here," my reflection sneered, turning my attention to that voice dripping with malice, each word like a dagger slicing through my confidence. "You're just a lowly Kin, a pretender with your power bound. You believe you can survive these trials? You think Reign or anyone else will care when you fail?"

The hissed words hit me like a punch to the gut. I swallowed hard, fists clenching as the mirrored version of myself circled me, her form wreathed in dark, writhing shadows. The air around her seemed to darken, as if she were sucking the light from the room itself.

"You're nothing," she hissed, her voice rising, the shadows swirling closer to my feet. "You think you're special? That the goddess chose you in her infinite wisdom? It was a mistake. You belong at the mercy of a Fae lord, nothing but a warm body to fill his bed." Cold tendrils snaked up my legs, nothing like the pleasant icy tingles Reign's shadows elicited, threatening to pull me down into the void.

"You, the child of the prophecy, will plunge us all into darkness."

"No, it's not me!" I cried. "It can't be."

"You can delude yourself all you want, Aelia, but you know the truth." My reflection stabbed a very real-feeling finger into my chest. Pure obsidian bled across the familiar blue irises, morphing them into liquid pools of night. "Despite the binds that steal your powers, you can feel it. There is real darkness inside you, waiting to break free. That is why your abilities were bound."

"No, you're wrong."

"Even Reign won't be able to help you. Worse, he won't want to."

"No..."

I forced air into my lungs, focusing on the countless hours of training. My *rais* surged to the surface, a shield of liquid light. I wasn't just a powerless Kin anymore; I was Light Fae, and possibly Shadow Fae. But more importantly, I was more than the doubts festering in the depths of my mind. Even if I was the child of twilight, I would choose my own destiny. I would never be the worst version of myself. My hand glowed with the faintest flicker of light as *rais* flowed through my veins, the warmth of it spreading from my fingertips, steadying my resolve.

"You're wrong," I said, my voice steadier now despite the panic clawing at my insides. "I've survived much worse than you. Or me, rather."

My mirror-self laughed, a cold, cruel sound. But I ignored it. I allowed the light to grow within me, forcing the shadows back. I was not just this broken version reflected in this cursed mirror. I was stronger than my fears, stronger than this illusion.

None of it was real.

From across the hall, I could just make out Ruhl battling his own inner demons, his *nox* penetrating the air. It washed over me, tangling with the *rais* rushing to the surface. The surge of power clashed, siphoning all the air from my lungs. I channeled the heady, icy *nox* and drew it inside me until the dark, smoky energy filled my core. My knees trembled, but I held fast, channeling the potent influx.

The light in my hand intensified, flooding the chamber with radiant energy. The shadows recoiled, and my twisted reflection began to waver. With a final push of *rais*, I splayed my fingers and flung the light toward the mirrors, the blinding flash shattering the illusion around me.

The glass splintered and fell, the entire chamber quaking at the explosive rush of energy. I dropped to the ground, shielding my face with my arms until the tremors subsided.

"What the realms was that?" a familiar voice growled from a few yards away.

I spun around to find Ruhl crouched beside a crumbling column, shards of glass strewn across the marble floor. I heaved in a breath as the air grew still once more, the oppressive weight lifting from my chest. Pushing myself off the floor, my heart racing, I surveyed the remaining fragments. Now the only image reflected was me.

My hair was disheveled, and I'd earned a few new scratches, but I'd survived. And I vowed in that moment that no one would ever force me to doubt myself again.

Ruhl stalked closer, dark eyes tapered at the edges.

A twinge of fear rekindled in my chest. Had he heard the whispers too? Did he know about the prophecy?

As he approached, a wild expression in his eye and his cheeks a sallow hue, my worries were assuaged. Whatever he'd seen must have been just as bad, if not worse, judging by the haunted look in his eyes. If I hadn't seen his fears, he must not have noticed mine either, right?

Pressing his palm to his chest, he moved his hand in a slow circle. Curses, had he felt me draw on his *nox*? His eyes sharpened as he regarded me. "It seems to me you've been holding out, little Kin." The darkness in his gaze relented, replaced by something more frightening still.

Curiosity.

Chapter Thirty-Nine

R^{eign}

You know Aelia is going to hate you for this, right? Phantom's question echoed through my mind as we soared over the deep greens of the Feywood Forest.

She may be displeased, but technically, I'm not breaking my very carefully formulated vow. I have no intention of physically harming the old man.

My skyrider snorted, whispers of dark smoke erupting from her immense nostrils. *You forget that I've come to know you quite well over the past ten years, my prince, and I know very well that you need not physically harm someone to do damage.*

The time for inaction has come to an end, old friend. With the Umbral Trials in full swing, it's only a matter of time before my brother learns what I've long since suspected. I'm honestly shocked it hasn't dawned on him yet. If I have any hopes of eluding the dire consequences of this prophecy, I must know everything about Aelia.

And if you find out that she is, in fact, the child of twilight, what will you do then?

Whatever I must to keep her alive.

But the king—

Whatever I must.

Drawing in a fortifying breath, I peered over Phantom's heavily scaled shoulder, focusing on the treetops growing ever closer. And at the edge of the woods stood a now familiar cottage. A trail of dark smoke curled into the sky from the small home I'd visited only six months ago. Never in a million years would I have imagined what that fateful day would bring.

Phantom curved her wings toward the ground, slowing their powerful flaps.

Land beside the forest and remain in the cover of the trees. We need not draw any more attention than necessary. And after Aelia's vivid story of the last time she arrived upon dragonback, I preferred to avoid a confrontation with Aidan out in the open.

Of course, my prince. She banked to the left and the grim browns and pale greens of the earth shot up to greet us. The moment my dragon's talons hit the soil, I leapt from her back. It was a short walk to the cottage, the sun's rays not quite as oppressive on this side of the Feywood Forest. I'd met Phantom across the river and flown over Shadow Fae lands for the bulk of the trip, reveling in the feel of *nox* once again free-flowing over my skin.

The glint of the silver bangles on my wrists soured my mood. For years, I'd prayed for the day I'd be able to complete the debt to my father and finally be free of the blasted cuffs draining my power.

Now, I feared that day.

The old wooden door of the cottage creaked open before I reached the stone pathway. Aidan stood on the threshold, the agony carved into his expression palpable. "What's happened?"

"Aelia is fine." Or at least she was when I skulked away from campus while everyone was otherwise entertained by the trial. It was a gamble, but regardless of what Aelia was to endure in that event, I was powerless to help her from the outside. "I've come to speak to you, Aidan." I paused a yard away from the entrance, calling back my writhing shadows.

His head dipped and he took a step back, motioning for me to enter. Still, his hand moved to the dirk at his hip as he led me to the small table in the middle of the space. I eyed the blade, and I couldn't help but wonder if it too was forged of infernium vein. I vowed to get that answer and more today.

I folded into the rickety chair at the table in the center of the chamber, the ancient wood squealing its protest, and Aidan settled in across from me. He eyed me warily, every muscle coiled and ready to strike. His posture, his very essence spoke of a seasoned soldier. I was embarrassed I hadn't noticed it upon my first visit, but with Lord Liander attempting to steal my acquisition, I'd paid little attention to Aelia's foster father.

"Why have you come, professor?" His gray eyes glinted as he regarded me.

Professor? Interesting. Had Aelia not shared my true identity with her beloved guardian?

"I have come to retrieve information Aelia is too kind to demand for herself."

A knowing smile lifted the corner of his lip. "She has told you about me then?"

I nodded slowly. "I hope that proves to you that she finds me trustworthy."

"She may, but she is also a young girl, clearly taken by her attractive and mysterious professor." He rubbed at his chin, eyes fixed to mine. "I am neither young nor taken by you, Reign Darkthorn. If there are answers you seek, you will have to prove yourself to me." His cold gaze raked over me, and for the first time since meeting this male, a swell of *rais* emanated from his aura. Was the spell binding his Light powers the same one used for Aelia?

"I know about the twilight prophecy, and my guess is that you do, as well, which is why Aelia's true bloodline has been kept hidden all these years."

The old male's face was a blank mask, not a twitch of emotion despite my goading. Yes, he was definitely a soldier in another life, and a faithful one at that.

"That does not prove anything to me, professor, other than the fact that you, too, are hiding secrets."

"What do you wish to know?" I ground out.

"For starters, what are your intentions with respect to my daughter?"

My jaw clenched, teeth still grinding. I could barely sort through the jumble of emotions that female elicited in my thoughts, let alone put them into words. Words that would need to assuage his very legitimate fears. "I wish to protect her." Not quite the full scope, but it was a start.

"Why?"

"Because I *care* for her," I gritted out.

His eyes narrowed, the unabashed scrutiny so piercing I found it difficult not to squirm. Which was very unlike me. Not even my father would get this sort of reaction out of me. How very peculiar...

"You're going to have to do better than that, professor." Aidan propped his elbows on the table, tenting his fingers. "You see, feelings between males and females are fleeting. You may want to protect her today, but what about tomorrow, or in a week or a month? What if she finally succumbs to your charms and you grow tired of her?"

"I wouldn't," I barked, unable to keep the anger of his insinuations at bay.

"Why not? Surely, she's not the first female that has caught your attention?"

"It's different with Aelia..."

"Different how?" he growled.

A flow of *rais* prickled my skin, piercing my flesh like a

thousand tiny blades. It infiltrated my veins, ethereal light rushing through my system and crawling into my dark depths. My *nox* surfaced, desperate to fight the unexpected onslaught, but it was too late. My tongue began to move before I could stop it.

"Because I love her!" I blurted. "Because I believe she could be my fated mate, my twin flame. I feel the ancient cuorem bond unfurling between us, and it's becoming harder to fight by the day." The moment the confession dribbled past my lips, I slammed my jaw down hard, the crack of teeth clashing reverberating through the suddenly silent space.

"Oh, gods, no," Aidan hissed, burying his face in his hands. "It cannot be."

I was still too shocked to utter a word. What had come over me? Why would I ever admit those things to this stranger?

My mind struggled with the facts, racing through the ancient tomes I'd studied in the Arcanum library. There could only be one reason.

Some Light Fae were gifted with a rare form of illumination sight, granting them the ability to not only discern the truth through light but force it out of other Fae.

"How did you do that?" I stuttered.

Aidan's hands fell to the table, limp. "Do what?"

"How did you compel that from my lips?" I had yet to admit to myself the overpowering feelings I'd been harboring for Aelia.

"I didn't force you to say anything, professor. I merely searched for the truth in your cold, dark heart."

Now, that sounded more like me.

He loosed a protracted breath, his entire posture crumbling. "This changes everything," he murmured.

"Why?"

"You are the catalyst, Reign Darkthorn. *You* are the one who triggers the prophecy."

My head whipped from side to side as the awful truth of his

words bled through the cage around my rapidly fluttering heart. "It can't be..."

"If you wish for me to divulge Aelia's secrets, then you must first share your own." He swallowed hard, eyes intent on mine. "There are very few souls who share the knowledge of the prophecy's existence, so tell me, professor, how did you become one of the chosen few?"

My jaw worked, indecision warring in my gut. Besides Gideon, I'd never entrusted the truth of my identity to anyone, let alone a rogue Light Fae. But if I had any hopes of protecting Aelia, it was necessary I discovered the truth, and this male was the only one who could give it to me.

"A binding oath?" I lifted a skeptical brow.

"If that is the only way..."

My chin dipped.

"And you must vow to keep what I am about to tell you from Aelia as well, if you truly wish to protect her," Aidan added.

My eyes widened, disbelief curving my mouth in shock. "You cannot be serious."

"I've borne the weight of this secret for decades, Reign. There were countless times I wished I could tell her the truth, but for her safety, I remained strong. Now it is your turn to bear that burden, if you truly love her."

The weight of his words pressed down on me, heavy and unrelenting, sinking deep into my bones. I loved her—gods, I did—like I'd never loved another. I had tried to fight it, to deny the bond growing between us, but it was futile now. There was no escaping the truth.

"I am ready."

Chapter Forty

elia

"Are you sure we should be here?" I whisper-hissed as Rue tugged me through the forest that encroached on the west side of campus. The same one that had hidden Lucian and Kian before the latter's untimely demise. My skin prickled at dark memories of the Fae who'd made my first few months at the Conservatory a nightmare.

Always avoid the Fae forests. It was a warning driven into my head by Aidan since the beginning of time.

"Yes, of course, we should!" Rue cocked her head over her shoulder, pulling me faster through the dappled light. "We survived the second trial without getting sent to Arcanum. I consider that a win that must be celebrated."

She wasn't wrong on that count. The idea of spending a day, let alone weeks at the ominous Citadel sent a wicked tornado of dread whirling through my insides. One of our teammates, Jacarta, had suffered such a fate and, according to Symon who'd heard from one of the Shadow Fae students, after only one night, she'd attempted to escape. Malakar caught her before she reached the river, and her punishment was to spend the night alone in the Twilight Forest. Another round of goosebumps rippled across my skin as memories of the gloomwhisper and its poisonous claws surged to the surface.

Poor Jacarta. Not that I'd ever been particularly close to the female, but I wouldn't wish death at the hands of that beast to my worst enemy.

"Come on, we're almost there."

As if confirming her announcement, hushed voices rushed across the crackling foliage overhead. A rainbow of leaves shielded us from the midday sun, blanketing the woods in a murky film. A chilly breeze lashed strands of dark hair across my face, reminding me winter drew closer by the day. Unlike in the Shadow Court, snow never fell upon the goddess-blessed soil here, but the temperature did drop according to Rue. In the past few days, the balmy weather had taken a decided turn.

"Where exactly are we going?" I huffed out.

"You'll see." *For someone with such short legs, the female was fast.* She jerked me forward, winding us through the sea of ancient, towering trees. If we hadn't been moving so quickly, I would have taken a moment to admire the colorful foliage and matching barks of every shade. From the deepest ochre to the most brilliant fuchsia, it was nothing like the common dark greens and patchy browns of the Feywood Forest.

The tangle of seemingly endless trees finally gave way to a clearing. The familiar voices rang out clearly now, one in particular. "Finally, you made it!" Symon waved from his perch atop a moss-covered boulder rimming a hidden gem nestled within the deep expanse of the forest.

A tranquil hot spring shimmered with an ethereal glow at his feet. Surrounded by a circle of trees whose multi-colored leaves filtered the sunlight into a soft, golden haze, the spring looked like a natural basin carved from the forest's heart.

"This is beautiful..." I murmured as Rue urged me closer.

The water, infused with a natural luminescence, radiated a soothing warmth, casting dancing reflections on the surrounding foliage.

"Come on, Aelia, the water is just perfect." Sy dipped a toe into the shimmering pond before jumping in.

My head bobbed up and down, releasing Rue's hand to join Sy along the water's edge. I moved closer, the air thick with the scent of wildflowers and the earthy aroma of damp undergrowth. I was so enthralled by the breathtaking scene that I hadn't paid any attention to the other initiates filling the spring, half-clothed and others already completely bare.

My beaming smile morphed into a scowl when my gaze landed on a familiar blonde male with plaited hair. Belmore. And Ariadne beside him. At least both were in swimming attire. A prickle of awareness skated up my nape, and I barely suppressed a groan. As if the idyllic tranquility couldn't possibly be further shattered, another familiar giggle twisted my lips into a full scowl. Liora. And who was sidled up beside her on the edge of the crystalline water? None other than *my* mentor.

My mentor, who'd mysteriously vanished in the middle of the Umbral Trial.

I supposed I should have been relieved they were both still clothed. Reign's eyes lifted to mine, and something unreadable flashed across the pulsing darkness. A hesitant smile slashed across his lips before he whispered something to Liora. Red-hot jealousy flared at the intimate gesture, igniting something dark and powerful in my murky depths.

"What are *they* doing here?" I hissed at Rue who'd joined me along the shore.

She shrugged. "Heaton probably invited Liora, but I'm not

sure why Reign would be here." She dug her pointy elbow into my side. "Maybe he came to see you."

I threw her my best eyeroll before plopping down on a moss-covered boulder, removing my boots and dangling my feet in the divine warmth. I nearly moaned when my toes hit the tepid waters.

Symon and Rue had already stripped down in that brief time span, both up to their necks in the spring, laughing and splashing water at each other.

"You're not going to join them?" Heaton sauntered over, dropping onto the giant boulder beside me.

"I didn't exactly bring any bathing clothes. Gods' forbid my best friend tell me where we're going so I can be prepared."

"That does seem like my sister, although it's not like she's bothered by such things." He wrinkled his nose before diverting his gaze. Rue had zero qualms about nudity, much like most Fae. Still, I couldn't imagine it was pleasant seeing your sibling bare in front of other males.

"What about you?"

He angled his body toward me, tiny droplets glistening across his bare torso, his trousers rolled up to his knees. "I've already been in, as you can see. Now I'm attempting to dry off so that I can return to campus. I only wanted to see you before I left."

There was something about his tone that had dread pooling in my core as my eyes rose to meet his. "You're leaving?"

He nodded slowly. "I received word yesterday. An envoy from the Royal Guardians will be arriving today to escort a few fourth-years to the front lines."

"Oh, gods, Heaton..." My hands curled around his, dropping them into my lap. "Where? And how long will you be gone?"

"I don't know," he murmured. "I assume we'll be stationed along the border of the Wilds. That's where the most fighting has been taking place."

"Against what?"

"Those horrible creatures our parents used to warn us about when we were only children." He shrugged.

"None of this makes any sense."

"As Draven said, it's not our place to question the king. He has asked for reinforcements along the border, so we are to obey."

I stiffened my bottom lip, forcing an encouraging smile—or at least trying to—despite my insides crumbling. "You're going to do great out there, Heaton. And you'll be back here before you know it, leading our team to the end of another term."

"From your lips to Raysa's ears." He squeezed my hands before releasing me, crossing his arms over his chest. "At the very least, I hope to find Lawson."

A dark shadow loomed closer, drawing the glimmering light from above, and I realized why Heaton had relinquished my hands. Reign stalked up, Liora no longer pinned to his side. A tiny petty part of me wished to snatch back Heaton's hand if only for Reign to feel an ounce of the envy currently consuming my chest. From my peripheral vision, I could just make out his precious new acquisition bare from the belly button up, splashing in the glistening pool with Sy. From the sound of it, my flirty male friend was laying on the charm. And for some ridiculous reason, it rankled my nerves.

"So now you're accompanying your acquisition to initiate get-togethers?" I smiled up at my professor sweetly, baring my teeth, completely bypassing any form of pleasantries. I knew very well how childish I was acting, but I simply couldn't stop myself. He'd never taken *me* to any of the gatherings my first term. Not to mention the fact that I was still angry about his disappearance yesterday. What if something had gone wrong? What if I'd needed him?

Heaton glanced between us before he slowly retreated. "I'll give you two a minute alone," he murmured as he slunk away.

That blanket of shadows curled around us as Reign perched

on the edge of the boulder, piercing gaze intent on mine. "I ran into her when I was looking for you in the dormitories. She asked me to accompany her, and I came, assuming you too would be here."

A likely story. A surge of jealousy filled my core, the likes of which I'd never experienced. What was happening? Why was I letting Reign get to me like this? Ever since that night at Melisara's, my feelings when it came to my professor seemed even more out of control.

"And what about at the trials yesterday? You were gone before I got out. Even Ruhl waited..."

His brows furrowed, the shadows keeping us hidden from curious eyes growing darker, more violent. "Ruhl did *what*?"

"I *may* have siphoned some of his *nox* during the trial. He waited for me when it was over and sort of... thanked me."

He barked out a crazed laugh, his head falling back with the sound, but the mirth didn't even come close to reaching those icy orbs. "Are you out of your mind? After everything I've gone through to protect your secret... Did he realize what happened?"

"I don't think so."

A snarl curled his lips as he regarded me, long and hard. "And Ruhl does not thank anyone. He was likely trying to discern what had happened by pretending to get in your good graces." He dragged a hand through his wild hair, tugging at the ends. "Gods, Aelia, how could you be so naïve?"

"I had no other choice. His *nox* called to me Reign!" Even hidden behind his shadows, I dropped my voice to a whisper before continuing my tirade. "And besides, if I hadn't ended the trial when I did, he would have heard what my mirror image was saying, about the prophecy, about my blood! Either way, the truth was about to come out."

"For Fae's sake, you should have come to me first thing this morning," he growled as he stood. "Now, I must go find him and discover if he's put any of the pieces together."

"Then I'll go with you." I slid off the mossy boulder and stood in front of him, toe-to-toe.

"No."

"Why not?"

"Because the more he sees us together, the clearer it will become."

"The clearer what will become?"

"My feel—that you're not simply some first-year I'm bedding, Aelia."

I snorted on a laugh, forcing myself not to focus on that tiny slip, on that sliver of hope it kindled. Sometimes I wished it were as simple as a physical attraction.

A moment of weighty silence passed between us. I could beg him to allow me to come, or I could simply follow him. Either way, I was too angry with him right now to beg so I'd have to find a way to skulk across the river later. "Where were you yesterday, anyway?" I hissed. "You never answered me."

His lips drew into a hard line. "I had an important matter to attend to."

"What was it?"

"Aelia, contrary to your opinion, not everything in my life revolves around you," he barked. "It was a private matter, just leave it at that."

His spiteful words stung, leaving an invisible lash across my heart. *Bastard prince.*

He must have read the hurt on my face, because he began to open his mouth—to say what I would never know, because in that moment, the thunderous flap of mighty wings drew my gaze overhead. From between the thick canopy of leaves, two forms took shape.

"Skyriders," I whispered.

Reign's eyes tipped skyward, following mine. "Not just any skyriders. Those are Royal Guardians."

My breath hitched, frantic gaze scanning the idyllic spring. "Where's Heaton?"

I sprinted across the mass of initiates gathered around the crystal-clear pool, my pulse rising with every step. He was gone.

Chapter Forty-One

R*eign*

"You better be careful, brother," Ruhl whispered, his dark eyes twinkling wickedly beneath the full moon. "With all this skulking around in Shadow territory, it's only a matter of time before you're caught." He leaned casually against the rough bark of the *gigantia* tree nestled within the depths of the Twilight Forest. "And then what would you do?"

"Don't worry about me, little brother." I stalked out of the shadows, eyes fixed on that irritating smirk. Ruhl was always cocky, and now with his recent triumphs at the Citadel, his arrogance had only heightened. "I've been doing this for a long time."

"A lot more, recently, in fact." He pushed off the tree and crept closer. "Late night visits to Gideon? Or is there some other female you're courting on this side of the river?"

I snorted. "You really are keeping close tabs on me."

"As, I imagine, are you. Or why else would you have requested this secret rendezvous?"

Clenching my jaw, I forced a calmness I did not feel. Just the idea that Ruhl could have overheard something about Aelia in the last trial had my nerves scattered. Surely, he would have told Father by now if he had. But I must be sure.

"I only came to ensure your mirror image did not divulge any secrets of mine in the last trial." I crept closer, erasing the distance between us. "I know how these events work, and if there was even a hint—"

"Relax," he barked. "Apparently, my own fears and weaknesses are more than enough to bring me to my knees. Yours did not need make an appearance."

A satisfied grin curled my lips. "Why, Ruhl, you have weaknesses? I don't believe it."

That smug smile vanished, a sickly pallor tingeing his cheeks. An odd sense of foreboding surged in my chest as I regarded him. "What?" I snapped. "What did you see?"

"I don't know..." The cocky brother I grew up with was gone, replaced by a serious male I barely recognized. That haunted look in his eye only intensified the dread uncoiling in my gut.

"Tell me."

"I already said I don't know." He paced a quick circle around me, dragging his hand through his hair in a move so similar to my own, it was oddly disturbing. "This dark, mirror-image of myself said things..." His lips thinned, words falling away. "I don't know what was real and what was simply the machinations of our twisted professors, but—"

"What did it say?"

"That both the Light and Shadow Courts would fall, and I would be too weak to stop it. That I would never sit the throne of the Court of Umbral Shadows."

I shook my head, driving back the ominous words. "It's only your own fears playing tricks on you, Ruhl."

"I'm not so sure." He lowered his voice to a deadly whisper. "My mirror image said it was the Court of Infernal Night to bring about our downfall. That I would die at their hands before I became king. Why would that be a fear of mine? The demons of the Night Court have been extinct for ages."

Icy fear crawled up my spine as Aidan's admission and Melisara's words echoed in my mind. *Zar. Aelia. The twilight prophecy. Noxus*, what if it was all true? What if Aidan was right, and I was the catalyst in all of this? This cuorem bond with Aelia would ignite the flame of an all-out war between the realms, because I would never let my father have her. I would rather plunge the entire continent into darkness than betray her again.

Which meant there was only one option left.

I spun on my heel, turning toward the river.

"Reign? Where are you going?" Ruhl trailed behind me, his frantic steps echoing the mad hammering of my heart.

"There's something important I must do," I called out over my shoulder. Ruhl lengthened his stride, running up beside me. I halted, fixing my gaze to his to impress the importance of my words, "Don't tell anyone else what you saw, brother, especially not Father. If what your mirror-self predicted was true, I believe I know how to put a stop to it."

"How?"

My head whipped from side to side, anguish eating at my soul. "I'll be in touch if I'm successful."

He slowed as we reached the edge of the forest, where the rushing river loomed just ahead. I could feel his dark gaze boring into the back of my head as my shadows hissed and spat before morphing into wings.

Leaping into the cool, night sky, I hazarded one more peek over my shoulder. Ruhl stared up at me, his dark eyes glinting beneath the pale light of the moon. There was no telling if he would keep quiet, which meant I had to move now.

Fate's pieces were falling into place with alarming swiftness, and if I wished to prevent plunging our courts into eternal dusk, Aelia had to make her choice tonight.

✕

I stole into Aelia's chamber, the spelled door easily opening with a wave of my hand. I knew granting myself private access would come in handy one day. Better to save my reserves of *nox* to shadowtravel us both back to my rooms once she was awake.

Both females were fast asleep, their quiet breaths filling the air. Creeping toward Aelia's bed, I avoided the faint rays of the twilit sun and bent over her still form. Her dark, raven hair spilled over the pillow in a perfect halo, the sliver of platinum bisecting her long locks like a streak of moonlight slicing through the veil of night.

I stood there for a long moment, just watching her, taking her in. Gods, Aelia was a marvel, not just in her breathtaking beauty, but also in her indomitable spirit and the relentless fire that blazed in her heart. I *loved* Aelia. For the first time in my tormented existence, I truly fucking loved.

And now, I may be forced to give her up.

Her dark lashes fluttered, fanning across the soft skin beneath her eyes. Slowly, they opened, lifting to meet mine. "Reign?" she whispered, her voice rough from sleep.

"I need you to come with me. It's urgent."

Her head bobbed drowsily as she drew the covers back, revealing a gauzy nightgown. Forcing my gaze to remain locked to hers, instead of wandering south like I truly wanted to, I offered her my hand which she surprisingly accepted. I pulled her close and my shadows closed in around us, their excited frenzy whenever she was near only solidifying my resolve.

Not a single doubt existed anymore. Aelia was my fated mate, my *cuoré*. And I would do anything to save her.

"What's happening?" Her sleepy gaze lifted to mine as we were plunged into darkness.

A moment later, my shadows dissipated giving way to the dim lighting of my bedroom. I drew in a breath, the cool darkness a respite from the eternal light of court. Aelia stepped free of my hold, her bright eyes alert once more as they scanned my chambers.

"What are we doing here?"

I motioned to my bed before thinking better of it. "Please, sit. We need to talk."

"That sounds ominous, Reign."

"I wish it weren't." I pressed my palm to the small of her back and steered her toward the oversized bed.

She dropped onto the edge of the mattress, one hand curling around the ornate bedpost. "What is it?"

Noxus, I'd had nearly a quarter of an hour to plan and practice what I wanted to say, and still, all the words stuck at the tip of my tongue. I folded down beside her, anxiety lashing at my insides like jagged lightning tearing through my beloved night sky.

She angled her body toward mine, fingers knotted in her lap. "You're making me nervous, Reign. What is going on?"

"I went to see Ruhl tonight."

Her brows shot up, nearly reaching her hairline. "And? Does he know? Did he hear my mirror image blathering on about the prophecy?"

"I'm afraid it's worse than that." My shoulders rounded, the weight of the entire realm poised on my back. With a steadying breath, I recounted the details Ruhl had shared.

When I finished, Aelia stared up at me, dark brows drawn. "You truly believe that there are Night Fae still out there somewhere simply because *zar* was used to bind my powers?"

I nodded. I didn't quite understand it myself, but I was certain somehow all of this was connected. Ruhl's vision, Aelia's *zar* and the rare cuorem bond between us.

"But how could it be, Reign?"

"I don't know."

"And what can we do to stop it?"

I took her hands, lacing my fingers through hers, then brought them palm up between us. Those familiar sparks skimmed over my skin, the ones I'd fought so desperately to ignore. "Do you feel that?"

Her cheeks rosied, chin slowly dipping. "I thought you didn't..."

"I've felt them since the very first day we met, princess." My lips slid into a smile, unbidden. It was true. I'd felt an instant connection with the formidable little Kin that day at her cottage, and it had only grown every day since.

"Why didn't you say something?" Her bottom lip trembled, and I could practically feel the rush of emotion surging between us.

"Because I didn't want to believe it was true. Because I didn't think it was possible."

"What is causing it?"

I held my breath, the air electric between us. "The *cuorem* bond, the Twin Flames. I'm sure you've heard stories of fated mates? It's a profound and mystical connection believed to exist between two souls, making them perfect counterparts of one another."

Aelia's mouth curved, a faint breath catching.

Forcing my tongue to move, I continued. "It's more than just a romantic or emotional attachment; it is a cosmic and spiritual link that ties two souls together across time and space. It is said that those bound by the cuorem are predestined by the gods themselves, their spirits eternally entwined."

"By the gods?" she squeaked.

"According to myth... A true cuorem bond hasn't been seen between Fae in decades." I shrugged, dropping my gaze to our intertwined hands. "I did some research."

"How long have you suspected?"

"It was actually Elisa who first mentioned it."

"The healer?"

I nodded again. "She noticed I was particularly taken by you from the start. But back then, we didn't know exactly what you were. A cuorem bond between Fae in general is unusual, but between Light and Shadow is unheard of." My thoughts flickered back to Aidan's admission.

Aelia was born of both Light and Shadow. Her parents were forced to go into hiding to protect her because of the prophecy. When they could no longer hide the truth, they bound her powers and left her in my care.

"So *we* are fated mates?" Her mouth curled around the words as if she were tasting them, rolling them across her tongue.

"I believe so—no, I'm absolutely certain of it." My lips melted into a smile once more. I hadn't realized how much keeping the truth from her had been weighing on me. Nor did I expect the rush of relief and excitement at finally telling her.

Her head cocked to the side, brows knitted. "How can you be sure?"

With our hands still interlocked between us, I leaned forward until our lips brushed. My heart punched my ribs, pulse hammering in my ears like a relentless drum. It took all my restraint to keep the kiss chaste and not fully capture those tempting lips with my own. Tiny sparks of *rais* and *nox* zipped between our palms, and a rush of heat raced below my waist.

"Because, princess, as heart-stoppingly beautiful as you are, and as mesmerizingly handsome I am, *that* is not normal."

Chapter Forty-Two

elia

I drew in a breath, the chaos of sensations warring in my chest impeding the normal functioning of my lungs. Reign and I were fated mates? *Cuore*? I couldn't seem to wrap my head around the concept, even with the inexplicable connection I'd felt to him from the start. And he'd felt it too?

My breaths continued to come fast and uneven as my heart stomped out an erratic staccato. Those dark eyes pierced mine, daring me to speak, to move, to do something. Another kiss could possibly help...

"Say something." Reign's request seemed to echo my thoughts.

"Can you read my mind?" I blurted.

The corner of his lip twitched. "I wish..." He lowered his hands, tugging mine along with them. With our fingers still linked together, his expression grew serious. "If we complete the bond, we would eventually be able to feel each other's emotions, hear each other's thoughts, and sense physical sensations from one another, regardless of the distance separating us."

My gods, I wasn't sure I was ready for Reign to have unfettered access to all my innermost thoughts and feelings. My expression must have painted a vivid picture of my fear because a curtain of darkness vanquished that hopeful look in his eye.

"You still don't trust me." His words were nothing but a faint whisper.

He dropped his gaze to our interlaced hands, mouth slanted in a hard line.

"It's not that simple," I murmured, tipping up his chin to force his eyes to mine. "I trust you with my life, Reign Darkthorn. There is no doubt in my mind that you would put me before anyone else, anything else, no matter the cost. The issue I have is with that cost. Your ruthless methods are what frighten me, and the lengths that you'll go to in order to protect me. I fear that you'll continue to keep truths from me in a misguided attempt to shield me from the harsh reality."

"It's Reign of Umbra," he whispered.

"What?"

"My name, Aelia. As a prince of the Court of Umbral Shadows, my name is Reign of Umbra, not Reign Darkthorn." He exhaled a pained breath. "Darkthorn is a surname I adopted to conceal my true identity."

Of all the truths he'd kept hidden, this seemingly insignificant one vexed me the most for some absurd reason. Of course, I'd considered it, much as I had questioned my own surname. But still, it only cemented the fact that I knew nothing about this male.

"Just as I assume Ravenwood isn't your true surname either."

And just like that, the irritation lessened because he had managed to read my mind once again, and he was right. If I wasn't born a Kin, my real family would certainly not have adopted the typical naming convention of the powerless born in Feywood.

We remained trapped in a void of silence for an endless moment, my spiraling thoughts providing more than enough company. A long minute later, I lifted my gaze to meet his tormented one. "What now?"

"Run away with me."

Reign had said it before, upon my return from Feywood, before I knew all his deepest, darkest secrets. I wasn't certain he truly meant it then, but this time, I could read the conviction in his unfaltering gaze.

He released one of my hands to caress my cheek, pinning those shimmering pools of midnight to mine. "It's the only way to ensure your safety and that of the entire realm. We can finally be together without the gods' forsaken prophecy looming over our shoulders."

"What does the prophecy have to do with us being together?"

His lips twisted, and darkness descended across his perfectly carved features. "I'm not certain, but—"

"You're not certain, or you're afraid to tell me?"

That façade, the calm and collected professor he frequently donned crumbled. A fury of emotions glistened in his eyes as he regarded me, clutching my cheek. "I'm so damned angry, Aelia," he cried. "I'm fucking furious and... and afraid of how much I love you and—" His mouth crashed into mine, the tempest of emotions clashing between us like a violent storm, unyielding and raw, threatening to sweep us both into its depths.

Logically, I knew I should stop him. There was more he was going to say, and I was certain I needed to hear it, but I'd lost all control of my senses. With Reign's tongue dancing with mine, his fingers diving into the hair at the back of my neck as he tilted my head to just the perfect angle, there was no room for thought.

It was only feeling, raw and powerful, like the untamable nature of our dragons. I was swept into the deluge with those three words that would lead to my undoing. Gods, it was all I ever wanted, to be loved by Reign. And to be free to love him back. And Raysa, I did love him. Too much. But everything I'd confessed before remained. How could you truly love someone you didn't fully trust?

Reign's free hand clamped around my waist, dragging me into his lap so that I straddled him. The proof of his desire glided against my apex, and an embarrassing moan escaped my lips. I could feel his own tip into a smile against my mouth.

"Let's complete the bond tonight, and we can be across the continent by morning," he breathed as he dropped kisses along my jaw.

"How does one complete the bond?" I panted, the haze of lust all-consuming. I'd blame the blooming cuorem, but attraction had never been an issue between us.

"I make love to you all night, *princess*, and we seal it with a blood vow."

Oh! My heart leapt at my ribs like a battering ram and fiery heat coiled low in my belly at his explanation.

With his hands now sliding down my back to palm my bottom, he pressed me more firmly against his arousal. Fire blazed between my thighs as he rubbed me against his hard length. My back arched, the frenzy of sensations taking over my body in complete control. I ran one hand through his dark, wild hair while the other explored the contours of his muscled back.

He paused the licking and nibbling to meet my gaze. "Aelia, what do you say? Will you be mine, forever?"

Gods, the 'yes' was perched at the tip of my tongue. I could not dream of anything better than a lifetime with Reign. But what of everyone else? If we ran away, I would never be able to see

Aidan again, or Rue and Sy, or any of my friends. And what of the prophecy? What if there was a way to be that beacon of hope? I couldn't just condemn the realm with my own selfishness.

Hot tears gathered in my eyes, a rush of emotion constricting my throat. "I love you, Reign Dark—whatever your name may be. I will *always* love you, in spite of all the terrible things you've done and all those you will continue to do in my name. But I cannot run. It is not in my blood. If I truly am this child of twilight, then it is my duty to reshape our destiny and bring forth a new dawn to our realm." A sob built in my chest, sending a tremor through my shoulders.

Reign's eyes remained pinned to mine, the light vanishing as I forced out the words.

"I love you," I kissed him again. "And I am so sorry."

He stiffened beneath me, the layers of armor he wore disintegrating.

"I just need more time to sort through all of this, to discover the truth of who I am and what it means."

"We don't have time, Aelia!" he growled, his hands sliding up to grip my waist. "If we don't leave now, it will be too late."

"But *why*?"

He gritted his teeth, the tendon in his jaw feathering.

"Tell me," I hissed, framing his face with my hands.

"Because all those years ago, when my father began training me for this mission, he forced me to make a vow, Aelia. Finding the child of twilight isn't only my duty, but a blood oath he forced upon me. Do you remember what it felt like when I bound you to our oath?"

Oh gods, no. Invisible bands laced around my lungs, growing tighter with every breath. The crushing weight pressing into my chest was permanently embedded in my mind. If I hadn't agreed to the deal the night of the Winter Solstice, I would have died.

"If the king has any inkling of who you are, he will call in my debt, and I will have *no* choice."

This could not be happening. It simply wasn't fair.

"So you would kill me?" The words came out surprisingly steady, considering the whirlwind of emotions battering my insides.

"Of course not," he hissed. "I could *never* hurt you. Which would leave me with only one option... to take my own life to keep my father from forcing me to steal yours."

Chapter Forty-Three

A*elia*

"No," I cried. "There must be another way." The murky insides of Reign's chamber blurred around me as I processed the devastating truth. One of us must die.

"There is no way out of a blood oath, Aelia. Trust me, I know. Ever since I suspected who you might be and, more importantly, who you might be *to me*, I've been poring through the ancient texts in the library hoping to find some sort of reprieve. The cuorem bond is sacred, gifted by the gods themselves. I cannot fathom them doling out such a cruel fate."

He curled his arms around my waist so that I was once more flush against the hard planes of his torso. The full body contact set my nerve endings aflame. He pressed his forehead to mine, our breaths mingling.

"Our only hope is to run. Please, Aelia. If my dying would save you from the prophecy, I would gladly offer my soul to Noxus, but I fear what will happen when I'm gone..."

"Don't say that." A single tear spilled over, then another. How could I be forced to choose between abandoning everything I've ever known and saving the male I love, *my mate*?

Reign swept his finger across my cheek, catching the first tear. Then he pressed his lips to my skin, kissing each and every one after. He held me tight against his reassuring form until I could cry no more.

Once the sobs sputtered away and my shoulders stopped trembling, he slowly unraveled his muscled arms from around my back. My body felt the loss of his acutely.

He pressed a chaste kiss to my forehead before shifting and dropping me onto the mattress beside him. "If you choose to stay, we will have to find a way to break the bond."

"W-what... why?"

"With all the time we spend together, it will become unbearable. Even incomplete, the effects will be debilitating for both of us. I can barely control myself as it is. Then there is always the possibility of undesirable side effects..." He shook his head, misery carved into his jaw. "The cuorem bond desires to be completed, it's practically a sentient force, compelling us together. If anything were to happen to me, I don't want you to suffer—"

"Damn it, Reign, it's not as if I can simply stop loving you."

"No, I imagine that will take time to wear off." A rueful grin ignited a spark in his dark irises. "But there are steps that can be taken to hasten the severing of the connection."

"Like what?" The notion sounded completely horrifying.

He heaved out a pained breath. "Like... developing feelings for another."

Pain lanced through my chest at the mere insinuation. Just seeing Reign talking with Liora had sent pangs of jealousy ripping through my insides. I couldn't imagine what it would feel like to be forced to stand by as he actively pursued someone else.

"No," I spat. "Absolutely not."

"There's no time to argue, princess. I'm afraid it's only a matter of time before one, if not both, of the kings discovers the truth. And when they do, we'll be out of options." He rose, the bed screeching beneath him, and offered a hand. "Come, I'll take you back to your room."

Maybe it was this burgeoning bond, or perhaps, I'd simply come to know Reign that well, but the agony in his gaze rooted my feet to the spot. When I didn't place my hand in his, those dark brows knitted as he regarded me.

My thoughts were tormented; denying Reign was the most difficult thing I had ever been forced to do. Under any other circumstances, I would have leapt into his arms and begged him to complete the bond. Claws of indecision lashed through my chest, tearing at my ribs. I wanted him, loved him, more than anything.

"Can we pretend, once more, just for tonight?" My words were a rushed whisper, as if speaking them more quickly would erase their very existence.

"Princess..." A rough growl vibrated Reign's chest as he stood over me.

"I'm not asking you for anything," I swiftly added.

"I know you're not. It's my restraint that worries me." A wicked grin crawled across his face, and gods, I just wanted to bask in its fierce beauty.

"Please?" I reached for his offered hand and when he reluctantly took it, I tugged him to the edge of the bed so that he stood between my legs. I needed this moment of intimacy, this final time together... for closure. I wasn't sure such a thing existed, but I had to try.

"This is the opposite of what we should be doing if we wish to break the bond."

I rose from the bed and onto my tiptoes and brushed my lips against his. A shudder raced through his body so violently it vibrated against my own. "Just. One. Night." I punctuated each word with a kiss.

By the time the last one fell, Reign claimed my lips with the ferocity of a storm of *nox* unleashed, each kiss a crashing wave, demanding and possessive, as if he could imprint his very soul onto mine. And a part of me was certain he already had.

We toppled back onto the bed, scrambling from the swirl of sheer power raging between us. Reign hovered over me, his corded arms pinning me to the mattress. A frenzy of shadows whipped around us, icy tendrils crawling over my skin. His lips ravaged mine, devouring my mouth, then moving down to nibble at the curve of my jaw and then down my neck. Every touch was pure heaven, like the gods-blessed *rais* raining down on me.

Reign wedged his hips between my thighs, his arousal rubbing exactly where I needed it. Gods, I wanted to shred the clothes between us. I needed to feel his skin against my own. A pulsing presence demanded it. It was as if Reign had unlocked something deep inside me when he explained the existence of the cuorem bond.

That pulsating, insatiable sensation had been there all along, only I'd never been able to put a name to it.

He rocked his hips against mine, igniting a fire that could set the entire campus ablaze. Gods, why was I fighting this again? Every touch, every breath, every moment with Reign felt so right.

As his lips assaulted mine, his hands traveled unexplored areas beneath my sleeping gown, leaving a trail of fire in its wake. "Oh, princess, the things you do to me..." he murmured, voice laced with desire. "You have no idea how frayed the fine tethers of my restraint are right now." His fingers crawled up the inside of my thigh until they found the soft silk of my panties. He ran his finger across the sensitive hollow, and I gasped as he hit the taut bundle of nerves at my core.

"I think I do," I rasped out. Knowing this could be the last time we were together only heightened the heated moment, magnifying every lingering touch. My hips thrust, unbidden, my body moving instinctively against his circling finger.

I reached between us, desperate to touch him. My fingers latched onto the hem of his tunic and dragged it over his head. My hand met warm skin, rippling with finely sculpted muscle beneath. I never thought it would be possible for such an unyielding form to bring so much comfort. He was everywhere, all consuming, his shadows icy tendrils licking over my heated flesh. As much as I reveled in their ghostly touch, nothing was better than his hands, his lips, all of his flesh and blood blanketing me in his essence.

My hand crept lower, fingers trailing each carved indentation of his abdomen until I reached his trousers. I wanted to feel him, revel in the touch of his desire *for me*. I slid my hand beneath the waistband, and he froze above me, his entire body going absolutely still.

"Aelia…" A warning growl parted his lips.

"I just want—"

"I cannot be held responsible for what comes next, princess. If you keep pushing me to the edge, it's only a matter of time until I fall. Or worse, jump."

A ridiculous smile melted across my lips to think I had that sort of power over him. The great prince of shadows was crumbling beneath *my* touch.

Before he could stop me, my hand closed around his silky hardness. A moan escaped through his clenched teeth followed by a string of curses to the gods, or maybe they were praises, I couldn't quite be sure in the thrill of the moment.

He thrust his hips, and I slid my hand up and down his length. He was slick with desire, and the thought alone had me giddy. I had no idea what I was doing, but he seemed to enjoy it. "It's your turn." A devious grin stretched across his face as his fingers slid beneath my panties and dipped inside me.

Now I was the one groaning.

Reign had been the only male to touch me there, to elicit

that sort of response from my body. It was incredible and terrifying, all in the same instant.

"Gods, you feel so good," he groaned. "If I close my eyes just right, I can pretend I'm inside you, claiming you as mine."

A sliver of my heart fractured at the confession. I wanted this, I needed him so badly, but I couldn't forsake everyone I loved... could I? There had to be another way for us to be together, and I would find it. Promises were broken every day in Feywood. Surely, there must be a way to sever a Fae blood vow.

Running away was not an option, but neither was losing the first male I loved. The male I was born to love.

Reign's movements grew more frantic, and his devastating fingers followed his pace, drawing me from my dismal thoughts back to the heated moment. That insatiable fire began to build, brilliant embers scorching through my veins. His eyes locked to mine, the dark abyss like molten obsidian, firelight dancing across the night.

I could feel his climax approaching, much as I could feel mine. The raging pleasure soared through me, stealing the breath from my lungs. A tremor surged from the base of my spine down to my toes and all the way up to my fingertips. For an endless minute, I didn't breathe, I couldn't think. I was nothing but pure pleasure, caught in Reign's adoring gaze.

He hurtled over the precipice an instant later with my name on his lips, his entire body shuddering above me, the intense vibrations coursing through my own. We remained there, locked in each other's arms, neither speaking nor moving as the echoes of pleasure thrummed between us.

Minutes passed—or perhaps even hours. I was too scared to move, to shatter this fleeting moment of pretend. Because once it was over, we would be forced to face the reality: Reign was still oathbound to kill me, and I still refused to run.

He was the first to break the heavy silence, lifting his hand to my cheek and caressing my flushed skin. "If that didn't change your mind, I'm not sure anything will." A sinful grin brightened the darkness settling into his expression.

"I love you, Reign, and I promise to find a way out of this, somehow. If the gods chose us to be fated mates, I refuse to believe they would be so cruel as to bestow this bleak destiny upon us."

"I wish I had your relentlessly optimistic nature, princess." He pressed a gentle kiss to the corner of my mouth, and my heart sputtered out a dismal beat. "But I don't... So I must be realistic about our future, despite the agony it will cause me."

"So our pretend time is over?"

"Soon, yes. But if this is truly to be our final intimate moments together, let us not waste them." He hauled me into his side, curling his body around mine. "Rest, starlight."

I must have fallen asleep because at some point in the middle of the night, Reign woke me. I watched him, still groggy from sleep, as he pushed himself off the bed, heaving out a breath. "Come, I'll take you back to the dormitory. The third Umbral Trial begins in a few days, and it will take place across the river. Everyone will be watching, Aelia."

And just like that, we were back to professor and student, mentor and mentee. After everything we'd been through, we were once again reduced to this. Clenching my teeth, I bit back another round of tears. I'd let them fall once I reached the privacy of my chambers.

I was Aelia, carved of stone, and I must find that strength if I wished to not only survive, but also to create a future worth living.

Chapter Forty-Four

elia

The days came and went, and with Reign doing his damnedest to keep his distance, every moment was excruciating. Despite his decree, he was still my mentor, which obligated him to spend *some* time with me. But he'd completely shut down, the cold Shadow Fae I'd met upon my arrival at the Conservatory was back in full effect.

I tried not to be bitter, to remind myself that in Reign's mind I had rejected him. He'd confessed so much, was willing to give up everything for me, and I simply couldn't reciprocate.

Gods, I wished I could see Aidan, talk to him, beg for his advice. Only a few more weeks until the term ended, and I'd finally be allotted my time off. I vowed to go directly to Feywood the moment we were set free.

All you have to do is survive the next two trials. Sol's voice cut through my mental musings.

Which I will, obviously. I stalked toward the flight field where my dragon awaited, talons pawing at the earth. Rumor had it that the final trial would be an airborne one, so Rue, Symon and I had planned to meet twice a week to practice aerial maneuvers with our skyriders in addition to our daily Offensive Flight class.

What's got you in a mood? I could practically see the twitch of my dragon's lips as I approached. He was the first to arrive, neither Griff nor Windy were anywhere in sight.

You know why.

If you're so heartbroken over your dear professor, why didn't you escape with him?

You can't be serious? You truly believe running is the answer?

Sol snorted and spirals of silver smoke drifted from his nostrils. *I didn't say that. I simply asked why you chose otherwise. A cuorem bond is a rare gift, one that is not easily returned to the gods.*

I thought you hated Reign. I reached the intolerable dragon and began to scale his leg, using the knobby protrusions as steppingstones.

I never said that, little Kin. I only warned you not to trust him. And I was correct, wasn't I? He was keeping yet another secret from you.

Multiple, actually. Not only did he suspect us of being *cuoré*, he conveniently failed to mention his mission to destroy the child of twilight was also a binding blood pact. *Did you know about the cuorem bond? Reign said one hadn't been seen among the Fae in decades, but seeing as you've been alive for centuries over the course of your reincarnations, surely, you had heard of it?*

I had, yes.

I slid into my riding position, nestled between the indents of his wing bones. *And?*

I may have suspected it.

Then why didn't you say something? Gods, why did everyone believe lying to me was the best way to keep me safe?

Because I feared what it meant.
That I had Shadow Fae blood muddling my veins?
Yes. Nothing good comes from inter-court mating.

A swell of irritation surged through our bond, bloating my chest. Of course, he would say that. It was the reason he and Phantom were torn apart.

Need I remind you that I could be a result of inter-court mating?

Exactly my point. I could almost hear the snicker. I bit my tongue, despite the desire to tear into him for lying to me and for his snarky comment. Now we would both be in foul moods.

"Getting a head start?" Rue's voice filtered through my thoughts, putting an abrupt end to our conversation. I twisted my head over my shoulder toward the Hall of Luce and found my roommate and Symon trudged across the field arm-in-arm.

"We missed you at supper time," Sy called out.

"I wasn't hungry." I nudged Sol in the side, forcing him to turn toward my approaching friends.

"It's the third meal you've skipped this week." Rue lifted an admonishing brow.

"Sorry, Mother, I promise I won't do it again."

It wasn't the first time my perceptive roommate had commented on my dismal state, but I'd brushed off her questions like I often did regarding all things Reign. I couldn't tell her about the cuorem bond without raising suspicions about my bloodline, so as usual, I was forced to lie to my closest friends. Which I hated.

"Someone is in a mood," Sy quipped.

A knowing glance passed between my friends. "Ignore her, she's been like that all week, but she refuses to say why."

"It's nothing," I snarled.

The flapping of wings turned my attention skyward where Symon's tawny gryphon and Rue's silver Pegasus appeared from between the fluffy clouds. Unlike Sol who was forced to nest far off in the Alucian Mountain range, my friends' skyriders remained in the stalls on the far side of campus. I often thought of poor Sol alone on the jagged peaks. Though Windy and Griff were no longer terrified of being eaten by him, they also weren't exactly playmates.

"So where shall we go today?" Sy asked as he mounted.

"Let's go to the north, toward the Darkmania Falls," Rue replied once she was seated atop Windy. "I've heard they're beautiful."

My heart skipped a beat at the mention of the waterfall along the Shadow Court border that I'd visited with Reign last term. Visions of his body blanketing mine in that cold cave surged to the surface. Dispelling the painful memories, I blurted, "Or we could go south, instead."

"I'd rather avoid the Wilds, if it's all the same to you." A jagged edge laced Rue's tone, and I felt awful. How could I have made such an inconsiderate comment when now both of her brothers had been called to fight along the border?

"I'm sorry," I murmured. "I didn't think—"

She waved a nonchalant hand. "No, it's fine. Let's not talk about it, okay?"

I exchanged a quick glance with Symon whose lips were pressed into a tight line. Gods, I was a terrible friend. I'd been so wrapped up in my own misery, I'd barely considered how she was faring without Heaton.

The thunderous flapping of our three skyriders broke the silence of the tense moment, and an instant later, we were all skyborne. With Sol's immense size, I was forced to remain a few yards away from my friends, while they flew side by side.

Throughout the thirty-minute journey, amidst occasional light-hearted banter, we practiced defensive and offensive maneuvers with and without the use of *rais*. By the time the towering crags of the Darkmania Falls loomed ahead, I was exhausted and depleted of energy. Even Sol's wingbeats seemed sluggish.

"How about we take a dip in the falls before we head back?"

I called out to my friends, the glittering celestial glyph I'd drawn amplifying my voice.

"Yes," they chorused back.

As we began the descent, the familiar sound of enormous pounding wings echoed overhead. I tipped my head back to search the darkening sky, but only shadows remained.

Sol, did you hear that?

His nostrils flared. *Yes, but whatever it was, it seems to have left already.*

There was only one other dragon I could imagine it could have been. *Phantom?*

Too far to tell.

"Come on, Aelia!" Rue's voice jerked my attention toward the quickly approaching ground. "Last one in is a rotten gryphon egg!"

Sol tilted his wings, and we barreled toward the earth, the cascades glittering beneath the moonlight of the Shadow Court. Despite the hollow carving out my chest at finding myself here once again without Reign, a tiny flicker of excitement propelled me forward. Spending a few hours splashing in the cool pond beneath the waterfall with my friends sounded like the perfect way to drown the dark thoughts of the past.

By the time I crawled down Sol's leg, Rue and Symon were already chin deep in the lagoon, their clothes scattered along the shore. Thank the gods we were on the dark side of the divide which allotted a modicum of privacy as I stripped down and ran into the glittering pool.

"That's my girl!" Rue cheered as I hit the water and sank beneath the swirling eddies.

The icy droplets rushed my skin, and I gasped the moment I rose to the surface. "It's freezing!"

"It's not that bad." A familiar voice erupted from the shadows, and every tiny hair on my body stood at attention. My head spun over my shoulder to the cavern behind the glistening waterfalls, the very one Reign and I had slept in all those months ago.

Ruhl emerged from the cascade, dark locks plastered to his face and as bare as the day he was born. He ran his hand through his hair, tossing the wet strands back and I kept my gaze pinned to his eyes, refusing to allow them to wander south. "Well, hello there, little Kin. Fancy meeting you here on my side of the Luminoc."

Rue and Symon froze, their wary gazes locked on the Shadow heir.

Of course, they had no idea we knew each other as anything other than rivals from the trials. No one did.

"Ruhl," I bit out. With a quick glance over my shoulder, I confirmed my daggers were still hidden beneath my pile of clothing behind the nearby brush.

He glided closer, a storm of shadows curling around his bare form. "Here for a leisurely swim without your mentor?"

"No, not exactly. We were out training and needed to cool off." I moved beside Rue and Symon, senses alert and ready to summon my *rais* to the surface. I never knew which version of Ruhl I'd encounter, the ruthless one whose dragon tried to incinerate me or the cordial one I'd chatted with at the ball at the commencement of the Umbral Trials.

"Mmm, interesting." His lips curled into a smile. "Where is that Shadow Fae traitor?"

"I have no idea, I'm not his keeper."

The smirk only grew bolder. He was taunting me, and I knew it very well. But if he dared speak the truth, it would only condemn him as well. From what I understood of King Tenebris, he'd murder his own heir if he dared to out Reign. Which left us at this awkward standstill.

"Are you prepared for the next trial?" His dark brow arched, trapping me in that hypnotic stare. "Perhaps, we'll be paired once again."

Realization slammed into me as I took in that devious

smile. He'd done it on purpose... somehow, he'd convinced Malakar to enlist us together in the trial. But why?

"Do you have any insights as to what the next trial might be?" Rue asked.

For a second, I'd nearly forgotten my friends were there.

His dark eyes narrowed as they regarded her, as if he too had forgotten her presence. "I may have an inkling."

"And... care to enlighten us?" Sy spoke up.

"Now, why would I do that? Any information I may have could lead to your advantage."

I fixed him in my steeliest glare. "Because you owe me after the last trial. It was my understanding that Fae weren't in the habit of taking debts lightly."

Ruhl clucked his tongue, drawing closer still, so that his silky shadows nearly touched my nose. It was becoming arduous keeping my gaze fixed to his, instead of dipping lower. "Touché. But if we're keeping score, you owe me from the trial before that."

Curses. Reign had been right. Ruhl had only helped in the gauntlet to force me into his debt.

"I suppose I could give you one little hint, but then the balance will tip in my favor once more."

My hand shot up. "No, keep your information to yourself." A sliver of darkness curled around my fingers, its frosty touch sending a chill up my spine, before returning to its master.

"It will take place in the Feywood Forest, just miles away from your hometown and the dreaded border of the Wilds."

Chapter Forty-Five

R*eign*

I stood at the back of the hall as Professor Litehaus droned on about lightweaving and all the advanced techniques used to form intricate patterns for various magical effects. It was this craft which created the wards that kept the student dormitories impenetrable. I'd added my own shadoweaving powers to Aelia's chamber to ensure she'd be protected the day she arrived at the Conservatory.

At the time, I'd done it for selfish reasons, to ensure the success of my acquisition. Or at least, that was what I had told myself. In retrospect, perhaps even then I already knew. I blew out a breath, knotting my arms across my chest. It no longer mattered what Aelia was to me, she had made her decision and now I had to find a way to live with it.

A part of me had hoped she would change her mind once she'd had time to process the truth about our bond, or even after that incredible night of pretend we shared. Instead, she had remained steadfast in her convictions.

Fucking hell, I was angry and... hurt. I tried my best to keep my careful mask in place, but her refusal had burned more deeply than the banished mark emblazoned into my chest. I had never dared love before her, and now, I understood why the Fae were so weary of it. Binding yourself to someone so wholly only left you vulnerable and weak. I would never let it happen again. Curling my fingers into fists at my sides, I searched for the icy calm I once possessed. Aelia had ruined me, tearing through every wall I'd ever built. Now, without her, I was nothing but a hollow shell, stripped of all that made me whole.

I would continue to protect her to the best of my ability until my dying day, but holding on to the love I had for her was too damned painful. She rejected me. She chose Aidan, her friends, the entire gods' forsaken realm over me. To say my ego was bruised was an understatement. And yet, that selflessness, that ever-shining light was what I loved most about Aelia. As much as I wanted to resent her for it, I simply couldn't.

I despised the notion of severing this bond between us, but I had no other choice. To live with the burgeoning, overpowering sensations it created would send me to an early grave.

The sharp scrape of chair legs across stone drew my attention to the front of the hall where the students now gathered showcasing their wondrous lightweaving abilities. Most practiced illumination sigils, drawing complex designs in the air or on surfaces that emitted specific effects when triggered.

My gaze instinctively tracked to Aelia where she stood beside Liora, watching as her finger traced the air that created a vibrant illusion of Professor Litehaus's form.

The old male clapped, laughing wholeheartedly. "Well done, Liora, very lifelike."

The other students marveled at her skill and a chorus of *oohs* and *ahhs* filled the hall. Had I truly been so blind to Liora's talents? For a first-year, she was quite advanced, oddly so.

Perhaps I needed to start spending more time with her to hone those talents. Not that I'd ever cared to offer more of my free time unless it suited me, but damn it, Aelia had changed me. I suddenly felt responsible for these students, for their lives. At the very least, I should keep an eye on my acquisitions.

"Miss Ravenwood, let's see what you can do." He ticked his head at Aelia, and pure white light sparked across her fingertips. Raising her hand, she drew a brilliant sigil in the air, the dancing glyph vibrating with power I could sense from all the way across the room.

Once it was complete, she turned to Liora with a disarmingly sweet smile. "Walk through it."

The first-year paused before glancing between Aelia and the professor.

"Go ahead." He nodded, urging her on.

The moment Liora's hand brushed the shimmering sigil, thunder clapped, reverberating across the entire hall, and a downpour of concentrated Light energy exploded across the room like a galaxy of shooting stars. Students ducked and dropped to the ground to escape the powerful influx of *rais*.

My mouth curved into a smile, unbidden. I still remembered the days she could barely summon a protective shield. Now, every day her power grew stronger, if not more volatile. Maybe I truly had made a difference in her life.

Professor Litehaus beamed at Aelia, despite the flecks of fiery light singeing the tips of his mustache. "Very well done, young lady. It's been some time since I've seen a starfall cascade."

She dipped her head, offering a small smile, then moved past the other students to find her seat.

"Next?" Litehaus called. "Who would like to demonstrate what they've learned?" As the other first-years scrambled to show off their talents, Aelia marched up the aisle to return to her seat only a row away from where I stood. Her eyes lifted to mine and held.

My heart rioted in my chest, slamming against my ribcage like a wild beast. It had been barely a day since I'd seen her last, but I ached for her. After giving in to that intimate moment last week, the dormant cuorem bond seemed to have awakened. And right now, it was angry, furious at being kept away from its mate.

I knew allowing ourselves that indulgence would only cause more pain in the long run. And still, I couldn't bring myself to regret it.

"Hi." She slid into the empty row, eyes still trained to mine.

"Princess," I whispered, dropping into a dramatic bow.

"Oh, stop that. If anyone should be bowing to anyone else, it should be the other way around." She kept her voice low, so quiet that if I weren't so attuned to her, I doubted I would have made out every syllable.

"After the other night, I'll never stop bowing to you." My jaw slammed shut, instantly regretting the outburst. Good gods, what was that? Clearing my throat, I waited for the blush to retreat from her cheeks. "Are you ready for the trial tomorrow?"

She nodded quickly before taking a step closer, and I wondered if she was even aware she'd done it. Only a single row of desks stood between us now. Was she feeling the pull as desperately as I was?

"I saw Ruhl."

"What? When?" I had to force my feet to keep still when they were begging to leap across the tables separating us.

"The other night when Rue, Symon and I were training. He said the third trial would be in Feywood. Do you know anything about it?"

The surprise must have shown on my face because she drew in a long breath. "Did he give you any more details than that?"

"No. We didn't stay long once Mordrin arrived."

I bristled at the mention of my brother's bloodthirsty

dragon, and fear lanced through my chest. I should have been there, damn it... I should always be there to ensure her safety.

"Sol does not seem partial to him," she continued, so I attempted to refocus on the conversation and forced back the pointless thoughts. "And the feeling appears mutual."

"Mmm. I'm not surprised. Phantom seems to despise him as well. There's some sort of history there, I'm sure, but my skyrider has yet to share. She is oddly reticent when it comes to matters regarding Solanthus."

"Don't you hate it when she doesn't tell you things? Sol finally admitted he suspected about"—she gestured wildly between us—"and never said anything."

"You, or rather we, need to remember that our dragons have lived for centuries through each incarnation. They carry the wisdom of the ages. As a result, they seem to think they know better than us." A rueful chuckle slid out despite the pit of unease lodged in the bottom of my stomach.

"I understand it in theory, but I still hate it."

The slap of footsteps lifted my gaze over Aelia's shoulder to a quickly approaching Liora. She stomped right past my mentee and jabbed a finger at my chest. "How come you taught Aelia to do that starfall thing and not me?" The hurt in her eyes shone as she glanced between us.

"I—I didn't teach her that. When I train with Aelia, we mostly work with my shadows." I dragged a hand across my nape. Had I been doing Liora a disservice by centering all my attention on Aelia? She was my acquisition and, apparently, quite talented. Not that I'd ever concerned myself with fairness before, but somehow Aelia's kind nature continued to rub off on me.

"Why don't you work with me one-on-one?" She inched closer, her hand flattening on my chest.

I could feel the heat of Aelia's glare searing into me from over Liora's shoulder. More than that, it twisted inside me like a poisonous serpent, writhing around my lungs and squeezing the air out.

"You're right, I should," I blurted and took a big step back, so her hand fell between us. Nearly immediately the pressure relented. I glanced up at Aelia and those silver-blue eyes lanced right through me. Continuing to backpedal toward the doors of the great hall, I called out, "We'll create a training schedule later this week after the next trial, Liora. Now, excuse me, but I must go see the headmaster."

Like an apparent coward, I turned tail, fleeing the hall with my shadows wrapped around me like a shield, instead of allowing Aelia to suffer through the jealousy. I pressed my hand to my chest, massaging the tightness away as soon as I stepped outside of the oppressive building. Noxus, as much as I despised the thought, I had to find a way to break this bond, or we would both lose our minds.

Chapter Forty-Six

The whispering forest of darkwood trees loomed only yards away, their leaves a deep, almost unnatural shade of green. It was surreal finding myself once again at the foot of the Feywood Forest for the third Umbral Trial, only this time with my entire first-year class, along with the horde of Arcanum students standing just behind Malakar near the foot of the Luminoc.

One familiar presence was markedly absent within our squad of initiates. Heaton.

It had been more than a week since the Royal Guardians came for him, and we had not heard a word since. He had promised Rue he would be back by the end of the term, and I prayed to all the gods he would keep his word. After this trial, only one more remained, and then within a few weeks, we will have survived our first scholastic year. I still couldn't quite believe it.

You still have this trial and the last to conquer before you can begin to celebrate, little Kin. Sol's voice streamed through my subconscious.

I glanced over my shoulder to the edge of the forest where he and the other skyriders were gathered. *Thanks for the vote of confidence.*

I do not wish to dishearten you, only to remind you that there is still much more you must overcome.

I'm well aware, Sol. As if the trials weren't bad enough, a void had opened up in the center of my sternum. It was a constant, living, breathing source of emptiness. I pressed my hand to my chest and rubbed a small circle. It appeared the morning after that incredible night with Reign and seemed to only grow larger and more painful every day.

It's the cuorem bond. It desires to be completed. Sol's voice was low, filled with anguish. As if he knew exactly what I was experiencing.

When will it get better?

He chuffed, the gruff sound echoing through my mind. *It will be appeased only when you've completed the bond, or eventually go silent if severed.*

I was afraid that was what he would say. *Reign is trying to find a way to dissolve it. He says it's the only way to survive our current predicament, but I refuse to give up.*

I assumed as much. The connection will go quiet in time if left unbound, but it can take years.

I love him, Sol. Gods, I sounded so weak and pathetic.

I know, little one. Even in my mind, his words were like a gentle caress.

I don't want to give him up. There must be some other way for us to be together without causing the utter destruction of our realm. I had confessed everything Reign and I had discussed to Sol once I'd stopped crying that next morning—not that I'd needed to, as I was fairly certain he'd heard it all.

I wish I had an answer for you. What I do know is that an incomplete cuorem bond can have terrible side effects. It is wise for

Reign to consider other alternatives. Then again, severing the tie forcibly can also prove quite uncomfortable for both parties.

"Wonderful," I grumbled out loud. *So we're doomed either way.*

"What's wonderful?" Rue appeared beside me, drawing me from our mental conversation. Symon moved into step beside her, along with the rest of Flare Squad who had assembled along the northern side of the Feywood Forest while I'd been otherwise occupied.

"Nothing," I muttered. "Sol and I were just strategizing." *Lie.*

"First, we must win this trial before we start preparing for the final, aerial one."

"You're right, Rue." I nodded and focused on the line of Shadow Fae assembled across from us. Then I searched the mass of bodies surrounding me for the one that made my blood sing, but Reign was nowhere in sight.

I faced the dark mass across the way once more where another pair of equally disarming orbs found mine and latched on. Ruhl. My heart leapt up, a twinge of fear and something else I refused to name, escalating my pulse. A predatory smile curved his lips, stealing the air from my lungs. I had thought his brother was mercurial, but the young prince was as unpredictable as they came.

Draven clapped his hands and sparks of luminescence rose high into the air, illuminating the murky sky and tearing my gaze free of Ruhl's invasive stare. Now, so close to the border of Feywood, Raysa's blessed light would no longer prove eternal, giving way to inky darkness once the sun set. A part of me looked forward to the moon-drenched, starlit sky, until I reminded myself we'd be spending the night in the dreaded forest.

"Students," the headmaster droned, "welcome to the third Umbral Trial, the Veil of Echoes."

Hushed murmurs rippled across the crowd of first-years.

"For today's event, you will navigate the Feywood Forest, where the boundaries between the past and present blur, and voices of the past guide or deceive. You have until morning to retrieve one of the sacred relics. As in the gauntlet, there are fewer relics than participants." A devious grin curled the corners of his trailing white mustache as he paused. "And this year, in an attempt to foster unity, each of you will be coupled with a student from the opposing academy. Unlike the Mirror of Illusions, you will be forced to work together."

"Oh, gods, not again," I muttered.

"At least you were already paired with the prince," Rue whispered. "What are the chances you'd get stuck with him again?"

"Stuck with who?" Liora poked her head between Sy and Rue, flashing perfectly white teeth. Gods, I hated how beautiful she was.

"Prince Ruhl," Symon replied.

Her lavender irises flicked across the line of Arcanum students to the prince. He stood tall, muscled arms pinned across his chest and clad in all black, much like the other initiates, and still, he stood out. The waves of *nox* leeching from his form so powerful, they reached across the divide.

"I wouldn't mind being paired up with him." A smile stretched across her face, lighting up the brilliant lavender flecks in her eyes.

Of course, she wouldn't. Clearly, she had a thing for Shadow Fae. I'd already witnessed her tireless flirtations with Reign. If she only knew they were brothers... I pushed the dangerous thought to the furthest recesses of my mind and locked it up tight.

Draven had continued to speak during our hushed conversation, but his speech seemed to be coming to a close. Malakar moved beside him and cut off his final words. "As always, there are no rules, other than to survive. The first-years who fail to retrieve a relic, will find themselves guests of the opposing academy for the next week until the trials end." With a dip of his head, he revealed a scroll from the inner folds of his onyx robe. "And now, the pairings..."

A thick silence descended over the crowd as names were called and students emerged from their respective groupings to join their new teammate.

"What is the point of this, anyway?" Symon hissed. "As if it's not bad enough that we have to watch our backs against other Light Fae, now we have to worry about a Shadow Fae partner?"

"I agree. It makes no sense." Not for the first time, I wondered what the headmasters were truly plotting. Or did this go beyond the academies, to the kings themselves?

"Aelia Ravenwood," Draven shouted, "And..."

I froze as the headmaster spoke my name, and my pulse thundered across my eardrums, drowning out all else. Somehow, I knew. I knew whose name would come next before he finished speaking the dreaded words.

"Prince Ruhl of Umbra."

Despite suspecting, my stomach still plummeted to the soles of my boots.

"Oh, Aelia," Rue grumbled.

"That cannot be by accident," Symon interjected. "What are the chances you'd be paired with the prince twice?"

My thoughts exactly. For once, I was relieved Reign wasn't here to witness this. He would have likely lost his temper in front of everyone, which would have done nothing to help our cause.

"Stay strong, little Kin." Symon gently caressed the rounded curve of my ear. I shot him a scowl, though my heart wasn't quite into it. "Just for luck." He smirked.

Rue spun me toward her, hands squeezing my shoulders. "You'll do just fine in there, A. Ruhl is the strongest Shadow Fae of his class, and Draven said you had to work together. This could be a good thing."

Rue was right, but she didn't know the whole story, and as always, I couldn't reveal it without putting her at risk. "As long as he doesn't try to stab me in the back with one of his umbral blades," I muttered.

Again, Reign had forced me to keep my daggers hidden in the safety of the dormitory, leaving me to wield unfamiliar short blades which I'd strapped at my hips. Either way, I'd need to count on my *rais* to win the trial. Searching for my necklace beneath my tunic, I rubbed at the worn medallion. Raysa, protect me.

Ruhl stepped forward, a trail of shadows surrounding him, and I forced my feet to follow. As I passed the row of Light Fae students, Liora popped out once again. "You're so lucky," she whispered. "With the prince as your partner, you'll surely win."

I wished I shared her enthusiasm. Instead, I only mumbled a weak, "Cheers." The female wasn't completely awful, and the only reason I truly disliked her was because of these uncontrollable feelings of jealousy. "Good luck to you as well."

And with that, I marched on and joined Ruhl at the foot of the ever-darkening forest. A line of other initiates had already assembled, most standing in silence beside their life-long enemies-turned-new-partners.

"Well, hello there, Miss Ravenwood." Ruhl dipped into a mocking bow. "Fancy meeting you, yet again. It seems as if fate is drawing us together."

I tensed beside him, curling my arms across my chest. "Fate or you? It seems like too much of a coincidence, wouldn't you agree?"

His dark brow arched, lifting the corner of his lip. "What can I say? The gods work in mysterious ways." That smirk, stars —it reminded me so much of Reign's my chest tightened at the sight.

"Why would you want to be paired with me?" I blurted. There was no point dancing around the topic. If it wasn't Ruhl who'd requested it, then Draven or Malakar were pulling the strings. And if it was the young shadow prince, did he already suspect I was the child of twilight, or was he only trying to get close to me to irritate his elder brother?

"How very arrogant of a simple little Kin to assume such a thing."

"You know very well I'm not a Kin," I growled.

"No, you're not, but you were raised here. I imagine of everyone assembled, you know these woods better than any other arrogant Fae here."

A surge of relief crashed over me before a hint of satisfaction seeped in. "So you did arrange for us to be paired together."

"Maybe, maybe not. I suppose you'll never find out." He smirked again, but this time, a hint of mirth lit up the cold darkness of those piercing orbs.

"Initiates, take your places." Malakar's voice boomed across the gathering crowd.

I glanced down the line and found Rue standing beside a willowy Shadow Fae female, and Symon farther down peering up at a towering male. I only hoped we'd all make it out of this forest alive.

While Ruhl was correct that I'd grown up nearby, what he did not know was how little I knew of the forest. I'd spent most of my life avoiding it at all costs thanks to Aidan's terrifying bedtime stories. In addition to the echoes of the past we would have to battle, we would also have to avoid a variety of bloodthirsty creatures, if the tales were true.

The sharp buzzer rang out, tearing my thoughts away from the grisly images my imagination had conjured. I swallowed hard, my pulse skyrocketing.

Ruhl extended a hand, dipping into a bow, and motioned toward a break in the thick foliage. "After you, duskling."

Chapter Forty-Seven

With the thrashing of bodies racing through the forest and the mad pounding of my heart, I barely had time to contemplate what Ruhl had just called me. *Duskling*? What in the realms was that?

The damp earth squelched beneath my boots as we treaded deeper into the shadow-drenched Feywood Forest. Now was not the time to consider my new nickname. We had until sunrise to locate a sacred relic and avoid all the nasties lurking under the cover of the woods. After my last experience in Mysthallia, I was anxious to be far from the dreaded poisonous trees and wicked creatures.

Ruhl moved silently beside me, his presence a constant reminder of the uneasy temporary alliance between us. I swung my head to the right to peer at the Shadow prince sprinting beside me. "Do you have any idea where the relics might be?"

His lips twisted into a frown. "No, why would I?"

"You seemed to have led your team through the gauntlet in record time, so I thought perhaps you had some sort of special insight."

"If I did, what would I need you for?" Again, that wicked grin.

I considered telling him the truth, that this knowledge he relied upon didn't exist, but instead, I ground my teeth, deciding that letting him think I was valuable would do much more to ensure my safety. "Just because I'm familiar with the forest, doesn't mean I can find these sacred relics."

"I'm aware of that." He began to slow, and I thanked Raysa, because there was no way in the realms I could keep up this break-neck pace for much longer. He wound through the thick copse of darkwoods and pressed his back to a tree, yanking my arm so I halted right beside him. A dozen initiates raced past us, oblivious that we had stopped. The whirlwind of shadows curving to his form began to peel away, tendrils of darkness stretching between the colossal trunks. "Which is why I'll have my shadows do the work for us."

Not for the first time, I was so damned jealous of the Shadow Fae abilities. As powerful as *rais* could be, it never seemed quite as sentient as those whispers of night. Or perhaps, I simply hadn't mastered them yet.

He still leaned against the tree, something predatorial about his stance. Though he seemed at ease, I could feel the buzz of *nox* skimming over my skin.

I took a step away, anxious to escape that invasive yet seductive energy. "What do we do now?"

"Wait until they find something and lead us straight to the relic."

I suddenly felt extremely useless. And if I wanted Ruhl to believe he needed me to win this trial, I had to prove myself valuable. "While you just sit there, I'll scan the forest with my illumination sight."

He released a bored sigh. "Fine, do what you'd like, but

please, try not to get eaten by any of the beasties. Reign is doing his best to convince me you mean nothing to him, but I fear he'd rip my head off if anything happened to you under my watch."

I froze mid-step and whirled around to face him. "He's not lying," I ground out. "There is nothing of substance between us."

"Then why can I hear your heartbeat quicken at the mere mention of his name?"

Heat raced up my neck, only elevating my pulse. "It's lust; that is what you're sensing."

A sinful grin melted across his face, and he pushed off the trunk and swaggered closer. "Well, then, if it's only lust, then I am more than willing to scratch that itch." A gasp escaped my clenched lips as a faint shadow slithered off his form and curled around my neck. "My brother isn't the only one who can command shadows to do his bidding. I'd wager I could have you writhing in pleasure without so much as laying a finger on you."

Oh, goddess. I swallowed hard and squirmed free of the shadow's icy touch. "That would be highly inappropriate," I hissed. Not to mention the fact that Reign would literally murder him once he found out. And still, I couldn't deny the allure of the suggestion. What was wrong with me?

Reign was my cuoré, despite his insistence on breaking our bond. I knew how hurt he was when I refused to run away with him, and I was fully aware that severing our tie was his misguided way of protecting himself. And me. But I still loved him, in spite of everything. So why, then, did I feel even an inkling of temptation?

The crunch of leaves underfoot jerked me from the completely inappropriate musings. *Stars, Aelia, focus!* Ruhl's head whipped over his shoulder, his entire body tensing. *Nox* surged from his pores, swirling with my *rais*, and energy budded in my core.

"What was that?" I whispered.

"I'm not certain, but whatever it is, it's coming."

A deep rumble reverberated through the earth, and my hands shot out to steady myself. The trees trembled and shook, and I watched in awe as their roots sprang up from the hard-packed dirt and began to move, walking on them like legs, much like Melisara's tree had done in Mysthallia. The dense copse literally parted right before us, revealing a clearing bathed in a ghostly silver glow from where the moon peered through the thick canopy. There, in the ancient grove, a creature coalesced through the darkness.

I hissed out a curse.

A hulking beast cloaked in shadows, with eyes like molten gold that glowed with anger emerged into the moonlit clearing. Its multiple limbs, each tipped with deadly claws, scraped against the ground, setting my nerves on edge.

Ruhl tensed beside me, a storm of shadows rising. "A Lurker, one of ours," he murmured, gravely, his voice low. "Ready yourself, duskling."

I nodded, though my distrust for Ruhl clawed at me as fiercely as the Lurker might. What better way to get rid of me than to allow that monster to kill me? The creature charged, a blur of shadow and fury. Ruhl acted first, extending his hand as dark tendrils of shadow sprouted from his fingertips like wicked vines. They raced forward, hissing and spitting, aiming to entangle the beast. But the Lurker was swift. It dodged the onslaught with a guttural snarl that raised the fine hairs on my arms.

Summoning my *rais*, my thoughts whirled back to my Lightweaver's Craft class. I focused, feeling the familiar warm surge of energy pooling in my palms. Light gathered, swirling into brilliant strands that I wove into a blinding net of radiance. With a sharp thrust of my hands, I cast it towards the creature. The light ensnared it, and the Lurker howled its fury as it thrashed against the luminous bonds.

"Now, Aelia! Trap it!" Ruhl shouted over the shrill screams, his own shadows creeping up to reinforce the bonds I had created.

I hesitated, my instincts screaming to flee now rather than trust Ruhl. Yet, with the creature fighting fiercely and the powerful *nox* skimming my *rais*, I knew our combined powers were necessary. Steeling myself, I channeled more light, enhancing the net into an unbreakable cage of brilliance. The creature's howls diminished under the intensity of the light, and its form began to dissipate as the shadows that composed its body melted away.

Ruhl watched, his expression unreadable in the dim light.

We remained silent for a long moment, until the Lurker vanished and nothing but torn shreds of light remained of the net.

"Not bad," he finally conceded with a grudging nod. His shadows receded like the tide, slipping back into his tense form a moment later.

I kept my guard up, still wary of Ruhl's true intentions, but at least I'd proven myself. "Let's move on," I grumbled, already turning away from the now-quiet clearing. "We need to find that relic before something else finds us."

⋈

As the hours passed, Ruhl's scowl grew more murderous. His shadow minions had scoured the forest, returning empty-handed each time. My illumination sight had done no better, unable to discern any traces of energy patterns or hidden magical sources.

Still, I kept moving because it was better than remaining in one place for too long and attracting the attention of some other fearsome Fae beast. Ruhl trudged on behind me, his footfalls growing heavier with each step. It said something of our maturing relationship that I'd allowed my back to him, completely exposed.

Not that I trusted him exactly, but he'd had multiple opportunities to abandon me or worse, and he had yet to act upon any of them.

Judging by the shards of pale blue light that snuck through the curtain of foliage overhead, the moon must have been high in the night sky by now. I was exhausted from the endless march through the forest, and I was also fairly certain we were moving in circles. If Ruhl hadn't figured out I knew nothing about these woods yet, he wasn't half as smart as Reign claimed.

"Are you purposely trying to get us more lost?" Ruhl's voice echoed from behind me, farther back than it should have been.

I spun around and found him seated on the damp earth a few yards back. He held a twig between his fingers, snapping it into smaller and smaller pieces, then tossing the shrapnel into the dirt.

"Of course not," I hissed as I marched toward him.

He swung his head at a giant darkwood and pointed at the deep charcoal bark. Three light slashes had been carved across the trunk. "We passed this tree hours ago," he grumbled. "Three times, to be exact."

Curses. Perhaps Ruhl was smarter than I'd given him credit for.

I slumped down onto the ground beside the tree and leaned my weary bones against the wide trunk. "Maybe we just need to take a little rest." Leaning my head against the rough bark, my weary eyelids drooped, but I couldn't quite relax enough to let them close. Allowing myself to be that vulnerable in the presence of the prince would be foolish. To keep the exhaustion at bay, I blurted the first thing that came to mind. "Don't you find it odd that we haven't encountered any of our teammates?"

Ruhl was now sprawled across the forest floor, staring up into the canopy of dark green. Clearly, he didn't feel the least bit intimidated by me if he was able to relax like that. "I wouldn't be surprised if the entire forest was cast in illusions. There could be another pair just on the other side of that wall of shrubbery for all we know." He shrugged and a swirl of darkness peeled off his form, twirling between his fingertips.

It certainly was a possibility, but I should have been able to pick up on something with my illumination sight. This entire forest was so damned disorienting.

"*Estellira...*" The unearthly hiss sent goosebumps rippling down my exposed arms. "*Estellira*, come to me."

I shot up to my feet, my head whipping back and forth amid the encroaching darkness. "Did you hear that?"

"Hear what?" Ruhl barely tipped his head up.

"*Estellira*, leave him, my darling. It's me, your mother, and I must tell you something." The voice sweetened, a timbre I was certain I'd never heard before and yet recognized all the same. All the air siphoned from my lungs.

"Mother?"

Chapter Forty-Eight

A^{elia}

My legs compelled me forward of their own accord and before I knew what had happened, I was sprinting through the darkness, gnarled branches reaching out and lashing across my face.

"*Estellira*, you're almost there..."

I followed the ethereal voice, blindly, heart thrashing at my ribs. A voice in the far corners of my mind warned me of my stupidity, but I ignored it, that oddly familiar voice drowning all logic and leaving it behind. Tears burned, blurring the edges of my vision, but still I kept going, running deeper into the heart of the forest. "Mother, where are you?"

Rais surged to the surface, that well of power in my core building and bathing my skin in radiant light. Illuminating the woods as I ran, I kept my gaze trained ahead, guided by an invisible tether. I vaguely registered Ruhl's shouts echoing behind me, but I'd lost all control of my limbs. I had no choice but to run toward the haunting, melodic tone.

The ancient grove parted into another clearing with dew-kissed grass and moonlight shimmering overhead. In the center, a spectral form appeared, wisps of midnight hovering just over the ground.

My pulse hammered in my ears like a relentless drum as I regarded the ghostly form wavering on an invisible breeze. "*Estellira*, you found me."

"Mother, is it really you?" I crept closer, my breaths coming fast and uneven.

"It is, my child." The apparition pulsed with shadows and something more. An unfamiliar suffocating energy floated in the air, thickening the atmosphere.

"Why did you abandon me?" The question fled my lips before I could stop it.

A warm chuckle set my frazzled nerves at ease. "Oh, silly girl, I never abandoned you. I only did what was necessary to save you. Believe me when I say that leaving you truly broke my heart."

Tears pricked my eyes, tightening my throat. I moved closer still, my hands twitching at my sides, desperate to touch, to confirm this insane illusion. "Save me from what?"

"From that cursed prophecy, *estellira*..."

A gasp pursed my lips, and my head began to spin. "It's true, then? I am this child of twilight?"

"You are, my love, but no one else can ever know the truth. It is why we fought so hard to keep you hidden."

"Well, that sort of went to shit," I hissed. "The goddess marked me. Everyone knows I'm Light Fae, Mother, and Reign thinks I'm Shadow Fae, and then Melisara, a Spellbinder, said my powers were bound by *zar*. How is that even possible? And Reign says we're cuoré and he's the catalyst in all of this, but I love him and—" All my fears spilled out, a torrent of all the crushing anxieties I've held at bay for months. "What am I supposed to do?" A sob wracked my shoulders, my voice trembling. "Help me, please."

The cloud of pure obsidian brightened with specks of starlight and surged closer. "Oh, my dear, *estellira*, I am so sorry. I wish I could be here for you."

"What happened to you? What will happen to me?"

The dark form wavered, then sputtered out, and the flicker of hope in my chest was snuffed out.

"Mother!" I cried.

"Curses, Aelia, never run off like that again!" That deep timbre squeezed the remaining air from my lungs.

I spun around to find the clearing dark once more, with the exception of the furious Shadow Fae looming at the edge of the woods.

"What in the realms made you take off like that?" Ruhl stalked closer, dark brows furrowed. "For a second, it was as if you'd completely vanished…"

Banishing all thoughts of the apparition, I swallowed hard. "I—I thought I heard something."

"Of course you did. This is the Veil of Echoes, or did you forget already? None of it is real, duskling. They are only voices meant to deceive."

But goddess, she seemed so real.

My shoulders rolled, caving in on me as Ruhl glared down at me like I was some disobedient child. A tear threatened to spill over, and mortification heated my cheeks. *Oh, gods, please don't let him see.*

His jaw twitched as his hard gaze tracked over the traitorous gleam in my eyes. I waited for him to say something, but he never did. Instead, he only whirled on his heel back toward the forest. Once he was a few steps ahead of me, he cocked his head over his shoulder. "Are you coming or not? I believe I've found a way to find those damned relics."

Drawing in a steadying breath, I forced my feet forward.

"I know you and my brother have a secret..." Ruhl's quiet voice sent my heart on a rampage as we strolled through the murky forest.

"There's no secret, Ruhl." I kept my gaze steady, focusing on the cluster of shadows we were walking toward. I was impressed with the calmness in my tone given my insides were a raging mess.

His footfalls suddenly stopped, and he whirled on me, a blanket of shadows descending over us. I sucked in a breath and reached for the blade at my hip, clenching it in my fist, poised to strike.

The corner of his lip tipped up as he regarded the knife. "Relax, duskling. I'm not going to kill you. As I said before, my brother clearly harbors feelings for you beyond what he's letting on. I've known the male my entire life, and I've never seen him like this. He tries to hide behind this false bravado, but anyone with eyes can tell he's completely taken by you." His eyes narrowed as if he were trying to discern the truth from the darkest depths of my soul. "The question is *why*?"

"I'm incredible in bed."

A deep chuckle broke the uneasy silence, and a flock of garblers took flight overhead, their wing flaps echoing the drumming of my wild pulse. "I don't doubt that." He smirked, eyeing my blade. "The violent ones always are."

"Why are you so interested in Reign's love life, anyway?" I sheathed the knife but propped my hand on my hip at the ready.

"You just answered your own question. *Love* life, duskling. He's never had one, never been remotely interested in a female beyond the carnal urges."

I couldn't deny the thrill of satisfaction that admission brought along with it. It wasn't that I questioned Reign's feelings, but a little reassurance was always nice. Instead of continuing this conversation—which had nowhere good to go—I deflected. "Why do you keep calling me duskling?"

He clucked his tongue, striding closer so that I staggered back into the trunk of a particularly large darkwood. "Duskling, a creature of the dusk, neither fully in the light nor completely in the dark."

A chill slithered up my spine and goosebumps cascaded down my arms. Crossing them over my chest, I rubbed away the damning evidence. "Cute," I retorted.

"I suppose it makes sense, given your upbringing in Feywood." His eyes searched mine, searching for a kink in my armor.

I would give him no such victory. "I've never believed anyone to be truly good or evil, light or dark, Ruhl. Even you must have some redeeming qualities. So, you're right, duskling does suit me."

His lips curved into a smile, and gods, if he wasn't such a bastard, I might admit how handsome he was, how much he resembled Reign.

I pushed off the tree and put some distance between us. "Not that I'm not enjoying this getting-to-know-you bit, but you said you had a way to find the relics?"

He ticked his head at the cloud of shadows hovering only a few yards away. "When you abandoned me earlier, I got to thinking. Why would Draven and Malakar force us to work together unless we needed both *rais* and *nox* to find the relics?"

"You know, you're smarter than you look, prince."

Ruhl grinned, the mirth actually seeping into his icy obsidian irises. "Just because I'm pretty doesn't mean there's not more behind the handsome mask."

"I'm beginning to see that."

"And I'm glad you agree I'm handsome." Now the smirk turned purely wicked.

With a dramatic roll of my eyes, I hissed, "You were saying..."

He motioned toward the murky swirling shadows. "I

suggest we combine our energy and send it out as one. Perhaps then, the ancient artifacts will reveal themselves to us."

I nodded despite the hint of unease. Would Ruhl be able to feel something different in my *rais*? Reign never had, but we had never used our combined powers like this. I had only siphoned from his *nox* to bolster my *rais*.

"Ready?" He dipped his head at the buzzing midnight cloud.

"Right." Summoning the radiant light deep within my core, I urged it to the surface until my fingertips glowed with power. Casting it toward the coiling shadows, the opposing energies hissed and crackled as they danced around each other. A swirling vortex of light and dark whipped and twirled into a tornado of power expanding to the treetops.

"Impressive..." Ruhl rasped. "I can't say I've ever seen or felt anything like that before."

"Neither have I." My head tipped back, taking in the storm of shadows and light as it spread across the forest. But it was nothing compared to the tempest roiling within.

Not more than a few seconds later, a satisfied smile curved Ruhl's lips, and he turned toward the south. Wrapping his hand around my forearm, he tugged me forward. "Come on, duskling, we've got something."

Chapter Forty-Nine

A *elia*

Ruhl raced after the coil of both light and dark energy, a living, sentient thing pulling us deeper into the gloomy woods. I sprinted after him, determined not to get left behind despite his longer strides. The farther we got, the quicker I realized we weren't heading toward the center of the forest as I'd first imagined. Instead, we were traveling toward the southern edge. Soon I was able to make out the rolling hills that encroached the border along the Wilds.

Stars, where had they hidden those relics?

As the looming trees began to thin out, muffled voices echoed at a close distance. Ruhl slowed, throwing his arm out so I nearly slammed right into it. "Shh," he hissed.

I drew in a deep breath to slow the rapid thrumming of my pulse after the sprint across the woods and moved into step beside him. We kept to the shadows rimming the ring of darkwoods along the southern edge of the thicket.

A familiar form coalesced just beyond the treeline and I muttered a curse. Lucian. Raysa, why did this male always appear in the most inopportune moments? Another blonde head of hair bobbed beside him, the gold circlets lining his pointed ear sending my stomach plummeting.

"It was a team event, you fool," Belmore hissed at his friend as he circled something on the ground. From this distance, I couldn't quite see below his kneecaps.

"Those Shadow Fae females were only slowing us down, and you know it. I did us a favor." Lucian kicked at whatever lay between them.

Ruhl inched closer, his icy breath spilling across the shell of my ear. "Do you know those two?"

"Unfortunately," I grumbled.

"Well, they're standing between us and the relic. Either they're too stupid to realize, or they're guarding it to keep others from finding it."

"My gildings are on the former."

He smiled. "Good, then let's claim what's ours." He strode forward, but I slapped my arm across his chest without thinking. His dark gaze whipped to mine, a mix of surprise and fury swirling through the darkness.

"Uh, apologies…" I slid my arm off his unyielding torso and tucked it behind my back. "It's only that Belmore, the one with the braids, is on my squad."

"So?"

"We aren't allowed to harm our teammates. Isn't that a rule at Arcanum?"

Ruhl snorted on a laugh. "That's cute, duskling. No such regulation exists at the Citadel. The only code of conduct we must abide by is *Strength from Darkness, Power through Pain.*"

Gods, that sounded awful.

"Either way, we cannot hurt him, understood?"

He nodded, begrudgingly. "How about the other one with the short hair?"

A devious smile parted my lips. "He's all yours."

Ruhl emerged from the cover of the trees, shadows whirling around him in a tight formation. I paused for a moment to take him in, a lither more elegant version of Reign. While his elder brother was raw power, the younger prince oozed grace.

"And Ruhl, feel free to make it painful," I called out after him.

He canted his head back, flashing me incisors. "I was right, you are a violent little thing."

I quickened my step to march beside him as we emerged from the edge of the woods into the valley at the foot of the hills. Both Belmore and Lucian spun in our direction the moment our footfalls crunched through the fallen leaves.

"Why am I not surprised you're with *him*?" Lucian snarled. "You have a perverse fascination with the Shadow Fae, don't you, Kin?"

"You're the only perverse one here, Lucian," I growled back.

From the corner of my eye, I caught the subtle shift in Ruhl's demeanor, the tensing of his posture, the flaring of his nostrils. "Son of Raysa," he gritted out, feet already moving.

I tried to follow his line of sight, and when I did, my stomach dropped to my heels. The thing the Light Fae males were circling earlier wasn't a thing at all, they were bodies, two of them.

Ruhl moved in a torrent of darkness, his *nox* bleeding through the air and thickening it so that it was impossible to drag in a full breath. Lucian and Belmore both staggered back as the wave of night pushed closer.

I darted behind him, nausea curling in my core, threatening to unleash the measly contents of my stomach. "Ruhl, wait!"

He slid down to the earth, fury surging from his pores in a deadly tangle of *nox*. I reached the bodies only a few seconds after him, and my gut twisted. The two females were strewn across the lawn, scorch marks mutilating their forms. Angry blistering skin covered their charred bodies, and the pungent odor of burnt flesh infiltrated my nostrils.

Oh gods, I was going to be sick.

"Clarys..." Ruhl snarled.

The name rang a bell, but I couldn't quite place it. I knelt down beside him, my hand twitching to squeeze his shoulder and impart some tiny bit of comfort, but I kept it still, thinking better of it. Ruhl was not my friend. He may not have been quite as terrible as I'd imagined, but I still had to keep my guard up. "Clarys?" I whispered.

"The female you saved in the Luminescent Gauntlet."

My thoughts swirled back to the chaos of the labyrinth of light and dark, and the Shadow Fae who'd staggered toward us with an ethereal blade lodged in her chest. I had no idea Ruhl knew her, or that he'd seen me tend to her wound.

Before I could get a word out, he rose, nothing but a torrent of pure night. His shadows surged forward. Belmore conjured an ethereal sword, but a shadow curled around the blade and ripped it from his hand. Lucian watched in horror as the tendrils of darkness surrounded him, twisting and coiling around the two males, until everything else fell silent beneath their screams.

Doubt warred at my insides as I watched the wicked shadows plunge into Belmore's ears, mouth, eyes—basically every open orifice. His lips curved in terror, eyes so wide they seemed mere seconds away from exploding from their sockets. Gods, it was horrible. Technically, I wasn't the one hurting him, so I wasn't breaking any rules. And still, that guilt surged. Even if I wanted to stop Ruhl, there was no guarantee he would listen. If I'd learned anything from my time at the Conservatory, it was that this sort of ruthlessness was commonplace among the Fae.

And still, the words popped from my mouth before I could stop them. "Ruhl, no! Not Belmore." *Ugh...* "And maybe

Lucian's had enough too." I muttered the last part so if he missed it, I'd understand.

"You cannot be serious?" he shouted. "After what they did to Clarys and Evin, they do not deserve your mercy, and they certainly will not receive mine."

My thoughts flew back in time, to Reign tearing out the life of that Shadow Fae who had caught a glimpse of my dagger's power, and my insides clenched. I couldn't simply stand by and allow it to happen again.

"Ruhl, I said *stop*!" I shouted louder this time, the rush of emotion inciting a surge of *rais* to the surface. My fingertips glistened, lighting up my entire form in the encroaching darkness.

He canted his head back, his hands still splayed, guiding his shadows. "Are you going to try and stop me, duskling?"

"If I have to..."

Without so much as a response, he turned his attention back to the writhing Light Fae who now hung in the air, suspended by the dark wraiths of death. That arrogant little bastard. Huffing out a breath, I summoned my *rais* then drew from the powerful *nox* thickening the air. My chest bloated, the mix of light and dark sending fiery energy through my veins and bursting from my splayed hands.

A wave of *rais* slammed into Ruhl's shadows, dispersing the shadowy minions into tiny fragments. Belmore and Lucian crashed to the ground, coughing and wheezing as inky, dark smoke puffed out of their mouths and nostrils. The reprieve was short-lived as the shadows re-formed and readied for a second surge.

"Please, no," Belmore cried, tears splashing down his cheeks. "It wasn't me. I didn't kill the females."

"Ruhl, enough!" I cried out. "You've taught them a lesson."

He spun on me, pure malice in his expression. "I'm not your professor, Aelia," he hissed. "I've come for their lives, not their penance."

A shadow slipped from his finger and curled around Lucian's throat, and I lunged for Belmore. I blanketed his trembling form with my own body as I summoned a radiant shield. Through the gilded haze, I could just make out the sickening crack of bones breaking.

Spinning toward the sound, I caught the vacant expression on Lucian's face an instant before he crumpled to the ground. He landed in a heap, his neck twisted in an unnatural angle. Oh, gods. Squeezing my eyes closed for only an instant, I whispered a quick prayer for his soul.

"Noxus's nuts," Belmore ground out as he eyed his friend, a sickly-green pallor coating his skin. "He snapped his neck."

"In Ruhl's defense, Lucian did murder two of his classmates." Every kill seemed easier, fazed me less. *Curses.* I was becoming like them, immune to the ruthlessness. "What the blazes happened?" I growled at Belmore. "Weren't we supposed to be *working together* with Arcanum?"

He shook his head, a tremor still vibrating his broad shoulders. "Lucian and his partner—Evin, I guess it was—were fighting about something stupid, and he lost his temper. My partner, Clarys, tried to step in to help her friend, and he lost it." His Adam's apple bobbed as he took in the motionless form beside us. "He may have been an asshole, but he didn't deserve to die like that."

"And neither did those females." I ticked my head toward the pile of little more than charred flesh, bones and ash. Straightening, the radiant orb popped, and Belmore grew paler still.

"What are you doing? He's going to kill us." He stood and started backpedaling toward the woods.

I fixed my gaze to Ruhl with Belmore's footfalls echoing behind me as the coward retreated into the safety of the forest. Already, I could feel the prince's fury dissipating, as if his devilish underlings had been somehow satiated by the kill. He stalked toward me, jaw clenched so tight it seemed carved of stone. Or maybe I was wrong... "Never do that again," he hissed.

"Do what, exactly?"

"Stand between me and my prey unless you wish to join them."

"That's exactly the problem, Ruhl. They weren't prey, they were Fae, just like you and me. And as terrible as they may have been, you don't have the right to steal their lives any more than I do."

Ruhl's shadows curled around me, trapping me against a wall of obscurity. "You're wrong, duskling. I am the prince of the Court of Umbral Shadows, heir to the throne and blessed by Noxus, god of eternal darkness. *I* choose who gets infinite sleep in his arms."

His words reverberated through the dense forest, every syllable thick with power. I held his gaze, unflinching, though my heart raced with a mix of fear and defiance. "And that," I countered, my voice steady, "is why your court will always be shrouded in true darkness, Ruhl. Not from the lack of light, but from the absence of compassion."

Ruhl's eyes flashed, the shadows retreating slightly, as if taken aback by my reply. For a moment, a flicker of something else crossed his features—surprise, perhaps, or maybe an unspoken respect. "Compassion," he scoffed, but his voice lacked its earlier venom. "Compassion doesn't rule Fae or prevent war; power does. And power demands sacrifice, Aelia."

I pushed against the shadows, feeling them give way under my determination. "Then perhaps it's time for a new kind of power, one that doesn't thrive on the sacrifice of innocents."

Ruhl watched me, his expression unreadable for a long moment. Finally, he stepped back, the shadows dissipating completely. "Perhaps," he murmured, almost to himself as he turned away, "but not today."

Chapter Fifty

R*eign*

Slivers of light stretched across the horizon, bathing the dark greens of the Feywood Forest in an ethereal glow. As the cool darkness gave way to the sunlight, I searched the tree line for any sign of Aelia, or worse, Ruhl. I'd spent the entire night sick with worry and completely helpless. Noxus, it was pure torture being forced to remain here, waiting and watching, unable to act, unable to protect her, unaware of what she was facing.

Aelia was out there somewhere with Ruhl at her side, plotting, strategizing for only the gods knew what. How my brother had managed to secure Aelia as his partner yet again was beyond me.

The Malakar I knew bent to no one, not even the heir of Shadows.

Could it be Draven, then? Had my deceitful half-brother found a way to bribe his way into his good graces?

I stalked a path along the edge of the trees, the same one I'd been trampling all night. What did it matter at this point how he'd done it? What I needed to determine was why. My little brother had shown far too much interest in Aelia already, and I needed to put an end to it, once and for all.

The familiar beating of wings sent my gaze skyward to a flock of skyriders approaching from the north. Without even getting a good look at the lead rider, I already knew who was to bless us with his royal radiance this morning. King Elian's *rais* filled the sky, casting swathes of glittering light in his wake. And behind him, his ever-faithful Royal Guardians, along with one sniveling headmaster.

Why was the king here today?

The flight of skyriders angled their wings to the ground in astonishing unison, and the wave of accompanying *rais* barreled over me as they alighted only a few yards from the forest where I stood in the shadows. Spending all night here was hardly part of my duties, as professor or mentor. The less attention I drew the better.

So, I watched from a careful distance as King Elian dismounted from his fiery phoenix. The royal oozed power, a shimmering, corporeal host of pure light. The king's mount was a borrowed creature, much like Pyra, as once a Fae lost their bonded skyrider, they were unable to bond again. According to old war stories Father had recounted, Elian's dragon had been killed in an attempt to save the prior Light king, Alaric, his brother. The beast was brought down, and Elian too nearly met his fateful end.

Instead, it was Alaric who died and, with no heirs, his brother, Elian, assumed the role of king upon his passing. Fate truly was a fickle bitch.

A sudden shift in the air jerked me from musings of the past and to the flicker of darkness pooling only a few yards from the entourage of Light Fae. *Nox* crawled across my skin, eager to break free of its skeletal confines, and my shadows raged at the sudden influx.

A cloud of pure onyx shadows burst from the ether, and my heart ground to a halt. Turbulent, overwhelming power poured over me, further inciting my shadows into a frenzy. The King of Umbral Shadows emerged from the swirling darkness, his Umbral Guard in tow, and the streaks of first light appearing over the horizon all but stilled at his presence.

What in all the realms was *he* doing here?

Father rarely left the comfortable confines of his Shadow Fortress. And now, he'd come twice this term. Was it truly to keep an eye on his great heir, or was it something else?

The king did not so much as spare a glance in my direction, which should have pleased me, but somehow it only rankled my nerves. Instead, he marched straight for King Elian, the typical swagger in his step. Even from this distance, I could see the Light royal's unease. Clearly, I wasn't the only one caught off guard by my father's arrival.

The crackle of leaves beneath heavy footfalls sent my head spinning toward the tree line, all thoughts of the royals forgotten. The hair on my nape prickled and an invisible tether forced my feet forward. My pulse ratcheted up as I fixed my gaze to the murky woods, waiting...

She stepped forth from the darkness, a beacon of shimmering light, and I could suddenly breathe again. Worse, I hadn't realized I'd ever stopped. Aelia strode toward me, cradling the artifact with a victorious smile etched onto her face.

I surged forward, barely able to restrain myself from touching her. She kept a careful distance, holding the artifact against her chest. The multi-faceted crystal was encased in a delicate frame of silver that twisted and twirled into intricate filigree patterns, resembling the branches of an ancient tree.

"Well done, princess," I whispered.

"Thank you." She inched closer, holding the relic between us as if it could somehow protect her. "Lucian's dead," she murmured on an exhale.

"What? How? Are you all right?"

Aelia nodded slowly, the satisfaction from the win fading. "Ruhl killed him."

"For attacking you?"

She shook her head. "No. Lucian slaughtered two Shadow Fae females from his team. I guess he actually cared about them."

I snorted on a laugh, rolling my eyes. "Ruhl doesn't care for anyone, princess. Don't ever make the mistake of believing otherwise."

A hint of irritation deepened the groove between her brows. "I don't think you know your brother as well as you believe you do."

Now I was the one becoming irritated. My fingers curled into my palms, nails biting into flesh. "You cannot be serious? You spend one night in the forest together and you think you know him better than I do? You forget that I have twenty years of experience with that little tyrant."

"Maybe," she muttered, "but he's not all bad, Reign. Maybe you should get to know this new version of him. Four years is a long time and people do change."

I couldn't believe we were having this discussion. It was completely absurd. Peering over the top of her head, I searched the dim woods for Ruhl. "Where is my new and improved brother, anyway?"

As if my words had summoned him, he emerged from the thick copse, hauling something over his shoulder.

"What in the realms?" I cocked a brow as he marched closer with an immense satchel woven of shadows slung across his back.

"Clarys and Evin, Ruhl's teammates and friends, as it seems," Aelia whispered as she began to turn away. My fingers ached to grab her arm and wrench her back, to beg her to understand what Ruhl was truly like. But I couldn't, not with so many spectators. Before she got far, she canted her head over her shoulder, bright eyes meeting mine. "You of all people should know how much these academies can change you, Reign."

Without another word, she hurried behind Ruhl to greet the royals and claim their win.

※

Hours passed before all the competitors emerged from the forest, some victorious and others... dead. The crowd grew ever larger, until nearly all the remaining students were accounted for. Draven and Malakar hovered anxiously over their respective first-years, counting and recounting to determine which academy would be victorious.

Aelia remained far away from me surrounded by her friends and teammates. At least she seemed at ease. I reminded myself that was all I wanted for her: to be safe and alive. Still, every so often her gaze caught mine, and I could feel something there. Something more she wanted to tell me, perhaps?

Ruhl, too, kept his distance, surprisingly. I fully expected the triumphant bastard to come over and gloat over his win. Not only had he and Aelia been the first to find their relic, but they'd also set a Conservatory record in how quickly they'd been able to retrieve it. A part of me needed to know how they had accomplished that.

Determined to find out, and also lacking any other good excuse to speak to Aelia, I forced my legs forward. Shoving by Belmore and Ariadne, I found the semi-circle gathered around her as they all recounted their exploits of the evening. Even Liora had pushed herself into the mix, squeezing between Rue and Symon to regale the others of her harrowing tales.

"Excuse me," I mumbled when I reached Liora.

She twirled around, a beaming smile on her face. "Did you see how well I did, professor?"

"Yes." I dipped my head. "A fine job, indeed." Clearing my

throat, I ticked my head at Aelia. "I need a moment with my other acquisition."

"Your *first* acquisition," Rue chimed in.

"And favorite." Symon threw me a cheeky grin.

"You know, I clearly remember a time not so long ago when you were both terrified of me." My shadows coalesced over my shoulders, stretching into looming wings over my head. "I believe I preferred those days."

"We didn't." Rue grinned up at me, but a tiny sliver of fear flashed as she took in the whirling mass of darkness over my head.

"Mmm," I grumbled. "Aelia?" Offering my hand out of habit, I nearly snatched it back, but she surprised me by placing her palm in mine. Perhaps, I was right and there was something more she wanted to tell me.

I led her to a small grassy knoll beyond the forest, well into Feywood land now. Just over the rolling hills, the Wilds extended—barren, untamed land to the south. Neither of us spoke until we reached a shaded spot beneath a sprawling willow where the land began to grow steeper.

Aelia dropped to the ground, leaning on the slight incline, gaze locked on the cottony clouds overhead. I folded down beside her, careful not to sit too close. We were far enough away from prying eyes, but one could never be too sure, especially with both kings in such close proximity.

Which reminded me...

"Did either of the royals explain the reason for their surprise appearance today?"

She shrugged, keeping her gaze trained to the pale blue above. "They claimed to have come to wish us well."

"And you don't believe them?"

She propped herself up on her elbows and swung her blue-eyed gaze at me. "Do you?"

"Of course not."

"Well, I think some of your cynicism has worn off on me, professor."

"I hope that's not the only thing."

"No, also your ruthlessness, savagery, and general disregard for life." Aelia blew out a breath, returning her gaze to the sky.

"Now, I know that's not true."

"I told Ruhl to kill him," she whispered, her voice so quiet I could barely make it out. "I wanted him to destroy Lucian."

I remained silent, allowing her to process the confession as I knew she needed to.

"But I changed my mind in the end. I couldn't allow Ruhl to go through with it." She paused, sucking her lower lip between her teeth. "I tried to stop him. I wasn't fast enough to save Lucian, but I did get to Belmore in time."

"You *saved* that arrogant Light Fae bastard after everything he's put you through?"

Her voice dipped, expression thoughtful. "I may be Light Fae, possibly even Shadow Fae," her voice dropped to barely audible levels, "but I refuse to be ruthless, savage, heartless—"

"You refuse to be like me?"

She sprang up, hands flailing at her sides. "Yes! Is that so wrong?"

A regretful smile spread my lips as I regarded the female the gods had chosen as my perfect mate. How could they have made such an error? She was everything I was not, everything I could never be. Maybe it would be a mercy to sever this bond between us instead of tying her to such a selfish and cruel mate.

"No, it's not wrong at all, Aelia. If there were more Fae like you, we would not endlessly find ourselves on the brink of war."

Her expression fell, the mask of confidence she'd learned to wear crumbling. She sank down onto her knees beside me, brilliant irises opaqued. "I am the child of twilight, I know it now. But I refuse to be the dreaded 'harbinger of oblivion' the prophecy speaks of. I will instead be a beacon of light with the power to reshape destinies for the good of all Aetheria."

A knot of tension coiled in my stomach. "How do you know?"

"My mother came to me in the forest. I know it sounds ridiculous, but it was her, I'm sure of it."

Chapter Fifty-One

A *elia*

Drawing in slow, deep breaths I focused on the shifting clouds in the sky, anything but the dreaded words I'd just spoken or the male sitting in front of me. I had barely begun to process the spectral sight of my mother, but the moment I breathed the words aloud it made them real. Reign eyed me warily, as if I'd left behind my senses in that dreaded forest.

"Aelia, you know that was part of the challenge... voices from the past meant to deceive."

"Or guide." I stood in front of Reign who still reclined against the grassy knoll. "The headmaster clearly said *guide* or deceive."

His shadows curled around the back of my legs, drawing me closer. Their icy touch awakened every nerve ending in their wake. "But they aren't real. They are mere hallucinations created by the brightest minds at the Conservatory."

"How do you know?" I bit out, ignoring the influx of sensations from those ghostly little fingers. "Can you say with absolute certainty that the shadowed, spectral form I saw wasn't my mother?"

Those dark tentacles wrapped around my legs, moving higher, urging me ever closer. I wasn't even certain Reign realized he was doing it. "Shadowed?" he blurted.

I nodded, begrudgingly.

"It's true, then, your mother was Shadow Fae just like—" His jaw slammed shut, the crack reverberating across the quiet clearing.

"Just like what?"

"Just like I am..." His aura darkened, those shadows slithering across his form in a weak attempt to conceal the obvious. "Which explains the cuorem bond."

"You're lying to me again, Reign," I hissed and staggered back.

He leapt up and curled his fingers around my wrist before I could get away. "I am not lying, I am Shadow Fae, am I not?"

"But that wasn't what you were going to say." I rose onto my tiptoes, glaring up at him. "You swore to me you'd never lie again."

"What does it matter now?" His jaw tensed, his eyes, dark as midnight, ablaze with a tumultuous storm. "You've made your choice, clear as daybreak. You chose the fate of the entire gods' forsaken realm over us, over *me*." Reign's voice was a serrated whisper, slicing through the tense air between us. "You rejected me as your mate, so why must I uphold my end of the bargain?"

"That's not what happened!" The words tore from me, raw and desperate, as emotions roiled between us, stealing the very breath from my lungs. "You asked me to run, Reign, to abandon all. That was the one thing I couldn't do. My heart never swayed; I never stopped wanting you, loving you with every part of my soul. You are my everything—my heart's *only* choice."

Gods, how did we always end up here?

I pressed my lips into a firm line, gritting my teeth to prevent further spillage of monumental declarations.

"I went to see Aidan after we returned from Mysthallia." Reign's voice was a harsh whisper, laced with the same emotion constricting my airways. "I made a vow not to repeat what he told me; not to you, not to anyone."

"He told *you*?"

"Only after he *rais*ed the truth out of me about the cuorem bond."

I swallowed down the lump growing in my throat. "Oh, stars, he knows about us?"

"Yes, which is why he rewarded me with the knowledge of your mysterious origins. He claimed that, as your cuoré, it was my turn to bear the burden of truth."

"Tell me!"

"I cannot, and before you ask, you know why. I am blood bound. I physically cannot tell you what he said."

"But he told you my mother was Shadow Fae?"

A barely perceptible nod, so faint I could have imagined it, except the sweat beading on his brow confirmed the strength it took for him to defy the vow, even in such a minimal way.

"So that means my father was Light Fae." *A child of twilight, born from the dance of light and dark.* I paced a quick circle, my mind buzzing in time with my footfalls. "And what of the *zar*?"

"I know nothing of *zar*."

At least I knew that part had to be true if he spoke it out loud, otherwise the vow would have forbidden it.

"Do you know anything else?"

The tendon in his jaw flickered but his lips remained still. There had to be more, but the damned vow was prohibiting him from speaking it. And without knowing what to ask, I would be going in blind. There was also the possibility that Aidan hadn't imparted all the information he knew, only bits and pieces to quell Reign's suspicions. My adoptive father was a wise old Fae, and he'd keep my family's secret to heart if he'd gone to such lengths for all these years to protect it.

I glanced across the hills to the east where our old cottage stood, not more than a half-day's journey on foot. I needed to talk to Aidan, to finally discover the truth. If he'd told Reign, then why didn't I deserve to know?

"You cannot go now," Reign murmured. "We are in the middle of the Umbral Trials."

"Can't you give me a special dispensation as my mentor?"

He slowly shook his head, something like regret in the rounding of his broad shoulders. "I am certain Aidan will tell you when the time is right."

I hissed out a curse, blaming all the gods and fates. I'd had enough of the lies, of the males in my life trying to protect me. It was time to ensure my own safety.

A loud boom to the south spun my head over the grassy peaks to the border of the Wilds. Reign's dark gaze followed mine, eyes intent on the hills and sparse forest that created a natural boundary between the two regions. Then another explosion and another, rapid fire. The ground trembled beneath my feet, sending my arms shooting out for balance.

A prickle of energy surged across my skin, the likes of which I'd never encountered. It wasn't the bright sunshine of *rais*, nor the dark void of *nox*, or even the smokey signature of *lys* I'd experienced in Mysthallia. But whatever it was had every tiny hair on my body standing at attention. "What was *that*?" I whisper-hissed.

"I'm not certain, princess, but we will not stand here waiting to find out." Reign's hand settled on the small of my back. "Come, it's time to go, surely all the initiates must have returned by now." He nudged me in the direction of the forest where the rest of the first-years were still gathered.

As we hurried across the clearing, my thoughts flew to Heaton and the other fourth-years deployed to the conflict along the border. Was Heaton out there fighting? Was he okay?

And more importantly, would he return before the end of the term as promised?

Please, Raysa, keep him safe.

A desperate swirl of misgivings wrestled in my core as we strode toward the remainder of Flare team. From the looks of it, everyone had made it out, thank the gods. Rue and Symon encircled me, their beaming smiles settling some of the unease swirling inside me.

Had they not felt the quake? Apparently not, as everyone milled around the edge of the forest as if nothing had happened, including the two kings. There was no point in worrying Rue right now. Perhaps, I'd ask one of the professors about it later.

When Liora crept closer to join the circle, I offered a faint smile, her presence not as bothersome now. Belmore cast a glance in my direction as my friends gushed about the trial, and instead of the typical hateful sneer, a faint smile lingered on his lips. Ariadne followed his line of sight, a confused expression pinching her heart-shaped face, but Belmore's smile only grew wider.

And gods, it felt good.

For the first time in a while, I'd done something I was truly proud of. I'd taken the first step in bridging the divide within Flare Squad. I only hoped the truce wouldn't prove temporary, and with Lucian and Kian gone, it felt like a very real possibility. With unequivocal certainty, I knew that whatever was unfolding across the border would demand a joint effort. Our success would hinge upon not only a unified Light Fae contingency, but also an alliance with our Shadow Fae counterparts.

I could almost feel a shift, the wheels of fate spinning and grinding forward, an inexorable force altering our future.

Chapter Fifty-Two

A *elia*

The toe of a thick boot slammed into my shin, and I hissed out a curse, lifting my gaze across the banquet table. "What the stars?" I squealed at Sy.

"Quick, distract her," he mouthed from across the assortment of platters. Glancing past the trays of Fae delicacies, I caught sight of the blonde, spikey-haired male who had run my best friend's heart through a meat grinder this term. Devin stalked by, his eyes red and swollen, as they had been for the last three days since his beloved Mariana failed the last trial and had been banished to Arcanum.

The sight of him pining over his girlfriend had driven Rue into an uncharacteristic state of sullenness. Turning my attention to my roommate, I blurted the first thing that came to mind. "Rue, do you have any lager left from home?"

She pushed stringer beans across her plate, staring listlessly at the deep green vegetable. "I'm not sure, why?" She didn't even look up at me as she spoke.

Which at least allowed for the moping Devin to pass by unnoticed.

"We have yet to celebrate our third win this term."

Rue blew out a breath and dropped her fork onto the plate, the clatter ringing out across the table. "I'm not sure if Heaton had any left..." Her bottom lip quivered, and my heart sank.

"Nice distraction, Aelia." Sy tsked, shaking his head. "As if bringing up her missing brother would help."

Ugh. "Oh, shut it, Symon." Wrapping my arm around Rue's slim shoulders, I drew her into my side. "I'm sorry. I—I didn't think. I was only hoping to get your mind off things."

"A night of drinking copious amounts of alcohol could help..." Sy threw Rue a devious smile, waggling his light brows. "It could be just the three of us."

"Yes!" I squeezed her tighter, and the faintest smile appeared.

"I don't know if we should. We have classes tomorrow, and the final trial is next week. Shouldn't we be in tip-top form?"

Sy's brow lifted into an incredulous arc. "Who are you, and what have you done to our friend Rue? Since when are you the responsible one?"

"Symon's right, and now that I think about it, why limit it to only the three of us? Maybe what you need is a little distraction from the opposite sex."

"Oh, yes, I concur." Sy's head bobbed up and down. "Forget a BFFF night, let's get drunk and have meaningless sex with other first-years before we all die."

A chuckle squeezed out as I regarded my ridiculous friend. "Wait a second, BFFF?"

"Yes, best Fae friends forever. Duh, Aelia, where have you been?"

"Too busy pining over a certain professor," Rue interjected. "I'm not the only one in need of a distraction."

"You know what they say," Symon interjected, "the best way to get over someone—"

"Is to get under someone else," Rue finished, cackling gloriously. She reached for her cup and downed the remnants of honey wine. "You know what? You two are right. This Devin thing must stop. There are dozens of eligible males at this academy, so why limit ourselves?"

"Or…" Sy's lips twitched into a mischievous smirk. "Why limit ourselves to this side of the river?"

"Wait, what?" I squealed.

Rue clapped her hands, the murky curtain across her typically expressive irises finally receding. "Yes! I am all in. Did you see some of those Shadow Fae males? There's something to be said about the bad boys, those sprawling midnight tattoos and muscles for days. They make Devin look like a pathetic, washed-out weakling."

I barely kept my head from bobbing up and down in agreement. Maybe it was the Shadow Fae in me, but there certainly was something about the darkness that called to me. Not that I'd ever admit it out loud, but there was even something about Ruhl… And with him, I couldn't even blame it on the cuorem bond.

Shaking my head to toss out the wild thoughts, I focused on this more important bit of insanity. "We cannot just sneak across the river and go hunting for Shadow Fae hook-ups. What are we going to do, just skulk into their dormitories?"

"That's exactly what we're going to do, my round-eared friend. With the Umbral Trials in full force, there are plenty of other Light Fae lumbering around the campus." Sy ran his finger over the shell of my ear. "And thanks to your newfound friendship with the Shadow prince, you are the one that will get us in."

I was already shaking my head before he finished the sentence, despite knowing how futile it was.

As it turned out, Heaton had left an entire barrel full of lager in his dormitory, and amid tears toasting our absent team leader, the three of us finished half of it before curfew. Rue's smothered giggles echoed across the foyer of the Hall of Glory as we tiptoed out the gilded doors.

The chilly air skimmed over my face, blowing strands of dark hair and the occasional platinum streaks across my eyes. Tucking the loose locks behind my ears, I led the way toward the Luminoc. As I brushed the rounded tip, I wondered if Melisara had been able to break the spell binding my powers, if my ears would sharpen to points like those of my friends.

Thumbing the warm medallion at my chest, I couldn't wait for this term to be over so I could confront Aidan once again. There was no reason for him to keep the truth from me any longer. It was clear I was the child of twilight, and whatever he was keeping hidden from me couldn't be worse than that.

"Eek, it's so cold!" Rue's shrill voice turned my attention to the present where she stood beside the river, dipping a finger into the murky waters. Arcanum Citadel loomed just across the narrow expanse, the spiraling turrets reaching into the starlit sky.

"Come on, Aelia, can't you whip up one of your luminous creations?" Symon stood at the edge, shivering.

"Why can't you?"

Symon leaned against Rue who had finally straightened, the pair staggering on the breeze. "Because clearly you had less lager than we did." They laughed, and then Sy twirled Rue in a circle.

I held my breath as she teetered on the edge, a second away from plunging into the frigid depths. "Okay, okay, I'll try. Just keep still."

Rue curled her arms around Symon, the two huddled together for warmth, and possibly more. Oh gods, I only hoped they wouldn't take things too far tonight and ruin a good friendship.

No, if all went well, they would each find a Shadow Fae to rub up against for a few hours, and we could make our hasty retreat back to the Conservatory before anyone was the wiser. And if everything went terribly... well, we could be spending the rest of the term stuck at the brutal academy.

"Come on, Aelia!" Rue cried out. "We have to get over there before my buzz wears off."

I didn't think there was any chance of that judging by her dreamy expression and the glimmer in her unfocused gaze. Drawing in a breath, I searched my core for the flicker of *rais* then turned my attention across the river. *Nox* pulsed from the earth, the dark vibrations skimming over my skin.

I barely had to call on my powers, energy erupting from my fingertips in a fiery surge of ethereal light. A luminous bridge spanned the dark waters, wide enough for us to walk two across.

"Raysa's tits," Symon blurted as the light formation appeared. "Looks like Lightweaver's Craft is really paying off."

I shrugged lamely. "Sure is." Steering my inebriated friends toward the bridge, I hurried them along the shimmering expanse. The moment my first boot hit Shadow Fae soil, a swirl of dark energy filled my core. Moonlight glistened across my shoulders, and I reveled in the sudden cool darkness after the overbearing sunlight. I could almost feel invisible curls of enticing *nox* invading my insides.

All the other times I'd traveled into the Shadow Court, I'd never felt anything quite like this. The energy expanded, growing and swirling with my *rais* in a tangle of heady sensations. It reminded me of the time I'd managed to siphon some *nox* from Ruhl in the Mirror of Illusions trial. A storm of power battled it out in my core, squeezing my lungs and quickening my heart rate.

"Hey A! Are you coming?" Rue's airy voice pivoted my attention from the brewing tornado within. She and Symon were already at the tree line, steps from the Twilight Forest that surrounded the citadel.

"Yes, be right there." Waving my hand, the luminous bridge disintegrated along with the vice grip around my lungs.

Good gods, what was happening?

The only thing that had changed since my last visit across the divide was that odd encounter with the ghostly version of my mother, which could have just been a hallucination. There had also been the revelation of the cuorem bond... Could either of those be the cause for my sudden surge in power?

As much as I hated the prospect given our current situation, I would have to consult Reign. My *cuoré* had remained as distant as ever after the revelation that Aidan had informed him of my mysterious bloodline. The fact that he knew more about my heritage than I did only infuriated me more.

A rustling of leaves from the forest had every hair on my body standing on end. Even Rue and Symon, despite the abundant amounts of lager they'd ingested, froze amidst the shadows.

"Well, well, well, what are you doing on my side of the Luminoc, yet again?" That taunting voice permeated the air an instant before its owner emerged through the dark copse. A whirlwind of shadows danced around Ruhl's form, a cape of utter darkness blanketing the shadow heir. A smirk pulled up the corner of his lip as he regarded me. "It would seem you're making a habit of this, duskling. Did you miss me already?"

Chapter Fifty-Three

elia

"Duskling..." Rue giggled.

I shot her a scathing glare that had her cheeks reddening. Thank the goddess she kept her mouth closed after that. I had told her bits and pieces of my night out with Ruhl in the Feywood Forest, leaving out anything incriminating of course, my new nickname being one of those things. She had been no help in trying to decipher the heir's hot and cold behavior. But she did say she liked him a bit more now that he had disposed of Lucian for us.

Ruhl stalked forward, umbral blades tucked in sheaths at his narrow hips. "So, to what do I owe this unexpected pleasure?"

"How did you find us?" I blurted, avoiding his question.

"You cannot truly believe a burst of power like that one would truly go unnoticed?" He ticked his head toward the river, where sparks of *rais* still glittered over the brackish depths. "It just so happens I was the one out on guard duty tonight, and I thought I sensed something familiar..."

A pit of dread sank to the bottom of my gut, and the swirling energy in my core only intensified. Gods, Reign was right. It was only a matter of time before his brother discovered the truth. If he hadn't already.

"Listen, dark prince..." Rue stumbled forward, a flirty smile skimming her lips. "We just came over here to have some fun. We heard the Shadow Fae know how to have a good time."

Ruhl's brow arched, following the corner of his mouth. He stepped closer, locking me in that dark glare. "Is that why you've come, duskling? Have you grown tired of the insipid Light Fae males?" His voice was pure danger, laced in venom.

"No," I ground out.

"Then what are *you* doing here?"

Raysa, this was a terrible idea. Why did I ever think, even for a second, that this evening wouldn't have disastrous consequences?

"We forced her to come with us," Symon replied, staggering between the prince and me, a valiant effort from my intoxicated friend. "We needed a little reprieve."

Ruhl barked out a laugh, the sound rumbling the air between us. "You know nothing about the Citadel if you believe skulking here in the middle of the night will grant you a reprieve."

Rue pushed her way between the males, placing her petite palm on the prince's chest. She thrust her bottom lip out, batting long lashes. "You're telling me the heir to the Shadow Court throne doesn't know how to have a little fun?"

"Oh, I do, sweetling. I'm only uncertain whether you and your friends could handle the sort of entertainment I have in mind." He cast a dark gaze over Rue's head, fixing those turbulent spheres on me.

Oblivious, Rue bounced on her tiptoes. "Oh, we can handle it."

A sinister smile crawled across Ruhl's face as he offered his arm to my roommate. "Then by all means, follow me."

I swallowed hard, that lump of dread growing to astronomical proportions as Ruhl took my friend by the arm and led her toward the Citadel. Symon whirled on me, a tangle of emotions playing on his handsome face. "Well, we've made it this far."

"This was such a bad idea, Sy."

He held his hand out, a sheepish grin curling his lips. "You know what they say about bad ideas, right?"

"No, what's that?" I grumbled.

"They often make the best stories."

I couldn't help the chuckle from tumbling out as I took his hand. "I can't argue with you on that one, my friend."

He hauled me forward, forcing me to lengthen my strides to keep up with Ruhl and Rue. I vowed not to let my roommate out of my sight now that she was in the prince's clutches. Though my opinion of Reign's brother may have been slightly upgraded, it didn't mean I trusted him with my best friend.

Ruhl led the way through an arched entrance at the back of the Citadel lined with vines so thick, I never would have found the door had I not known it was there. *Nox* pulsed all around us, the thick, pungent feel of it pressing into my skin.

Goosebumps cascaded down my arms, beneath the thin fabric of my tunic, as Ruhl waved his hand across a rune, and the door ground open.

"Are we allowed to be here?" I blurted as we neared the threshold, my mind fleeing back in time to my arrival at the Conservatory and crossing through the Veil of Judgement.

"We won't be smote down by Noxus or something, will we?" Sy interjected.

Ruhl canted his head over his shoulder, grinning wickedly. "I certainly hope not."

A blast of cool air flitted across my flesh as Symon and I squeezed through the entrance together. Rue was chattering on, completely oblivious, but at least I was happy she was enjoying herself. It was the most animated I'd seen her in days.

A labyrinth of dark stone hallways that absorbed light stretched out before us. The torches along the walls appeared as mere flickers against the oppressive darkness. Black marble, veined with streaks of silver that shimmered faintly covered the floors, reflecting any stray beams of light.

"It sure is dark in here," Sy quipped.

"Umhmm." Not only was the darkness oppressive, but the silence was unbearable.

We walked beneath towering arched ceilings, supported by columns adorned with intricate carvings of the Citadel's history and the Two Hundred Years' War. Everything about the academy was foreboding in its grandeur, adding to the ominous atmosphere.

"Why is it so quiet?" I whisper-hissed.

Ruhl spun around, eyes flickering with mirth. "I don't know how they do things at the Conservatory, but here, we have a curfew."

Right. Of course. Why did I assume the school would be a lawless, free for all? I cast a wary glance at Sy. "We never should have come," I mouthed.

His shoulders lifted before slumping back. "At least Rue seems to be having fun."

After traversing endless dark corridors, the obsidian walls obliterating all traces of light, Ruhl finally stopped in front of a door. I drew in a breath as the prince's hand closed around the ornate knob. Soft footfalls echoed behind us, freezing his movements, and I spun my head around in time to see a dark figure at the end of the hallway. He paused, stared in our direction, then scurried around the corner.

"Is that going to be a problem?" Symon asked.

Ruhl waved a dismissive hand and opened the door behind him, offering a glimpse of the grand chamber within. Not a sound erupted from the all-out rager surging beyond the threshold.

My jaw nearly unhinged. Some sort of sound-cloaking spell. It had to be.

"Don't be so surprised, duskling." Ruhl smirked, the wicked grin a painful reminder of Reign. "We must find our own ways to break the monotony and strictness of our rigorous training."

He took a step back, motioning for us to enter. I hesitated on the threshold for a long moment. Nothing good would ever come from this evening of debauchery. But maybe Rue wasn't the only one who deserved a night off. Forcing my legs forward, I entered the decadent room draped in black silk and dark velvet, with silver and purple accents that caught the flickering light from the candles ensconced in twisted iron holders along the walls. Strings of faintly glowing dark crystals hung in intricate patterns across the ceiling, casting a mesmerizing light that mimicked the starry night sky of the Court of Umbral Shadows.

"What is this place?" Symon stared at the enormous chamber, his lilac irises luminous beneath the faint light.

"It's our entertainment room." Ruhl shrugged as he led us farther into the space.

Like the rest of us, Rue took it all in, mouth gaping. The haze of liquor seemed to wane amidst the foreign splendor unfolding before us. Dozens of Shadow Fae initiates filled the chamber in extravagant attire. I suddenly felt severely underdressed in my typical linen tunic and suede leggings. Voluminous gowns and doublets threaded with spider silk and moonlight danced across the room, while others wore less, adorning themselves with only mystical tattoos that writhed on their skin, alive with the beat of the music.

"I've never seen anything like this," I murmured.

"Of course you wouldn't have. You grew up in Feywood, and then had the misfortune of landing across the river." His lazy smile grew feral. "If only Noxus had blessed you, instead of that dull, lifeless Raysa. Everyone knows what happens in the shadows is far more entertaining than in the light."

I swallowed thickly at the dark gleam in his eyes.

He led us toward a long table with an abundance of exotic Fae delicacies and

decanters of rich, dark wine. An array of shimmering potions lined the dark planks, their potent aromas mingling in the air.

"What are those for?" Rue pointed at the small vials.

Ruhl curled his arm around my friend's shoulders. "Various enchantments to enhance pleasure, of course."

Rue's slim shoulders trembled, a smile slashing across her lips.

"Help yourself." He motioned toward an ampule with a glittering purple liquid. "I hear this one does wonders to increase a male's size." Then he ticked his head at Symon. "I don't have an issue in that department, but perhaps it could help you."

Sy stiffened beside me, his gaping smile hardening to a harsh line. "I have yet to hear a complaint."

"From Light Fae females but trust me when I say the Shadow Fae are much more discerning."

"Enough," I hissed at Ruhl. "No one will be indulging in any—"

Rue uncorked a bottle and downed the dark contents.

"No!" I squealed, but it was too late. She'd already swallowed down the last drops. I grabbed the vial and sniffed. "What was in this?"

Ruhl snatched the container from my hand and dragged his tongue along the opening. "*Corinthia* tincture." With a grin, he arched a dark brow. "Your friend should be feeling *very* good soon."

Oh, gods.

"I'd find her a willing male before she takes matters into her own hands."

Rue draped her arms around Ruhl's neck and fitted her nose in the crook of his shoulder. "You smell so good," she whispered.

"And so it begins," Symon muttered.

Ruhl untangled her arms and handed her over to Sy. "I'm afraid not, sweetling. Your kind doesn't do it for me."

"But..."

I clapped my hand over Rue's mouth before she could embarrass herself. "Maybe we should just go." I eyed Symon as our friend started to toy with his nipples through his linen tunic.

"But we just got here," she murmured beneath my hand. Her eyes were bright, shimmering beneath the flickering lanterns.

Ruhl's fingers clamped around my arm and spun me toward him, forcing me to release my drunk best friend. "She's right. You can't leave yet."

I tensed beneath his touch, an instant away from ripping free of his hold, when a familiar icy shadow swirled around my neck. Instantly, my body was at ease, and a strange rumble echoed in my throat. Was that a purr?

As if Ruhl had heard it, his dark eyes widened, smoldering into dark, oily pits. His fingers uncurled, and he regarded me for a long moment without speaking a word.

That dark tendril lifted the hair on the back of my neck, before surging higher around my ear. "I need you to listen to me very carefully, princess, before I lose my shit and barrel into that room, destroying everything my father has strived to accomplish in the last twenty years."

The barely restrained violence seeping through Reign's shadow messenger stopped my heart mid-beat.

"I don't know what you wanted to accomplish by going to Arcanum to see my brother, but you have my attention, Aelia.

If you do not walk out of there right now, though, I will storm in myself, or worse, have Phantom raze the entire Citadel in dragonfire. Do you have any idea what goes on in those shadow bacchanalias?"

The "what?" died in my throat.

A part of me wanted to rebel and fight him on this possessive streak. First of all, I did not come here to see Ruhl, and secondly, who was he to tell me what to do? But the other half, the sane one, knew this was a terrible idea from the start.

I sidestepped Ruhl and latched onto the sleeve of Symon's shirt. "We should go."

"But why? Things are just getting interesting." He tipped his chin at Rue grinding on some Shadow Fae male.

"Symon! You were supposed to watch her!"

"I'm sorry, she got away. She's a strong little thing." My brow quirked, knowing full well he could have stopped her had he chosen to.

Ruhl appeared beside me and nudged his elbow into my side. "We could join her on the dancefloor."

"I swear to all the fucking gods, Aelia," Reign's shadow minion hissed in my ear, "if you don't get out of there *right now*, I'm coming in. My father will banish me for real this time, he'll see you, and everything we've fought for, everything we've given up will be for nothing."

"I have to go." I hissed at Ruhl before spinning at Symon, eyes pleading. "I can't stay here or something *very* bad will happen," I whispered, dragging him away from the prince so we could speak in private.

"Reign?"

I nodded quickly.

"Then go."

"I can't leave you two here."

Symon grinned as he reached for a flute of dark liquid from the table. "We'll be fine, little Kin. We don't need you to babysit us, I promise."

Indecision warred at my insides. I hated the idea of leaving my friends here, but apart from making a scene and hauling them out forcibly, I didn't have a choice. I'd experienced the choking hold of the cuorem anytime Liora was near, and if Reign did rush in here like a possessive lunatic, it would ruin everything.

I squeezed Symon's hand and lifted onto my tiptoes. "If you're not home in two hours, I'm coming back for you."

"Deal."

"And please, keep an eye on her."

"Of course." He pressed his hand to his heart. "If I don't, may Raysa strike me down."

"Please be careful."

"You worry too much, Aelia. We'll be just fine."

"Also, please wait to explain to Rue why I've gone until you've left the Citadel." The last thing I needed was my professor's name mentioned within these hallowed halls.

With one final glance at Rue and the handsy Shadow Fae male, I spun for the door. I didn't make it more than a step before firm fingers closed around my biceps.

"Running off already?" Ruhl stood over me, gaze pinned to the shadow swirling around my neck. "Let me guess, my brother called you home? And now you must go running to him like a good little whore?"

My hand moved before I could stop it. The sharp sting across my palm registering a moment too late.

Ruhl glared down at me, fury carved into his fine features, and a tornado of shadows cloaking him in darkness. His eyes were a storm of emotion, a tempest intent on destruction. If it hadn't been for those rioting minions sheltering us from curious eyes, I was certain the entire room of Shadow Fae would have whirled in our direction.

As if Reign had felt the shift in the atmosphere, his shadow expanded, then buzzed around me, enveloping me in a shield of darkness.

"Get out of here," Ruhl barked. "Before I do something we'll both regret."

Gritting my teeth to keep the expletives poised on the tip of my tongue at bay, I spun on my heel and marched out. I whipped the door open and cocked my head over my shoulder. Those penetrating orbs were still pinned in my direction. "If anything happens to my friends, I'm coming for you, Ruhl."

He barked out a laugh, the tense set of his jaw softening a touch. "Why would I harm them, when it's you I want, duskling?"

Chapter Fifty-Four

R*eign*

A lethal mix of red-hot fury and piercing jealousy surged through my veins, lighting up my entire body despite the cool night at my back. I paced the length of the riverbank, the usual reprieve from standing on Shadow Fae soil doing nothing to quell my temper tonight.

When Gideon sent word he had seen Aelia in the Arcanum dormitories, I'd nearly lost my mind. I was certain he'd made a mistake, that my cuoré would never be so stupid. Imagine my surprise when I'd found her chamber empty and followed her scent to the Luminoc. From there, my shadows had easily found her.

With *him*.

Ruhl seemed to conveniently pop up everywhere she was lately. It was more than a coincidence; I was sure of it. And what about Aelia? Was she seeking him out too?

My movements grew more violent, more impatient with

each lap along the river. Once I'd come to terms with this cuorem bond and then suffered Aelia's rejection, I had spent hours in the library researching all I could about the ancient Fae binding. It was rare, but in some cases, a familial tie occurred through blood. In other words, Ruhl and Aelia could find themselves drawn to each other simply because of the bond Aelia and I shared. The similarities in the blood running through Ruhl's veins confused things.

For a sacred gods' blessed bond, it seemed quite fickle.

Realms, what if she was attracted to him?

Just the thought had another wave of anger rolling over me. I'd rip his head off if he so much as touched her.

The hair on my nape prickled, and my gaze swung toward the tree line adjacent to the Citadel. A familiar figure emerged from the gloom, her arms knotted across her chest and a swirl of my shadows as her entourage. A male appeared behind her, and I tensed for an instant before recognizing the dark-haired Fae.

"Gideon," I breathed. If he hadn't spotted her, who knew what sort of disastrous evening would have ensued.

Aelia stomped toward me, a tangle of *rais* and *nox* emanating from her strained form.

"How could you be so irresponsible?" I barked when she was still a few yards away.

"Oh, stop it, Reign," she snarled right back. "There are countless Light Fae initiates roaming the halls of Arcanum because of the Umbral Trials. My life was hardly at risk."

Gideon stood behind her, lips pursed, but it was impossible to ignore the spark of amusement in his dark gaze.

"Thank you for accompanying her, Gid. I mean it, I am forever in your debt. Now, feel free to show yourself back to the Citadel."

"And miss this?" He chuckled, dark navy streaks of hair glowing beneath the moonlight. "I don't think so."

"Gideon," I growled.

"What? Is it so wrong for your best friend to want to meet your cuoré?"

Aelia's eyes widened, the silvery-blue twinkling beneath the moonlight. "You told him?"

"Yes," I gritted out. "As I've told you before, Gideon has access to an entire library I do not at Luce. Since you're so adamant about severing the bond, I required some assistance."

"*Me*? I'm not the one that wants to break the gods' forsaken bond, Reign, that's *you*!" She closed the distance between us and glared up at me.

"No, you just expect me to stand by and watch and wait for disaster to unfold."

"Why does it have to be a disaster? Why can't we forge our own fate?"

"She makes a valid point," Gideon interjected. "You always assume gloom and doom."

I glared at my friend over Aelia's head. "Oh, be quiet, Gid, before I loose my shadows on you."

Aelia jabbed her finger into my chest, drawing my gaze away from my now former-best friend and down to her fiery one. "You never even tried to fight, your answer was simply to run. I'm only asking for a chance to avert this oncoming oblivion."

"There is no stopping it." I clutched her shoulders, desperate to shake some sense into this stubborn female who was filled with foolish hope. There was nothing more dangerous.

"Well, then, that's the difference between you and me, Reign of Umbra. I don't give up when the situation seems hopeless. I only choose to fight harder. Do you think it was easy growing up with the knowledge that at the age of twenty I would be sold off to a Fae lord? Should I just have given up back then, too?" She paused, searing me with that piercing gaze that could reach all the way down to my soul. "The day you found me you told me I had two options: rise to the occasion and succeed or do nothing and spend the last few months of my miserable existence being tortured at the hands of both Light and Shadow Fae."

A rueful smile crawled across my lips as vivid memories of the day I'd saved her from the clutches of Lord Liander coalesced.

"And what did I choose?" She slapped her hands on her hips, defiant as all the realms.

"To fight," I gritted out through clenched teeth.

"Say it again, professor, I don't believe our friend Gideon heard." She canted her head over her shoulder to where my friend stood watching us, completely enthralled by the show.

"You chose to fight," I growled in frustration.

"So fight with me, Reign, damn it." Her hands slid off her hips and found mine, weaving between my fingers. "Please." Her eyes were filled with so much damned hope I couldn't bear the thought of denying her.

Gods, the odds were stacked against us, but she was right, they'd always been against her and somehow, she had survived. She always survived.

"So what do you say, my prince?" Gideon flashed me a smirk, knowing good and well what my decision would be.

"I. Will. Fight." I echoed the words Aelia had spoken all those months ago on that fateful day in Feywood.

As soon as the last word slipped past my teeth, Aelia's mouth was on mine. It was a swift kiss, no more than a quick brushing of our lips, but gods, the fire behind it sent heat racing down my breeches.

"And, that is my cue to leave."

I barely made out Gideon's declaration over the sudden wild pounding of my heart. Forcing my scattered thoughts from the blazing sensations, I glanced over Aelia's head at my best, arguably only, friend. "Thank you, again, Gid."

He waved a nonchalant hand. "If you keep thanking me for saving her, I will have to take advantage of you."

"Well, it seems as if you've found my weakness." I curled my arm around Aelia's waist and drew her into my side. My shadows buzzed in relief at the feel of her body pressed to mine.

"I promise not to use it against you." Gideon winked and turned toward the looming shadow of the Citadel. He took a few steps before spinning back, navy irises bouncing between us. "I wouldn't be your best friend, Reign, if I didn't say it. You two are a perfect match, clearly destined for each other. Don't let something as fickle as fate stand in your way."

I nodded slowly, unanticipated emotion tightening my throat. I never doubted Aelia was the female for me; despite my reluctance to admit it, I'd always felt it in my soul. But we had bigger problems to contend with—my brother only the first in a long line of many.

I watched in silence for an endless moment as Gideon disappeared beneath the shadows of the Citadel. Once his footsteps fell away, I turned to Aelia and blew out a breath.

"Why did you come here tonight?" I whispered, attempting to keep my temper from rising.

"Mostly for Rue. She needed an escape, and somehow, Arcanum seemed like a valid option at the time."

"Mostly?"

She shrugged, gaze pinned to the fortress towering over us. "Ever since I discovered the truth about my mother, I can't deny I've felt more drawn than ever to the shadows."

"Mmm." I paused, holding my breath before I gathered the courage to ask. "And drawn to Ruhl, perhaps?"

An interminable moment passed before she tipped her chin up, brilliant irises meeting mine. "I don't want to lie to you, Reign." She chewed on her bottom lip, expression pensive. "Maybe, a little... Why do you think that is?"

"I fear it is because of the cuorem bond. Whatever is tying us together, it is also linking you to my brother."

"That makes no sense."

"I've told you before, some say the cuorem is practically

sentient. Its only purpose is to make a connection. With the tie incomplete, it searches out another, the closest link."

"Well, I suppose it kind of makes sense." A deep groove formed between her brows, and I wondered how profoundly her feelings had taken root.

I dared not ask for fear her answer would compel me to snap my brother's neck.

"The gods certainly do like to test us and watch as we fumble and flail, don't they?" Her gaze was pensive as she fiddled with her fingers.

"It seems pretty twisted if that is the case." I ran my hand up and down Aelia's shoulder, reveling in the feel of her. "It should only be temporary, princess. If the bond is completed, all the other side effects will vanish."

"Just like that?" She glanced up at me, shards of moonlight alive in her eyes.

"Yes."

"Then let's do it, Reign, please. I want to complete the cuorem bond. I refuse to believe that tying myself to the Fae I love would lead to the downfall of our entire realm. I need something good and genuine in my life, something to cling onto, to carry us through the challenges ahead."

Chapter Fifty-Five

A *elia*

Reign paced the length of his dimly lit chamber, the tendon in his jaw twitching and feathering like mad. He hadn't said a word since I spoke the life-changing words, pleading with him to solidify our bond. He merely scooped me up into his arms as his shadows shifted along his broad shoulders, creating the wings to carry us back across the river.

Seconds later, we landed in his room and the manic pacing began.

I shifted on his bed, the silky sheets gliding beneath me. If the tension in the air hadn't been quite so thick, I would have gladly sprawled across the immense mattress. Though I hadn't had quite as much as my friends to drink, I had enjoyed a full tankard of lager, and combined with the late hour, my lids were beginning to grow heavy.

"Reign?" Sliding to the edge of the bed, I waved a hand,

attempting to get his attention. "Are you going to say something?"

"I can't. I'm thinking."

"I didn't think the two were mutually exclusive."

He cocked a dark brow in my direction, the ghost of a smile pulling at his lips.

"How about you share with me what you're thinking?" I patted the empty spot on the mattress beside me.

Reign slowly shook his head, a sharp exhale pursing his lips. "If I let myself near you, especially while you are on the bed, I fear I will have no control over what happens next."

"But I want it to happen," I murmured.

"Because you are scared of whatever it is you're feeling toward my brother?" he snapped.

"No!" The word whooshed out. But... wasn't I? I couldn't deny I felt something...

He stalked closer, dark tendrils of night clinging to his powerful form. His *nox* skimmed over my skin, compelling a swell of goosebumps. "Then why the sudden change of heart?"

"There was no change, Reign. I love you. I've loved you for much longer than I dare admit."

"But only a week ago, you refused me."

"For the love of Noxus, why must you be so dense? I did not refuse *you*. I refused to run! How many more times must I say it?"

"Until you convince me it's true." He closed the distance between us in one long stride, and I parted my legs, allowing him to fit perfectly between my thighs.

"Then that's what I will do." I reached for his face, caressing the dark smattering of prickly hair on his cheek. He bent lower, placing his palms on either side of my thighs, trapping me on the bed.

"Gods, princess, I want you so badly." His eyes locked on mine, twin orbs of pure midnight searing to mine. "There is nothing I'll ever want more than to be one with you, to complete the cuorem bond and spend forever worshiping you, my cuoré."

I swallowed hard, the intensity in his gaze stealing the air from my lungs. "But?"

"I'm terrified of what will happen when my father discovers the truth and forces me to complete my blood vow."

"Please, let's not worry about something that has yet to happen. What if he never finds out at all?"

He scoffed, blowing dark strands of hair across his brow. "It's inevitable, Aelia; as inescapable as you and me and this pivotal moment."

I slid my hand from his cheek down to the leather laces of his tunic and untied the knot. "Then, if our fate is truly sealed, let's make our final stand spectacular—a blaze of glory that will echo through eternity."

That elusive smile melted across his face, the kind that lit up his eyes more brilliantly than the star-studded night sky of the Umbral Court.

"Noxus, Aelia, when you put it like that, you make it nearly impossible for me to say no."

"Then don't." I pressed my finger to his lips and slipped my free hand down his torso to the hem of his linen tunic. "I love you, Prince Reign of Umbra, and if all we have is a few days or a few weeks of happiness as cuoré, I'll take it."

"Realms, Aelia, I would cherish just a few gods' blessed hours entwined with you, completely—mind, body, and soul." He slipped his hand behind my back and moved me farther up the bed before trapping me beneath his massive form once again.

Before his lips claimed mine, I drew the dark fabric over his head revealing the intricate canvas of runes across his chest. The mark of the banished pulsated, the grisly carving a terrible reminder of all he had endured at his father's hand. I ran my finger over the marking as his lips devoured my own. The *nox* used to create the mystical engraving pulsed beneath my fingertip, calling to something buried deep within.

Heat skimmed across my flesh, and Reign must have felt it too because his lips drew back, freeing my own. His heated gaze flickered between the mark and my mouth, as if he couldn't quite decide where to focus his attention.

"Do you feel that?" I whispered.

"Mmhmm," he murmured. "But you will have to be more specific, because I'm feeling *a lot* right now." He thrust his hips, his arousal rubbing right where I needed it.

My back arched off the bed as a thrill of sensations streaked down my lower half. "Me too," I rasped out.

He pressed his forehead to mine, a faint smile playing on his lips. "It is said that once cuoré are bound, their powers are amplified, and that mates can draw from each other."

"That should be interesting given my muddled abilities."

"It will be spectacular." One hand moved from the side of my head to the hem of my tunic. His deft fingers slid beneath the light linen and found the swell of my breasts. I let out a moan as he toyed with my nipple, drawing it to a hard peak. An influx of pure pleasure radiated from the sensitive tip, surging down to the tips of my toes.

"Oh, Reign," I groaned.

He lifted my top up and over my head, releasing a hiss as that heated gaze raked over my bare torso. A scrap of fabric lingered over my breasts which he quickly disposed of with a swirl of his shadows.

"Raysa, you are beautiful, my princess. You are pure starlight forged into flesh, so radiant you are nearly painful to behold." He pressed a gentle kiss to my lips then more along the curve of my jaw. "I cannot wait to make you mine. Forever." His hand slid between our bodies, finding the waistband of my leggings. Excruciatingly slowly he dragged the suede down my thighs.

Once I was bare, with the exception of my lace panties, I reached for his breeches, the impressive bulge beneath the laces sending another thrill up my spine. It seemed as if I'd been waiting my entire life for this moment, to be claimed by this beautiful, powerful male who had once starred in my nightmares and now was on the verge of making all my dreams come true.

I made quick work of his pants, sliding them down his powerful thighs and freeing his arousal. I sucked in a breath as I took him in, much like the first time. I should have been scared by his size, but instead only a rush of certainty overtook me. Reign was mine, and I was his.

Cuoré. Cuoré. The word hissed through my mind, growing faster and more forceful with each iteration.

What in the stars?

"Do you hear that?"

His eyes brightened, the midnight pools shimmering. "You heard the call of the cuorem?"

"I think so... You didn't?"

Reign shook his head. "The bond is typically initiated on the male's side, which is likely why I realized first, then it is the female who must accept the call."

A silly smile spread across my lips as I regarded the dark furrow of his brow. "I accept."

His expression mirrored mine, the hard set of his jaw softening and genuine happiness radiated from those mesmerizing, bottomless orbs. He slid his hand between my legs, a growl vibrating his throat as he found me already slick. "We have to make sure you're ready for me, princess. I don't want to hurt you..."

My head bobbed as he dipped a finger beneath my panties and found that taut bundle of nerves aching for his touch. "You won't," I whispered as the devastating pleasure began to build.

"But this is your first time and—"

"You won't." I pressed my finger to his lips. "We were made for each other, right? Forged by the gods themselves?"

He nodded and captured my mouth once more with the fiery intensity of a thousand suns. Between his tongue and his fingers and our bare flesh finally against each other, a plethora of sensations whipped through me, more powerful than the mightiest storm's winds tearing across the open sea. Each touch carved deeper into my soul, leaving a trail of heat and shivers that defied the calm before the tempest.

"I think I'm ready," I whispered against his mouth, his kisses growing more ravenous by the moment.

His dark, turbulent eyes fixed to mine, the torrent of emotions streaking through the abyss breathtaking. "I don't want you to *think*, princess. I want you to feel it, to know without the shadow of a doubt that you are ready to bind yourself to me for eternity. Regardless of the consequences."

I lifted my head off the mattress and captured his lips, pouring every ounce of love, fear and uncertainty I felt into the kiss. After an endless moment, I drew free of his mouth and found those stormy eyes. "I have no idea what the future will bring us, but I know that I want to spend it bound to you."

A smile so brilliant it put Raysa's blessed sun to shame spread across his handsome face. "Gods, you are absolutely perfect for me." He crawled down my body, his cool shadows dancing across my heated skin, leaving a trail of goosebumps in their wake. Their icy fingers found the waistband of my panties and slid them down my legs, leaving me completely bare.

Reign dropped his head, his nostrils flaring as he breathed me in. "Memorizing your scent as mates often do," he whispered, his voice laced with desire as he echoed the sentence he hadn't finished the last time we were together.

Drawing him farther up my body, I reached for him, wrapping my fingers around his silky hardness and positioning him at my entrance. "I'm ready for forever," I whispered against his ear.

That smile grew somehow more radiant, eyes twinkling

beneath the flickering torch overhead. "I will go slowly, tell me if it hurts."

My head bobbed up and down as he nudged at my entrance, igniting every nerve ending ablaze in anticipation.

A shrill blast tore through the lusty haze sending my racing heart catapulting against my ribcage. Reign hissed out a curse, echoing my sentiments exactly.

"What is that?" I clung onto him, despite knowing full well our moment had been irrevocably shattered.

"It must be a Shadow Fae raid," he snarled before a slew of curses dribbled from his lips. "Gods be damned. It would seem someone is trying to keep us apart, indefinitely." Dropping a kiss to my forehead, he whispered, "I'm sorry, princess, but it seems as if we will have to postpone this momentous occasion."

"Must we?" I pouted, sticking out my bottom lip and wrapping my arms more tightly around his neck. "Would anyone even notice if we weren't there?"

"I'm afraid they would." He offered a hand and pulled me up off the mattress as I continued to scowl.

Reign dragged his pants on, leaving his underclothes on the floor, and jerked his tunic over his head. Then he tossed me my clothes, frowning. "This isn't over, Aelia. Gideon was right, I will not allow fate or some ancient prophecy to dictate our destiny. I will make you mine, I swear to it."

Pulling my tunic over my head, I rose onto my tiptoes and pressed a kiss to his lips. "I will hold you to that vow, my prince."

Chapter Fifty-Six

A flurry of students fled the Hall of Rais after Aurora Weaving class, reminding me of the night before last when the alarms had been triggered in error. Our grand moment had been interrupted for nothing. Hundreds of students, initiates and fourth-years alike had charged down the steps of the Hall of Glory prepared to fight invaders only... none ever came.

As we'd retreated into the dormitories an hour later, I caught sight of a familiar gray dragon circling. There was only one skyrider of that hue that existed in these parts—Mordrin, Ruhl's dragon.

Reign had been certain his brother had set off the alarm, but to what end?

The chaos it had caused had been temporary and no damage had been done. The whole thing was a mystery.

Rue raced up behind me and pushed off my shoulders, launching herself up and over my head. The glittering celestial glyph shimmering on her back giving her the added momentum to nearly achieve flight. As much of a disaster as our escape into Arcanum had been, I couldn't deny that my friend seemed much happier since that night.

She'd made quite an impression on Blyte, the Shadow Fae initiate she'd met at the bacchanalia. So much so, that I'd caught an errant shadow creeping across the river onto our training field only yesterday. The little dark messenger had been sent by the male from Phantom team, whispering sweet nothings in my roommate's ear as we practiced with luminous shortswords.

Rue had tried to play it off as nothing, but whatever he'd whispered had my friend's cheeks flaming. And that did not happen often.

"I can't wait for tomorrow!" Rue squealed as she circled back.

"For the last trial, or because you'll get to see that hot, broody Blyte again?" Symon's eyes sparkled as he regarded the faint crimson tingeing her face.

"Both." She shot him a smirk. "Please, don't act as if you didn't enjoy yourself with that female from Shade Squad."

Symon grinned, looking smug as a bug. "I did enjoy myself immensely, but I didn't go as far as exchanging names with the female. Everyone knows that relations between Light and Shadow Fae are strictly forbidden."

My stomach plummeted like a stone. Not only had my parents been guilty of the great sin, but I was also following in their footsteps. Although, technically, since I was part Shadow Fae, it was a bit of a gray area.

"And you know rules were meant to be broken." Rue ruffled Sy's perfectly styled hair. "Speaking of Shadow Fae..." Rue waggled her brows at me. "Where is our favorite professor?"

"Oh, are we speaking to him again?" Sy threw his arm around my shoulders. "I simply can't keep up with the two of you."

"I think they're doing more than *speaking*, right, A?" Her light eyes twinkled with mirth at my expense.

After the false alarm, all the staff had been called into a meeting with the headmaster, leaving me all hot and bothered and with a desperate need to divulge at least something to someone. Luckily, Rue and Symon had stumbled home shortly after the commotion, providing the perfect cover for their return. I had filled in my roommate on bits and pieces of my reunion with Reign.

"We're taking it slow," I whisper-hissed. Which felt like a much bigger lie than it was. I hadn't actually seen my mentor for more than a few rushed minutes in the past two days. Suddenly, Draven had enlisted him to take on all sorts of inane projects, including preparations for the end of the term. Then there was Liora, who abruptly needed him by her side every moment of the day.

Reign's faithful shadow messengers kept me company, but they were a poor substitute for the real thing. I was trying not to let it get to me, but after finally making the decision to be with Reign, despite the possibly disastrous consequences, I simply wanted to be with him already. The cuorem bond itched beneath my skin, begging to be completed. After we'd come so close the other night, the mystical tether seemed beyond frustrated. And it wasn't the only one.

The past two nights I'd heard the call of the cuorem, the relentless drumbeat pounding across my skull. I had become so agitated I'd considered sneaking into his room and forcing him to make love to me simply to make it stop.

Only the fear of getting caught so close to the end of the term had halted my feverish thoughts. Tomorrow was the final trial, and soon we would be granted leave once again. Perhaps, it would be better to wait so that we could enjoy a week together without being forced to skulk and hide.

"Aelia, are you even listening to me?" Rue flashed her hand

across my face as we walked across the flight field, nearly hitting my nose.

"Sorry, I was distracted."

"Clearly." She shook her head, smiling. "Are you sure you're up for one more practice flight before the final trial tomorrow?"

"Yes, I'll be fine."

"Oh, did you say you're flying?" A familiar female voice echoed from behind, and I suppressed the urge to groan.

I spun around to find Liora jogging after us, her perfect hair plaited into a crown around her head. "Yes, we are." Forcing my mouth into a smile, I attempted to look sincere.

"Would you like to join us, my lady?" Symon bolted in front of me, dipping his head into a ridiculous attempt at a curtsy.

She giggled and Sy preened like a peacock. "I would love to. I still haven't quite gotten the hang of the commands. Fuego still thinks he's in charge, and frequently I have little say in the matter." Liora had been gifted a phoenix at her Choosing Ceremony, and quite an ornery one from what I had seen.

"Oh, that is terrible." Sy tsked dramatically. "Shouldn't your mentor be helping you with that?" He cast a playful smirk in my direction, and it took all my willpower not to hurl an obscenity. Instead, I settled on a pinecone which bounced satisfactorily off his head.

Sy grimaced, but easily recovered as I cackled internally.

"Reign is just always so busy." She stuck out her bottom lip, and I barely restrained an eyeroll.

"Where is our Shadow Arts professor anyway?" Rue asked.

"I'm not sure." She shrugged. "He was supposed to meet me this morning to train, but he never showed up."

A hint of unease unfurled in my gut, but I shoved it down, convincing myself Reign was likely tied up with Draven, as he had been for days preparing for the end of the term. There was to be a grand ball at Arcanum after the final trial—assuming we all survived—and apparently, Malakar had requested some assistance from the Conservatory's staff.

Rue's worried gaze chased to mine. It seemed I wasn't the only one that found it strange.

"Maybe I should go—"

"Relax, my little round-eared friend, I'm sure our *professor* is just fine." Symon's eyes flickered to Liora who was regarding me curiously.

Did I look panicked? At times it was easy to forget that amidst all the countless reasons Reign and I couldn't be together, the fact that he was my professor was still at the top of the list.

"Right, I'm sure he is."

"He can certainly handle himself, that's for sure," Rue added.

A familiar presence soothed the building turmoil, and I glanced up to the edge of the flight field. Sol pawed at the earth, his talons sinking deep into the dew-kissed grass. Griff and Windy stood on either side of him, both seeming as anxious as he was.

Are you ready for a ride? I threw my voice across the mystical tether between us. I hadn't seen Sol in days, and that familiar longing to be in his presence returned at the sight of him.

I am. As apparently you were only two nights ago.

Heat raced up my neck, warming my cheeks at the insinuation. *Excuse me?*

I heard you nearly completed the cuorem bond with Reign. Don't you think it was something you should have discussed with me?

I bristled at his tone. *I thought you knew everything, Sol? Aren't you some sort of all-powerful, omniscient creature?* Even through the bond I could hear myself shouting.

As I've told you before, I attempt to block you out so I'm not privy to every whiny moment of pining over that Shadow Fae traitor.

I halted mid-stride, his words like a knife to the heart.

Gods, Sol, tell me how you really feel.

I'm sorry, Aelia, but I do not believe you are thinking clearly. There are far-reaching ramifications—

Like what? You've skirted around the subject for months now, Sol. I know there's something you're not telling me. Please, stop hiding the truth from me!

Can't you simply trust me?

No! Is this about the prophecy? Is that what has you frightened?

The connection between us cut off, the shimmering, mystical ties going silent once more.

Sol?

I glared up at the stubborn dragon with my hands on my hips, but his golden irises glazed over. Symon barreled into me from behind, chattering away with Liora, tearing me from our mental argument.

"Sorry," I muttered at my friend, canting my head over my shoulder.

"You okay, A?" Rue inched closer, our skyriders only a few yards away now.

"No," I gritted out. "I'm sorry, but I can't fly today, after all."

"What? Why not?"

I scowled at the enormous dragon, his scales aglow beneath the luminous sunlight.

"Is it because you're worried about Reign?" Rue whispered.

"No." Stiffening my spine, I cast one last furious glance at my dragon before whirling on my heel. "I simply remembered there was somewhere important I needed to be."

The moment the last word was out, the pounding of wings lifted the hair on the back of my neck. I didn't bother turning around because I knew Sol would already be gone.

What was wrong with him, and why was *he* so angry? And most importantly, what in all the realms was he keeping from me now?

Chapter Fifty-Seven

A*elia*

Sitting on the edge of my bed, I tugged on the bodysuit that had magically appeared in my armoire this morning. The material was crafted from luminous, silver-threaded fabric that glinted subtly beneath the rays streaming in through the skylight. The suit was like nothing I'd ever seen before, lightweight yet resilient, designed to protect against the harsh elements and the rigors of high-altitude winds. Along with it, I'd found an armored vest made from some mystical alloy that was as strong as steel but felt as light as feathers, as well as a set of bracers and greaves with shimmering runes.

Rue sat across the room with her back to me, examining her new suit and all the accouterments that came with it. A ripple of nerves made my movements shaky and agitated as I strapped on each piece. The final Umbral Trial was here. As if that weren't enough to scatter my nerves, the fight with Sol had my insides in a terrible tangle.

I'd never quarreled with my bonded skyrider before, and it was nearly worse than my fights with Reign. Those shimmering mystical strands that linked us were dim, and an impenetrable wall had been erected between us, severing our connection. It felt as if one of my arms had been cut off.

A sharp gasp from across the room tore me from my dark musings. I jumped up, spun around, and nearly tripped over my own feet, forgetting my suit was only a quarter of the way up. Pulling the light material up the rest of the way, I rushed over to Rue's side of the chamber. She sat on the edge of her bed, now fully dressed, staring at a scrap of parchment.

"What is it?" I asked as I folded down beside her.

"A letter from Heaton."

I expected delight in her eyes, or at least relief, but I saw neither. "What's wrong?"

"I don't know." She frowned, staring at the dark scrawling across the yellowing page. "It just doesn't sound like Heaton at all. It's so formal, so bland." She handed me the scroll. "Take a look for yourself."

Dear Rue,

The situation on the border is worse than expected. The enemy is looming ever closer, so you must prepare for what is to come. I am safe with my unit and pray to Raysa I will remain that way. Rest assured, I will return before the end of the term.

I hope all is well with you.

In Raysa's blessed light,

Your brother, Heaton

I read over the message twice, searching for a hint of the team leader, the loyal friend or the doting older brother. Rue was right; it didn't sound like Heaton at all.

"He didn't even mention Lawson," she added. "How could he not? He was all we talked about before he left."

"Can you send a letter back?"

She shook her head. "I don't know how. I have no idea how the letter appeared on my nightstand. It was just suddenly... there."

"We'll ask Reign after the trial. Maybe he can get a message to Heaton through his shadows."

My best friend's pale blue eyes lit up; that spark that had recently returned fading with the arrival of the letter. Somehow, it found its way to the surface once more. "Do you think he would do that for me?"

"Absolutely." I would make sure of it.

She threw her arms around my neck and pulled me into a hug. "Thank you, A. I'm just so worried about him."

"I know you are. I am, too, but Heaton is strong and capable. He'll get through this and be back at the Conservatory before we know it. I'm sure of it."

"Yes, you're right. There are only a few days left."

"Exactly." I nodded aggressively then tugged her off the bed. "Now, we have a final trial to get to."

※

The brilliant sun streamed down on my shoulders through the new bodysuit as Rue and I marched toward the flight field. Even at this distance, I easily found Sol standing amidst the line of skyriders. His glistening golden form towered over all the others, standing proudly, his snout tipped toward the endless blue.

I searched our bond for any sign of him, but it was quiet.

How was I expected to pass this trial if he refused to speak to me? Not that I was in any particular mood to be all chatty with him either. His words yesterday stung, and what was worse, knowing he was still keeping something important from me was the ultimate slap in the face.

The crunch of grass from behind registered an instant before Symon swung one arm around me and the other across

Rue's shoulders, squeezing his way between us. "Good morning, ladies! Who's ready for the big day?"

We both grumbled in response.

"Good gods, what is the matter now?" His worried gaze bounced between each of us.

"It's Heaton," Rue murmured.

"And Sol," I added.

His cheery smile evaporated. "Do I even want to know?"

"Heaton's okay, for now, and he promises to return for the end of the term. There was just something about his letter that seemed off." She waved a dismissive hand. "Something to deal with after the trial."

He swung his head in my direction. "And Sol?"

"We're not speaking." I had already filled Rue in on some of the details of our argument the night before without going into the specifics. I hated to continuously lie to my best friend, and I vowed that once we survived this term, I would talk to Reign about telling her the truth. Maybe not all of it, as the last thing I wanted was to paint a target on her back, but at least some.

"What, why?" he asked.

"Basically, he doesn't approve of Reign," Rue replied for me. Which was much simpler than the lengthy answer I'd conjured up.

Symon released a dramatic sigh before squeezing us into a Fae sandwich. "Oh, ladies, after this trial is over, we'll sort everything out over a full tankard of lager."

I couldn't help the chuckle from spilling out. Of course, Sy would find an easy answer to our *trivial* little problems.

"Sol will get over it because he's not going to risk your life up there." His eyes ticked to the sky before turning to Rue. "And Heaton will return as he promised; and if he doesn't, we'll simply go find him." He offered us each an indulgent smile before releasing us. "Now, get your head in the game so that we can win the final trial and avoid spending our week of respite at Arcanum."

My heart leapt up my throat. "That's the punishment for the losing team?"

Symon nodded. "That's what I've heard."

We had yet to be told much of anything about the final trial. With Heaton absent, no one had shared any details. After last term's ambush by Arcanum, we had all been on high alert last night. Reign had spent all night on our doorstep, despite my urging to come inside. He had insisted he would be unable to remain in the same room as me all night without acting upon the cuorem bond's primal urges.

Just the thought sent a delicious shudder up my spine. Besides the obvious reasons for wanting to succeed in the final trial, I couldn't wait for the term to be over so Reign and I could finally complete the bond and enjoy a few uninterrupted days together.

The steady rumble of voices drew me from more pleasant thoughts to the present. Dozens of initiates littered the clearing, making their way toward their skyriders. I had been dreading this moment since I walked off the field yesterday.

On the far corner, a dais had been erected with a billowing white canopy. Beneath it stood the distinguished faculty of the Conservatory, Reign included, along with a special guest. A shimmering golden orb encased the platform, powerful *rais* pulsating in the air. A troop of Royal Guardians surrounded the stand where King Elian sat atop a high-backed chair. Draven stood beside him, his trailing, snowy mustache twisted in disdain.

I wondered what had our headmaster in a huff.

In answer to my unspoken question, a wave of pure night blotted out the shimmering sunlight. The horde of Shadow Fae descended in a surge of *nox*, sucking all the light from the midday sun. Among the crowd, blanketed in hissing shadows, stood none other than King Tenebris.

My gaze shot across the field to Reign, where I instinctively knew he stood along the dais. His dark eyes chased to mine, and even from this distance, I could feel his entire body stiffen at his father's presence.

Drawing in a steadying breath, I forced my gaze away before curious eyes followed my line of sight. Because I could already feel *him* too. Ruhl appeared from within the cloud of sheer darkness, his contemptuous glare heavy on me.

My heart revolted at the sight of him, an erratic thumping against my ribs. This was the first I'd seen him since the night of the bacchanalia. My thoughts flew back to the false alarm and that slate dragon flying in the distance. Why would Ruhl have set off the wards? If he'd intended to strike, had he changed his mind? Or was it something else entirely?

Not for the first time, I contemplated what Reign had told me about the cuorem bond and the blood attraction. I should have been relieved to know that the tangle of emotions Ruhl brought out in me were mystically explainable, but instead, I only felt more confused.

That powerful force of *nox* sifted over my skin as Ruhl's intense gaze bored into me. I refused to meet it, refused to face what I knew I would find. It would not only be anger there, but something else. Something far more frightening.

I had yet to speak my most terrible fears out loud, but what if Ruhl and I were meant to be cuoré, and the bond was confused about Reign? The thought alone felt traitorous, but I couldn't deny its existence. When fate was pulling all the strings, how could one truly be sure of anything?

No, it couldn't be... what I felt for Reign was more powerful, more visceral than any mistake. Gods, I simply wanted to complete the bond so that we could finally truly be together. There was nothing I wanted more.

"Welcome, Light and Shadow Fae initiates to the final Umbral Trial," Draven's voice boomed across the field.

I pivoted my gaze only to be caught in Ruhl's dark one. Those icy obsidian orbs drilled into mine from across the divide of Light and Shadow Fae students. The faintest twitch of his lips trapped my attention. "Good luck, duskling," he mouthed.

Forcing my lips to stretch into a smile, I nodded. "Same to you," I replied soundlessly.

"For today's final trial, each Light Fae squad will be pitted against a Shadow Fae team. Therefore, unlike the last Aerial Combat, one academy will not be the overall winner, but rather it will depend on each individual squad."

Malakar nudged Draven in the side and interjected, "Unless, of course, there is a clean sweep by either side." A wicked gleam lit up his dark eyes.

Ignoring the Shadow Fae headmaster, Draven cleared his throat and continued. "Points will be awarded based on time remaining in mid-air, and of course, the final initiate and skyrider flying from each team wins, earning a bonus one hundred points for their squad. As always, you must remain within the aerial boundaries, but besides that, anything goes. Does everyone understand?"

Muttered yeses rolled through the crowd.

"And now, the team pairings."

A whisper of unease crept up my spine as Malakar produced a scroll from the dark depths of his robe. My eyes flickered to Ruhl's as the headmaster slowly unrolled the parchment. Oh gods, please tell me he didn't. I shot the Shadow heir a questioning glance, the unspoken words caught in my throat. His barely perceptible nod a long second later stole the air from my lungs.

I should not have been surprised. I wasn't, not truly.

A terrifying smile jerked up the corners of Malakar's lips as he read from the scroll. "The first squads up are Flare team from the Conservatory of Luce, and Midnight Squad from Arcanum Citadel."

Chapter Fifty-Eight

A*elia*

Despite knowing it was coming, the tiny flare of hope Symon had instilled a few moments ago deflated as Malakar spoke the dreaded words. Today, I would be forced to fight the prince. In front of everyone. Worse, the moment the proclamation was out, King Tenebris materialized on the dais, inching closer to the two headmasters, his entourage of dark minions coiling and twisting around his ominous form.

He didn't speak, didn't utter a sound. Instead, he only stood there, his intense glare razing over each member of Flare Squad before settling on me. Heady, overwhelming *nox* polluted the air, pressing against my burgeoning *rais*. Every hair on my body stood on end as shards of ice surged through my veins at that piercing stare.

Frosty tendrils raced across the shell of my ear, followed by Reign's agitated voice sailing across my eardrum. "Do not engage Ruhl, Aelia. Do you understand me? Do what you must to keep your distance. I don't care if you must lose to avoid him. There is a reason my father is here, and I guarantee it is not to cheer on his favorite son."

I nodded ever so slightly, worried the king would notice the swirl of darkness churning around me. His gaze never deviated, never confessed whether or not he had noticed Reign's ghostly messenger.

The king's heavy stare grew more suffocating, as if a bubble of *nox* surrounded me, squeezing the air from my lungs. My *rais* blossomed, surging below my skin, eager to fight the invasive intruder. Just when I was certain I couldn't stand the onslaught for a moment longer, Ruhl appeared by his father's side, diverting his attention.

Finally free of that overwhelming presence, I heaved in a breath, and my lungs began to function once more. Sweat slickened my brow, tiny droplets slinking down my back from the strain. Stars, that male was powerful.

"Now, it is time for the first two teams to take their places!" Draven bellowed.

I attempted to move, but my feet were rooted to the spot. Ruhl still stood beside the dais, speaking to his father, and Raysa, I wished I knew what they were saying. I briefly contemplated a celestial glyph to bolster my hearing, but the last thing I needed was for Draven to catch me listening to the Shadow royals' conversation.

Ruhl's gaze flickered in my direction for an instant as he turned away from his father and marched across the field to where Mordrin stood in front of the assembly of Shadow skyriders.

"Aelia, come on!" Rue waved at me, now a few yards down the field. Symon had already mounted as I stood there frozen.

"You can do this, princess." Reign's deep voice flitted across my ear. "I have the utmost faith in you."

"How am I supposed to win if I cannot engage Ruhl?" I gritted out through clenched teeth, hoping no one was watching me talk to myself. "You know he will come after me."

"Find another way, Aelia, please. This is the first time you've been forced to battle directly against Ruhl in the trials. If he feels the true extent of your offensive power, he will know, if he doesn't already. And he'll run to my father who will call in my vow. We cannot let that happen, no matter the cost."

"So you'd rather I lose and spend the week at Arcanum?"

"I fear it's the lesser of two evils."

Gods, this was impossible. Blowing out a breath, I tried to force my legs to move. And to my surprise, they finally obeyed. A flurry of motion drew my attention across the field as Light and Shadow Fae initiates scrambled to board their mounts. Eight of us remained from Flare team, thanks to the addition of Liora, against the ten from Ruhl's squad. I supposed I should have been appreciative to Lucian for taking out those two females in the last trial or we would have been even more outnumbered.

As I marched closer to Sol, I searched our mental link. It seemed quiet, but a hint of light trickled through. *Sol?*

Yes, Aelia?

Oh, good, I'm glad you're still there.

I couldn't very well abandon you, now, could I? A plume of silver smoke billowed from his wide nostrils.

I wasn't sure after yesterday...

I apologize for my outburst. It had little to do with you, and more to do with my frustration with our current predicament.

And what is that? I closed the final distance between us and stared up at his looming shadow.

I'm not even certain where to begin.

I suppose now isn't the best time to discuss it anyway.

No, it is not. Right now, we must destroy that savage bastard. His reptilian irises narrowed to furious slits as he glared across the divide between the Light and Shadow teams.

Ruhl?

No, Mordrin. I had a chat with Phantom after our disagreement yesterday evening, and she brought certain truths to light.

A follow up question lingered on the tip of my tongue, but I never got the chance to voice it because a buzzer rang out, interrupting our mental conversation.

"That's the warning bell," Rue called out from Windy's back a few yards away.

"Good luck, Rue!" I shouted.

"Same to you, A."

Symon darted by, Griff's wings already pounding the air. "I'll see you ladies in the winner's circle."

A smile curled my lips despite the building tension as I waved one final time at my friends. Sol extended his leg, and I quickly climbed up, expertly avoiding the jagged protrusions. Once I was firmly seated between his wing bones, I cocked my head over my shoulder. Ruhl sat atop Mordrin, the smoky gray dragon glaring in our direction.

One day soon you're going to have to fill me in on your history with that one.

Hopefully after today, I won't have to suffer Mordrin's presence any longer.

Unease rolled through me as I processed the lethal edge to his tone. I had never heard or felt that depth of fury from my dragon before. It was more than alarming.

"Initiates, take to the skies!" Draven called out.

I hazarded a quick glance at Rue, then Symon, and my heart pinched. Belmore, Ariadne and Liora were all nearby aboard their skyriders, and I sent each a tight smile. The mad pounding of wings beat the air into a whirlwind, echoing the escalating drumbeats of my pulse. This was it.

The buzzer rang out, and chaos erupted around me like a violent storm unleashed.

My stomach dipped when the winds roared past me as Sol spiraled upward into the cloud-marbled sky. Below, the vast expanse of the forest surrounding the Conservatory blurred into a sea of greens and browns.

Reign doesn't want us to engage Ruhl. I sent the thought through our bond, dreading Sol's response.

Of course he doesn't, he snarled.

To protect me.

He snorted his reply, more dark smoke muddying the air.

The sound of growling beasts and metal clashing resonated from below as we climbed higher. I kept my gaze fixed on the mystical border outlining the aerial battlefield, one half bathed in light, the other in murky shadows. After our last mid-air encounter with the Arcanum first-years, I'd spent many excruciating hours growing accustomed to the thinner air at these heights. I would not be caught off guard this time.

The steady thrashing of wings turned my attention over my shoulder. Curses. Ruhl and Mordrin cut through the clouds like a shadow at dusk. Sol roared a fiery challenge that resonated across the vast sky, his wings beating with a fury that matched the pounding of my heart. We had trained for moments like this, to face the Shadow Fae and their mounts in battle, yet as I clamped my thighs tight around Sol's neck, a surge of apprehension washed over me.

Ruhl's dark eyes caught mine across the expanse of blue, and Reign's warning echoed through my thoughts. *Do not engage*, I growled through our bond.

Still, Sol surged forward, his wingbeats growing more frantic as Mordrin hurtled toward us.

Sol!

Don't worry, little Kin. We won't be needing your powers today. I will be the one to ground Mordrin with my bare fangs and claws, once and for all.

An unexpected pang shot through my chest at the vivid image of a broken and battered Ruhl plummeting from the sky. When had Reign's brother become someone I no longer despised, in spite of everything?

You cannot kill Mordrin without taking Ruhl down with him.

And why is that a problem?

The distance between the two dragons grew smaller with each massive wing flap, and my heart hammered more erratically with each yard closer.

You simply cannot Sol. To kill the Shadow heir would only escalate the tension between the two courts. You could start a war.

The heir knew very well what he was getting into when he enlisted at the Citadel. Sol roared, unleashing a wave of dragonfire that lit up the sky.

Gods, Sol, what did Mordrin do?

Not now, Aelia!

Mordrin dove, evading Sol's flames with an agile grace that contradicted his massive form. Ruhl glanced upward, his piercing gaze meeting mine. In that brief look, I felt the unspoken challenge along with an echo of the tumultuous connection that neither of us could deny. He was the enemy, the prince of the Court of Umbral Shadows, one wrong move and he could be my death sentence. And still, I couldn't be the cause of his end.

"Sol, easy," I murmured. He snorted, his fiery breath a brilliant contrast against the cooling air as we grew closer to the border between the courts. Mordrin retreated to the darkness and Sol followed, the tension radiating from his scales seeping through my skin.

Ruhl and Mordrin ascended swiftly, looping over Sol in a daring arc. Ruhl's dark gaze was fixed to the starlit sky, his body moving in perfect sync with Mordrin. They were a formidable pair, and every innate instinct urged me to end this threat, to protect myself and my secret at all costs.

Letting Sol end both their lives would have been the smart decision, the ruthless way of the Fae. I didn't doubt that Reign would understand. Even Ruhl would take some sort of twisted pride from it.

Yet, I held Sol back as we soared higher. *Not a kill, Sol. We only need to incapacitate them.* I only hoped my dragon understood my internal conflict. He growled his response, a rumble of disgust, as his eyes locked on Mordrin once more.

Sol plummeted, a spiral of light chasing shadow, the distance closing between us with heart-stopping speed. Mordrin swerved at the last moment, but Sol was faster, and his talons grazed the slate dragon's hide. An unearthly roar shook the heavens, vibrating the air whizzing by. Ruhl shouted at his dragon, a sound lost to the wind, and for a moment, my heart plunged along with our diving forms.

With a powerful thrust of his wings, Sol pulled up, and we hovered, watching as Ruhl regained control. His eyes found mine again across the turbulent air, dark and intense. There was no hatred as I'd imagined, only the heavy burden of duty that shadowed his features.

The battle calmed as both dragons circled warily, each of us contemplating our next move under the weight of potential loss. I breathed deeply, feeling the chill of the altitude seep into my bones, mingling with the heat of adrenaline.

Below us, few riders remained. I sent a quick prayer to Raysa that my friends were safe. With the intensity of the battle, I hadn't had a free moment to search for Rue or Symon, let alone the other members of Flare Squad.

"Ruhl," I called across the wind, my voice steady despite the turmoil inside. "Stand down!"

A sharp chuckle iced the blood in my veins. "I'm afraid that's impossible, duskling." He ticked his head below, to the mass of remaining battling bodies and beyond that to the canopy where the royals convened. "Only one of us will be the last to fall today, and it *must* be me."

"Sol wants Mordrin dead!" I shouted. "You know that doesn't bode well for you."

"Then let him try." With a wink, he turned his dragon, urging him farther into the depths of the Umbral Court. He likely thought my *rais* would diminish the deeper we went. Little did he know my powers only came alive beneath the cool darkness.

Curses... A whisper of fear throttled the air from my lungs. What if Ruhl suspected the truth? What if he was drawing me farther into the Shadow Court to test his own theory?

You could be right. Sol's reluctant tone echoed through my mind.

So now what do we do?

End them both.

Chapter Fifty-Nine

R *eign*

Solanthus and Mordrin sailed across the infinite sky, where light battled shadow. The deadly dance of dragons and riders had my heart in a choke hold. I forced my lungs to continue expanding despite the fury and suffocating fear crushing my chest. Standing here, completely helpless was pure torture.

I should have been up there. It was my duty to protect Aelia.

Now flying above Shadow lands, if she attempted a direct strike, Ruhl would figure it out, he would sense the tangle of *rais* and *nox* as I had. If he hadn't already. And I strongly suspected that he had. With all the time he'd spent with her as of late, I wouldn't be the least bit surprised. My brother was many things, but stupid was not on that list. What I did not understand was why he still kept the truth, or even his assumptions from Father?

Or perhaps he had not, and my sire was simply waiting for an opportune moment.

I hazarded a glance over my shoulder at the king. The male who had made me a ruthless monster. Maybe Ruhl *had* shared his suppositions about Aelia, which explained his unexpected presence here today. Had he come to see her in action for himself?

Solanthus soared across the clear blue giving chase to Mordrin who had crossed the boundary into night. *No*! If Aelia's volatile *rais* was loosed in Shadow lands, Ruhl's assumptions, which up to now would have been just that, suspicions and suppositions with no proof, would surely be confirmed.

Phantom, where are you?

Close, just behind the Darkmania Falls, per your orders. Ready to swoop in and save the day if necessary.

Good.

If Aelia were somehow exposed, I was ready to step in. Phantom was prepared to raze both academies to the ground, and I would throw my stubborn *cuoré* over my shoulder and escape to the farthest corner of the continent, all else be damned. I would *not* lose Aelia today. Not ever.

My heart hammered against my ribcage as my gaze tipped skyward once more. Aelia soared above the spiraling turrets of Arcanum before diverting back toward Light Fae lands. *Good girl*. The sunlight glinted off Sol's iridescent scales, a beacon of the power she wielded. Below, the dark form of Ruhl on Mordrin mirrored my own turmoil. He was holding back, but why?

They rose into the cloud banks, a tempest of motion against the serene backdrop of the late afternoon sky. As they emerged, Solanthus gave chase once again. Every fiber of my being wanted to shout for her to pull back, to not engage, but this battle was hers to command, not mine to govern.

As they ascended, Sol's wings beat with a rhythm that pulsed through the very air, powerful and commanding. Aelia maneuvered him with the expertise of a seasoned rider, her body leaning into each twist and turn as they hunted Ruhl through the sky. Mordrin dodged each blast of Sol's fiery breath with a desperate precision. Ruhl's face was set, focused, the embodiment of the shadows he commanded.

My thoughts flitted back to Aelia's words after the last trial. Could it be true? Had my brother actually changed in the past four years? No, it wasn't possible. He was Tenebris's heir, raised for one thing only. He wasn't capable of change, of kindness, of growth.

A screech echoed across the sky, and my heart catapulted across my chest as the golden dragon attacked. Another wave of dragonfire burst from Sol's maw, singeing Mordrin's left wing. This time, the screech came from my brother's mount, one of excruciating pain. He dropped a few yards, his wing flaps slowing.

The tension was palpable, a living thing that wrapped its fingers around my throat. I watched, stunned, as Sol gained the upper hand, his massive body outmaneuvering Mordrin with that injured wing. Sol was ruthless, striking again. The slate dragon banked to avoid the brunt of his jagged talons across his good wing.

Ruhl's grip slipped, his body arching away from Mordrin's. He fell in a slow, horrifying descent toward the forest below.

My breath caught. "No!" The word was torn from me, an unexpected near-silent scream that Aelia must have somehow heard above the roar of wind and wing. In a heartbeat, she directed Sol in a steep dive, her own life suddenly secondary to the male who had haunted us both.

Sol's talons stretched out, grasping, as Aelia leaned far over his side, her hand extended. I watched, paralyzed, barely breathing, as the tips of her fingers brushed Ruhl's arm. Then, with a strength that contradicted her slender frame, she caught him. Ruhl's body jerked violently as he was pulled against Sol's warm hide, clutched in Aelia's determined grasp.

Good gods. She saved him.

Relief flooded me, sharp and sweet, but it was laced with an ache that throbbed deep in my soul. Why had she saved him? She risked everything, not for the glory of the win or the sanctity of her court, but for Ruhl—my brother, her enemy.

I always knew her compassion bordered on the point of recklessness, but was there more to this? Had the cuorem bond actually spun true feelings for him?

No. It couldn't be. As I watched the pair descend, I tossed the fear aside. It was simply Aelia, exactly what I loved about her, the depth of her courage and the boundless expanse of her heart.

Sol landed in the middle of the flight field inciting a tremor across the verdant land. Overhead the battle had grown quiet with no remaining members of either squad still left to vie for the final spot and a chance at victory.

Aelia had won her match.

From across the way, I could just make out Ruhl's scowl as he slumped behind Aelia between Sol's impressive wing bones. Her expression was unreadable, and a pang of uncertainty trampled across my insides. I watched from the dais, keeping my countenance an expressionless mask, torn between surprising gratitude and a gnawing fury.

Movement across the platform turned my attention to Father who barreled by his guards and leapt onto the lawn below. *Curses.* I rushed down the steps behind him, keeping a few strides between us. Aelia was my acquisition and mentee. It made absolute sense that I would go to her. Or at least, those were the lies I told myself, because staying away from her at this critical juncture was impossible.

"Ruhl," Father bellowed, the wrath and disgust in his tone palpable. A torrent of shadows trailed his form, blanketing him in endless night. "What in Noxus's name was *that*?"

Moving out from behind Aelia, Ruhl slid down Sol's leg and faced our sire with surprising calm.

Oh gods, Ruhl knew somehow. That could be the only reason he would act so composed in the face of the king's ire.

"I fell." His shoulders lifted calmly, as if falling from his dragon was a common occurrence.

A vein popped across the king's brow, his entire demeanor edging on the brink of total rage. His shadows whirled faster, a wave of *nox* draping the air in dark energy. "What do you mean you *fell*?" he gritted out. "You've trained your whole life for this moment, Ruhl!" His roar echoed through the trees, powerful and deadly. "Did I choose unwisely in selecting you as my heir? Perhaps I should have designated your brother…"

I halted midstride, all the air expelling from my lungs at the word.

"I'm sure Dom will make a fine king one day." Ruhl's reply forced my errant organs to once again comply. Of course, Father was speaking of Dominion, his youngest heir, certainly not me, the bastard. "And I'm sure even great kings occasionally fall from their dragons. In fact, I remember such a royal in recent history, King Alaric of Ether. Surely, Father, you remember the name?"

Noxus, perhaps Aelia had been right, and the sniveling child who doted on Father's every word had changed. I had never seen him speak to the king in such a manner.

"Excuse me, I must tend to my student," I muttered through a gritted jaw. Forcing my legs to move around the arguing royals, I marched toward Aelia, compelling my face into a mask of calm when all I wanted to do was run to her and drag her into my arms. She slid off Sol at my approach, wiping the perspiration from her brow.

"Are you all right, Miss Ravenwood?" I managed.

She dipped her head. "Yes, professor."

"You did quite well up there. You were the last student from Flare team left airborne."

"I was." Her eyes chased over my shoulder to where Ruhl and my father stood, tangled in a hushed, heated debate, then began scanning the field around us. "Did everyone else from my team survive?"

I could read the fear in her eyes for her friends. "Yes."

"Thank the goddess."

"Did anything of consequence occur that you need to share?" Namely, did my brother discover your secret? The real question sat poised on the tip of my tongue.

Aelia released a careful breath before shaking her head and meeting my eyes. "No, nothing that we cannot discuss later."

"Very well."

"I suppose I should meet this valiant Light Fae initiate who saved my heir's life." The king's voice over my shoulder iced the blood in my veins.

No. No, damn it, Ruhl.

I cast a murderous glare in my brother's direction as he and the king stepped closer. The little bastard's smirk remained perfectly in place.

"As I told you, Father, I was paired with Miss Ravenwood in the last trial. She proved quite a worthy partner, despite her Lightness."

The shadow of a smile cracked my father's thin lips. Dark tendrils of *nox* oozed from his pores, circling Aelia. "Isn't that interesting?"

Get ready, Phantom. I shot the command through our mental link, prepared to take on my father and his entire retinue of Umbral Guards if that was what it took to keep Aelia safe.

Ready when you are.

Aelia dipped into a quick curtsy, her gaze remaining pinned to the grass, but the flare of *rais* was unmistakable. It seemed I wasn't the only one prepared to fight our way out. "An honor to meet you, Your Umbral Highness," she murmured.

"Yes, I suppose it would be." He tipped her chin up, forcing her gaze to his curious one. Nostrils flaring, his cold, hard eyes razed over her.

Every muscle in my body coiled, poised to strike. My

shadows twisted along my arms, gathering across my shoulders. She was within arm's reach. I'd grab Aelia and shoot into the night sky before Tenebris could strike.

The air crackled with intensity. I barely dared to breathe at the slow, agonizing scrutiny. Noxus, how I wished I could tear these damned manacles off. Even now I could feel their siphoning energy inhibiting my power. An endless moment later, the king released her, drawing in a slow breath. "I do hope you'll attend the celebratory ball at Arcanum this evening, Miss Ravenwood?"

Aelia's wary gaze flitted to find mine then pivoted to Ruhl's. A barely perceptible nod from my brother.

"Of course she'll be there," he replied. "It's poor manners to deny a prince."

"Or a king," Father snapped.

"Of course." Despite the calm edge to her tone, tension vibrated from her aura. Her fingers lay mere inches from her blades, and I could practically feel them twitching to reach for their comfort.

As if one royal wasn't enough, I barely restrained a groan when I caught a glimpse of glittering movement over my father's shoulder. King Elian, in all his radiant splendor, marched toward our semi-circle with an entourage of Royal Guardians.

"Tenebris," Elian grumbled. "I believe you've harassed my citizen enough for the day. The female initiate only just finished a trying battle, defeating your great heir. Perhaps, you should allow her to be dismissed with the rest of her team, so that you too may return to your side of the Luminoc."

Father's eyes narrowed to tiny slits of darkness. "If I didn't know better, Elian, I would think you were trying to dismiss *me*."

A tight smile crept across the Light Fae king's lips. "I would never be so ill-mannered."

"I didn't believe so." Tenebris glanced to Ruhl before

turning to his guards. "I suppose we should return to Arcanum to ensure Malakar has everything ready for the grand feast tonight."

Not once in the entire conversation did my father's gaze flicker to mine. Did he truly believe me to be so inconsequential, or was his control simply that impressive?

Either way, I was certain of one thing. If I wished to pose a challenge to my father when the fateful day came that he discovered the truth about Aelia, I would need to be at full power. And the only way to do that was without these damned cuffs.

And with my *cuoré* at my side.

Chapter Sixty

A*elia*

"Why did you save him?" Reign stood across from me beneath the shadow of a sprawling lightwood, pure torment etched into his jaw.

The sounds of deadly combat surged overhead as the final Light and Shadow teams battled it out. All first-years were forced to stay and watch as our fellow initiates endured the final Umbral trial. As of yet, Sol and I were in the lead for longest flight time. I should have been pleased, but the triumph felt hollow.

In a few short hours, all the anguish would be forgotten, the pointless lives lost ignored, and we'd spend the night reveling in some undoubtedly grand chamber in the lavish halls of the Citadel.

I still couldn't quite process it all.

I had spent the past hour dreading this moment, feeling the turmoil in Reign's gaze from across the field as each team took to the skies. The truth was, I still hadn't been able to answer the question myself.

When Reign's willpower had shattered as the final teams were called, he grabbed my arm and toted me to this quiet copse of trees on the outskirts of the training field, hidden from view. All the while, I'd felt Ruhl's dark gaze tracing our movements until the enormous willows closed around us.

It wouldn't seem so odd except that I *felt* him watching me. I never turned to confirm my suspicions because there was no need. Much like I knew when Reign entered a room or was within a mile radius.

Whatever mystical confusion was happening with the cuorem bond, it was accelerating. It would no longer be ignored.

"Aelia?" Reign obliterated the space between us, a storm of shadows forming a protective barrier around us before he clamped his hands around my shoulders. "Talk to me."

It wasn't a question. It was a command. And for a second, I saw the ruthless, cold Shadow Fae I had met in my cottage all those months ago.

He deserved the truth; after all we'd been through, I wouldn't lie to him about something so important.

Lifting my chin to meet a pair of fathomless midnight orbs, I steeled my nerves. "I saved him just as I would have saved any other Fae had it been within my power."

The hard line of his jaw softened a touch as I paused.

"But there is more..."

The shudder that rippled up his spine, pulsing across his broad shoulders, deepened the ache in my chest at the words I was about to speak.

"I've been feeling things for him—not anywhere close to what I feel for you, but there is something there."

He hissed a curse, squeezing my shoulders so hard, his nails dug into my skin. "It's the damned cuorem, Aelia. It is exactly why I wanted to leave this place, to be free to be together without all the other interferences."

"I know," I mumbled.

His strong hands framed my face, piercing irises locking to mine. "This has gone far enough. We seal the cuorem bond tonight after the ball." A glimmer of uncertainty settled across his brutally handsome face. "Unless... you have changed your mind."

"Of course I haven't. I love *you*, Reign. I want *you*." I pressed my hand to his heart as I dropped a hasty kiss to his lips. "I know all of this is merely some mystical trickery the gods have concocted to test us. I simply don't understand why."

"I wish I knew the answer." He swept a lock of platinum hair behind my ear, the gesture so gentle, so intimate, it had my heart staggering. How could I be so confused one moment and so certain the next? When I was with Reign, not a single doubt existed, but when I found myself in Ruhl's presence, I couldn't deny the pull.

"There is one more thing..."

His dark brows furrowed as he regarded me, a trickle of tension igniting once again.

"With the fickle nature of the blood attraction of the cuorem bond, is there any way—" I paused, unable to form the traitorous words.

"Is there any way, what, Aelia?"

"That it's a mistake," I forced out.

"You and me, a mistake?" His voice was nothing more than a jagged whisper. "There is no world that exists in which you and I were brought together in error, Aelia."

Reign tightened his grip ever so slightly, the earnest intensity in his eyes searing into me. "Our bond, this connection—it transcends the uncertainty, the fickle will of gods and the cursed prophecies. You are the truth in my heart, the calm in my storm. Trust in that, Aelia, trust in us, and all else be damned."

His words cascaded over me, a gentle balm that eased the

storm raging within. He'd always possessed this uncanny power over me, even from those turbulent first days at the academy. His mere presence—his potent nox that should have sent me running—was the only thing that could tame the spiraling chaos inside. I loved this male, and I always had. Bond or no bond, Light Fae, Shadow Fae, whoever I was. My soul had known his from the start, bound by something ancient, undeniable. Nothing, and no one, could touch what we had.

I drew in a steadying breath, feeling the decision harden within me like tempered steel. "You're right. I know you are. So, whatever comes, we face it together. I trust you, Reign, with every fiber of my being. And I love you... more than I ever thought I was capable of."

He smiled then, a true smile that reached those deep, soulful eyes. "You are my everything," he said, pulling me close. "Tonight, we become unbreakable. Tonight, we defy the gods, the prophecies and all odds."

The certainty in his tone, the promise in his embrace strengthened my resolve, confirming what I knew deep in my soul all along. Tonight, after the ball, Reign and I would finally seal our cuorem bond. The unbreakable vow would be held unwavering by the sheer force of our determination, our love.

"Okay," I breathed.

His mouth captured mine, hungry and insistent, his firm hold tethering me to him in the chaos of the moment. One hand drifted down my neck, fingers diving into the hair at my nape, tilting my head to deepen the kiss. The dangerous, forbidden moment stretched on for an eternity and still it was nowhere near enough.

My body, heart and soul craved Reign's, compelling me to seal the sacred bond between us. I wanted this more than anything. I had been a fool to think I could simply walk away from this male who had become *my* everything. When he finally pulled away, my shoulders sagged at the loss of his comforting warmth and unyielding strength.

"I cannot wait to make you mine forever, princess."

"I was about to say the same, my shadow prince."

The mood in our chamber as Rue and I dressed for the final ball at Arcanum was nothing like the one that started the term. With my thoughts on the ramifications of sealing the bond with Reign and facing King Tenebris again, and Rue's fear for Heaton mixed with dismal memories of Devin, the silence in the room was smothering.

I wished I could avoid the ball all together, but with the Shadow King expecting me, doing so would be a blatant show of disrespect. And if catching Tenebris's interest was bad, earning his hatred would have been countless times worse.

A soft sigh tumbled from Rue's lips, turning my attention from the array of lavish ballgowns hanging in the armoire to my friend.

"Are you all right?" I whispered as I walked toward her.

"No." She slumped onto the bed, clutching a glittering, sequined gown. "I'm just so worried about Heaton. I can't even explain it. It's this terrible feeling in my gut."

"I'm so sorry, Rue." I folded down beside her and bent my forehead to hers. "I don't have siblings, so I cannot imagine what you're going through, but I do know that Heaton is strong and resourceful. He will survive whatever he may be facing in the Wilds."

"What if he doesn't?" Her voice trembled.

"Then like Symon said, we'll simply go in there after him."

A tear streamed down her cheek before she could sweep it away. "Thank you, Aelia. You are the best friend I've ever had."

"As are you." I pressed a kiss to her forehead, then squeezed her into a tight embrace. "Now, are you going to wear something over the top gorgeous tonight to have all those Light and Shadow Fae males salivating over you?"

A giggle erupted from her lips as she swept back the remaining tears. "I should, shouldn't I?"

"Absolutely, you should."

She groaned. "I almost forgot Devin will finally get to reunite with his true love tonight. I'm not sure I can watch that."

"Then don't. You give him your own show to watch. I'm sure Blyte will be more than happy to comply."

Rue chuckled again, a devious one this time. "What I did with Blyte beneath the cover of darkness at a bacchanalia is not quite the same as a ball for both academies where all will be watching."

"Who cares? Isn't it time to end this divide between Light and Shadow Fae? Shouldn't we focus on the real threat in the Wilds?"

"Are we talking about me or you, A?" She shot me a knowing smile. "I saw you sneak off to the woods with our broody professor earlier."

A silly smile parted my lips, despite the instant rush of butterflies the mention of his name caused.

"Is everything okay between you two again?"

My head bobbed, and I vowed to find time to discuss Rue with Reign. I refused to lie to her anymore. "I think I'm finally going to—" Heat spread across my cheeks at the embarrassing confession.

But it felt good. Felt right to finally share some bit of truth with my friend.

She let out a squeal, reading the words I was too much of a coward to say out loud, then tugged me into her chest, wrapping her slender arms around me. "It's about time! I am so happy for you, A. That male is crazy about you. I said it from the start."

"I love Reign." The confession instantly lifted the weight from my shoulders. Finally, I could tell her something. "And he said he loves me." Now, I was surely grinning like a fool.

"Love? That brooding, grumpy, sometimes terrifying male actually used the word *love*?"

My head bounced up and down. "Multiple times."

Rue clapped our hands together, pulling me to my feet as she began to spin in a circle. "Oh, Aelia, this is the best news I've heard all term. Just wait until Symon hears he's lost his chance with your virgin rounded ears."

A laugh pealed out, my head falling back as a cackle vibrated through my chest.

"Mark my words, Aelia, tonight will be a night none of us will ever forget."

Chapter Sixty-One

The monstrous darkwood doors swung open, and my fingers tightened around Rue's hand as a blast of frosty air and a healthy dose of *nox* skimmed across my bare shoulders. My jaw unlocked, head tipping back to take it all in. The ambiance of Arcanum's grand hall was otherworldly, the ceiling mimicking a twilight sky filled with swirling constellations and a full moon. The obsidian walls flickered with gentle, luminous orbs that hovered like wayward stars, casting a soft glow over the assembled crowd.

"This is unreal..." Rue murmured.

A warm arm laced around my shoulders, chasing away the chill. "Much more grand than that clandestine bacchanalia the other night." Symon grinned wickedly as he sandwiched himself between us.

"Are you going to find that special someone again?" I cocked a brow at my friend. Rue's eager gaze was already scanning the sea of swirling colors as students danced to a symphony of mystical musical instruments.

"Many someones." That devious grin only grew wider.

"Why are Light and Shadow Fae relations forbidden?" The question popped out as I focused on the raised dais at the front of the room where the Light and Shadow Fae royals sat atop gilded thrones divided by a throng of guards.

A tiny voice in the back of my mind whispered the dreaded word: the prophecy. If the two courts never intermingled, the chances of it coming to fruition lessened.

Symon shrugged, Rue's attention still captive across the room. "I'm not certain, to be honest. It's simply always been that way. I suppose the war had a lot to do with it, but prior to that, who knows? I would assume intermingling would dilute our powers, and no one wants that."

"Maybe there was a time when the courts were free to mingle."

Rue finally returned her attention to our conversation. "I'm sure it's in the history books. After all, we were three courts once, and from what I understand, the Shadow and Night Court were long-time allies."

She was right, perhaps it was time to learn more about my Fae ancestry.

"Anyway, I don't know about you two, but I did not come here to discuss boring history." Symon's lively lilac irises flickered across the dancefloor to where Liora, Sylvan and Zephyr stood, swaying to the hypnotic tune filling the air.

"Same here." Rue offered her arm. "Come on, A, if I can't find Blyte, Sylvan will certainly do for the night."

I laughed, shaking my head at my friend. It was good to see her in high spirits once more. Threading my arm through hers, I let her lead me through the mass of twirling bodies. Shimmering gowns and suits that reflected light sparkled brilliantly with every turn, while Shadow Fae students embraced the darkness with velvety, dark fabrics adorned with shadowy motifs, creating a mesmerizing interplay of light and darkness.

We walked beneath a grand, crystalline chandelier which cast radiant beams that mingled with the deliberate shadows, creating a dance of light and dark, mirroring the students' quick footsteps across the floor. The entire ballroom was spectacular, the perfect blend of both courts.

A strange yearning bubbled up inside me, a need to feel the unmistakable presence of *nox* and *rais* together, intertwined.

"There she is! The resounding winner of Aerial Combat!" Sylvan hauled me into an unexpected embrace. As he pressed me to his chest, the scent of honeyed wine and something more potent reached my nostrils. "Not only was she the last one mid-air, she even saved the great prince of Umbral Shadows."

Zephyr offered me a congratulatory pat on the back. "You should have just let the arrogant bastard die. One less Shadow Fae royal, the better."

I bit back the retort poised on my tongue. This was not the time or place to express my traitorous tendencies.

"Yes, well done, Aelia." Liora offered a tight smile. Reign's *other* acquisition had done decently for someone so new. Speaking of my cuoré, where was he? I'd been certain he would have remained glued to my side all night after I'd caught the king's attention.

As the others continued to chatter on about the final trial, I searched the dark recesses of the ballroom for any trace of Reign's shadows. When I found none, my wandering gaze widened its scope to search for the *other* prince.

Ruhl and I hadn't exactly left things on a good note when last we saw each other. Instead of a thank you when I'd risked my own life to save his, I'd received a brusque, *you should have just let me die rather than suffer the embarrassment of being rescued by a lowly Kin.*

I'd bristled from the insult for only an instant before the

ground rushed upon us, and all was forgotten once we landed on the field only to be welcomed by the Shadow King.

Rue grabbed my arm and toted me to the center of the dancefloor, forcing away all thoughts of King Tenebris to be dealt with later. Symon was right, tonight was a celebration. Months ago, when I first set foot on this gods-blessed land, I never would have imagined how far I would come.

I should have been thanking my lucky stars.

Along that thought, I allowed the blend of haunting melodies and lively harmonies to move my stiff form, until my hips swayed, and I became lost in the moment. Sylvan, Zephyr and Symon formed a circle around us, and within our happy bubble, I felt free. Rue laughed, head tipped back to the midnight sky as Sylvan twirled her across the dark marble floor. The warm sound was a balm to my weary soul. Thank the gods we'd seen no sign of Devin or Mariana to ruin her fun.

"May I have this dance?" The rich velvet sound had every nerve in my body standing at attention.

I whirled around to find Reign in a formal suit, the material spun from pure night clinging to the broad expanse of his shoulders. My heart punched my ribs, a desperate attempt to breach the divide between us. He held his hand out, a rare unguarded look in his eye.

I glanced around the teeming dancefloor at the dozens of curious gazes slanted in our direction. "Do you think this is a good idea?" I whispered.

"I don't give a flying fuck, Aelia," he growled. "If one of these Shadow Fae males lances one more hungry look in your direction, I'll take out the whole damned lot of them." Dark tendrils of power crisscrossed the sleek fabric of his jacket, growing more frenzied with each ragged breath.

A chill raced up my spine at the violent edge to his tone.

He snatched my hand and dragged me to his chest as a whirlwind of shadows consumed us. "I am your professor, I am your mentor, and soon, I will be *much more.*" Heady *nox* skimmed my bare arms, and we were enveloped in darkness before we were catapulted across the room.

When my eyes dared open once more, Reign held me flush against him in a shadowed niche in the far corner of the grand hall. Glistening orbs danced over our heads, casting his hard expression in a swirl of light and dark.

"How much longer must we be here?" His eyes blazed, a mixture of fury and desire bleeding through those fathomless orbs.

"We just got here." A smile tipped up the corners of my lips.

"I'm not sure how much longer I can wait, Aelia." He dipped his head to my neck, warm breath spilling over my skin. "Every moment I spend with you, but not *inside* you, is pure torture."

A surge of heat raced to my core, flooding every inch of me with desire.

He dragged his tongue across the sensitive skin of my collarbone, winding his arm around my waist so that our bodies were flush. I could feel every inch of his desire pressed against my belly. A faint groan mingled in the air between us as his tongue continued its dangerous path to the sharp dip of my neckline.

I was suddenly very thankful Rue had insisted I choose the glittering strapless, corseted gown which allowed Reign full access. As we swayed to the slow, ethereal music, his tongue trailed a scorching path across the swell of my breasts, spilling over the fine satin.

A torrent of heady sensations swept over me, a second pulse throbbing between my legs. The cuorem bond pulsated between us, a ravenous beast with only one thought in mind. To claim, to possess, to unite.

Cuoré.

Cuoré.

The hypnotic hiss echoed the mad thumping of my raging heartbeat.

"Did you hear *that*?" I blurted.

His lips lifted from my chest, turbulent eyes meeting mine. "No, but it's a good sign that you are." His smile was devastating. "You will continue to hear it until the bond is complete."

Reign captured my lips with the force of a thousand suns, each one more brilliant than the last. I staggered back from the onslaught until he had me pinned against the sleek obsidian wall, the cool stone sending chills across my heated flesh.

His muscled arms caged me in, shadows swirling around us at a fevered pitch. All-consuming energy surged between us, billowing from our hidden niche. "*Noxus*, Aelia, I wish I could have you right here, right now. You make me absolutely mad." His hand slid from the wall, down my back and curled around my behind. Firm fingers kneaded my sensitive flesh before skimming down my thigh and lifting my leg to wrap around his hip.

The new position drove his arousal just where I needed it most. I groaned at the building pressure, the swell of unfettered energy erupting between us. A devastating tornado of *nox* and *rais* twirled around our forms, light and dark dancing perfectly entwined.

"Do it," I breathed. Only a few layers of clothing stood between us now, and gods, I wanted this too. I needed the security, the certainty of Reign. Once we were bound, nothing else would matter.

He halted, tearing his mouth from mine so those blazing orbs locked on mine. "*Noxus*, I love you, princess. You deserve more, so much more than a rushed, tawdry encounter for your first time. I want it to be absolute perfection, a moment in time we will remember forever."

Pressing a soft kiss to my forehead, he blew out a resigned breath. "And because of that, we should probably slow down before I am no longer able to control myself."

"Control yourself from doing what, brother?" Ruhl's voice scattered Reign's shadows, dousing the building fire and smothering the embers with that icy tone. He stalked closer, tendrils of darkness beating the air around him.

Reign gently let my leg slide off his hip before he took a protective stance in front of me. "What do you want?" he snarled.

"Only a word with your acquisition. I scented her from all the way across the chamber." His dark eyes sparkled with wicked mirth. "Or is she your mentee, or the female you're bedding? It's so hard for me to keep up with the nuances."

Reign lunged at his brother, but I caught his arm before he pummeled into the prince and ruined everything we'd fought so hard to keep hidden.

"So touchy..." A sneer curled Ruhl's lip.

"Don't, Ruhl. Please." I stepped between the two snarling males, placing a hand on each prince's chest. Both heaved beneath my palm, the mad thunder of Ruhl's heart catching me off guard.

Ruhl ticked his head up and over my bare shoulder. "I need a moment alone with Aelia."

"Absolutely not," Reign scoffed.

"Do you really think I could hurt her in a room full of Light and Shadow Fae, not to mention all the royals and guards?"

"No, I don't believe you could because I would rip off your head before you dared."

"Violent too... Typical, I suppose, for this sort of situation." His dark gaze dipped to mine. "Trust me, duskling, you are going to want to hear what I have to say."

Reign's body tensed behind me, every sharp, muscled plane pressed against my back. "What did you just call her?"

Drawing in a steadying breath, I twirled around. "It's okay. He won't hurt me."

"Are you mad?" A sharp laugh burst from Reign's clenched teeth. "How do you know that?"

"For the same reason I could not allow him to die."

The hard angle of Reign's shoulders rounded, his chest deflating as he hissed out a curse.

"Trust me," I mouthed.

The tendon in his jaw fluttered, a rhythmic pulse moments from detonation.

"Please." I laced my fingers through his and squeezed.

"Fine, I'll give you five minutes, but I won't be far." He leveled a murderous glare at his brother. "If your shadows so much as twitch, it'll be the last move you make on this gods-cursed earth."

A half-smile tugged at Ruhl's lips as he bent his head. "Whatever you say, brother."

Chapter Sixty-Two

A^{elia}

The moment Reign disappeared into the shadows, Ruhl stalked closer. I found myself once again pressed against the smooth, chilled obsidian walls of the ballroom.

"Why did you save me?"

The question caught me so off guard, I balked and bumped the back of my head against the unforgiving wall.

"Stars," I hissed, rubbing my skull. "This sounds remarkably much like a conversation I just had with another prince."

"And what answer did you have for my brother?"

My stomach twisted into knots as Ruhl's presence bored into me. I understood why the cuorem was confused. The shadow siblings were more alike than not. Besides their resounding good looks, their minds worked similarly. Perhaps, that was one of the greatest reasons for their shared animosity.

"I'm just a lowly Kin, right? Ruled by my emotions. I'm not

like you ruthless Fae. The idea of allowing you to die simply didn't sit well."

The shadow of a smile crept across his mouth. "Well, I know you didn't save me for my brother. In the last few seconds, he's threatened my life twice." He paused, flicking his tongue out across his bottom lip. "I don't blame him really. If you were mine, I'd likely feel the same."

A river of heat seeped up my neck, coursing across my cheeks.

"You're not what I expected, duskling." He inched closer, erasing the minute distance between us. "For years, I'd listened in as Father instructed Reign about the child of twilight—"

My heart stopped mid-beat, lungs flailing.

"You know, I was jealous of him. The king spent countless hours in his instruction, while I was only a boy, ignored and left with the royal nannies. As soon as I came of age, I vowed I would be the one to find the child of the prophecy and prove to my father that I deserved the role of heir."

"I have no idea what you speak of," I sputtered, cursing Reign for not allowing me to keep my favorite blades sheathed beneath my skirts.

"Of course you do." He lifted his hand, thumb caressing my cheek. "And more importantly, so does Reign. I wonder how long he's known..."

"You're wrong," I gritted out.

"I wish I were." His eyes chased to mine, and I almost believed him. "You see, I'd been curious as to why a Kin had my brother in such a state, so I bided my time, attempting to learn all that I could. Then the other night, when you disappeared from Arcanum, I caught a glimpse of Gideon lingering in the halls. It occurred to me that if anyone knew more about you, it would be my brother's best friend. So I waited until he was asleep, then infiltrated his study. And guess what I found?"

I swallowed hard, my desperate heartbeat roaring across my eardrums.

"A slew of ancient tomes about the cuorem bond." He wagged a finger, a sly smile spreading his lips. "I spent a few hours scanning the text and then it all made sense. Why my brother would shirk his duty, why he was so clearly obsessed with you and, more importantly, why every time I attempted to fill my father in on my suppositions about you, my lungs failed to function, and my heart felt as if steel bands held it prisoner."

Oh gods, this wasn't happening.

"Not only has my brother found himself tethered to you, but I, too, seem to have been caught up in the mystical web."

"Ruhl..."

He lifted a hand, pressing his finger to my lips. "Do not worry, duskling. I have no intention of divulging the truth to my father. I only ask one small favor in return."

"What is that?" I breathed.

"Simple, you refuse to complete the cuorem bond with Reign."

My mind spun, palms sweating as I emerged from the hidden nook, desperate to find Reign. Ruhl knew the truth, and the moment we had feared had finally come. Only I never expected *this*.

I scanned every corner of the elegant space, gaze drifting from clusters of Light and Shadow Fae dancing, drinking, and reveling in the night of peace. But no such peace existed for me. *Damn it, where are you Reign?*

He never would have gone far, leaving me at the hands of his brother. Unless... I searched the endless chamber for King Tenebris. His throne atop the dais was empty, leaving only the queen in her chair beside his with King Elian on the opposite end.

What if King Tenebris had already discovered the truth? If

Ruhl had, there was no telling what resources the royal had at his disposal.

"There you are!" Symon raced by cradling an unconscious Rue in his chest.

"Oh gods, what's wrong with her?"

"Nothing life threatening, hopefully. She merely enjoyed too much of whatever concoction the Shadow Fae were handing out." He shifted Rue in his arms, throwing her limp body over his shoulder. "In any case, I'm going to bring her home. Are you coming?"

I hesitated, my heart torn between my roommate and the disaster possibly unfolding at this very moment. I couldn't simply leave Reign. Then again, if Tenebris had discovered the truth, perhaps a quick escape was the best option at this point. Reign would find me, he always did.

My head bobbed up and down. "Yes, let's go."

The dark halls of the Citadel passed in a blur as I followed Symon down the winding corridors. Before long, we emerged along the river where a luminous bridge which had been erected for the evening awaited us at the crossing. A few Light Fae students meandered across the glowing structure, all unsteady on their feet.

At least I hadn't indulged in too much of the foreign liqueurs. The last thing I needed was to be caught off guard tonight.

"Is that Rue?" A familiar voice echoed from behind, and I paused, swinging my head over my shoulder. Devin raced up, light brows puckered in concern. "What happened to her?"

"She just had too much to drink." I couldn't contain the sharp edge to my tone. This male had broken my friend's heart. And now he was worried?

"And she's heavier than she looks," Symon grumbled. "So if you don't mind, I'd like to keep moving."

"Here, let me help." Devin held out his arms, and I eyed him warily.

"What about Mariana?" I snapped.

He scrubbed his hand down his nape, wincing. "She met someone while she was at Arcanum. Some Shadow Fae male; it'll never work out, clearly. But..." He shrugged. "It was never about her, honestly. It was always Rue. I only gave in to Mariana's advances because your friend refused to commit. It was stupid and petty, but I was jealous, so I'd hoped to get her attention by pretending to be interested in another."

"Well, it worked," I hissed. A little too well. Rue had been heartbroken for weeks over this idiot.

"Fine, you can have her." Sy rolled her into Devin's awaiting arms.

"Symon!" I squealed.

"She's heavy..." he whined.

"She's half your size!"

"And must be pure muscle by the feel of her." He stepped into stride beside Devin as we crossed over the bridge, finally reaching Light soil.

The remainder of the hike back to our chamber passed in a rush of chatter. Devin admitted how taken he was by Rue, and by the end of the conversation, I had almost forgiven his stupidity. *Almost.* But more than that, he had succeeded in distracting me from my own troubles.

As I swept my palm across the rune at the door to our chamber, all the fear and turmoil came rushing back. A part of me had hoped to find Reign waiting, but the room was empty.

"Ugh..." A groan slid through Rue's lips as Devin carried her across the threshold.

"It's okay, Rue, I'm here." His muttered reassurances were surprisingly sweet. Maybe these two would be able to work it out.

Her lids slowly opened, focusing on Devin before darting to me.

"It's okay, Rue, we're back in our dormitory." I pressed a

hand to her feverish brow. "Devin helped carry you because, apparently, Symon is a sad little weakling."

"Hey!" Sy grumbled as he folded onto the settee by the flickering hearth. "We all had a long, trying day today."

Wasn't that the truth?

Devin carried Rue to her bed, gently laying her onto the mattress as he recounted the same story he had told us about his true feelings for her. I watched every move, waiting for my best friend's reaction to her ex. She must have still been feeling the effects of the potent draughts, though, because she only stared up at him dreamily.

"What's this?" The high pitch of Devin's inflection sent my erratic pulse skittering.

Even Rue snapped up from the pillow, her eyes wide and suddenly clear as they took in the luminous scroll which had appeared on her nightstand. I darted across the room and snatched the parchment from Devin's grasp.

I scanned the familiar dark scrawls, my heart pitching with every word.

Dear Rue,

I hate to write this, but I am afraid I have no other choice. The situation is desperate. My squad has been decimated, and I am the only one left standing. Nigel is dead. If I abandon my post, I will be banished, marked a traitor, but no other option remains. Please, save me. I'll wait for you by the western border of the Wilds for as long as it takes.

In Raysa's blessed light,
Your brother, Heaton

"What is it?" Rue cried, the fear in her expression likely mirroring what was now my own.

"It's from Heaton," I whispered.

She ripped the letter from my grasp, any hint of the potent fog lifted. Her eyes scanned the note, and I could practically see the resolve in her clear gaze once she dropped the parchment. "I have to go."

"No, Rue, you can't!" I caught her arm and yanked her toward me.

"What is happening, now?" Sy scrambled off the settee and read the letter from over Devin's shoulder.

"I must, Aelia, it's Heaton."

"Then let's wait for help. Surely, someone at the academy knows what is happening along the borders. Both kings are just across the river as we speak. Let's go to them and seek their assistance."

Rue slowly shook her head, tears brimming in her eyes, but sheer determination was set into the hard line of her jaw. A part of me knew there would be no waiting or changing her mind. "Aelia, you of all people should know how insignificant we are in the eyes of the royals. King Elian won't raise a finger to help my brother. He's nothing more than fodder for his battles." She slipped from my grasp, marched to the closet and began shedding her gown.

"Then I'm going with you," I announced. "And Sol, we'll definitely need him."

Rue spun at me, half-undressed, and laced her slender arms around my neck. "Thank you, A."

"Well, it's not as if I could let my best friend go off on a rescue mission without me."

"And, I certainly cannot let the two of you go alone." Symon slid between us, pulling us into a tight embrace. "Plus, Griff would feel so left out."

"I'll go, too," said Devin. "It's the least I can do after how I acted." He glanced at Rue, a sheepish grin curling his lips.

Unraveling herself from Symon's long arms and my embrace, she swept the remaining tear from her cheek and gritted her teeth. "I appreciate all of you, I truly do. Now, let's get Heaton back."

Chapter Sixty-Three

A^{elia}

For the record, I do not condone this unsanctioned, and quite frankly, foolish outing. Sol's gravelly voice vibrated my skull as I followed behind Rue and Devin through the quiet hallways of the dormitories. Symon was silent beside me, likely also discussing our trip to the Wilds with Griff, because otherwise the chatty Fae would never be so quiet.

Noted, I shot back to Sol through our link. *But this is for Heaton, Sol. We cannot simply abandon him out there.* I slid my hands to the sheaths strapped to my hips, running my fingers over the smooth leather where one of *my* daggers and one blade I'd acquired from the academy rested. Without knowing what we would find tonight, I needed the solace only my dagger afforded.

You can and you should leave him out there. It is his duty to face whatever lies in the Wilds. Not yours.

A prickle of fear resonated all the way down to my bones. *Are you saying you will not come?*

I did not say that. I only wish to make it abundantly *clear that I disapprove, and I cannot be held accountable for what may occur as a result of this foolhardy mission.*

You've made it clear. And nothing will happen. We will simply meet Heaton on the border and bring him home. We will return before morning and anyone realizes we're gone. I huffed out a breath as we reached the front steps of the Hall of Glory. Through the light spray of the glittering fountain, Arcanum loomed across the river, sharp turrets like skeletal remains reaching into the night sky. It had been over half an hour since we'd left the Citadel, and still, I'd heard nothing from Reign.

Another bout of unease kicked up, twisting my stomach. Tonight was supposed to be a night of celebration. How could it have turned into such a complete disaster? First, Ruhl, and now, Heaton. Ruhl's ultimatum had been entirely unexpected. I'd fumbled and flailed, attempting a satisfactory response that would buy me some time. Not completing the bond with Reign would shatter his heart, as well as my own, and likely drive us both mad, but if Ruhl confessed the truth to the king, both of our lives could be forfeit. I needed to speak to Reign to decide our next move.

But where was he?

I squinted to make out a familiar blonde sauntering up the stone pathway, hidden beneath the trellises of wild ivy.

"Liora?" Symon blurted, and our entire impromptu rescue party came to a halt.

Oh gods, not her.

She emerged from the shadows, holding up her voluminous skirt to reveal bare feet. Her delicate chignon had come undone, wisps of blonde hair framing her weary face.

"Are you all right?" Symon rushed over.

A tear rolled down her cheek and a spasm of regret tightened my chest. Maybe I'd been a little unfair to the female since her arrival. I'd never even given her a chance because of my irrational jealousy.

"What happened?" I inched closer, joining Symon and the others beside her.

"I'm not sure." Liora choked back a sob. "One of the Shadow Fae initiates offered me something from a little vial. It tasted absolutely wretched." She gagged, her mouth twisting from the memory. "The next thing I knew an hour had passed, and I found myself alone in a corner of the dormitory hallway. I have no idea what happened."

Symon swung his arm around her quivering shoulders and tucked her into his side. "You are all right now, and that is all that matters."

"What if they did something to her?" I whisper-hissed to Rue.

"Then we will make them pay tomorrow. Besides, hopefully her hazy memory will return by then, and we'll discover exactly what happened." My best friend shifted from foot to foot nervously, her gaze darting across the flight field to the encroaching woods. I followed her line of sight, squinting at where Windy and Griff already awaited beneath the cover of trees. With a steadying breath, she turned to Liora, a tight smile on her lips. "You'll have to excuse us, but we are under a time constraint."

"Where are you going?" Her glossy eyes darted between us.

Rue's lips slanted into a hard line, and I avoided her questioning glance, searching for Sol behind the tree line. Keeping my friends' mounts hidden was much easier than my enormous dragon.

"We—" Symon started but Rue cut him off with a narrowed glare.

"No, no one can know."

"Know what?" Liora's eyes were red and swollen, bottom lip jutting out. She looked absolutely pitiful.

"There's something we need to do," I muttered.

"And no one else can come." Rue knotted her arms across her chest.

"Oh, please let me come." She wiggled free of Symon's hold and reached for Rue's hands. "Whatever it is, I won't tell anyone, I promise. I simply cannot be alone right now."

Devin shrugged, glancing at Rue. "Maybe she can help."

Rue's eyes flicked to mine again, an unspoken question hanging in the air between us. Hesitancy wavered in my chest as I regarded the female. Bringing her was no riskier than allowing Devin to come. I didn't fully trust either of them.

Worst case scenario, I could have Reign erase their memories should the need arise. *If you find him.* An unfamiliar voice of doubt squirmed through my thoughts. Shoving it back to the dark recesses where it belonged, I nodded quickly at Rue. We would find Heaton and bring him home. By the time we returned, surely I'd find Reign waiting. There was no reason for anything *else* to go wrong tonight.

The thunderous flap of mighty wings turned my attention skyward. Sol's gilded appendages glistened beneath the sun's sinking rays. Twilight approached, the rare hour when the blessed sun sank low behind the Alucian Mountains. The light never fully disappeared, but this was as close as it got. It was now or never.

"We must go, now," Rue announced.

"Just let her come," said Symon. "She can ride with me."

"Fine," she gritted out. "But you're responsible for her."

Sy nodded and pressed his palm to the small of Liora's back, guiding her toward the field where our skyriders awaited.

I marched to the dragon towering over the other mounts, dark smoke lifting from his wide nostrils. His agitation surged through our bond, a tangle of his and mine. *Sol, I hate to ask, but I need you to check on Reign through Phantom.*

He snorted, and brilliant ochre flames burst from between his fangs.

Windy let out a shrill whinny, pawing at the ground as the fire danced in the air a few yards above her head.

Please, Sol. I wouldn't ask if it wasn't important.

Fine, but only because I hope he can talk some sense into you and keep you from this fool's errand.

He stretched out his leg, and I climbed up the spiky protrusions, avoiding the nastier spikes and using the stubby ones as hand holds. Scaling the enormous beast had become second nature, a feat I would have thought impossible only a few months ago.

Once I was seated between his wing bones, I glanced below, where Rue, Devin, Symon and Liora were already mounted on their respective skyriders. As I watched Symon and Liora whispering, I wondered how much he had divulged of our covert operation. Deserting a squad of Royal Guardians was tantamount to treason. Once we found Heaton, he would be forced to run or pay for his disloyalty with his life. The thought had my stomach in knots once again. I couldn't imagine the next year at Luce without him as our team leader.

Sol? Any luck?

Phantom is not answering.

Does that happen often?

I would not know, Aelia, I do not often attempt to speak to her.

That swirl of fear ignited, churning into a frenzied storm of worry. *Keep trying.*

As you wish. His grumble of annoyance seeped through the bond, only intensifying my unease.

"Everyone ready?" Rue called out as Windy's wings beat the air, bringing the silver Pegasus to Sol's eye level within seconds.

A chorus of yeses swept through our small rescue squad.

"We should find Heaton within the hills of the western border between Feywood and the Wilds." Rue jerked on the reins, turning her mount's head south. "Let's go." Beyond the Feywood Forest, full dark had set in, Raysa's endless light reaching only as far as the court's southern border with Feywood.

Sol's massive wings thrust us into the sky, my stomach dipping from the speedy ascent. Once in the air, he flapped leisurely, staying well above the others to avoid their getting caught in the backdraft from his powerful beats. The sprawling landscape below, a tapestry of dark, whispering forests and rugged mountains, still seemed distant, but felt threatening, nonetheless. What was out there? What could have destroyed an entire squad of Royal Guardians?

The flight across the Court of Ethereal Light was a quick one, my spiraling, dismal thoughts more than enough company. Between my worry for Heaton and strangling fear for Reign, my heart leapt around my ribcage, battering my bones with lethal force. On the bright side, I hadn't once thought about my own perilous predicament.

Chapter Sixty-Four

A^{elia}

Sol's mighty wings sliced through the chilly air, soaring high over the Feywood Forest. Just beyond my home, the rolling hills of the Wilds threatened ever closer. The sky darkened, Raysa's blessed light finding its boundary, and a deadly silence descended over the lot of us.

From below, I could just make out Rue's glittering celestial glyph before her voice rose over the roaring winds. "We'll land at the edge of the forest and go the rest of the way by foot, so we don't attract too much attention."

"Okay," I shouted back. Again, hiding a dragon would prove much more difficult than the other skyriders, which would force Sol to remain in the cloud-covered skies nearby.

Sol tilted his wings toward the earth and we began the slow descent. The dark hills of the Wilds tumbled across the border between our lands, and my thoughts skittered back to the last time I was here. To that loud rumbling beneath the earth and the odd sensation that had accompanied it as I sat on the knoll with Reign discussing our dismal future. Summoning my *rais*, I traced the glittering lines of a celestial glyph to amplify my sight. *Where are you, Heaton?*

I searched the horizon, my vision augmented by the *rais* skimming over my skin. Nothing but endless night stretched out toward the hills and beyond. *Still nothing from Phantom?* I focused on our bond, nervous for the answer.

I'm afraid not.

Keep trying while you circle. I'll let you know as soon as we find Heaton.

Very well, Aelia.

The minute Sol's talons hit the ground, I slid off his leg, eager to join the others.

Be careful, little Kin. Sol's gruff voice echoed in my mind, the hint of some deeper emotion I couldn't quite decipher flooding our link.

I whirled around to find him watching me, the typically smooth line between his reptilian orbs furrowed. "Always," I replied aloud.

With one last, meaningful glance, his majestic wings unfolded and his enormous body catapulted into the night sky.

"Come on, Aelia!" Rue called out, turning my thoughts away from my dragon and back to the matter at hand.

I quickened my steps into a jog and raced after Rue, Devin, Symon and Liora who had already reached the edge of the clearing where the terrain began to slope upward.

"Where exactly are we going?" I asked Rue, fingering the crystal encrusted into the hilt of my blade, its familiar presence comforting after so much time apart.

"How about over there?" Liora interjected as she signaled over the ridge to a cluster of darkwoods. "Judging by the thick foliage covering the terrain, it seems like a good place to start."

She wasn't wrong. Their oversized leaves and sprawling

branches would provide good natural shelter and a decent place to hide.

Rue narrowed her eyes, scanning the darkness. A long minute later, her shoulders lifted before falling back reluctantly. "Sure, we can start there."

"I'll lead the way." Liora stepped forward with an eager Symon by her side.

"I suppose it's a good thing we brought her, after all," said Devin as he moved into place on the other side of Rue.

"I'm sure we could have figured it out without her," I grumbled. The moment the words were out, I wished I could take them back. I had to stop being so unfair to the female who, through no fault of her own, was merely unfortunate enough to be Reign's acquisition.

The five of us marched up the steady incline, a heavy silence filling the space between our ragged breaths. The darkwoods loomed ever closer, a strange energy pulsing in the air. The foreign sensation prickled the hair on my arms and a chill raced down my spine. The unearthly power pressed into me, an icy blast sending my *rais* surging to the tips of my fingers.

"Do you feel that?" I whispered to Rue.

"What, exactly?"

"That power..."

Instinctively, I reached for my necklace, needing the comfort of its touch. I thumbed the medallion and nearly squealed as the metal burned my fingertips. Muttering a curse, I dropped it, and the medal slid down the chain and fell back onto my chest. I waited for the sharp burn, only it never came. What in the realms?

"Look, over there!" Liora motioned through the thick trees to a figure huddled on the ground in the shadows.

"Heaton!" Rue darted ahead, and I pushed my legs to keep up with her sudden sprint.

"Wait, Rue! Wait for us!" I shouted, but it seemed as if my friend had suddenly grown wings.

A booming tremor shook the earth beneath my feet as I raced after Rue. My arms shout out to steady myself, but my boot caught on a gnarled root and I sailed forward, my chest hitting the ground with a thud. All the air siphoned from my lungs at the impact, and I was left gaping, struggling to draw in a blessed mouthful of air.

The sky darkened suddenly, as if a blanket of pure obsidian had decided to fall atop the typical night. Except... no, it was the opposite. A veil had been lifted, the mystical curtain covering the horrors that hid just beyond the border had only now been revealed. My heart leapt into my throat when I saw them. An army clad in armor as black as a raven's wing, riding creatures that resembled enormous, smoke-like serpents. The beasts moved toward us with terrifying speed and coordination, more akin to Reign's shadows than flesh and blood.

I simply lay there, frozen and unmoving, gaping at the truth behind the Wilds.

"No!" The cry of a familiar voice tore my gaze from the army of darkness. Heaton appeared on the ridge, bloodied and bruised, waving his arms frantically. "What are you doing here? Run! Get away from there!"

As if his words shattered the spell I was under, I pushed myself off the ground just in time to see Rue's form crumple a few yards ahead. Her knees gave way at the sight of her brother, a devastated cry tearing from her lips. "Heaton! We came for you!"

"Go, now!" he shouted again. "You have to get out of here!"

But it was too late.

The serpent-like beasts were upon us, shrieking and spitting a caustic black liquid that scorched everything in its path. But it was their riders from which I could not force my gaze away.

Torn straight from the history of the Courts of Aetheria, I stared in awe and terror at the Demon Fae. Even astride those terrifying beasts, I could make out their tall, sinewy forms that moved with an unnatural, eerie grace. Their skin ranged from dusky crimson to a glossy obsidian, shimmering with a faint luminescence that seemed to pulse with darkness. Their eyes were the most striking thing about them, though: a deep ruby, vibrant lavender, or glowing citrine, they lacked any whites at all, giving them a haunting, predatory look.

Raysa, help us, how was this possible?

The Court of Infernal Night had been decimated decades ago in the Two Hundred Years' War.

"Rue!" I cried out. She and Devin huddled on the ground, encased in a glittering orb.

Beasts and riders with sinewy, bat-like wings zipped by, hissing and shouting in a rough, guttural tongue I could not comprehend. They repeated the same phrase over and over, their chant growing to a fevered pitch.

Infantum od twilit. Infantum od twilit. Infantum od twilit.

I tried to run toward my friends but that odd surge of power crept over me once again, a tidal wave of dark energy with a hint of sulfur coating the air. *Zar.* The word formed in my mind then spilled from my tongue. "It's *zar*," I breathed. The mystical energy I couldn't decipher wasn't *nox, rais* or even *lys*, it was *zar*, and gods' damn it, I should have recognized it.

My medallion pulsed as if echoing my sentiments.

Aelia, what is happening down there? I felt a burst of energy... Sol's frazzled voice filled my subconscious.

It's the Night Court, Sol. They're alive, and they're angry.

I'm coming, little Kin. Run!

Gods, why did everyone keep saying that?

I glanced between the edge of the forest a few dozen yards away and my friends, who were caught in a tornado of shadowy serpents and fierce Demon Fae. All of my friends, except for Liora—where was she? Streaks of brilliant *rais* streamed through the wave of darkness as they attempted to fight off their attackers, but for every one they took down, another appeared in its place. I couldn't simply abandon Rue. Or Sy, or Heaton, or even Devin, for that matter. I *wouldn't*. Digging deep into my core, I searched the deep well of energy where my *rais* resided. Instead of the radiant light, though, I found nothing. A vast chasm of emptiness.

No. No. No. This wasn't happening.

The crack of mighty wings flapping sent a surge of hope rushing through the void in my chest. Tipping my head to the infinite darkness, a spark of gold lit up the night across the horizon. *Sol.* And just behind him, a sleek obsidian dragon; Phantom's eyes were glowing like twin stars, bathing the fathomless night. Reign? They were still too far to tell.

We're coming for you, little Kin.

The ground trembled beneath me once again, shooting my heart up my throat. A fissure raced across the earth, spilling the pungent scent of sulfur, and from the dark depths, a figure coalesced. A torrent of ancient power pressed into me, drawing the remaining air from my lungs.

A towering male appeared, his hair a striking silver with skin the color of midnight, shimmering with a subtle, menacing glow. His eyes, deep set and fiery, burned with the intense red of smoldering coals. The Demon Fae was dressed in armor that seemed forged from the night sky itself, decorated with intricate runes that writhed and shifted in the low light. A distinctive cloak hung from his neck, the shadows of forgotten souls—if my memory served correct—moving as if still alive.

Oh, gods. The legendary King Helroth of Infernum. My fingers tightened around the hilt of my dagger.

A wicked grin curled the corner of his lip as those burning, crimson orbs raked over me. "There she is, the promised one— *infantum od twilit.* Oh, how I've waited for your arrival."

In a heartbeat, he erased the distance between us, and his hand jutted out, thick fingers wrapping around my throat. I gasped as his unyielding grip crushed my windpipe. No. This was not how I died. After everything I had survived, I would *not* die at the hand of an extinct Demon King.

His free hand found my medallion, fingers grazing the engraving. "I knew it was you," he hissed.

Twisting my wrist, I jabbed my blade beneath the scales of his armor, hitting the soft part of his belly between the flaps of his gambeson, the padded jacket. A grunt pursed his lips as his eyes widened into terrifying pools of blood.

Then that sinister smile returned, bolder than before. Releasing my necklace, but still holding me by the throat, he wrenched my dagger free from my knotted fingers, twisting my wrist until the pop of bones breaking crackled through the air. I bit back a scream, refusing the monster the pleasure of my pain.

Muddled shouts resounded around me, the familiar cries of my friends drowned out by the frantic drumbeats of my heart. Oh, gods, please let them survive this.

The Demon King lifted my dagger, eyeing the blade, then ran his tongue over the blood-spattered metal. "Infernium vein. Just as I suspected." The droplets of deep crimson that coated the weapon floated into the air, then amalgamated into a figure eight. I watched, dumbstruck, as the circlets of blood closed around my wrists, and pure agony streaked through my veins. "And now, it's time to take you home, princess."

The king bent down, his arms curling beneath my thighs. I struggled and kicked, but the mystical manacles tightened and a raging fire seared my veins, blocking everything else out. Oh gods, it hurt. Blinding pain surged through my bones, reaching into my marrow. I couldn't breathe, couldn't see. There was only pain. I searched the bonds that tethered me to the ones I loved, but the agony was too much.

Sol?

Reign...

The king's arms tightened around my shattering form, and my stomach catapulted up my ribs as he leapt into the bottomless fracture in the earth. A flicker of movement over his head of silvery hair caught my eye, and a heart-wrenching howl echoed over the chaos.

Reign's panicked eyes met mine for an instant, his shadows a fury of dark power as he soared toward me, still too far.

"Reign…"

His name was the final word on my lips before I plunged into the infinite pit of darkness.

To Be Continued…

Please don't hate me! I know that was a BIG cliffy but I promise the wait will be worth it :) Book 3 of the Courts of Aetheria, Crown of Wrath and Ruin will be out next year and you can preorder it now. Can't wait for the next book? Join my Patreon at patreon.com/GKDeRosa to read all the chapters as I write them plus get early access to all the things and other exclusive goodies! Or for a sneak peek of the first chapter, join my Facebook group, GK DeRosa's Supe Squad or my VIP reader newsletter at https://landing.mailerlite.com/webforms/landing/b7f8p7 or visit www.gkderosa.com.

And while you're waiting for the next book, check out all of my complete series from the world of Azar. Start with the super fun paranormal reality TV show dating game Hitched: The Bachelorette :)

One innocent human girl.
Twenty-five supernatural bachelors.
Six weeks to choose The One.

When struggling actress Kimmie-Jayne Starr discovers she's snagged the starring role on the next huge reality TV show, Hitched, she thinks all her dreams have finally come true.

But as soon as she lands on the beautiful island of Mystic Cove, something feels wrong.

Sure, the twenty-five bachelors are heart-stoppingly gorgeous, but she's certain they're all hiding something—something supernatural. As she gets to know the guys, protecting her heart proves impossible when she finds herself irresistibly drawn to more than just one.

As a string of strange accidents on set grow deadlier, Kimmie realizes there's much more to this dating show than she ever could've imagined. If she can't figure out who's behind these incidents, she'll end up risking more than just her heart.

Guide to the Courts of Aetheria

Court of Ethereal Light

King Elian of Ether

Light fae, beings associated with illumination and radiant energy, possess a variety of magical powers aligned with the forces of light and positive energy through *rais*.

Light Fae Abilities

1. Photokinesis:
The ability to manipulate and control light.
2. Healing Light:
The power to harness light energy for healing purposes.
3. Luminous Wings:
Only extremely powerful Light Fae can sprout ethereal, radiant wings that allow them to fly gracefully through the air.
4. Illumination Sight:
The ability to see beyond the visible spectrum, allowing Light Fae to perceive things such as auras, energy patterns, or hidden magical forces.

5. Solar Empowerment:

Drawing strength from sunlight, Light Fae experience enhanced abilities, increased vitality, and heightened magical powers when exposed to sunlight.

6. Prismatic Manipulation:

The power to control and manipulate prisms and rainbows.

7. Radiant Shields:

The ability to create protective barriers or shields made of radiant light.

8. Solar Flare Burst:

Unleashing bursts of intense solar energy, powerful Light Fae could create blinding flashes or focused beams to repel adversaries.

9. Light Infusion:

Infusing objects or individuals with radiant energy.

10. Harmony Induction:

The ability to radiate an aura of peace and tranquility.

11. Illuminate Knowledge:

The power to gain insights, visions, or access to hidden knowledge through the illumination of light.

Court of Umbral Shadows

King Tenebris and Queen Vespera of Umbra

Shadow fae, beings associated with darkness and shadows, possess a range of magical powers aligned with the forces of shadow and concealment through *nox*.

Shadow Fae Abilities

1. Umbrakinesis:
The ability to control and manipulate shadows.
2. Shadow Travel:
The power to traverse through shadows, allowing mature Shadow Fae to move swiftly from one shadow to another.
3. Cloak of Invisibility:
The ability to wrap themselves in shadows, becoming invisible to the naked eye.
4. Umbral Constructs:
The power to shape shadows into solid, tangible forms.
5. Fear Induction:
The ability to manipulate the fears and anxieties of others.
6. Eclipse Manipulation:
Control over celestial events, particularly eclipses.
7. Shadowmeld:
The power to merge seamlessly with shadows, becoming one with the darkness.
8. Umbral Blades:
Conjuring weapons made of solid shadow.
9. Whispering Shadows:
The ability to communicate through shadows.
10. Nightmare Weaving:

Crafting illusions and dreams that induce nightmares.

11. Corruptive Touch:

The power to taint or corrupt objects with shadows, extremely rare.

Also by G.K. DeRosa

<u>Courts of Aetheria</u>
Crown of Light and Shadows
Crown of Flames and Ash
Crown of Wrath and Ruin

Forgotten Kingdoms (Shared World Stand Alone)
Of Dragons and Desire

<u>Hitched Live</u> (World of Azar)
Sweet Revenge
Wicked Games
Savage Love
Sweet Temptation
Dark Desire

<u>Of Gods and Wolves</u> (World of Azar)
Death's Captive
Death's Fate
Death's Mate

<u>Vampish</u> (World of Azar)
Vampish: The Hunt
Vampish: Kiss of Death
Vampish: Blood Bonds
Vampish: Blood Mate

<u>Wolfish</u> (World of Azar)

Wolfish: Moonborne
Wolfish: Curseborne
Wolfish: Mateborne
Wolfish: Fateborne

<u>Darkblood Prison</u> (World of Azar)
Darkblood Prison: Demon On A Dime
Darkblood Prison: Demon Double-Agent
Darkblood Prison: Demon At Large
Darkblood Prison: Demon Dark Lord

<u>Royally Hitched Series</u> (World of Azar)
Royally Hitched: The Fae Prince
Royally Hitched: The Fae Twins
Royally Hitched: The Fae Princess

<u>Darkblood Academy</u> (World of Azar)
Darkblood Academy: Half-Blood
Darkblood Academy: Supernatural Slayer Squad
Darkblood Academy: Demons
Darkblood Academy: Prophecies

<u>The Hitched Series</u> (World of Azar)
Hitched: The Bachelorette
Hitched: The Top Ten
Hitched: The Final Five
Hitched: The One

<u>The Vampire and Angel Wars</u> (Stand Alone Series)
Wings & Destruction
Blood & Rebellion

Souls & Salvation

The Vampire Prophecy (Stand Alone Series)
Dark Fates
Dark Divide
Dark Oblivion

The Hybrid Trilogy (Spin Off of the Guardian Series)
Magic Bound
Immortal Magic
Beyond Magic
Magic Bound: The Hybrid Trilogy The Complete Collection

The Guardian Series
Wilder: The Guardian Series
Wilder Destiny
Wilder Revelation
Wilder Legacy
Wilder: The Guardian Series The Complete Collection

Acknowledgments

A huge and wholehearted thank you to my dedicated readers! I could not do this without you. I love hearing from you and your enthusiasm for the characters and story. You are the best!

A special thank you to my loving and supportive husband who always understood my need for escaping into a good book (or TV show!). He inspires me to try harder and push further every day. And of course my mother who is the guiding force behind everything I do and made me everything I am today. Without her, I literally could not write—because she's also my part-time babysitter! To my father who will always live on in my dreams. And finally, my little hellions, Alexander and Stella, who bring an unimaginable amount of joy, adventure and craziness to my life everyday.

A big thank you to Stefanie from Seventhstar Designs, for creating a beautiful book cover, to Samaiya Beaumont for the lovely header designs, character art and all the swag. I could never come up with all the ideas that you do! Thank you to my editor Rachel for not only questioning all the things but also getting a laugh out of me every time. And a special thank you to my dedicated beta reader and best VA ever, Sarah. You've been my sounding board on everything from cover ideas, blurbs, and story details. Not to mention doing everything behind the scenes. And to my ARC readers who caught spelling errors, and were all around amazing.

Thank you to all my family and friends, author and blogger

friends who let me bounce ideas off of them and listened to my struggles as an author and self-publisher. I appreciate it more than you all will ever know.

~ G.K.

About the Author

USA Today Bestselling Author, G.K. De Rosa has always had a passion for all things fantasy and romance. Growing up, she loved to read, devouring books in a single sitting. She attended Catholic school where reading and writing were an intense part of the curriculum, and she credits her amazing teachers for instilling in her a love of storytelling. As an adult, her favorite books were always young adult novels, and she remains a self-proclaimed fifteen year-old at heart. When she's not reading, writing or watching way too many TV shows, she's traveling and eating around the world with her family. G.K. DeRosa currently lives in South Florida with her real life Prince Charming and their little royals.

www.gkderosa.com

Made in the USA
Monee, IL
10 June 2025